KINGDOM COME

KINGDOM COME

Lynda Rose

HEADLINE

First published in 1996 by
HEADLINE BOOK PUBLISHING

10 9 8 7 6 5 4 3 2 1

British Library Cataloguing in Publication Data

Rose, Lynda
Kingdom come
1. English fiction - 20th century
I. Title
823.9'14[F]

ISBN 0 7472 1854 4

Typeset by Avon Dataset Ltd, Bidford-on-Avon, Warks

Printed and bound in Great Britain by
Mackays of Chatham PLC, Chatham, Kent

HEADLINE BOOK PUBLISHING
A division of Hodder Headline PLC
338 Euston Road
London NW1 3BH

For my mother and father

Chapter One

Father Trumpington was what you might call an old-fashioned kind of priest. He prided himself that throughout the deanery his was the one church still remaining that practised true Anglicanism. It came as a surprise therefore when he announced to the world at large, and the Parochial Church Council in particular, his intention of taking a woman for his next curate.

The motives underlying this decision were somewhat complex. Father Trumpington had something of a bad track record with curates. Within his own little empire he was god, and he demanded unquestioning and absolute obedience. To his mind a curate had to be a self-effacing individual who bore the brunt of parish work. But, at the same time, the curate must not commit the sin of becoming too popular within the parish. If his commandments were transgressed, whether consciously or not, the not-so-good Father reacted viciously and with a deviousness that made Machiavelli appear on a par with Mary Poppins. In fact, sad to say, he had treated his last curate so badly that within only five months he had reduced the poor man to a gibbering wreck and catapulted him into a state of religious doubt that had resulted in his leaving the Church to become an insurance salesman.

After that particular fiasco the Bishop had said that Father Trumpington was never to have another curate again. This, however, had displeased Father Trumpington, who was congenitally incapable of seeing that he had done anything wrong. He had at first stormed, then wheedled, and finally produced a mild heart attack as evidence that he could not cope alone, at which point the Bishop had relented sufficiently to issue an ultimatum: a woman or no one at all. To do that poor and much beleaguered man justice, he had assumed that Father Trumpington would reject such a proposal out of hand with horror. He had then hoped, even prayed, that Father Trumpington would quietly go and begin the job he had originally been ordained to do. In the

1

event, he found what happened a severe test of faith because Father Trumpington accepted – and with what appeared to the Bishop to be almost unseemly alacrity!

When Father Trumpington had agreed to the Bishop's ultimatum he had had not the slightest perception of what he would get. The whole question of women's ministry had never bothered him in the least. Women by definition, in his view, were inferior to men; not before God of course – theologically speaking (which he rarely did) – but in strength, intellect and temperament they were simply, well, how to put it tactfully? Weaker perhaps. It was just a fact of existence; unfortunate no doubt, but inescapable. Women were made to bear children and to provide a stable environment for a man. They were of course not to blame for the defects in their faculties, but clearly the fact that it was so made the whole question of their ordination to the priesthood ridiculous.

Yet Father Trumpington was in desperate straits. For the first time in thirty years he had found himself forced to take on pastoral work, and he did not like it. And then, when he thought about it a bit more, and gently mooted the issue to one or two of his colleagues, he discovered he did not greatly mind the idea of women being deacons, so long as they did not go any further. After all, what was a deacon but a servant – and what had God put women upon the earth for but to serve? And so after a while, when he had thought about it, and in the absence of any more congenial alternative, he thought perhaps he would not mind. In fact by this time he might well have agreed to a proboscis monkey if it had been demonstrated to him that they could do the job. But when he had agreed he had envisaged a meek and retiring gentleperson of indeterminate years who would wait upon his every whim, rather like the good and elderly ladies of his congregation. Ladies who, without exception, dressed in grey coats and headscarves and who happily undertook the cleaning of the church and arrangement of the flowers, and minded not a jot when he peremptorily ordered them to remove themselves from the vestry. What he got, however, was something entirely different.

Her name was Antonia Beecher-Henty – a mouthful by any

standards! Father Trumpington first made her acquaintance one grey Tuesday morning in early January, when a fine drizzle was falling and the whole world seemed cloaked with crystal-tipped gloom. She arrived ten minutes late. Father Trumpington, who was always late himself, disliked intensely unpunctuality in others, and especially when that other was a subordinate. He also liked his curates to be neat, respectable, and preferably wearing open-toed brown leather sandals and charcoal socks. It had occurred to him, prior to her arrival, that he might have to make some slight concession on this latter ground – for example substituting thick woolly tights for the socks. But in the same way that it had not suggested itself to him that she would not be overweight, fifty, and dressed in grey, so it had not seriously occurred to him that she would in other respects differ fundamentally from any of his other newly emergent ordinands. Her appearance, therefore, came as something of a shock.

Father Trumpington had been sitting on the lavatory, whence he had withdrawn in petulance as the minutes ticked by, when the doorbell rang. As its sonorous tones pealed through the vicarage he waited for a count of thirty seconds, slowly rose to his feet, adjusted his dress, and sallied forth magisterially, intent on intimating in no uncertain terms his displeasure at having been made to wait. He was totally unprepared, however, for the sight that met his eyes. Gathering himself up, and puffing out his chest in angry self-importance, he swung back the heavy oak door . . . to be greeted by one of the prettiest, most Madonna-like creatures he had ever seen.

The girl standing before him was about five foot two. She was very slender, and there was an insubstantial quality about her, as if she was so delicate that an extra strong gust of wind might blow her away. Her hair was a mass of long dark curls that framed a serious, very still face, as if the girl was watching, but watching what Father Trumpington had no idea. He wondered briefly if perhaps she was short-sighted. Whatever the cause, there was something about the look in her eyes that disturbed him; it made him feel uncomfortable, as if he had been caught out in some misdemeanour. And then after a moment he took in the rest of her appearance more fully, and his sense of unreality was intensified because she was dressed with all the casual elegance of one of the models who adorned his daughter's more expensive magazines. It was at this moment that Father Trumpington decided he had made a mistake and that this was not his prospective curate after all. In fact, on reflection she was probably some poor waif from too good a life who had come seeking spiritual succour – and fortune was smiling upon him because she had come to him. Father Trumpington's eyes gleamed, and he prepared himself to be at his most charming. 'Yes, my dear,' he said, 'can I help you?'

The vision, for this was what Father Trumpington was beginning seriously to suspect it was, appeared to find this faintly amusing. A smile curled her lips and she held out her hand. 'I hope so,' she said. 'I'm Antonia Beecher-Henty, and you, I presume, are Father Trumpington of St Godric's.' Her voice was perfectly modulated, with an accent that spoke of croquet on the lawn, Hampstead, and champagne and strawberries for tea.

Father Trumpington gaped as the truth forced itself upon him. He had not made a mistake after all and now it was too late to express his displeasure! He found his hand firmly shaken as he waved it uncomprehendingly in the air, uncertain what to do. He opened his mouth feebly, and then shut it again quickly, aware that he could think of nothing to say. But Ms Beecher-Henty seemed unperturbed by this fact. Gathering her coat more closely about her against the cold, she stepped forward through the door, and Father Trumpington suddenly found that she was in the hall, and the door shut behind her. He had the sudden, inescapable – though perhaps not unpleasurable – feeling that she had likewise stepped into his life. Conflicting emotions raged through his breast, and were still raging some three-quarters of an hour later when she emerged before him from the study.

Without quite knowing how it had happened, he discovered that he had agreed to everything she asked and that she would begin in the autumn, following on a late ordination – Father Trumpington had wanted somebody in June. He also discovered that he had agreed to allow her two days a week to study for a Master's degree and, worst of all, that she be allowed to set up a fellowship group. Of all the things that Father Trumpington hated,

4

fellowship groups came at the top of his list! In his view they bred an unhealthy desire for participation on the part of the congregation, functioning like subversive cells that provided a seedbed for unhealthy fanaticism. To Father Trumpington's mind, all fanaticism was unhealthy but none more so than that of religion. A man of temperate, even indifferent, belief himself, he deplored its fervent expression in anyone else. On the whole he enjoyed clerical life, yet he had entered upon it not because of any overwhelming religious conviction but because overall the lifestyle appealed to him more than any other. He revelled in the sense of importance he derived from walking around in his thick white collar, and the way lesser mortals deferred to him because of his obvious status. He firmly believed that he was God's spokesman upon earth – at least, the particular bit of earth that comprised his parish, and he did not relish the prospect of the status quo being disturbed by a group of unruly, power-seeking individuals who claimed they had the mandate of the Holy Spirit. Father Trumpington himself had never had much acquaintance with this latter exulted being – he supposed it existed, but he certainly did not believe that it had anything to do with what these awful people who claimed to have been 'born again' were on about. God could not possibly have such appalling taste.

He had in the past successfully resisted fellowship groups, along with such things as a family service (because he disliked noisy children in church) and the inclusion of popular choruses in worship, on the grounds that such things were the thin edge of the proverbial wedge. And yet, he had just agreed to Ms Beecher-Henty setting one up. Father Trumpington felt a sudden, momentary wave of terror as the full impact of what he had done was borne in upon him, but then another thought occurred. Antonia Beecher-Henty might not conform to his ideal image of a curate, but she was clearly a well-bred kind of a girl, obviously of good family, public school; clearly she would know all the right people. It was ridiculous to worry that she would let things get out of hand. And he suddenly felt much better.

As she stepped out into the murky gloom of the drizzle, a positive glow suddenly suffused him. Of all men, he, *he*, was going to have this wonderful creature as his curate. He would be the first vicar in the deanery to have, if he might use so indelicate an expression, a woman. And such a woman! The others would be green. Just for a moment, and for the first time in his life, Father Trumpington almost approached heights of religious ecstasy. Perhaps after all, he thought, God really did exist and, as confirmation of his presence, in the twilight of Father Trumpington's declining years, had taken it upon himself to smile.

He wasted no time therefore in phoning up the Bishop and, to the latter's astonishment, poured forth a positive eulogy upon the merits of the delightful Ms Beecher-Henty. How wonderful and merciful was God, he said, to provide him with so tailor-made and amenable an answer to his needs. How intelligent was Ms Beecher-Henty (dare he call her Antonia?), how refined, how... how just what the Church of England needed! He could not see what all the fuss about the ordination of women to the diaconate was. In short, he had said that he would be delighted to have her – more than delighted in fact – and that he could envisage not the least possibility of there ever being a hint of trouble. He had positively purred. He had not actually said it, but he had hinted that the angelic looking Ms Beecher-Henty was perfection personified.

The Bishop, immediately sensing trouble, had at this point attempted to draw back. 'Er, look, Dick,' he said, 'don't think you've got to be too hasty about this. I find we might be able to let you have a male curate after all.'

But Father Trumpington would have none of it. 'No, there's no need for that,' he said decisively. 'Ms Beecher-Henty will be fine – and why not? I'm not prejudiced against women! I don't think they'll be priests of course, at least I hope not, and I trust my views will be noted when the issue comes up in Synod next year! But I see nothing wrong with their working as assistant curates. I'm sure we're going to get along just fine!'

And on that ominous note the Bishop had retired, defeated. Not so, however, Ms Beecher-Henty's Director of Ordinands, the Reverend Elizabeth Marshall. She was horrified when she received a note a couple of days later informing her of developments and phoned up the Bishop in fury. 'What on earth do you mean, allowing the poor girl to go there?' she demanded.

6

'What are you playing at? The man's a menace!'

The Bishop ummed and aahed and, despite the fact that he was an ardent supporter of the ordination of women, wished devoutly that all females of the species would be content to be wives and mothers, and that all Father Trumpingtons could be quietly pensioned off to grass.

'It's not good enough!' bellowed the revered lady, by this time thoroughly exasperated. 'He'll slaughter her!'

'I had something of the impression people feared it might be the other way round,' he ventured.

'Don't be ridiculous!' came the angry retort. 'You've got to stop it. You're the Bishop!'

'Oh?' The Bishop sounded surprised. 'Yes, but Dick . . .' He trailed off.

'Well, if you won't do anything,' fumed the Reverend Marshall, 'I will. I'm going to see him.' And the Bishop was left holding a phone that buzzed in angry emptiness.

True to her word, Elizabeth Marshall descended on Father Trumpington. She did not conform to Father Trumpington's idea of female clerics either, not so much because of her obvious femininity, as in Ms Beecher-Henty's case, but rather because, with her iron-grey hair and muscular frame, she looked as if she hefted weights in her spare time and worked out with all-in wrestlers. In fact, all in all the Reverend Marshall was an intimidating sort of woman, made all the more so at that precise moment because of her obvious anger. She rang a peremptory summons on Father Trumpington's doorbell, casting around an angry look that seemed to make the snowdrops, valiantly struggling to poke through by the front door, wilt. No so Father Trumpington. He opened the door, took one look, and prepared himself for battle.

She swept past him with a glance of contempt and headed for the study. 'It won't do!' she bellowed as he bristled. 'It really won't do!'

Father Trumpington and Elizabeth Marshall were old sparring partners. As one of the two Diocesan Directors of Ordinands it was part of Elizabeth's duties to see to the pastoral care and oversight of all deacons in their first two years of ministry. She had therefore had dealings with Father Trumpington in the unfortunate affair of his last curate. In fact it had been she who had recommended that he never be allowed to have another curate again – male or female she had not bothered to stipulate, as it had not seemed to her even remotely conceivable that he would at any time contemplate having a woman. But of course that had been before he had managed to produce his heart attack.

Father Trumpington was fully aware of what he saw as her act of sabotage and, being a man to bear grudges, he had plotted ever since how to engineer her downfall, concocting in bed at night, as he lay beside the inert form of his wife, wild schemes that bore not the remotest chance of success because, though colourful, they had very little connection with reality. It had certainly never previously occurred to him that providence would itself provide the means of retaliation. But now, as he glowered after her black-caped back, he realised that fate had placed in his hands a perfect means of revenge. He was going to enjoy this.

Several minutes later his wife, Dorothy, tiptoeing past the study, heard their voices raised in angry confrontation. 'Antonia will come here only over my dead body,' she heard Elizabeth Marshall exclaim loudly, and then her husband, slightly quieter but equally venomous, 'An eventuality not perhaps to be ruled out if that's what is takes! The Bishop has said he thinks it an excellent idea – the perfect answer, in fact!' Dorothy sadly shook her head, aware of the untruth, and tiptoed on.

She was not to escape so easily. A creaking board underfoot at that moment betrayed her presence and a peremptory voice called out, 'Dorothy! Is that you? Come in here, please. Elizabeth says she would like a word.'

Poor Dorothy's heart sank. But thirty years of not very happy marriage had taught her unquestioning obedience and the ability to close her eyes to most of what her husband said and did and which once, in her younger days of faithful idealism, would have caused her outrage. She had long ago, when the real character of her husband had at last been inescapably and painfully borne in upon her, abandoned both faith and idealism. There was a time once when she had worshipped him and the image he projected but his petty deceits had gradually grown too big to be ignored and, rather than acknowledge what she realised to be the truth and have to face her own awful mistake, she had deliberately shut her eyes and devoted herself instead to the maintenance of an illusion. For long grey years she had had as little contact with the people of his parish as possible and, in so far as she was able, with him as well. Now, hearing his voice, her face dutifully assumed the mask of gentle solicitude which she habitually adopted when forced into any kind of contact with his official life and which she felt befitted a vicar's wife. Repressing a slight shudder, she went in.

'Oh, there you are, Dorothy,' he said as she came in. His voice was suddenly all false bonhomie and she felt a chill up her spine. He was sitting opposite Elizabeth Marshall. Both were in easy chairs; both decidedly uneasy. There was something in the tension of the room, unacknowledged but potent, that momentarily frightened Dorothy and she glanced from one to the other of them uncomfortably, the mask, despite all her efforts, briefly slipping. 'Elizabeth was just saying she felt she ought to talk to you about your reaction to my having a female curate. I said that of course you liked the idea because you felt women's ministry was such a good thing.'

They both looked at her, obviously expecting her to speak, he smug now in his complacency, clearly anticipating her support, the woman seated opposite him looking as if she was about to explode with fury. Though Dorothy knew her husband was expecting her to jump unquestioningly to his support, her tongue momentarily froze. It was not his lie that had upset her, she was used to that, but the fact that she was being asked a question, and a question where it actually mattered what she felt! The novelty of the experience made her reel.

In the silence, she struggled to think. The ticking of the hall clock sounded unnaturally loud and Father Trumpington began to drum his fingers on the arms of his chair in angry impatience. But for once she ignored him. She was so unused to being consulted about anything that she was finding the effort to decide what she did think difficult, but she was determined to try. She thought back to the beginning of the whole affair. She had not seen the girl, which was how Dick had described her. When

Antonia came, it had been one of her mornings for working at
the bank, and afterwards Dick had not really been very
communicative – but then he never was. He had just said that
she was the usual sort of thing, what you would expect really of
a woman in the Church, and she had accepted it unquestioningly,
as she always did. If she had thought about it at all, she had rather
thought that the girl would be some dowdy, nunnish individual
who would be terribly earnest, and it had even occurred to her
that they might be friends. Dorothy did not have many friends.

But there was so much palpable tension in the air that, almost
unconsciously, Dorothy found herself looking at the situation
again. She could not understand why the two of them seemed to
be rowing. Was there then something here that she ought to mind?
she wondered.

She cast vaguely around in her mind, thinking of past curates
her husband had had. Always respectful to her, nice young men,
they had trailed around dutifully after her husband, even
attending him at the rugby matches he liked to frequent, and
invariably tagging along to the choir to which he belonged.
Patiently biding their time, she supposed, until their next appointment. She knew they had none of them been very happy. Would
this girl do all that? she wondered. Would she go along to the
rugby matches and the choir? Surely not. But, it suddenly struck
her, what if she did? Despite herself, and faced with Elizabeth
Marshall's clear but angry gaze, Dorothy faltered. She began to
wonder if maybe she ought to mind.

Growing impatient, Elizabeth suddenly launched to her feet.
'Yes, Dorothy,' she boomed, 'I wanted to talk to you. I really must
know how you feel about all this.'

Dorothy looked at her blankly and heard her husband tut in
annoyance.

'It's very different, you know,' continued Elizabeth, 'when a
man has a woman for his curate, because there's still that close
working relationship. It can make a wife feel very excluded, even
jealous. Have you thought about how you're going to react to
that?'

Dorothy pulled herself together. She had to say something. 'Oh,
well, I—'

'Have you met Antonia yet?' Elizabeth swept on. 'She's very pretty of course, and she's extremely clever too. Are you going to be able to handle having a woman in a position of authority like that?'

Dorothy stopped listening. She had been asked, true, but she felt as if no one ever listened to a word she said. Yet Elizabeth's words, by contrast, were striking home. Antonia. She explored the name. Until that moment she had never even heard it before. Dick had referred to her only as Miss Beecher-Henty. And she was pretty, Elizabeth was saying. What did that mean? And clever.

'Are you saying you haven't met her yet?' Elizabeth's voice suddenly exploded, her fragile hold on her anger snapping. Dorothy jumped. She had not realised she had betrayed anything. 'But your husband's offered her the position, and this really is very important! It could produce untold tension if you and she don't get on.'

'Oh, come now,' broke in Father Trumpington, 'you really mustn't exaggerate. This is purely a working relationship, in no way different from those I've had with male curates.'

Elizabeth flinched at mention of male curates, as if that was a subject that in itself did not bear close examination. Undeterred, however, she bore on. 'No, I'm sorry,' she said, 'but the relationship is not at all like that between a vicar and a male curate. For one thing you cannot ignore the fact that you're a man and she's a woman, and that you're going to be working in the kind of relationship that in some respects is closer than that of marriage. In that situation it's absolutely vital that the vicar's wife and the curate get on well, so that there's absolutely no possibility of jealousy.'

Father Trumpington unkindly reflected that it was always the women who looked least attractive who imagined sexual misconduct at every turn, but then, happening to glance up, he caught sight of his wife's stricken face and a guilty flush suddenly flooded his neck and lower face. 'Preposterous!' he snapped, taking refuge in bluster.

Elizabeth blinked. 'Well, of course Antonia is engaged,' she conceded.

It was Father Trumpington's turn to look taken aback. Engaged!

He had not known that. He recovered quickly, swift to take advantage of his enemy's perceived weakness. 'There you are, you see,' he said, triumph in his voice, registering at the same time the way in which his wife visibly relaxed, as if she found some indescribable comfort in the announcement. 'And are you insisting that he meet me too, so that he does not indulge in any misplaced fits of jealousy either?' Father Trumpington had played a trump card and he knew it. It was Elizabeth's turn to flush uncomfortably.

'Well, no,' she said, 'it hadn't actually occurred to me but—'

'There you are then!' snapped Father Trumpington. 'Let's have a little common sense prevail in all of this.' He glared over at his wife, defying her to protest. 'Dorothy trusts me absolutely, don't you, dear?' It was a command. 'You can't be married thirty years and not get to know each other.'

His wife summoned up the courage to whisper, 'Very true, dear.' They had not wanted her opinion after all, she realised, but she felt perturbed. For years she had lived in a kind of glass house of carefully protected delusion, but just for a minute, with Elizabeth's questioning, she had looked at a part of her life that she tried very hard to ignore. What if . . . what if . . . But then, shaking herself, she firmly pushed the unwelcome thoughts and sensations away. No, she would not face that, not yet, not ever. If she denied such doubts they could not harm her, they had no substance. 'Of course I don't mind,' she said firmly – and she meant it; she would not allow herself to mind.

Father Trumpington smiled grimly, aware that he had won. 'If Miss Beecher-Henty is happy to come here – as I pride myself that she is – then I fail to see what objection there can possibly be. The Bishop is happy, and as you've just heard for yourself Dorothy too is more than happy. She trusts and relies upon me implicitly.' Dorothy looked at him. 'I'm very pleased that we've been able to have this frank talk, Elizabeth,' he continued. 'I hope you are now totally reassured.'

Elizabeth Marshall was not in the slightest bit reassured, but for the time being she was forced to acknowledge defeat. The man was impossible, she reflected. There seemed to be nothing she could do, and his wife was clearly totally under his thumb.

To think that she had not yet met Antonia! How on earth would she react when she did? It crossed her mind then to insist that she should herself arrange a meeting, but a quick glance at Father Trumpington's face told her that he would oppose the suggestion and that she would have little chance of success. So instead she withdrew, leaving Father Trumpington triumphant on his doorstep, all too obviously preening himself at having successfully repelled attack. In that moment she loathed him. It was an emotion that Father Trumpington, glaring after her retreating back, fully reciprocated.

Chapter Two

Antonia had not at first particularly wanted to go to St Godric's. Within the city the church had the reputation of being dead. A kind of spiritual no-go area, from which, it was rumoured, God had been excluded but which functioned as a kind of mediocre social club for the elderly that met every Sunday morning. There was, however, Henry.

Henry was now nicely established as a junior partner in Bartram & Crackitt, the firm of solicitors that he had joined, in hot pursuit of herself, when she had left the Bar and begun her own training at Becket House, the theological college in Carberry. Not that she had been at all averse to his pursuit. In fact it had been only some three months later that they had become engaged, a state that had agreed with her. So much so, in fact, that she was at present unwilling to exchange it for marriage. But though she was not yet ready for anything more permanent, she did not really want to be parted from him, and so St Godric's had seemed in every sense to be heaven sent.

Despite her initial lack of enthusiasm, however, as time passed Antonia found she was beginning to look upon the appointment as a challenge. She felt that God was perhaps calling her there for a specific purpose; and she began to dream of the Holy Spirit falling one day on the assembled church in power, so that St Godric's became a byword for spiritual renewal and revival, talked about throughout the land.

Antonia herself had come to faith some eight years before, and as a result of her sense of God's power, and of his purpose for her life – which she saw as in any case belonging to him – she was absolutely committed to serving him, and to being obedient to whatever it was she felt he was asking her, no matter how impossible it seemed. She indeed had something of the strain of a martyr in her. Had she felt the Lord was calling her to it, she would have walked through fire, and come out smiling the other side.

She was not, however, prepared for the Reverend Marshall's visit. That lady, having failed so dismally with the gentleman in question, lost no time in hastening round to see her. It was unfortunate that her opening salvo was perhaps rather lacking in sensitivity, because it had the effect of antagonising Antonia from the outset. Thus, what had been intended as a reasonable discussion centring on the latter's welfare rapidly deteriorated into something akin to armed confrontation, with Antonia left wondering why on earth the Reverend Marshall seemed to dislike her so much.

Elizabeth began by explaining in great detail why it was that Antonia could not possibly go to St Godric's. It was not Father Trumpington's turn to have a curate, she announced. There was the quota to be thought of. Carberry was fully staffed at the moment and there were at least two other priests in the city who were in line for curates, well ahead of Father Trumpington. And besides all that, Father Trumpington had not gone about it in at all the right way. He had ignored the proper channels. Elizabeth's chin had projected itself at this point. He had never once seen fit to consult her but had just phoned up the principal of Becket instead. Really, the man had come out of the ark.

Antonia, who knew very well the workings of the Church of England and that many priests still went about getting their assistants in the way Father Trumpington had, was left wondering what on earth was going on. She apologised sweetly, however, and smiled, and said that she was very sorry but she did not really understand, and she thought, on balance, given that the Bishop did not seem to mind, that she would still go.

Elizabeth swallowed. 'My dear,' she said, 'it would be an entirely unsuitable place for you to serve your first curacy.'

'Why?' demanded Antonia, the smile slipping.

This was dangerous ground; Elizabeth did not want to admit publicly that Father Trumpington was a swine, and besides, she did not think Antonia would believe her. 'He can be . . . difficult,' she temporised.

'In what way?'

Something about the set of the girl's jaw made Elizabeth foresee stormy waters ahead. 'He likes his own way,' she said.

'Don't we all,' said Antonia sweetly.

Elizabeth ground her teeth. 'He upsets people,' she said.

'U . . . um,' said Antonia.

Elzabeth thought she would try another tack. 'We have to be very careful in placing our women deacons,' she said. 'You know, there can be untold problems. It's such a very close working relationship, and the wife may not understand this. Indeed, the curate may not, and it is a situation in which jealousy can very easily arise. We have to be very careful to safeguard against that. I mean, have you even met Father Trumpington's wife yet?'

Antonia blinked. What on earth was the woman talking about? Did she think she was going to try and seduce the man? Had she seen him? But Elizabeth appeared not to have noticed her expression of blank amazement. 'As women,' she was continuing, 'we do have to be especially careful, my dear, because we don't always realise the effect that we're having . . . After all, we may be arousing deep feelings for which the other person just cannot be held responsible . . . because of their vulnerability . . .'

Antonia stared at her, taking in the grey hair swept severely back and the bright pink lipstick. Her gaze travelled slowly down, resting briefly on the black clerical shirt and severe pleated skirt, before descending to the tough, no-nonsense brown brogues on Elizabeth's large, no-nonsense feet.

'Are you trying to tell me,' she said, dangerously quiet, 'that you seriously imagine I am about to embark on something improper with Father Trumpington?'

'No, of course not, my dear!' exclaimed Elizabeth. She was beginning to dislike intensely the turn the conversation was taking; in fact she was beginning to wish she had never embarked upon it. 'But I am saying there's no knowing how he'll react, or his wife, and we have to be very careful because of that . . . and you are extremely attractive.'

'But this problem could arise anywhere.'

'Of course it could, my dear!' Elizabeth began to feel that she was making headway.

'So on that basis, you wouldn't be willing to place me anywhere.'

The words fell like ice. 'No!' Elizabeth protested as their

meaning sank in. Really, this was all getting too much. 'I don't mean that you can't go anywhere. Only that we have to be very careful, and that you yourself have to be alerted to the dangers so that you won't inadvertently do anything that might arouse such feelings and cause trouble.'

Antonia gazed at her with cold eyes. She had the distinct impression that Elizabeth Marshall did not want her in the diocese and for some reason would do all in her power to block her appointment. 'I think I am warned,' she said coolly, 'and I shall certainly take great care to see that I don't in any way lead Father Trumpington astray.'

Elizabeth swallowed. She was not quite sure how, but she felt she had some time ago lost control of this interview. It had not gone at all the way she had planned. She felt angry with Antonia for being so obtuse but then, as she glared at her, a wave of pity suddenly swept over her. Almost without thinking, she said abruptly, 'My dear, why don't you just marry your fiancé? Henry could take care of you and then there wouldn't be this problem.'

It was the worst thing she could possibly have said. It had somehow never occurred to her that, married or not, Antonia would still want to work and, what was more, would want to be paid for the privilege. Elizabeth had always wanted very much to be married herself and to have children, and she still had the old-fashioned idea that husbands 'took care' of their wives. If questioned, she would have said that she thought Antonia extremely selfish even to want a paid job, if she was in that situation, when there were so many in the country who were unemployed. She could of course work voluntarily in a local parish until children came along (as in God's mercy they ought to, speedily) but she should not want to be a burden to the Church financially when there was no need.

Antonia, however, did not think like that. Whether or not she married Henry, she wanted, first and foremost, to do the job to which she felt called. And she wanted to be taken seriously. In some respects wise to the ways of the world, she knew that financial reimbursement would inevitably colour the attitude of others to what she did, and in Church circles she knew that a stipend meant status. If she did not have a fixed appointment or get paid, she would be relegated for ever to the ranks of virtuous and godly women, of value for their endless charitable acts and dispensing of largesse but of no real standing or power.

'I appreciate your concern,' she said through gritted teeth and striving to keep her voice even, 'but I fail to see how my marriage to Henry is at all material to the situation. I do not regard my appointment to St Godric's as simply a way of filling in time and something I'll give up as soon as I get married. I see it as a part of God's calling on my life, as something he has trained me for. And if I were to opt out now simply because you don't like the way Father Trumpington has gone about things, I would see that as unfaithfulness.'

Elizabeth was taken aback. She sensed, rather than saw, Antonia's anger, but for the life of her could not understand what had provoked it. She bit her lip. 'Well, I shall have to go back to the Bishop then,' she said. 'It is of course his decision. But you will certainly not go there with my recommendation!'

After Antonia had made her views plain to Elizabeth Marshall, there was very little that anyone could do to stop her appointment, although as events turned out it began to feel to her as if God himself was having second thoughts about the move. Everything seemed to go wrong. First, the salaries allocations board raised queries about the scale on which she was to be paid. She could not, they said, be paid out of the amount set aside for curates because that had already been allocated. The church she was going to would therefore have to pay. At this Father Trumpington objected. St Godric's already paid more than its parish share to the diocese, he announced, so all things being equal, the diocese should pay for his curate. No, said the salaries allocations board. Father Trumpington raged. The Bishop quailed . . . and a glimmer of hope dawned in Elizabeth's breast. But, after much argument, it died again, because the board came up with a compromise. Antonia could go to St Godric's, they said, but her stipend would have to be entirely separate from the fund allocated for the payment of curates. She would have to come under the old measures relating to lay women.

The argument took in all about six weeks, during which time

Antonia began to wonder whether after all she was going to be allowed to go. However, she had just resigned herself to looking for something else when suddenly, somehow, it all became magically settled.

The second obstacle, however, was if anything even more wounding. For the past ten years, St Godric's had been the proud possessor of a rather fine curate's house. Up until then the curate had had to make do with lodgings, but Father Trumpington had decided that this state of affairs reflected badly on his dignity. His assistant, he announced to a surprised PCC, should be accommodated in lodgings more befitting the position. St Godric's was important, he said. It was a large church serving a large community (he did not mention the fact it was usually three-quarters empty). It was simply not right that his assistant should have to be 'put up' here, there and everywhere like some itinerant broom salesman. They should build a house. So that was what they had done, with endless jumble sales, coffee mornings, gift days, and not a few Masonic gifts, and the result had been a rather palatial three-bedroomed detached house with a large garden, standing next to the church hall. It was into this house that Antonia had had every expectation of moving. However, some two months before she was due to be ordained, Father Trumpington phoned her.

'Hello, Antonia,' he bellowed. 'We've had great news! That organist we've been trying to entice has agreed to come. He should be starting a couple of weeks before you.'

Father Trumpington's pride and joy was the church organ. Only some two years previously St Godric's had had a rather mean looking, dilapidated specimen that had tended to wheeze at inconvenient moments. It had been serviceable but uninspiring. Father Trumpington had always disliked it, not only for its lack of size and power but also because he had a genuine passion for music. While in the evenings most other vicars were off to prayer meetings and worthy discussions about the latest missionary endeavours, he took himself off to the local choral society where he sang a lusty bass and terrified the conductor.

It had always irked him that St Godric's did not have an instrument worthy of his own swelling talent, so when one of the pipes cracked following a break-in at the church, he seized his opportunity and, instead of initiating repairs, persuaded the PCC that the offending instrument should be replaced. This proposal, needless to say, did not meet at first with the unqualified enthusiasm he had expected. Not a few parishioners, with rather more Christian commitment than himself, felt that any spare money could more properly be expended on causes of a more Christian nature. It was also forcibly pointed out to him by the then Treasurer that the church did not in fact have that amount of spare cash to hand, as necessary repairs to the church roof had for a while left them considerably in debt, a state from which they were only just beginning to recover.

Father Trumpington had thought of that one. He announced magisterially that it was their Christian duty to do all within their power to build up the 'body', a word of which he was fond and by which he meant the fabric rather than the fellowship. The cracking of the pipe, he said, was a sign. It was God's will that they acquire something more capable of rendering him praise. St Godric's was very large, he pointed out, they had always needed a bigger instrument. It was the penny-pinching ways of the last vicar that had been responsible for burdening them with something that was entirely inadequate to the size of the building.

At this there were mutterings; no one else had been especially aware that the organ was inadequate, and the last vicar, Father Trumpington's predecessor by twenty-five years, had been a saintly man, beloved by all. He had, sadly, suffered an untimely death at the age of thirty-six and left behind him a grieving congregation which had long held his example as a pattern of holiness to which they all aspired. But Father Trumpington would have none of this. It was his private opinion that Father Coddington had been a wet, while he thought his predecessor's predilection for giving away money to the Third World had been nothing short of criminal, given his responsibility to St Godric's which all too patently he had neglected. No, they should acquire something more fitting, and as to finance, well, there was really no problem at all, he said, because he had already worked it all out – which to the amazement of the assembled company it transpired he had.

His proposal was that they take the £9,000 already in the fabric fund, which they had been laboriously collecting to repay the loan for repairs to the roof, and that they borrow a further sum from the bank. There was an outcry at this because it would double the original debt, but again he was ready for them. He himself, he announced, would stand surety for £5,000, and his Masonic Lodge – which he had already approached – would stand surety for the rest (a huge sum of over £150,000). The PCC was flabbergasted, but there was more to come. Not only would the Lodge stand surety for any amount they borrowed, he told them, but they had further agreed to make a donation towards the cost of another £3,000 and had entered into negotiations on his behalf to sell their present organ to another smaller church where the tradition of music was not so highly valued.

At this, pandemonium broke out, headed by the Treasurer, who by this time had decided that he smelt an extremely unpleasant rat and was going to have none of it. But, yet again, Father Trumpington was ready for him. He had long disliked the Treasurer, who tended to display an unhealthy tendency to want to talk about God and who always attempted to block his more grandiose designs. He had therefore conceived a scheme some months before for his removal, and to this end had been quietly infiltrating on to the PCC some half-dozen Masonic cronies, whose contact with the church otherwise was minimal (indeed they had agreed to come along and join the congregation only to add their support to himself because he had confided he was having problems). Six were all he needed to sway any vote his way, because the majority of the PCC, he knew from experience, would do as they were told – as he told to be precise. After some argument he therefore engineered a vote of no confidence in the hapless Treasurer, who almost before he realised what was happening found himself voted out of his position and off the PCC, and one of Father Trumpington's cronies voted in.

After that there was no problem, and in what to the congregation seemed an amazingly short time they found themselves the not very proud possessors of a brand new organ, almost cathedral sized in its dimensions, and with an overdraft of £125,000. Father Trumpington was delighted, and he held a special service of dedication to which both the Bishop and the Mayor were invited, along with a whole host of other civic dignitaries and leading businessmen of the city – and they all came because they wanted to see the fruits of their investment. Yes, it was a glorious day, though the Bishop obviously was slightly mystified by the grandeur of the occasion.

But having got the organ, Father Trumpington then found that the organist was deficient. He played well enough on the old instrument, but only because his mistakes were not so apparent. Now, however, they were glaringly obvious, and Father Trumpington rapidly realised that he had to go. Moreover, not only was he not very skilled on the organ, but his efforts to organise the choir were a disaster.

Father Trumpington effected his removal by a campaign of bitter complaint and general suggestion that the poor man was wholly unsuited to his task. Fate then played into his hands with the untimely death of the organist's mother, which really did for a while make him unsuited for everything except mooning around and feeling sorry for himself. That worthy, at around this time, conceived the notion that everyone was against him, a feeling which, in his current state of emotional precariousness, he found unbearable. It then only needed Father Trumpington to criticise him publicly twice and suggest he was emotionally unstable (which by this time he was) and he resigned. Father Trumpington could hardly believe the ease with which he had accomplished the whole operation. Ever since, he had been looking round for someone more worthy of the calling, by which he meant someone of concert standard.

The individual he had fixed upon was a young and struggling composer, trying desperately to make a name for himself as a serious artist and performer. Norman Pilkington was a mere twenty-six but already married and with two children. Father Trumpington had heard him one night on the radio, and inquiries had elicited the information that he was resident organist at a church in Birmingham and struggling to make ends meet by giving music lessons on the side. A few judicious questions had elicited the information that the young couple were heavily in debt.

Dreams of glory began to form in Father Trumpington's mind.

He began to harbour visions not only of having an artist worthy of his beloved organ at St Godric's, but of St Godric's being the home and encourager of a major new talent. The church would become famous. *He* would become famous. He would be the Svengali to Norman Pilkington's talent. Christmas concerts would be broadcast from his church, recitals on Radio 4 would become a regular feature, and St Godric's would become a household name, along with King's College, Cambridge, or Christ Church, Oxford. Why, he might even get a bishopric out of this! Father Trumpington had always harboured designs of being a bishop, but so far that state of elevation had eluded him. If, however, he achieved the feat of making St Godric's a household name, they would have to give him preferment of some sort, surely. Father Trumpington had even begun to wonder which see he would prefer.

His first overtures were rejected. There was a limit to the amount of cash he could offer, and the figure he named did not prove sufficiently enticing. Father Trumpington had to cast around for some other allure. Lying awake one night, unable to sleep as he concocted and discarded scheme after scheme, he suddenly hit upon the most brilliantly simple idea. It was so simple, yet so perfect, he could not understand why he had not thought of it before. He wasted no time in the morning in ringing up the young man and putting the scheme to him. He actually got hold of his wife at first, but a brief chat with her only strengthened his position and, under the combined pressure of them both, the organist finally capitulated. It was this Father Trumpington was now phoning Antonia about.

'Wonderful news,' he repeated.

Antonia dutifully made appreciative noises.

'There's just one slight problem,' continued Father Trumpington. 'He's agreed to come only on condition that we provide housing.' Antonia said nothing as the first faint glimmerings of suspicion began to form in her mind, and Father Trumpington continued hurriedly, 'Of course I did try to reason with him, my dear, but he was absolutely adamant, and you can see his point. After all, he has got a wife and two children to support, and I knew that you wouldn't mind. After all, if there's just you by yourself, what would you want with a three-bedroomed house? Much too big . . .'

Antonia thought rapidly as he paused. 'You're trying to tell me,' she said finally, 'that you've said he can live in the curate's house.'

'No, of course not, my dear,' protested Father Trumpington, at his most benign. 'It's simply that he's left us with no alternative. He'll only come *if* he has the curate's house to live in. I don't *want* him to have it! It's just that we have no choice.'

There was silence, then, 'What about me?' she inquired icily. 'Where am I going to be expected to live?'

'Oh, don't worry about that,' said Father Trumpington airily. 'We always used to manage before we built the house. We'll find you lodgings with one of the good ladies of the parish. In fact, all in all it might turn out to be much better this way. You won't be lonely racketing around in a great big empty house all by yourself, and at the same time you'll be company for some poor soul who might also be lonely on her own. It'll be an extension of your pastoral concern. Wonderful training!'

Antonia wanted to protest that she did not really want that kind of training, and that she had been rather looking forward to 'racketing around' in a three-bedroomed house all by herself. It had actually seemed just about the only draw to the job, over and above its proximity to Henry. But Father Trumpington gave her no chance.

'I'm so pleased you understand,' he boomed. 'But I knew you would. And don't worry about lodgings, I'll find you something suitable – though of course, there'll be the cost to think about.'

Antonia almost choked, and Father Trumpington seemed to realise he was on dangerous ground. 'But don't worry about that,' he continued hastily. 'In the circumstances I expect the church will see to all of that. So glad you understand. Really is wonderful news, isn't it? Cheerio!' And he rang off, not giving her the chance to say a word more.

Antonia was seething, but there was very little she could do. A complaint to the Reverend Marshall only brought forth the comment, 'Well, we never wanted you to go there in the first place', which, though true, did little to ease the situation. Henry also proved unsympathetic; in fact if anything he merely seemed annoyed at the inconvenience to himself. 'You mean I won't be able to visit you,' he said crossly, and then he brightened. 'Never mind, you'll just have to come round and stay with me!' Antonia gave him a look that spoke volumes, and they ended up by having a row – rows seemed to be erupting between them with increasing frequency these days.

In the end, there was absolutely nothing she could do about the situation. If she still wanted to go to St Godric's – and there was certainly nothing else on the horizon – she would just have to resign herself. A feeling of gloom had engulfed her. While everyone else at college was eagerly preparing for their various ordinations and swapping excited tales about the parishes to which they were to go, she began to feel like some kind of ecclesiastical pariah, unwanted by God and man alike.

Even that, however, was not an end to her troubles. Two weeks before her ordination she arrived back late one night at her room in Becket to find a note pinned to her door. 'Dear Antonia,' it read, 'I find that I shall be unable to attend your ordination as planned as I have been asked to conduct an important Masonic service at Clapham. I am sure you will understand. We look forward to seeing you at St Godric's the following day. Your lodgings are all arranged (an address was included). Every blessing, your sincere friend, Richard Trumpington. P.S. I have asked an old curate of mine who lives locally to perform my part in the ordination ceremony.'

Antonia could only stare at the note in disbelief. She had never before heard of such a thing. The vicar of the parish to which an ordinand was being licensed always attended – but not, it appeared, Father Trumpington. She refolded the note and noticed for the first time the envelope in which it had arrived. It had already been used once. On the front was Father Trumpington's name and address, hastily crossed out, and her own name scrawled in pencil across the top. 'Bloody typical,' she muttered, looking at it with disgust. She wondered briefly if Norman Pilkington was ever the recipient of such missives, and then dismissed the idea bitterly; he would be far too important a personage for Father Trumpington to risk such treatment. 'Sod it!' she said aloud. 'And sod Father bloody Trumpington!' She felt slightly better. She apologised to God, then screwed up the letter and the envelope and threw them both into the bin.

Chapter Three

Years later, when Antonia looked back on her first service at St Godric's, she wondered if some premonitory spirit had not been trying to warn her of the awfulness to come. She arrived some twenty minutes early, with Henry in tow, feeling both excited and nervous and as if everyone was staring at her shirt. There was a short, rather blowsy-looking woman with bleached, straw-coloured hair and an unwelcoming expression at the door, handing out books. She eyed Antonia narrowly, her full, impossibly cherry lips pursing into an expression of obvious disapproval. 'I suppose you're the new deaconess,' she said, her eyes resting briefly on Antonia's collar.

Her tone was cold and Antonia bristled, but she forced herself to smile. 'Deacon,' she corrected, 'I'm ordained. And if the measure goes through Synod this session, I'll be priested next year.'

The woman looked unimpressed. 'Hum,' she said. Then she shrugged and held out her hand. 'I'm Gloria,' she announced. 'Mrs Sunnington to you. I'm one of the churchwardens. We hope you'll be very happy here.' Her expression seemed to suggest the reverse, and at her side Antonia felt Henry stiffen. 'I'm sure you'll find you will be,' she continued, 'so long as you don't do anything to rock the boat. We've got a very strong *Anglican* tradition here. In fact, some of us feel we're the only really Anglican church in the city.'

There was an uncomfortable silence and then Henry asked, 'And what exactly do you mean by Anglican?'

'I mean,' she said tartly, detecting something of opposition in his tone, 'that we value our traditions. We do things properly here, none of that nonsense that seems to be happening everywhere else. And we don't like it when people try and disrupt us.' She glared at him, as if challenging him to disagree, but then suddenly her manner changed and she gave Antonia an oily smile. 'But I'm sure *you're* not like that, dear,' she said pointedly.

It was a warning and Antonia knew it. Gloria Sunnington, all four feet eleven of her, had apparently made up her mind to dislike her. They looked at each other measuringly, and then Gloria said, 'And who is this? Your young man? We heard you were engaged.'

Knowing it was expected of her, Antonia introduced Henry, but her eyes wandered almost unconsciously down the church. It looked almost as grim as Gloria. At that hour of the evening St Godric's was gloomy, illuminated by a kind of murky half-light. As far as she could make out all the lights were on, but there was still a 40-watt feel about the place, as if it was struggling along on half power, and the air felt clammy and cold, like a house that has stood empty for years. She shivered involuntarily.

'What's wrong, dear?' inquired Gloria, noticing. 'Someone walk over your grave?' And she laughed loudly, the odd metallic sound somehow contributing to the macabre atmosphere.

'What a harridan,' muttered Henry, as soon as they were out of what he judged to be earshot. 'There seems something positively malevolent about her.'

Antonia shrugged. 'Maybe she just doesn't like the idea of women in the Church.'

He looked dubious. 'I don't know,' he said, 'it felt like more than that. She was almost vitriolic.' He paused. They were about five rows from the front. 'I guess I'll sit here,' he said, his tone unenthusiastic.

Her eyes followed his gaze over the empty pews. So far the entire congregation was made up of only six people. Four were women, the youngest of whom was about sixty, and two were men, both of whom looked to be in their eighties. All six sat by themselves and at a safe distance from everyone else and, in the gloomy light, there looked to be an air of defeat about them.

'Well, you're certainly not going to be restricted for choice,' Antonia said drily. She pulled his head down towards her and gave him a quick peck on the cheek. 'Wish me luck,' she muttered. 'I think I'm going to need it.'

If the church was depressing, she discovered that the vestry was even worse. The light, if it was possible, was even murkier, and there was an air of untidy, neglected dilapidation about the place, as if it had not seen a duster in years. Against one wall stood a battered desk, its top strewn with yellowed books and bits of curling paper. In the corner beside it was a massive safe, easily as tall as herself and with a huge handle and dial on the front. It was the one thing that looked to be in working order in the whole church, and she stared at it in amazement, wondering what on earth they kept in it. She found it hard to imagine that the register of births, deaths and marriages warranted this kind of security. Perhaps, she thought, they stored bodies of parishioners there if they died during the service. She began to wonder, yet again, if she had made the most terrible mistake. At that moment, however, the door opened behind her and a little whistle of cold air blew in. 'Ah! Good evening, you made it!' boomed a voice. And the vestry was suddenly full of a swirling, black-caped figure, with a Russian fur hat perched on top of its balding head. Father Trumpington had arrived.

From that moment the service took on a kind of nightmarish quality. In a blur of growing misery Antonia found herself told to read the epistle and lead the prayers. 'None of your extempore stuff,' boomed Father Trumpington. 'Use this.' And he produced a little, dog-eared book of prayers which, when Antonia surreptitiously glanced at the flyleaf, yielded the date 'November 4th, 1920'. Under strict instruction, she prayed for the state of the nation, those engaged in caring for the sick (because, as Father Trumpington explained, they had a hospital in the parish), and for provision for the deserving poor. The response on the part of the congregation was not, she felt, one of unmitigated enthusiasm, but Father Trumpington assured her that that was what they liked; all eighteen of them. The congregation had grown while she had been in the vestry. Meanwhile Father Trumpington preached an inspiring and lofty sermon (to his evident opinion, at least, though it did not appear to be a view shared by the congregation) on the importance of Elgar. Afterwards he invited them all back for coffee to meet the new curate, at which point somebody snored.

Antonia discovered, however, that she had been wrong in imagining the congregation to be composed entirely of geriatrics. At least, to be strictly accurate, the congregation *was* composed almost entirely of geriatrics (with the exception of Henry, Gloria

Sunnington, and a girl who looked to be about her own age and was heavily pregnant), but the choir was rather more diverse. To her surprise she discovered two men, both of whom appeared to be in their thirties and one of whom sported a blue lay reader's scarf, three women, and five small boys aged between about nine and twelve. These last behaved appallingly throughout the service and sang indifferently, if at all, yet this latter fact did not seem to bother Father Trumpington. He appeared in fact to be blissfully ignorant of what was going on behind his back, and from the expression on his face during the anthem, which he joined in lustily, one would have imagined that he heard the supernatural strains of angelic choirs.

It was the women, however, who drew Antonia's attention the most, or rather one of them. Two of them looked to be in about their twenties. One was very earnest, with brown bobbed hair and glasses, and the other was a fresh-faced sturdy looking girl with curly blonde hair and an upturned nose, who grinned at her in a friendly way. The third woman was rather older. She was, Antonia judged, in her mid to late forties, and she evidently thought herself to be extremely smart. She was tall, about five foot ten, with impossibly black short hair and arresting blue eyes, the lids of which she fluttered repeatedly in an appealing sort of way whenever they were turned in the direction of one of the men. She looked, Antonia thought, like the archetypal vamp from a silent movie, mysterious and aloof; but at the same time there seemed something ominously chilling and cold about her. Like Father Trumpington, she sang lustily, and once Antonia saw her lean forward and tap one of the boys sharply on the head. Antonia she ignored.

Afterwards Antonia collected Henry and the two of them (Father Trumpington not having deemed it necessary to wait for them) went to the welcome evening at the vicarage. It was a dismal affair. About half the congregation had made the effort and come along, and there were around a dozen other faces there as well that were entirely new to her, so that there were about twenty-five of them gathered in all. These, Father Trumpington explained, were habitués of the morning service and were mainly on the PCC. They appeared to be rather younger than the

32

evensong brigade but again, with a couple of exceptions, the youngest was about fifty, and the women by far outnumbered the men.

Although she had not been at the service, Father Trumpington's wife, Dorothy, was also there, handing round plates and supervising the disposal of sausage rolls. Apart from one brief encounter on the doorstep, and despite Elizabeth Marshall's oft-repeated protestations, it was the first time that Antonia had had the chance properly to meet her. 'Hello,' she said as they came into the rather gloomy hall, preparing to be friendly, but Dorothy gave her an affrighted look and leapt about a foot back, almost dropping the plate she was carrying.

'Oh dear, you startled me,' she said, disapprovingly. And Antonia was surprised to see her face suddenly flush scarlet, while her anxious eyes seemed riveted on some point beyond Antonia's shoulder. In spite of herself Antonia half turned, trying to see what was engaging the other woman's attention. Behind her she found the three women from the choir, and an elderly lady with a Zimmer frame, but she was not sure if they were what Dorothy was looking at or not. Indeed, when she turned back, she thought she must have been mistaken, and that it was herself Dorothy was reacting to, because her face now bore a look of faint but unmistakable hostility. 'Well, come along in then, do,' she chided impatiently. 'We thought you'd be here before now.'

Antonia muttered something about having had to take off her robes. 'Yes, well,' Dorothy seemed unimpressed, 'you'll find Dick and everybody in the sitting room.' Her manner, while not exactly unfriendly, was distinctly chilly. In fact, she seemed ill at ease, and having delivered this salvo she scuttled off in the direction of the kitchen, her cheeks still pink.

It did not seem the most auspicious of starts. Antonia had been told beforehand that the event was to welcome her and Henry to the parish, but she rapidly discovered that the main purpose of the evening seemed to be rather to welcome the new organist. She was virtually ignored by Father Trumpington, while every so often his voice would boom across the room, 'Have you met Norman and his wife yet?' A few people came up to her and introduced themselves, but by and large she was left to herself to make the overtures, while several times she was conscious of Gloria Sunnington's eyes fixed suspiciously upon her, although the other woman made no further attempt to approach her. Then, about halfway through the evening, a small, plump woman with a jolly face came up and drew Henry aside. 'You look after her,' she said confidentially. 'Tell her to stand up for herself. He'll destroy her otherwise. Likes too much of his own way, he does!'

'Pardon?' said Henry.

The woman seemed totally oblivious of there being anything odd about her remark. 'Tell her not to let him browbeat her,' she said emphatically. 'I've known him since he was a boy. He grew up here, you know, and he was always a bully. I can't understand what made him go into the Church, but there you are. I sometimes think he'd have been better off as a bank manager, but then I suppose the life wouldn't have suited him.'

Henry was by now looking appalled. Although all of twenty-eight and, as he prided himself, wise to the ways of the world (indeed, he had a flourishing criminal practice growing up), he retained a perhaps oddly moral attitude to life and had a very strong sense of right and wrong. To describe a priest in these terms was unthinkable. He gaped at the woman in astonishment, temporarily bereft of words.

Perhaps fortunately, it was at this point that Father Trumpington chose to address the assembled company. He had seized hold of an empty coffee cup and was banging it noisily with a teaspoon in order to gain everybody's attention. In this he was not entirely successful, because one old lady continued oblivious with a monologue on the state of her corns, until peremptorily shoved in the back by Gloria Sunnington and loudly told to 'Sshh'. After that silence fell, and Father Trumpington beamed round.

'Friends!' he began. 'It is with truly great pleasure that I welcome you all here tonight on this joyous occasion. Indeed, we have a double cause for celebration, as I'm sure I don't need to tell you. Last week, our new organist, Norman Pilkington, took up his appointment with us, and I'm sure that you'll all agree that under his magic touch, our organ, gained by my efforts . . . and of course your support, sounds truly magnificent. The life of our church can only be enriched, and we expect great things of him.'

At this point, one of the men from the choir coughed noisily as if in protest, and Father Trumpington glared at him. But, determined to let nothing interfere with his mood of bonhomie, after a moment he continued, 'So it is with great pleasure that we welcome Norman here tonight, together with his wife, Gudrun, and we hope that they will be very happy here with us.'

The pregnant girl from the congregation now came forward and slipped a hand through her husband's arm. Her cheeks were slightly pink, as if she found the attention difficult, and she beamed self-consciously. Beside them stood the black-haired woman from the choir. She was simpering in an odd sort of way, and she suddenly said, 'Oh hear, hear!' Then, to everyone's surprise, she started to clap.

There was a moment's embarrassed silence and then, as if not quite sure of themselves, a few other people joined in, while the rest stood silent and still.

'Yes, well,' said Father Trumpington after a minute, 'let's move on. Our second cause for celebration tonight is the appointment of our new lady curate, the Reverend Antonia Beecher-Henty.' He beamed, evidently tremendously pleased with himself. 'Antonia is of course the first woman we have ever had at St Godric's, and she also has the honour of being the first woman appointed to the deanery.' He smiled smugly, or was it maliciously? Antonia was not quite sure which. 'Of course St Godric's is something of a trendsetter in this respect,' he continued, 'and it is undeniable that there are those within the deanery who oppose the ordination of women as priests. But we must, I say, move with the times, and Antonia, as a former barrister, is more than suitable for the fine tradition of Anglicanism that we have at St Godric's.' He had moved smoothly into Winston Churchill mode. 'As rector of our little vessel I feel it incumbent on me to be in the forefront of reform. We must look to the future, and I take it as a duty to give a lead to my fellow clergy. With our fine new organ and organist of inter-national repute, St Godric's will now give a lead to the city!'

There was no welcoming applause for Antonia at the end of Father Trumpington's introduction. Indeed, the priest gave no opportunity because, having once again alluded to his organ and the brilliance of Norman Pilkington, he went on to remind people that they still had an outstanding debt of £96,000 to pay off. If any of them should feel moved to contribute generously before the evening was over, he would be more than happy to receive contributions. This, perhaps unsurprisingly, had a rather dampening effect on the assembled company, and when he finished there was an awkward pause, broken by Gloria Sunnington who suddenly trilled, 'Perhaps we should have a concert!' Her words fell like lead into a murky pond, but Father Trumpington started, as if he had had sudden and unexpected divine revelation.

'A concert! Of course!' he said. 'Perhaps we could get the BBC . . .'

Antonia and Henry endured it for another hour, and were just gathering themselves up in readiness to slip away when a small grey man in his early sixties elbowed his way towards them. He caught Antonia's arm and hissed, 'We've been praying for you!'

Antonia, in the act of drawing on her jacket, jumped. 'Pardon?' she said.

'We've been praying for you,' the man repeated, 'a group of us. We've been asking God to send us someone. God promised that he would.'

'Did he?' said Antonia.

'Yes,' continued the man. 'Some of us were here before his mightiness arrived. Neville Coddington was vicar then, wonderful man, he was, really close to God. St Godric's was different then, things were happening. But then he died, and after that Dick came, and he was a very different kettle of fish. All he's ever cared for is what he calls his plant!'

For Antonia, it was one of those surreal moments when you have not the slightest idea what the other person is talking about but strongly suspect, from their general demeanour, that they may be mad. 'Plant?' she echoed.

'Yes, you know,' said the man, staring at her earnestly, 'the building. New doors, the church clock, the organ. None of us wanted that. It was him, said we had to have it. The money it cost! We've had three years fund-raising already, and all so as he can say he's got the finest organ in the city. Pah! But we've been praying for things to change.' He leant forward and Antonia felt his warm breath on her cheek. 'St Godric's was very different once,' he said softly, 'and some of us still remember that, whatever he thinks.' He indicated Father Trumpington with a jerk of his head. 'He can't put the light out, no matter what he does. God won't let this go on!'

Suddenly, Antonia became aware that a hush had fallen on the room and that people were staring uneasily over in their direction. She looked up in time to catch Father Trumpington's gimlet eye fixed upon her. He looked annoyed, though she could not imagine why, and his lips were pursed angrily. He was standing beside Gloria Sunnington and Antonia saw him mutter something to her and then detach himself, heading purposefully in their direction like a particularly belligerent man-o'-war. Her companion became aware of him in the same instant and pulled a wry face. 'He won't like me talking to you,' he whispered. 'He's afraid what I might say.' And then aloud he exclaimed, 'Dick, I was just telling young Antonia here about all that you'd done for St Godric's, and about our prayer group.'

Father Trumpington smiled evilly. 'I'm sure you have been, Ken,' he said, 'but I think we ought to let Antonia settle in and find her feet first before we burden her with the entire history of the church.'

'But I'm interested,' Antonia protested, wanting to hear now what the man had to say.

Father Trumpington, however, placed a firm hand under her elbow and began to propel her none too gently away. 'Come and meet our Treasurer before you go, my dear,' he said, in a tone that brooked no argument. 'You must get to know the important people of the church.'

'Right,' said Antonia. Her feet skipped as she found herself yanked away. 'Nice to meet you ... er ...' she called over her shoulder to the man.

'Ken Brown,' he supplied. 'I'll see you again.'

Antonia awoke the next morning to a grey day. She had drawn back the faded dahlia-covered curtains the night before, and now the tired morning light was attempting to crawl dispiritedly in through the murky panes of glass. They looked as if they had not been cleaned since Mrs Earnshaw, her landlady, had first taken up residence some thirty years before.

Mrs Earnshaw, Father Trumpington had informed her, was a lady truly in need of pastoral care. As Antonia understood it, she had attended St Godric's regularly for the past seven Christmases. Only at Christmas, never at other times during the year, but that, to Father Trumpington, made her a stalwart of the church. He had asked her to provide lodgings for Antonia when she had given him a cheque for £10 on the last St Godric's gift day. He had waylaid her on her way home from the shops as he sat at his little table outside the church, demanding money from passers-by. Father Trumpington, it should be said, thought he had a talent for fund-raising. Who else with a congregation of only seventy could manage to raise over £5,000 at a church gift day each year? Because of this, his standing in the diocese was, he thought, impeccable. Others could collect souls, but he would collect the money that would allow the ship to sail on!

In Mrs Earnshaw's case, she had been too embarrassed to refuse because Father Trumpington had shown every sign of not allowing her to continue on her way until she had put something in the box that he had rattled ostentatiously under her nose. Besides which, she was carrying a bag with 'Liberty' stamped all over it, and was acutely conscious of the skirt costing eighty pounds inside. It should be understood that for Kathleen Earnshaw to have spent this kind of money on clothes was not at all normal; in fact it was distinctly unusual and she was already steeped in guilt. So when Father Trumpington jumped up, she had the unpleasant feeling that he knew exactly what she had bought and how much it had cost, and that he disapproved. It was for that reason alone that she had grudgingly pulled out her cheque book and, without thinking of the consequences, written him a cheque.

She could not afford this cheque, just as she could not afford the skirt, but buying the skirt had been like an act of miserable defiance made to an uncaring world. She knew she could not afford it. She knew she had only ten pounds left for food for the last ten days of the month – one pound for each day. But she was so depressed by the endless struggle to make ends meet that she simply no longer cared. It had been a long time since she had had anything new, and she had thought to herself, 'I'll buy that skirt and to hell with it!'

However, misery fell into step beside her as soon as she got down from the bus. She knew it was no good. By the time Father Trumpington leapt up from his seat on the pavement, startling her like some particularly nasty imp, she had sunk into a mood of black depression that the Archangel Gabriel himself would have been hard put to shake. It need hardly be pointed out that Father Trumpington bore absolutely no resemblance to the Archangel Gabriel at all, and his motive in stopping her was clearly not to alleviate despair – in fact, he did not even notice there was anything wrong (although if he had, it is extremely doubtful that he would have behaved any differently). But in the mood she was in, Father Trumpington's demand seemed almost like retribution from an all-seeing God, and so it felt only right that she should sign away her last ten pounds and resign herself to returning the skirt straightaway. Her act of defiance had died.

But as she was turning away to go on, and Father Trumpington was congratulating himself on yet another addition to the fund, both she and he were astounded to hear him say, 'I don't suppose you'd like a lodger, would you, in that rambling old barn of yours?' Father Trumpington was not at all sure what possessed him to say that at that precise moment. Antonia was the last person on his mind, and besides, he had rather thought to place her under the beady eye of Gloria Sunnington, but the words just popped out before he was conscious they were even in his mind and, to his intense surprise, he had found himself looking uncomfortably straight into Mrs Earnshaw's startled eyes. And wishing for all the world that the words were unsaid.

Mrs Earnshaw could only blink at him in amazement, wondering if she had heard aright. It had never occurred to her to take a lodger – after all, you never knew about people. Besides, she was not sure she wanted that kind of invasion into her life. On the other hand, she was desperate for money, and she suddenly realised, with a start, that she was also desperate for a reason to live.

She had gone as a bride to what Father Trumpington described as her 'rambling barn' thirty years before, at the age of twenty-eight. From the start it had not been a happy marriage and when Martin, her feckless younger husband, had left her after only some three years of what had turned out to be unadulterated hell, no one had been surprised, least of all herself. In fact, she had been secretly glad. But he had gone leaving her with a mountain of debts and with the paint firm he had been working for in angry pursuit because he had taken one of their cars.

She had not been able to sell the house because it was in his name and he had simply disappeared at that point – no one knew where. In fact he had run off to India with some bizarre notion of joining a commune and discovering the meaning of life, but that had not emerged until a long time after, and meanwhile she had gone back to work as a shorthand typist, determined, if at all possible, to pay off all the debts. Eight years later, just as she was beginning to surface, she had had news of his death, of a brain haemorrhage. Only then had it emerged that his mind had been damaged years before, following an accident from which he had never fully recovered. She had never realised, had never even known about the accident or the steel plate fitted in his head. The news of his death brought her indescribable sadness, because only then had she begun to have some inkling of the demons with which he had lived. But by then, of course, it was too late. Too late to help. Too late to escape the pain.

To her surprise, she discovered she had inherited the house – the house on which she had paid the mortgage. Martin had at least thought to make a will, and she had a dim idea that he had been trying to make amends. She could have sold it then, of course, but because she had nowhere else to go, she stayed. And, living frugally, she had managed.

That, however, had all changed two years before, because the firm she had been working for had gone into receivership, and in the process they had somehow managed to wipe out the staff pension fund along with all the assets. At the age of fifty-six, Kathleen Earnshaw had found herself without a job and with very little money in the bank. She had no family, and no close friends, but she still had her pride, and so, yet again, she had begun the struggle to survive. Only now she was older, and she no longer had any hope. She found a friend in the occasional tipple of cooking sherry, and grimly hung on. But that morning, when she went into town and made the disastrous purchase of the skirt, she realised that she was on the point of giving up.

Thus it was, to the intense surprise of them both, that she heard herself saying, in an odd little voice, 'Why, yes, I might very well be interested in a lodger.' And then her cheeks suffused with colour and she muttered incoherently, 'Becomes so lonely, you know, and the dark nights.' And so, as simply as that, it was settled.

That first morning, however, Antonia did not feel exactly conscious of divine purpose at work. In fact she felt rather depressed with everything, and as if God had forgotten her. After what felt like the fiasco of her parish welcome the night before, she and Henry had parted, yet again, with 'words'. He had been angry at what he felt to be the slight dealt her by Father Trumpington and she, irritated at what she felt to be his interference, had forbidden him to speak. 'It's all very well,' he had complained, 'but this man treats you like that, and I'm supposed just to stand by and say nothing. But we're engaged, Antonia. I'm going to be your husband. I'm supposed to look after you!'

'Oh, for heaven's sake, Henry!' she had snapped. 'Stop sounding so medieval. You don't understand how the church works! You'll just cause problems. Grow up!'

He had stormed off angrily, and she had gone to bed feeling sick because she had felt just as annoyed and upset as he had over her 'welcome' but had not the slightest idea what to do.

In the grey light of the morning, all of Elizabeth Marshall's warnings came back to her, but she was acutely conscious, as she dragged herself out of bed and showered and dressed, that there were no alternatives. It was either St Godric's or nothing.

It was, therefore, in a mood of grim determination that she arrived at the church that first morning for the early morning office. She arrived before Father Trumpington and so had to stand outside, waiting for him on the pavement. The church was locked at this early hour, and Father Trumpington had not yet seen fit to entrust her with a key, although he had already given a full set to the organist. It was distinctly chilly in the early morning air, and the skies overhead were now black and overcast, as if a storm was pending. Then, in the distance, there was a low rumble of thunder, and the first heavy drops of rain began to fall in large, isolated splodges on the pavement. Antonia huddled back under the shelter of the door, and cursed the fact that she could not get in.

Father Trumpington saw her as he rounded the corner and strode jauntily down the street. He seemed totally oblivious of the rain, which was by now falling in earnest, and was swinging his arms briskly. He had on a long grey coat buttoned tightly over his chest, and his fur cossack hat was perched, as ever, rakishly on the side of his head. 'Good morning, good morning!' he boomed when he came within twenty-five yards of her.

He was quite obviously feeling good. The weather might be overcast and grey but his manner seemed to suggest that, after a long gloomy night, he felt the sun was once again rising on his little empire. He surveyed his new curate with satisfaction, the warm glow in his chest intensified by this tangible reminder of his victory over the Reverend Marshall. 'Come along, my dear,' he said jocularly. 'Let's bustle on in. Beautiful morning!'

It had been cold the night before and the church felt freezing, with a kind of dank, funereal chill that penetrated through to the bones. It was, thought Antonia, a rather ugly building, with its deep red bricks and the pale turquoise carpet that led up the nave. The colours jarred. There were stained-glass windows down the sides and over the altar, but they were somehow colourless and stern. The saints engraved upon them looked miserable, and the light that filtered through gave off an unhealthy glow, adding to the general feeling of cold. 'Attractive place, isn't it?' bellowed Father Trumpington. 'We spent a fortune on the carpet. But it was worth it!'

He led the way briskly down to the Lady Chapel and, seconds later, Antonia found herself installed in a heavy, and extremely uncomfortable, oak chair before the tiny altar. Father Trumpington himself sat on a kind of ornate bishop's throne, the seat made easy by a large velvet cushion, upon which he planted his equally large behind with a sigh of content. He thrust a copy of the 1662

Morning Office into her hands. 'You can read the lessons,' he announced, 'and I'll say the office. We'll say the psalm together.'

And he was off at lightning pace, charging through the words, investing them with a total lack of meaning that left her feeling dazed. 'Lord, have mercy,' he intoned loudly. In face of such a peremptory command, Antonia felt that the Lord would not dare do otherwise. The whole office took nine minutes – she timed it – and at the end Father Trumpington sat back with a sigh of relief. 'Good bit of discipline that,' he said. 'Now, let's give you your duties for the day. Oh, and by the way,' he fished in his pocket and held out to her what looked like a rough scrap of paper, 'here's your timetable for the week.'

Antonia looked at it, taken aback. Written in heavy black pencil was '1. Visit all members of PCC', followed by a list of twelve names. Then underneath, set out in rough columns, one for each day of the week, she read: 'Monday, day off; Tuesday, morning, Ambleside House, visiting the elderly; afternoon, old people's home; Wednesday, rehabilitation centre for the disabled at St Thomas's; Thursday, morning, assist with home Communions in hospital; afternoon, old people's home; Friday, visiting down Greystoke Road; Saturday, old people's home. Morning office daily at 8.30 in church, evening office Tuesdays and Thursdays, chapel of Ambleside House.' 'Are there a lot of old people's homes in the parish?' she asked uncertainly.

Father Trumpington looked surprised. 'No, just the two. Ambleside House and the other place.'

'This is what you want me to do this week?'

Father Trumpington stared at her. 'No,' he said. 'I just explained, this is your weekly timetable – every week.'

There was a small silence and then Antonia said, 'Isn't that rather a lot of visiting to two old people's homes, three times every week?'

Father Trumpington snorted. 'My dear Antonia, I'm what you call an old-fashioned sort of a priest. The stable I came out of, curates did as they were told. This is what I want you to do, so you do it! That way I know what you're doing. I'll know you won't be wasting time. And I've given you Greystoke Road because I know you like evangelism.' He made it sound as if it was a treat.

'But what about the rest of the parish?' she asked. 'When am I to visit them? Aren't there mums and toddlers and things that I can go along to? Aren't there any existing prayer groups?'

Father Trumpington grunted in dismissal. 'I see not the slightest necessity for you to go around visiting people will-nilly in the parish,' he said. 'Greystoke Road you'll find very nice. A challenge. It's on the council estate.' Father Trumpington pronounced this last as if it was somehow distasteful. 'None of them come to church from down there, they're a bit of a rough bunch, but I'm quite happy to let you try and evangelise them. But I don't want that sort of thing going on in the rest of the parish. Causes havoc! And they're a nice little crowd in the old people's home, you'll like them there. You'll soon get to know them. They'll make you cups of tea and things.' He beamed. 'I'll come with you the first time and introduce you.'

Antonia digested this. 'Is there a weekly service at either of them?' she ventured at last. She had not the slightest idea what she was supposed to do but was trying very hard not to antagonise him.

Father Trumpington almost exploded. 'Good heavens, of course not. If they want a service they can come to church. And no home Communions either, unless they're dying! But first of all, I do want you to get to know everyone on the PCC.'

There was a brief pause, and then finally she said, 'What about study time for my MA? We'd agreed I'd have time for that. And what about the fellowship group you said I could start? You haven't timetabled it.'

Father Trumpington assumed an air of injured puzzlement. 'I've given you time for study,' he said. 'Wednesday afternoons. And what do you mean about a fellowship group? I recollect us talking about the possibility of one, but I don't remember anything being settled.'

'You said I could start one,' she said indignantly. 'We talked about it when I first came over, and you definitely said that if I came I could start one up. And forgive me for pressing this, but you also said I could have two days a week for study and sermon preparation. I can't possibly complete my MA with just one afternoon a week.'

It was the moment Father Trumpington had been trying to avoid. He was perfectly aware of everything he had said at his first meeting with Antonia, but he had not the slightest intention now of honouring his words. He smiled at her patronisingly. 'All in good time, my dear.' He laid a paternal hand on her knee. 'I'm not at all averse to you fitting in little bits of study wherever else you can you know. You should have plenty of time for that. And you can always prepare your sermons in the evenings – when you're not doing anything else.' He gave her knee a squeeze. 'But the most important thing of all, at first, is that you should familiarise yourself with the parish. Why, you don't even know if we need a fellowship group yet.' His tone implied that she would soon discover that they did not. 'Plenty of time,' he said, now oozing bonhomie. 'Let's get your evangelism of Greystoke Road off the ground first. See if you can win any souls!' And he smirked, finally releasing her knee and resolutely turning his face away, as if to signify that that was an end to the matter.

Antonia bit her lip, stifling an angry retort. She was absolutely furious, offended as much by the patronising hand on her knee as by his words. But she realised that success would demand a little bit of guile here. She decided to bide her time. 'I'll visit the PCC,' she said.

Chapter Four

It was a quarter past five. The soft notes of the organ echoed through the gathering gloom and then hung shimmering in the air, before dying gently away. A thrill of pride ran down Father Trumpington's spine. He had come into the vestry as Norman Pilkington first struck up, about ten minutes before. The organist was unaware of his presence. Father Trumpington had intended merely to pick up his surplice so that Dorothy could wash it in readiness for the coming week, but as the notes swelled out he had hung on entranced, captivated by their sheer beauty and power. This young man was going to go far, he was sure; and the thought occurred to him yet again that St Godric's was going to go far too, pulled along on the coat tails of Norman Pilkingon's fame. A leader, he reflected smugly, commands able men. And, not for the first time in recent weeks, Father Trumpington saw again in his mind's eye the faint outline of a bishop's mitre and staff. It might still be possible, he reflected, even if he was sixty-two.

Sighing gently, he turned away. Just at this precise moment he had other concerns, and not even the allure of episcopal elevation could long hold his attention in face of this other far more important issue.

Stuffing the surplice into his briefcase, Father Trumpington stole quietly out of the vestry, his mind reverting again to the question of whether or not to go and visit Jackie Newberg. This was not a pastoral visit, it should be said. Jackie Newberg was the suave seductress from the choir who had caught Antonia's attention on her first evening, and Father Trumpington was in love. He knew it was madness. Compared with himself, Jackie was a mere girl, forty-eight to his sixty-two; besides which she was married, although her husband was working out in India, and had not been much in evidence in the parish for the past two years. Whether his feelings were reciprocated, Father

Trumpington was not yet sure, though that she was interested he was certain. He had taken to visiting her regularly over the last couple of months, every two or three days in fact, and for weeks past she had kept glancing at him coyly from her seat in the choir. Then, only the other Sunday, at the welcome for Norman Pilkington and Antonia, she had come up to him breathlessly and said, 'Oh Dick, what a wonderful sermon. Elgar! How uplifting! I really think you ought to compile a book. Such a comfort...' And to his amazement and startled delight, a tear had formed in the corner of her left eye and spilled delicately over on to her cheek. What it signified he was uncertain, but she had instantly and deftly wiped it away, before it could damage her mascara. 'You're such a comfort,' she had continued, catching her breath. 'Where would I be if it weren't for you?'

At that moment Dorothy had come up and they had both started guiltily, before Jackie had turned away and begun talking, equally beathlessly, to Edgar Slynne, a fellow member of the morning choir. But Father Trumpington had been left with the delicious sense of naughty and clandestine passion, and he had gone slightly pink, for all the world like a schoolboy caught out doing something he should not. Dorothy had evidently felt the same, because she had looked at him sharply before banging down a plate of sausage rolls on the table and scurrying away.

It did not occur to Father Trumpington that he owed his wife any loyalty in this matter and that he should, from that moment, avoid Jackie Newberg like the plague. If he thought about it at all afterwards, it was to tell himself that he deserved a little pleasure in life. Dorothy, as he not infrequently pointed out to her, was a disappointment to him. She did not understand. She was drab. And he craved a little bit of excitement in life. He needed it, like he needed red meat – and his appetite had been too long denied. Father Trumpington's blood, as the saying goes, was up and from that moment he had begun to scheme how best to stalk his prey and at the same time avoid being found out.

The air was chill as he emerged on to the dark pavement. Father Trumpington shivered with suppressed excitement and made up his mind. Yes, he would visit her. She would be back from work by now, probably just making herself a cup of tea. What more natural time was there to drop by? He set off briskly, humming. Dorothy might have been on a different planet for all the thought he gave her then.

His ring on Jackie's doorbell was peremptory, and he was rewarded within seconds by the sound of her eager footsteps in the hall. 'Oh Dick,' she simpered as she opened the door. And she fluttered her eyelids appealingly, like a timid schoolgirl with her first beau.

Her eyelashes, he thought, should be classified as a deadly weapon. 'Hello, Jackie,' he growled. 'Thought I'd just drop by. Thought you might offer me . . .' he paused, 'a cup of tea.'

Heaven, Father Trumpington reflected a quarter of an hour later, would be just like this. He was ensconced in an overstuffed armchair in Jackie's lounge, chocolate cake at his elbow, a cup of steaming tea on his knee. After the welcome party of the other night, both seemed to be conscious of a change in their relationship, as if they had crossed over some invisible Rubicon. Jackie was all fluttering and breathless delight.

As he sat there, she began dewily to tell him of her problems, all of which, as he rapidly discovered, revolved round her absentee husband, Malcolm. Malcolm did not understand her, she confided. He was possessive and demanding. He wanted to lock her away from the world, especially from other men. Whenever he was there, he nagged. It occurred to Father Trumpington that actually he was not there, but she explained this. The marriage was over, she said. He had gone abroad to work after having given her an ultimatum: give up her work and stay at home, or that was it. Of course she had not been able to accede to that, and as for India, there was no way she could live in such a hot and dirty country! Father Trumpington sympathised. Malcolm had not accepted it yet, of course, Jackie continued. He kept giving her just one last chance, but she could never, ever contemplate living with him again. And her voice shuddered at the thought.

In all of this Jackie was not being entirely honest. She did not, for instance, share the interesting detail that while they had lived together she had been constantly unfaithful, and that it had only been the discovery of her latest affair that had finally caused Malcolm to leave. Neither did she feel any compulsion to mention to Father Trumpington her husband's grief at separation from their little girl, Elspeth. She dismissed his fumbled attempts at reconciliation; in fact, each time he wrote, she stuffed his letter unopened in a drawer. But in one thing at least she was being entirely truthful – she did not want to live with him ever again.

Throughout all of this Father Trumpington sat there entranced. When at last she paused, a question occurred to him. 'Have you ever thought of divorce?' he ventured. Not having any very strong religious conviction himself, it seemed to him the most obvious solution.

Jackie looked horrified. This was rather anticipating her planned scenario. On no, she protested hastily, her faith . . . her child . . . and her finances! There was no way she could contemplate 'divorce'. She gazed at him fixedly and then, to his intense surprise, seemed suddenly to spring forward, perching precariously right on the edge of her seat, her chest throbbing with barely suppressed emotion, so that his heart lurched. Her involvement with the church, she whispered breathlessly.

Father Trumpington blinked. Jackie was undeniably wonderful, but the logic of this conversation was causing him some problems.

Jackie, if she realised this at all, was wholly unabashed. Malcolm had always been jealous of the church, she confided. He had never understood her love for it, nor her deep faith. He resented the time she spent there, her involvement with the choir. But she had to have some interests in life! In short, she was a wronged woman and her husband a beast, but she knew Father Trumpington would understand.

He did. Completely. His blood boiled at thought of the wicked treatment meted out to Jackie by the insensitive lout who dared call himself her spouse. But of course he quite understood why she did not want divorce too. Poor, poor woman, what a dreadful problem. So sympathetic was he that he reached out a hand and laid it on her knee. 'There, there,' he said. Jackie wriggled and smiled bravely, and it suddenly occurred to Father Trumpington how similar they actually were. Just as Malcolm did not understand her, dreary Dorothy misunderstood him. She had held him back, he reflected bitterly. She, too, had always resented the time he spent away. She, too, nagged. And he, too, had been unable to contemplate the spectre of divorce because of the damage it would do to his career – his sacred calling, as he phrased it. In that moment of sensual delight, Father Trumpington suddenly realised all of poor Dorothy's failings. He was injured, he was wronged, she had stifled him and destroyed his career!

Suddenly he was sharing with Jackie all his pent-up rage and frustration. 'We have a common bond between us,' he announced loudly. And then – he was not quite sure how it happened – they were sitting side by side on the sofa, the tea and chocolate cake forgotten. 'We are ships of the storm who can take refuge together and comfort one another. I, too, know the suffering you endure.'

Jackie gave a little squeal. 'Ooh, Dick,' she whispered, 'I knew it! I felt it all along. Twin souls!' And she buried her head in his shoulder.

The scent of her perfume hit Father Trumpington straight between the eyes, sweeping him along on a tide of passion. His lips sought hers, and locked on to her opened mouth.

At that moment the door suddenly flew open. 'Mummy,' said a small voice, 'can I have some tea?'

The pair catapulted apart to either end of the sofa, Jackie trying hastily to rearrange her hair and fasten her blouse, which in their embrace had come undone. 'Oh, Elspeth,' she gasped, 'darling . . . you startled me.'

The child stared at her with liquid eyes, and then turned her impassive gaze on to the flustered priest. A shadow of suspicion crossed her six-year-old face as she absorbed the scene. 'Why was he cuddling you?' she demanded.

Jackie had the grace to blush. 'I was upset,' she stammered. 'He was comforting me . . . it's his job.'

A note of desperation had crept into her voice and the child looked unconvinced. Her lower lip jutted and she stared at Father Trumpington belligerently. 'I think he should go,' she announced.

Father Trumpington was not noted for recklessness. He went, but not before he had exacted from Jackie a promise to come along with him to the West Carberry choir. They were currently preparing the Messiah and Dorothy, he was certain, could not object if he recruited Jackie to their ranks and gave her a lift to and from meetings. It was perfectly reasonable to invite the poor woman, he told himself. After all, she already sang in the church choir, she was lonely, and it was his pastoral duty to give her care.

Dorothy, Father Trumpington knew, would not be an obstacle to his helping Jackie in her time of need but, as he drove along to the meeting of his Masonic Lodge later that night, he pondered a far more difficult problem. Elspeth, the child, had made her disapproval patently clear. Beneath her gaze Father Trumpington had felt extremely uncomfortable. It was not so much what she had said, because she had said very little, but the way she had looked at him, her dark eyes seeming to stare deep into his soul and to see something there of which she strongly disapproved. It had made him inwardly writhe. He wondered if there was any way in which he could win her approval, and was still turning over in his mind various strategies when he arrived at the Lodge.

The Freemasons, along with the organ and choir, were currently Father Trumpington's overriding passion in life. In fact he joined in the meetings with almost religious zeal. He had, he knew, long since lost whatever Christian faith he had had, though truth to tell that in itself had never been very much. He had 'joined the Church' as he put it, thirty-eight years before because it had seemed to him a pleasant lifestyle and to hold out the offer of power. But the teachings of Christianity had long since begun to weary him, while the emphasis on love and forgiveness seemed to him insufferably naive. People needed to be realistic, he was fond of saying. It was no use walking around with your head in the clouds.

So it was that Alan Gunningham's suggestion that he should join the Masons, when he had been casting around for ways to raise money some years before for some other grandiose project he had launched, had come as manna into the aridity of his spiritual desert. It had been just what he needed. He loved the camaraderie and sense of brotherhood with like-minded men, he delighted in the way they stood by each other, and he found their teachings far more sensible than some of the more unacceptable extremes of his own professed faith. He liked, for example, the idea of one supreme being, known by many names. He liked the assurance that there was no out-and-out condemnation – it seemed so silly anyway. He truly believed that men and women were the architects of their own fate but that, if they got it wrong, that did not mean total obliteration. It simply meant that they had to work that bit harder to retrieve the situation and achieve their own little bit of salvation.

'Dick!' A voice hailed him as he crossed the marble threshold that formed the entrance to the Lodge. It was a large, imposing building, standing in its own grounds, a monument to the wealth of the city, and the power and influence of the men who followed the Craft.

Father Trumpington turned, startled. 'Oh, hello, George,' he responded, as a figure detached itself from the shadows and came forward. 'I didn't know you were going to be here tonight.'

Professor George Bullen was head of St Thomas's Hospital which lay within the parish boundaries of St Godric's and just down the road from the church. For the past fourteen years Father Trumpington had held the appointment of chaplain to this august institution, but it was a position he fulfilled with only limited enthusiasm. He had never liked hospitals very much. It was not that he was frightened of sickness, but to be physically ill lay beyond his personal experience, and he did not readily feel sympathy with those who were in pain. Because of this, he was accustomed to delegate whatever day-to-day duties there were to his curate, while he confined his own activities to attendance at hospital social functions and regular use of the large staff swimming pool. He was a firm friend of Professor Bullen, a relationship that had deepened considerably since his initiation into the Brotherhood and discovery that the professor was a Master Mason and Junior Warden of the Lodge.

George Bullen now clapped a hand on his shoulder. 'Dick,' he said again, conspiratorially, 'I've been wanting to have a word with you.' His voice sank even lower, and Father Trumpington found himself being propelled back into the shadows. 'It's rather quick, we know – people have to wait years for this – but we wondered if you might like to become a Companion of the Holy Royal Arch of Jerusalem. We have all been watching you and are most impressed.'

Father Trumpington's heart leapt. This was an honour to which he had not even in his wildest imagination dared yet to aspire. He was aware that there were other degrees of Craft Masonry he could himself decide to take, but to become a Companion of the Royal Arch was by invitation only and the initiate had to have demonstrated a real commitment to Masonic ideals in a way that impressed the higher echelons of power within the Lodge. He felt his face suffuse. 'George,' he said, 'I don't know what to say. You've taken my breath away.'

George squeezed his arm. 'Say yes, Dicky,' he urged. 'This is an honour. But, my friend, you deserve it.'

The darkness seemed to swirl in a hymn of triumph around Father Trumpington's ears. In his euphoria it felt almost tangible. 'Well, of course, George,' he stammered. 'How could I refuse? But such an honour. I hadn't even dared think . . .'

'Tsk,' said Professor Bullen. 'We know a good man when we see one. We need men of your calibre. I'll be very proud to introduce you.'

Sitting in the customary ceremony some few minutes later, prior to dinner, Father Trumpington could hardly believe the turn his life had taken. The professor had suggested to him that he be admitted to the order in five weeks' time – just before Christmas in fact. It seemed somehow appropriate. Christmas he usually found rather boring. Hard work and too many mince pies, and he found himself forced into Dorothy's company rather more than he liked, with all the worldly emphasis on family fun. But this Christmas was going to be different, of that he was absolutely sure. In fact, God seemed to be showering him with gifts a trifle early. And there was another cause for satisfaction, because as they had walked up the stairs together after their hurried conversation in the hall, Professor Bullen had grunted, 'I say, Dick, I hear your new curate's a woman. How about getting her to do the Christmas service up at St Thomas's this year? Be a nice change to see how a female performs. Make the show a bit different, don't you think? And then you could pop along with Dorothy for the drinks after.'

The only fly in the ointment of this suggestion was the reference to Dorothy but that, Father Trumpington supposed, could not be helped. After all, it was Christmas. But the suggestion that Antonia should take the service delighted him. The St Thomas's Christmas Day service took place every year at eleven thirty. St Godric's Christmas offering, just as regularly, began at ten thirty. Father Trumpington always tried to keep it as short as he could but, even so, it meant a tremendous rush for whomever then went on to the hospital. He had done it himself in the past, when pushed, but more normally he tried to offload the service on to someone else, either the poor curate or some retired priest who would not then be forced to attend both.

The only problem each year was persuading St Thomas's that his personal attendance, as chaplain, was not vital. Every year he brought up fresh excuses why it would benefit the patients to see a face other than his own, but every once in a while he was still forced to undertake the duty himself, and he had rather thought that this particular year might be one of those occasions, as it was now five years since he had last presided. To have the irksome duty thus lifted from his shoulders, and to be able at the same time to appear magnanimous, was an unexpected gift. 'Well, George,' he had replied, 'I'd rather thought to do it myself this year. It's been five years since I was last with you all for that particular service – terrible pressure of duties you know, Christmas morning. But I had thought that this year . . .' The professor had looked at this point as if he was about to agree and, worrying he might have overplayed his hand, Father Trumpington had hastily continued, 'But I'm sure it would be a wonderful experience for Antonia, and in the circumstances I'll be only too pleased to allow her to take the service instead.' And he breathed a sigh of relief. This Christmas was going to be quite unlike any other Christmas he had ever had.

Chapter Five

Gloria Sunnington picked up her Scarlet Sahara lipstick and purposefully slashed a deep, garish line across her upper lip. Surveying herself critically in the mirror, she smacked her lips together, welding the colour on to her mouth, and then stood back to scrutinise the effect. Curling false lashes fluttered dreamily back at her, but there was nothing soft in her expression. Gloria was preparing for war. Giving a final tug to a stray blonde curl, she smiled spitefully at her reflection. 'It's time,' she breathed softly, 'to act.'

At that precise moment her husband, Griff, lumbered clumsily into the bedroom behind her. 'What are you tarting yourself up for?' he demanded cantankerously. He stank of stale beer and smoke and Gloria suppressed a shudder of disgust. Thirty years ago she had been rather taken by his rough, slightly uncouth manner. He had ridden a motorbike then and she had liked the prestige of being 'his girl'. But thirty years on, minus the bike, he had changed only in the fact that he drank more and had a paunch, and now his beery vulgarity disgusted her.

'I'm not tarting myself up!' she retorted, eyeing him in the mirror with distaste. 'It's the PCC meeting, that's all. I'm simply getting ready to go out.'

Her reply incensed him and his baffled resentment, always simmering just below the surface, erupted. 'Bloody church,' he snapped. 'You're always round there these days. I suppose that means you're going to be out all night – just like every other night! I'm beginning to think you've got a fancy man round there!'

'Ooh, thinking are we?' she snapped back. 'Well, it would serve you right if I had! Any kind of a man would be a change after you!'

Her husband's hand raised itself. Violence was his invariable response to anything he disliked and, indeed, he had been in trouble with the police several times, but it did not frighten Gloria.

Four foot eleven she might be, but she was more than a match for him, and they both knew it. Now she whirled on him and he cowered back. 'Oh yes! Hit me, would you!' she screamed. It was not a question, more a challenge. 'That's all you're good for, isn't it? Frightening defenceless women.'

In the dim recesses of his brain, it occurred to her husband that there might be many epithets to describe Gloria but defenceless was not one of them. His hand fell. 'I ... I'm sorry,' he stammered.

'So you bloody should be!' she said remorslessly. She turned back to the work in hand and again crimped out the hair on either side of her head. Her handiwork obviously satisfied her because she turned then and shrugged on her coat. 'You should be careful,' she said self-righteously, 'making comments like that. God hears, you know! He doesn't pay his debts with money!'

With that, she spun on her three-inch stiletto heels and flounced out of the door, leaving him staring after her in uneasy bafflement. But he had been closer to the mark than he knew, because Gloria had come to a decision that night.

Gloria had initially started going to church to spite Griff and get out of the house, but also, in the latent places of her soul, she had wanted to better herself. At the age of fifty-three, she had pretensions to be middle-class. She was bored with Griff. Working-class he had always been, hero never, and his lack of intelligence had become more obvious with the passing of the years. On top of that, she hated the way he belched loudly after meals. She hated the way he drank, she hated his fondness for the dogs, and she hated his friends. And so, in inarticulate rage and wanting to hurt him, she had gone along to St Godric's where she had discovered, not God, but Father Trumpington.

If it had been any other church and any other vicar, the phase would probably have lasted a couple of weeks, and then she would have enrolled at night classes and maybe had a fling, maybe even have left Griff completely. But the first time she had seen Father Trumpington, vague resolutions had started to form in her mind. There was something in his character she was drawn to and she had sensed that under his burly exterior he was a deeply sensual man. But, more than that, he was a priest. And with that fact alone, something in her was riveted. If she could catch him. If she could steal him away from his God . . .

The fact that Father Trumpington was married did not enter into her thinking at all. In Gloria's estimation the priest's wife was a pathetic doormat of a woman. She did not deserve to keep her husband if she could not stand up for herself a bit more. And so, cold-bloodedly, she had begun to lay siege.

Griff, with some kind of dormant, animal intuition, had known immediately that something was wrong but she had beaten him down with angry piety and, in face of her pretended fervour, he had not known how to proceed other than with sulky belligerence. Once he had changed tack and offered to go with her to a service one night, thinking that perhaps he had been unjust and that there was something in her conversion after all – something even for him. But she had rounded on him angrily and with a touch of fear. Reconciliation between herself and Griff was not one of the fantasies that figured prominently in her mind.

Gloria had begun her campaign by telling Father Trumpington that her husband was a brute and an alcoholic who neglected and abused her. Father Trumpington had sympathised, and promptly signed her up to help with the church bazaar, which she had felt was a promising start. But though she had pursued her campaign from that point with energy, taking on more and more tasks, Father Trumpington had proved unexpectedly slow to respond, and recently she had begun to consider the possibility that she was perhaps being a shade too subtle. The possibility that he might not be attracted to her never occurred to her. Antonia's arrival, however, had precipitated in Gloria something of a crisis. The girl was undeniably attractive, and she was young; and the first time Gloria had seen her a green-eyed monster had reared its ugly head in her chest and gripped her by the throat. Dorothy she could discount, but in Antonia she sensed a threat. She was not about to allow this girl to steal Father Trumpington from under her nose. So it was in a mood of determined belligerence that she set out for the PCC.

The hall was quiet when she got there and she set about putting out the chairs round the table. She had almost finished when Jackie Newberg arrived. 'Ooh, it's cold out there,' announced

Jackie to no one in particular, but striking a pose of helpless femininity just in case as she came through the door. Then she saw that it was only Gloria there and became immediately far more matter-of-fact. She only bothered to exercise her air of dewy fragility when men were about.

Gloria was unimpressed. 'Umm,' she responded vaguely, preoccupied with trying to decide how best to restrict Antonia's activities while, at the same time, appearing to hold the best interests of the church at heart. She wondered whether she should feign friendship and try and influence her through advice, or let her displeasure be apparent from the outset. On balance she thought she would prefer the first option. It would, after all, be far better not to reveal her antagonism. And there were some in the church already who were openly hostile to women's ministry, so Antonia might be glad of an apparent ally. But deep down Gloria worried that this was not going to work. She really did dislike the girl. She was not sure if she could pretend to be her friend like that. Her jaw tightened at the thought. It was the voice, she decided, that was the worst thing, so obviously middle-class and superior. And her clothes! What right had she to dress as fashionably as she obviously did? Stuck-up bitch! she thought viciously. Ms La-de-da, double-barrel Beecher-Henty! And she banged down the last chair so ferociously that all the others rattled in sympathy.

'Golly,' giggled Jackie, 'you sound as if you mean business tonight!'

Gloria scowled, but the younger woman was impervious. She took off her coat and slid carefully into the chair which would be immediately on Father Trumpington's left. She had on a short, black, rather elegant lycra skirt which left very little to the imagination and which Gloria, painfully aware of her own rather pudgy legs and wrinkly knees, felt was indecent. The church-warden gave a faint 'Tck' of disapproval and in turn sat down, ostentatiously smoothing her long skirt about her ankles

Jackie smiled. 'So what do you think of our new curate then?' she inquired chattily.

Gloria had long since decided that Jackie was a bit dim. 'Not a lot,' she replied sharply. 'I don't really hold with women taking over men's jobs. I don't think they can do it.'

The fact that the uncouth Gloria disapproved of something immediately aroused Jackie's support for it. She was fully aware that the other woman had designs on Father Trumpington, and now she felt a kind of smug spite, knowing that she was on the brink of seizing the prize.

'I don't see why a vicar has to be a man,' she said vaguely, keeping her voice deliberately sweet. 'After all, we've got women doctors and things, haven't we? And I thought her first sermon last week was rather good.'

Gloria's eyes took on a steely glaze and her face went bright pink. She had hated Antonia's sermon. When the girl had spoken about genuine commitment, Gloria had felt dimly she was being got at. She was, however, saved the necessity of answering by the arrival of Edgar Slynne.

'Oi think she's jolly nice,' he said, overhearing. 'Jus' what we need. A bit o' young blood. An' she's a looker too. Bit of all right. Hear, hear! That's what oi say. Jolly good luck t' the girl!' He blinked, becoming uncomfortably aware that both women were glaring at him. This bothered him, because for the last three months Slynne had been stalking Jackie with the assiduity of a Scottish beater on the trail of grouse, hoping indeed that in the not too distant future – after, of course, she had got her divorce – there would be wedding bells in the air. The fact that he was seventy-three, five foot six to her five foot nine, and of singularly unattractive appearance, he did not see as a bar. Slynne had an optimstic nature.

'Oh, oi didn't mean that you two aren't lookers,' he said hastily, trying desperately to salvage the situation. 'It's jus' that she's young, see, an' well . . . we're all getting a bit long in the tooth, aren't we?'

To his surprise, Jackie did not appear mollified by this comment. Her face, on the contrary, froze and then she sniffed disdainfully and turned away, at the same time smiling at Gloria and beginning to chat to her animatedly. Momentarily cowed, Slynne went and sat at the far end of the table and began to plot how best to get back in Jackie's good books.

The rest now began to trickle in one by one.

61

'Seen 'Itler yet?' Slynne called out to Ken Brown as he and two others came in through the door. Slynne was rather in awe of Ken, who was the manager of Carberry's one and only Christian bookshop and who, it was generally agreed, was a very saintly kind of man.

In spite of himself, the bookseller smiled. 'Oh, hello, Edgar,' he replied. 'No, I haven't seen him yet, and you really shouldn't call Dick that, you know.'

Unabashed, Slynne grunted. 'Don't see whoi not!' he banged back. 'That's what 'e is, after all.' He beamed hopefully at Jackie at this point and she, hearing Father Trumpington's name, turned the full force of her lashes upon him. Pleased at having caught her attention, Slynne decided to follow up the sally. 'What 'e says goes, dunnit?' he chuckled, in what he hoped was a matey voice. 'Allays got t' 'ave his own way, or 'e won't play.'

Jackie smiled thinly. 'Well, he is very masterful,' she purred. Deliberately, she let the tiniest shade of displeasure creep into her voice, but it was lost on Slynne.

'Masterful!' he bellowed derisively. 'Oh, 'e's that alroight! An' a bit beyond if you ask me. Gets 'is own way a bit too much.'

The whole room was riveted and, unable to help herself, Gloria now launched in. 'He happens to be a very good organiser,' she sniffed.

This was too much for Slynne. 'Organise!' he exploded. ''Im? The only thing 'e can organise is the money outta our pockets!' He glared round at the assembled company, as if challenging them to disagree, but two or three nodded in sympathy. 'It's the only thing as 'e cares about,' he complained, slightly mollified. 'Money!'

Jackie had just begun to explain to him that Father Trumpington was really a deeply caring and spiritual man, when Antonia arrived. The curate had dressed for her first PCC with care. She had put on a plain black pinafore dress and clerical shirt, and a large, rather severe looking Celtic cross hung down her front. The effect was to make her look rather like a medieval nun, but the dress was also obviously expensive and Jackie and Gloria, who had instantly priced her outfit, glared.

'Some people,' said Gloria sotto voce to her neighbour, and

nodding meaningfully in the direction of Antonia, 'some people who ought to know better, given their calling, spend a great deal too much on the way they look.' She appeared to find nothing incongruous in the fact she had bought a new blouse for the meeting herself, and was rewarded by seeing Antonia flush.

Father Trumpington himself arrived just as the church clock was striking eight. 'Come along, come along, everyone,' he said testily, flinging in through the doors and striding purposefully up to his seat. His manner seemed to suggest that they were all late and that he was the one who had been kept waiting, and Edgar Slynne gave a snort. 'We've got a very busy agenda tonight,' the priest went on, 'there's a lot to get through, and I really would like to be finished by nine.' He glared around at them as if expecting a storm of protest, but the only sound was Ken blowing his nose. Father Trumpington handed round the agenda sheets he had brought with him and cleared his throat noisily, before launching forth.

First on the agenda, Antonia discovered, was the Christmas bazaar and party. Jackie volunteered to organise the entertainment at the latter, and Edgar Slynne, who prided himself on his organisational abilities, immediately offered to help.

'No, that's all right, Edgar,' Father Trumpington announced, 'I'll help Jackie this year. I've got one or two ideas I thought might be good.'

Jackie beamed and Slynne looked incredulous. 'You?' he demanded. 'You don't normally 'elp organise the party. You've allus said as you're too busy!'

'Yes, well, this year I thought I would.'

But Slynne was not to be put off. 'Whoi?' he demanded.

Father Trumpington looked shocked. 'Are you trying to tell me, Edgar, you don't wish me to be involved?'

'Well, no,' said Slynne. 'Of course not. Oi'm just a bit surprised, that's all. Oi 'elped last year!'

'Well, this year you can do something else,' said Father Trumpington testily. 'I don't think we ought to do the same thing every year. People get stuck in a rut that way.'

'Well, then, Jackie shouldn't do it neither,' said Slynne. 'If oi need a change, she oughta 'ave a change too.'

'I could do it,' offered Gloria. 'Jackie could organise the food this year.'

Father Trumpington began to look annoyed. 'Look,' he said, 'I didn't say everyone had to change. I simply said that I could do something different this year.'

'But you said as oi 'ad to do something different too!' said Slynne belligerently.

Everyone looked at Father Trumpington expectantly. 'Well, yes, of course,' he said patiently. 'If I help with the entertainment, you'll have to do something different. We can't both do it.'

'No, but oi don't see why it 'as to be you as does it,' retorted Slynne. 'Oi like 'elping with the entertainment.'

'Oh, for heaven's sake!' snapped Father Trumpington.

'I've got a suggestion,' said Ken. 'Why not let Antonia help, and both of you do something different?'

Antonia suddenly found that they were all now looking at her. 'Oh. Yes,' she said. 'I'd be happy to—'

'Well, in that case,' breathed Jackie, 'I think I might quite fancy a change myself. Perhaps Gloria would like to take it over after all?' She looked annoyed.

Gloria smiled a smile that lifted the corners of her mouth but left her eyes, fixed upon Jackie, completely dead. 'I don't wish to take anything from you, dear,' she said silkily.

'Oh, but you won't be. Really,' said Jackie. 'I only offered because I thought someone was needed. But if someone else would like to do it, then I'm very happy to stand down.'

'Well, I'm not happy at all,' suddenly snapped Father Trumpington. The unexpected turn of events had temporarily bereft him of the power of speech, but he had evidently decided it was time to reassert himself. 'I'm very happy for Jackie to take over the entertainment again this year, and there is absolutely no need for Antonia to help because I am going to. Edgar, your efforts were much appreciated last year but I think it would be good for you to try something different this year. I thought perhaps you could be in charge of setting out the hall for the bazaar.'

If he had expected this to settle the matter, he was doomed to disappointment, because Slynne was even more enraged and for a good five minutes pandemonium reigned, brought to an end only by Ken saying loudly, 'I think we should pray.'

Father Trumpington looked as if he was about to explode, but the little woman on Antonia's right breathed a sigh of relief. 'Oh yes,' she said gratefully. She had appeared very distressed ever since the argument had first broken out, and Antonia noticed Ken now lean across and briefly squeeze her hand. 'It's all right, Phoebe,' she heard him say. 'The Lord's in control.' And then he closed his eyes and began to pray aloud, not giving anyone else a chance to speak.

'Father Almighty,' he said firmly, 'we don't seem to be able to see eye to eye here, and perhaps we're letting other considerations get in the way of our duty towards you, so we just want to give this question over to you now. We're very sorry where we've been a bit hasty with each other. We ask you to forgive us, and we ask you to help us to forgive each other, and we pray that for the rest of our meeting tonight we may put you first, and be able to agree.'

'Can we vote?' broke in the little woman Antonia had just heard called Phoebe.

'I think that's a very good idea,' said Ken. 'Everyone in favour of our curate organising the entertainment.'

A flurry of hands went up round the table, while Father Trumpington and Slynne glared at one another stonily.

'I think that's carried,' said Ken.

Antonia's heart sank. She was beginning to know Father Trumpington well enough to realise that this would not be received with approbation but, after all that had just happened, there seemed nothing she could do. Almost unconsciously, she began mentally to brace herself. However, an uneasy kind of peace now prevailed, as if the main protagonists were circling warily round each other, working out their next move, and the next few items were got through without mishap. The bazaar, the party and the Christmas services were all arranged, with Father Trumpington firmly stating that he did not wish the children in any way to be actively involved.

'Oh, but,' said Phoebe, 'Christmas is a time for children. Couldn't they at least do something? Sing a carol maybe in the carol service?'

'No,' said Father Trumpington. 'The last time they did anything like that it was a disaster. They don't remember the words or what to do. Half of them stand up, and the rest sit down. The whole performance last year was thoroughly embarrassing!' On this point he proved adamant, glaring at Slynne, as if daring him to protest. But Slynne merely sniffed.

'No use lookin' at me,' he muttered. 'Oi don't care about kids either way, jus' so long as oi'm not asked t' organise 'em.'

'Good,' said Father Trumpington. 'Any other business? No? Right.' He shuffled his papers together, signalling the end of the meeting, and began to push back his chair.

Antonia jumped. She had talked to him again about a fellowship group earlier in the day and had been told her proposal would be brought up at this point under any other business. She suddenly realised that the meeting was about to close without it having been mentioned at all. Not for one moment did it occur to her that the priest had omitted to mention the group deliberately. Maybe he had forgotten, and would be grateful to her now for reminding him. So that was what she did.

Father Trumpington's eyes glazed. 'Ah, yes . . . a fellowship group,' he said. He stared at her coldly.

'Yes, you know, we talked about it this morning.'

'Did we?'

'Well, yes.' She gazed at him, perplexed. In her years at the Bar, Antonia had come across several villains who had lied almost without thinking in an attempt to evade imprisonment but she had always felt there was a kind of honesty about them. Their attempted subterfuges had never offended her because she had never expected anything different. They were honest villains. But of a priest she did expect something different. She expected honesty and openness. And she suddenly saw before her, trying to mask itself, something that she recognised from of old; something that was not honest, that was, on the contrary, little and evil, and would do anything to get its own way.

She was so shocked that she just stared at him, and then, becoming conscious of the silence, swallowed. 'Yes,' she repeated. 'I asked you if I could start a fellowship group, and you said that we'd discuss it tonight.'

'Oh, that sounds a good idea,' said Ken immediately.

She glanced at him gratefully and, without looking again at Father Trumpington, began to explain. They could meet weekly, she said, do a Bible study, pray and just generally try and get to know each other better. The aim would be to deepen one another's faith and support each other. Lots of parishes, she said, had them. As she finished, she stole a glance at Father Trumpington from under her lashes, and was in time to see a quick look pass between him and the Treasurer. She saw the latter shake his head slightly.

'Yes, well,' said Alan Gunningham smoothly, 'I've heard of these things, of course, and I suppose they're all right if people want that sort of thing, but do we need that kind of a group at St Godric's? I'd have thought we were a bit too Anglican for that.'

'Oh, Anglicans have fellowship groups,' said Ken. 'They're quite respectable. And we even had them at St Godric's a good few years back, when Neville Coddington was vicar, although of course they weren't called fellowship groups then. We had six of them altogether, I remember. I think it would be excellent to start them up again.'

'Well, of course you may be right,' said Alan Gunningham agreeably. 'I was simply questioning whether there is actually a need at St Godric's today. After all, we have a central focus in the music of the church. Dick has worked very hard to build up our choral tradition. In fact I think I'm right when I say we're the only church in Carberry, apart from the cathedral, with a full choir and 1662 choral evensong every Sunday.' Father Trumpington nodded his head in agreement and the Treasurer continued, 'With Norman Pilkington here I would have thought we could expect our reputation in that direction to grow, and surely the last thing we want is anything that is going to divert energy from that. We wouldn't, for example, wish people not to join the choir because they felt they had to commit themselves to a fellowship group. It's simply a question, I would have thought, of defining ourselves and of seeing where our strengths really lie, and of then concentrating in those areas and refusing to be diverted.'

'Alan, I think you've explained the position extremely well,' said Father Trumpington. 'We are a choral church. That's what we're known for.'

Antonia could not help herself. 'But there's no reason why a fellowship group should detract from that,' she blurted. 'In fact, if anything it ought to help, because small groups meeting for prayer and fellowship ought to help strengthen the church.'

'And for those of us who aren't musical, it would be very nice to have something we could be a part of,' said a small voice.

Father Trumpington breathed heavily. 'Phoebe, you're already involved in all sorts of things.'

'Well, yes, I know, but I really would love to be part of a fellowship group.'

People on all sides began to proffer their opinions, to Father Trumpington's increasingly obvious displeasure.

'Oi think we should 'ave one,' suddenly announced Slynne. He had been watching the debate closely and, in particular, he had been watching Father Trumpington. His enjoyment had increased in direct relation to the latter's annoyance. Now he smiled maliciously. 'Atter all, it's what churches are supposed to 'ave – prayer groups. An' Phoebe's roight. Not everyone is musical. There oughta be somethin' for them.' He turned abruptly to Jackie who was absently fiddling with her rings, her expression vacant. "Ow about you, Jackie?' he inquired sweetly. 'Do you think you'll join? Oi could give you a lift if you'd like to go.'

She jumped. 'Me?' she squeaked, surprised. 'Oh no, no. I'm definitely on the musical side. Not quite my thing really.' She fluttered her lashes in the direction of Father Trumpington who glared at Slynne.

'Yes, well,' the priest growled, 'we clearly need to give the issue more thought.' He rose to his feet with determination. 'For now, I'm declaring this meeting closed. Next meeting, as arranged, on February the twenty-fourth.' Abruptly he turned to face the opposite direction as Antonia also rose to her feet.

Noticing the movement Gloria's spirits soared. Almost, she thought, she could really begin to believe in God! Antonia was clearly not the threat she had felt her to be, after all. Obviously the girl was not about to embark on a torrid affair with Father Trumpington. In fact, if anything, it looked as if World War Three might break out between the two of them, if something did not happen to settle this dispute. Good, she thought buoyantly, hostility between the two would suit her very well. It would give her the chance to become more obviously Father Trumpington's ally.

Chapter Six

Kathleen Earnshaw discovered, with surprise, that she was happy. Three months before and she would not have believed it possible, but in some mysterious way having a lodger had given meaning to her drab life. She discovered that she had a reason to get up in the mornings, and suddenly she began to plan little treats for supper. Would Antonia like chops? she wondered. Or should she be really adventurous and do coq au vin? She had not cooked for years, there had been no reason to, but now she began to experiment with all sorts of exotic dishes; though not always, it should be said, with success. But she blossomed with the pleasure of having someone to fuss over.

She knew it was silly and that to an outsider it would have been difficult to comprehend the change that had come to her life. But Kathleen had lived on her own for so long that the mere presence of another human being in her echoing and gloomy house radically altered everything. It was as if something almost tangible and incredibly alive was there. But it was not, she decided, simply that there was someone else in the house. Rather, she thought, it had to do with Antonia herself. And Kathleen found herself pondering this, unable, at first, to account for it.

She had always, she acknowledged, been rather a chilly individual. This, of course, had not been helped by what she now thought of as the fiasco with Martin. But right from the beginning there was something about Antonia that caught her – that was unthreatening, and that she liked. The girl had not been installed five minutes when, to her intense surprise, Kathleen had found herself laughing. It had been so odd that she had almost felt for a minute that the house recoiled with shock. But laugh she had and, even more amazing, she had found herself the next instant telling Antonia all about Martin, and about the interminable struggle she had had over the years to make ends meet. To many, of course, this would have seemed utterly trivial, but for Kathleen

71

to share what she regarded as the most intimate details of her life was extraordinary.

As she thought about it later, she wondered if maybe the ease with which she had come to regard Antonia as a friend had something to do with the fact that the girl herself was physically so tiny. The first time Kathleen had met her she had thought to herself in surprise, 'My goodness, she looks as if a puff of wind would blow her away!' And she had looked at the huge figure of Father Trumpington standing at the girl's side, and the unwelcome thought had suggested itself to her that, if the priest wanted, he could reach out his fist and squash his curate without a second thought. Quite why he should want to squash Antonia it had not occurred to her to wonder. It was simply that, looking at them standing together in her narrow hall, she had been suddenly seized by a nameless and quite irrational dread. She rather thought later that it was then that, in some strange way, Antonia became for her the daughter she had never dared admit she had always wanted.

Be that as it may, the next thing that happened was that she had begun on a more regular basis to go to church. She had always found faith a very difficult thing. She rather thought, on balance, that there was a God but, after all that had happened, she found it difficult to believe that he was at all interested in her. It seemed, however, to be somehow bad-mannered to have Antonia in the house and not to go with her. Every Sunday morning, therefore, she had donned her best skirt and hat and had begun to go along. She had not enjoyed it very much at first. Going week by week, she had actually begun to listen to what was said, and she had found the language both archaic and unintelligible. Why, for instance, did they have to pray for government ministers and those in authority to minister justice 'indifferently'? It felt like praying for someone to do a bad job.

She had said as much to Father Trumpington once as he stood in the church porch shaking hands after the Communion, and he had given a patronising smirk and boomed, 'Oh no, dear lady, the sense is impartially!'

'Then why not say so?' she had retorted tartly, but he had seemed unimpressed.

'It is the ancient beauty of the language,' he had responded. 'To change the word would change the flow.'

She was not convinced, but in some strange way, after that, she had begun to have a sense of God, and of his being there, and deep inside her she had begun to feel a kind of rage at the priest's cavalier attitude. There he was, she thought to herself, earning a very comfortable living looking after what was supposed to be the house of his God, and he cared not twopence what it all meant. It was outrageous. It was like the janitor of some old and beautiful stately home refusing to allow the owner to come in and live there. If God did exist, she decided, this was no way to treat him. And all her pent-up rage at the rejection she had suffered suddenly erupted. Not visibly of course, but internally, and she had looked at the priest with real fury.

From then on, whenever she went into the church building, it was as if she could sense God there at her side, not a huge and powerful creator God who was there as of right, but a stuffed in the cupboard, apologetic kind of God who, she felt, would have very much liked to have come out and said hello to everyone, only he was not allowed because Father Trumpington held the keys.

When it came to the Communion, she walked up with her God-in-the-cupboard and she imagined him taking the bread and giving it to her, and then lifting the cup up to her mouth. And she felt he smiled. Then one day, as he held out the cup to her, she felt she saw a look of such sadness in his eyes that she said involuntaritly, 'Good heavens, Lord, what on earth's the matter?' He did not reply. Instead he simply gave her the cup to drink, and all the way back to her seat, stunned, she found herself repeating, 'Lord, what on earth is wrong?'

When she sat down, she felt him sit beside her and after a minute, as she sank to her knees, she felt him breathe, 'Kathleen . . .'

'What is it, Lord?' she asked.

She felt what seemed almost the lightest of brushes on her cheek, like a faint breeze, and then she felt him say, 'My child, I grieve at your separation. Come to me.'

She was riveted. Never before had it even occurred to her that

God might respond or take some part in her one-sided chats. She had not even known he could. It struck her like a blow between the eyes. She knew that some people would say she was mad, but she was absolutely convinced that the words were real, and that it was Jesus himself who had spoken them to her. But she had no idea what they meant.

What had begun as an idle fancy, with her vague imaginings of God locked in a cupboard, suddenly felt horribly, intensely real, but she was no longer sure who had put him there. She felt such a terrible grief that she wondered, at the end of the service, if she would be able to stand. She was convinced that she had to do something, but she had no idea what.

All that day she kept sending up to some vague place above her head little pleas for clarification. But there was never any reply and she began to feel like a child who has done wrong, whose parent refuses to talk to her until she has apologised and tried to put matters right. But how could she put things right when she was uncertain what she had done wrong? And then she began to feel exasperated. Really, this was unreasonable of God. It went against all the basic principles of justice. If she had done wrong and upset him, then she was very sorry, but really he would have to tell her!

So she began to feel enraged, and then she told him how petty she thought he was. And then, as if that was not enough, she told him all about how she had suffered in life, and where had he been then, thank you very much! And in her mind she suddenly found herself screaming at him, 'You never cared about me then, did you? Where were you? Didn't I deserve a bit of love too?'

Still nothing and by nightfall, when she retired to bed, all she could do was cry. She felt as if she had had an argument with someone who had become a very valued friend. 'Lord,' she said into the silence, 'I really am so sorry, but I don't know what I've done. Please, just show me, and I'll try and put it right.'

Some time later, still crying, she fell into an uneasy sleep. How long she slept she had no idea, but at some point she became aware that she was dreaming. It was an odd experience because, in the dream, she was divorced from herself. There was a character who was herself and who was a part of the action; and then there was her real self, consciously separate from the dream and watching critically what was going on.

She found she was in a car, driving along a badly lit road at night. Suddenly, and completely without warning, the engine began to make a grinding noise, and the next moment the car gave a kind of lurching jump and came to a stop. The character that was herself swore softly and went to restart the engine but, as she turned the key in the ignition, the headlights, which she had left on, flickered and then also died, and she found herself enveloped in an intense, dark silence.

Kathleen felt uneasy at this but she knew it was a dream and that she could, by effort of will, change the sequence of events. Concentrating hard, therefore, she willed the internal car light to come on and, after a moment, it began very dimly to give off a pale glow that barely illuminated the interior of the car. Try as she might, she could not manage to make it any brighter. Her functioning self, however, seemed inordinately pleased with what illumination there was, although she could tell that it, too, was now beginning to feel afraid. Apprehensively, she peered through the car windows, trying to make out where they were, but all she could see were the dark shapes of swaying trees. Then, as she brought her gaze back to the inside of the car, her eyes fell on a portable phone. Her functioning self was already reaching for it, and she watched with a sense of relief, unable to rid herself now of the terrible feeling that something threatening was close behind. She watched herself punch in a number, and then lock the doors as she waited for it to connect. After a minute a voice responded on the phone, 'International Breakdown, how may I help you?'

She was conscious of a most tremendous sense of relief, but now her dream character seemed to be quite unreasonably dragging her feet. 'Yes, hello,' she said. 'I've broken down. I wondered if you could help.'

As herself she became conscious of headlights coming up behind, picking their way steadily along what she now realised was a winding road, as though searching. Her dream persona seemed unaware of them. She watched as they came closer, a feeling of dread rising in her throat. She knew that they intended harm.

The person on the other end of the line was meanwhile asking for details. What was wrong? What was the make of the car? Where was she exactly? To all these questions she heard herself reply clearly and deliberately, but at the same time she knew now that her dream self had seen the lights and was also beginning to feel afraid. And then she heard the voice at the other end of the line say, 'Can I have your membership number, please?'

Within the dream there was a moment's heart-stopping silence, and then she heard herself say, 'Actually, I'm not exactly a member.'

A dispute broke out, the headlights all the time drawing nearer behind. She heard herself protest that she had made inquiries years ago, that she'd always intended to join but somehow she'd never got round to it. The lights grew dazzling in the mirror. The voice at the other end of the phone laughed. 'Intending to isn't the same as actually joining,' it said. And then she woke up.

She struggled out of her sleep in absolute panic, certain that something horrendous was about to grab hold of her. The room was dark and still and she lay shaking, sweat pouring from her body, for a minute not daring to move as the reality of the dream still gripped her. She had not done something! The thought boomed through her mind. But what was it? Taken out membership? For a minute she hung between the dream and the darkness of the room, unable to disentangle herself. Surely, she thought distractedly, all these motoring organisations would come out in an emergency and you could join then? But then, as she became more awake, another thought struck her. 'I am a member,' she said aloud, confused.

The reality of the dream was so strong that, even though she now knew she was awake, she felt compelled to get up and go to search in her little bureau to check the relevant documents. Yes, there they were, her membership was fine. It was not due for renewal for another five months. Relief flooded over her and, as the monstrous but unknown spectre from the dream receded back into its murky lair, she chided herself for a fool. But still she felt shaken as she clambered back into bed, and she deliberately left the light on, drawing her knees up under her chin and wrapping the blankets tightly round her skinny frame. Unbidden, the memory of the grieving Christ who had walked beside her up to the Communion earlier that day suddenly came back to her. 'I grieve at your separation.' Almost as if something from beyond herself was directing her thoughts, she began to ponder the dream.

The breakdown man had said he could not help because she was not a member. And she had said that she had always intended to join. It was almost like that with her faith, she thought. Never, in all her life, had she really committed herself to God. Oh yes, she had gone along to church occasionally, and she called herself a Christian if anyone ever bothered to inquire, but mentally she had always somehow held back. She had always shied away from the intrusion into her freedom that she felt an active commitment to God would mean.

Hot shame flooded through her as it struck her that, over the last few weeks, since Antonia had come to live with her, she had obediently walked up to the Communion rail every Sunday but never once had it occurred to her really to think about what she was doing. She took the bread and the wine because it was expected of her. But, she suddenly realised, she was not even confirmed. She remembered dimly, from her lessons at school half a century before, that in the Anglican Church you were expected to be confirmed before you received the bread and the wine. The thought came to her that she was like a child, stealing in through the fire exit at the cinema to see the latest film but not actually having any right to be there because she did not have a ticket.

It had been a long and tortuous path but suddenly, in the lonely quiet of the night, she felt she had arrived somewhere. The shock was so great that she sat up. Of course. God was telling her that she had to commit herself! In the same instant such a flood of love seemed to engulf her that, without realising, she began to cry, great racking sobs that tore at her body. 'Oh Lord,' she whispered, gulping in between her tears, 'what on earth have I done to you?'

Without more ado, she scrambled out of bed, pulled on her dressing gown, and knelt on the floor, hands clasped in front of her. She felt that she must look very stupid, but she dismissed the thought. This moment felt more real to her than any other moment in her entire life. She felt alive. 'Oh Lord,' she breathed, 'forgive me. I really want to know you. I love you.' And with a jolt, she knew that that was true. 'I want to follow you, Lord,' she said. 'Come into my life. Please.' Immediately, it was as if blinding light and warmth and the most indescribable peace flooded her. It actually physically made her gasp, and she slipped down on to her side, and then laughter welled up in her, and in that tired little bedroom she reached out her hand ... and put it into the hand of God.

The next morning she was a changed woman. She waited for Antonia to come down to breakfast in a mood of excited determination. She felt she knew exactly what she had to do, but she also felt it was not going to be very easy. 'Good morning, dear,' she said as Antonia came in. She did not look at her. Her heart was in her mouth as she poured out coffee and made some toast for them both and then, when they were both seated, she said, 'There's something I have to tell you.' Even to her own ears her voice sounded odd, but she ploughed on, undeterred, before Antonia could interrupt. 'It's a confession really,' she said. She swallowed. She was aware of Antonia putting down her cup and looking at her with concern. In her lap she clenched her hands and then, not giving herself time to think, she blurted, 'I'm not confirmed. I want to be confirmed. I *must* be confirmed.'

'Good heavens,' said Antonia.

Once she had started, Kathleen found the words came easily. 'I don't really know how to describe what's happened,' she said, 'but I know I've done wrong. I know now I shouldn't have been taking Communion all these years, and I want to put it right.'

There was a small silence as she gazed at Antonia, waiting for her to respond. Antonia for her part could only stare back wordlessly. She looked perplexed. At last she said slowly, 'If you've been taking Communion all these years, why is it so important now to be confirmed?'

'Because I didn't know then,' said Kathleen immediately. 'I didn't realise.'

Antonia looked at her. 'What didn't you know?' she asked. 'What didn't you realise?'

Kathleen felt that on her reply now the whole of the rest of her life hung. 'I didn't know what it meant,' she said earnestly. 'I didn't really think that any of it mattered, but now I understand what faith is. I *know* that it's a relationship and I shouldn't have been taking Communion without that relationship. But I've got that relationship now and I want to make a commitment. And it's got to be a public commitment. I want to put everything on a proper footing. I've got to . . . and that means I've got to be confirmed before I can take Communion again.'

A look of amused understanding settled on Antonia's face. 'I see,' she said smiling. 'Something *has* happened, hasn't it?' Then she came to a sudden decision. 'Of course you must be confirmed,' she said firmly. 'I'll speak to Father Trumpington.'

The wheels once set in motion, Kathleen felt she could relax, but she was still nervous. It was a big thing, she felt, asking for confirmation at her age. Everyone was going to know now that she had never been confirmed and she was certain they would condemn her. She herself was so convinced of having done what she now believed was wrong that a part of her dreaded the truth becoming known.

True to her word, Antonia spoke to Father Trumpington. 'Funny old bird,' he said, when he heard. 'Whoever would have thought it. Not confirmed!' He thought for a minute. 'You know, Antonia, I'd just tell her not to bother if I were you. After all, what is she, late sixties? She's been taking it for years! I can't see that it really matters. She might just as well carry on.'

'No,' said Antonia firmly. 'I know what you mean, and I know some people don't bother with confirmation anyway, but it really matters to her. You should have seen her when she told me. She was really . . . I don't know, gripped. And she was talking about making a public commitment. I really do think that's what she needs. It's her way of putting things right.'

'Oh Lord,' said Father Trumpington. He looked put out by the whole business. 'Well . . . Oh, I suppose so! You'd better prepare her then, and I'll find out where the next confirmation is in the diocese. We won't be having one till next autumn, and I don't suppose she'll want to wait that long. And besides, it'll mainly be the girls from Tuffington School then. She'll be like a fish out of water if we put her in with that lot, and I'm not sure the headmistress would like it anyway.'

With that Antonia had to be satisfied, although she felt it was something of a slight to Kathleen. Kathleen, however, was overjoyed when she learnt that it was to be Antonia who was to instruct her, and even more delighted when she learnt that the confirmation itself was not to take place at St Godric's. 'Oh no, my dear,' she assured Antonia when she was told, 'I was positively dreading it. I feel God has been rather good. And you'll be with me, won't you?' she asked pleadingly.

Antonia nodded. 'I wouldn't miss it for the world,' she said, and she meant it.

Antonia was discovering that, although life at St Godric's was very far from being a bed of roses, there were very definite compensations, and what had happened to Kathleen Earnshaw was one of them. Another was the enthusiastic response of the greater part of the congregation to her preaching, although she was aware that Father Trumpington was very far from pleased. That worthy had taken to turning his back on her whenever it was her turn to preach, and now sat through her sermons staring stonily up at the altar, as if saying to the congregation, 'I entirely dissociate myself from anything and everything that she says!' He had also begun endlessly to criticise her whenever they were alone; and this noticeably increased the more people said how good her preaching was. As if by way of compensation for this, she began to discover an unexpected dimension to visiting.

When she had been at college, she had hated evangelistic missions. Once every year, for a couple of weeks, they had been sent out in teams to parishes that needed help. While there they were expected to put on various events designed to draw people to church, and would often also go visiting door to door, trying to persuade people to come along to a Sunday service. On one memorable occasion in her second year she had been placed with an earnest but rather insensitive young man who wore open-toed sandals in the depths of winter and a large cross. His dress sense had rather offended Antonia, but even worse had been his manner of approaching people.

Each time anyone had opened the door in response to their

knock, he had literally leapt forward, hand outstretched, and demanded, 'Do you know Jesus Christ?' The first time he had done it she had thought it was a rather tasteless joke, designed to elicit an amused response and so open up the way for them to talk. It had been rapidly borne in upon her, however, that this was not so, and that he was in earnest. After the fifth door had been slammed in their faces, she had refused to go on. She had hated street visiting ever since, and had ended up having a row with her college tutor who had accused her of being judgemental.

Not surprisingly, she had not been looking forward to her visiting in Greystoke Road. She discovered, however, to her great surprise, that it was rather fun. People actually seemed to want to talk, while the circumstances of their lives often meant that there was real need and she could actually do something practical to help. In particular, she befriended a young unmarried mother named Jude, living in council-run bed and breakfast and at her wits' end trying to bring up two tiny children of mixed race, aged one and three. Jude was only twenty-two and had been knocked about by the children's father, with the result that in the end she had run away and taken shelter in a women's refuge. Greystoke Road was her first attempt to live on her own after that experience, and she alternated between paranoid dread that Cy, the children's father, would find her, and wild euphoria at having made it into a bedsit on her own.

But as Antonia rapidly discovered, she clearly also found being stuck on her own with two small and demanding children difficult. She wanted to be out enjoying herself, she said, and it became all too obvious that what she most wanted was a man. She had never really been on her own before, she confided. When she was a kid, there had been her mum and her big sister Rachel. But that had come to an end when her mum's boyfriend had moved in when she was fourteen, because he had resented her and Rach and one night he had, as she put it, tried it on. The result was she had run away. But she had taken up almost immediately with a bloke called Bill, a traveller, and for a couple of years they had wandered around the West Country. It had been good at first, she said, but he was a crackhead, and after a while he had gone off his head. That in itself would have been all right, only he had frightened her because he had started going on about the devil, and had taken up with a really weird crowd. So, when the opportunity had come up, she had dumped him.

The opportunity had been Cy. She was seventeen by then. A look of dread would come over her face when she talked about Cy now. 'He's a bad 'un, 'e is,' she would say with a shudder, puffing at one of her endless cigarettes as she sat and talked to Antonia. On one occasion she suddenly said, 'Look wot 'e did to me!' And she angrily pushed back the sleeve of the shirt she was wearing to reveal an old livid scar going up the length of her arm.

The first time Antonia called, Jude had wanted to talk. She had wanted to talk about God. The next time Antonia called, she had almost dragged her in excitement into the tiny room. 'There's something I want to show you,' she said mysteriously. 'I bought it!' And to Antonia's amazement, very proudly, Jude brought out an old battered copy of the *Good News Bible*. 'It was in the Oxfam shop,' she explained, 'in the window. I saw it after we talked, and I thought it was a sign. So I went and asked 'ow much it was, an' they said fifty p. An' that was exactly 'ow much I 'ad, see, in my purse.' She beamed triumphantly. 'I think God wanted me to 'ave it!'

Antonia had taken to dropping in on her regularly, and their friendship had steadily grown. Jude had even begun to talk vaguely about coming along to church.

Tonight, having told Kathleen of Father Trumpington's decision, Antonia thought she would go and see Jude. She would have liked most of all to have seen Henry, but he was away on business up in Manchester and would not be back till the end of the week, so Jude seemed a happy compromise.

A light drizzle was falling as she set out and it felt cold, but the worst thing of all was the wind. It buffeted and tore at her, and by the time she arrived at the top of Greystoke Road, she was soaked through and dishevelled. Worse was to come, however, because just as she turned the corner, the wind gave an extra strong blast and, battling to keep upright, she somehow managed to fall off her bike. She fell into a very large, muddy puddle, in the process ripping her tights and badly grazing her right shin. Antonia was not happy. It was, however, too far to go back, and so she completed the rest of the journey on foot.

Her destination was the middle house of an old three-storey Victorian terrace. The upper end of Greystoke Road was made up of modern council-owned semis, but at the lower end, where Jude lived, the last remnants of dilapidated and ravaged Victorian gentility grimly hung on. A hundred years ago they would have been quietly gracious town houses, lived in by doctors or solicitors perhaps, with a maid and a cook in residence in the attic rooms upstairs, but their quiet respectability had long since been obliterated, and the houses had fallen into filthy and unloved decay. Those who could not find a home anywhere else lived here, and all sorts of dark and secret goings-on took place behind the battered doors and grimy windows.

Jude's room was on the ground floor, on the left of what had once been an imposing front door. As the wind shrieked maniacally, a dull, dispirited light trickled feebly out through the gap between the grubby curtains, and Antonia breathed a sigh of relief, glad at least that someone was there. Her leg was stinging painfully, and all she wanted just at that moment was to sit down and rest, with a cup of coffee or tea.

As she chained her bike to the railings, the first really heavy drops of rain began to fall and from somewhere above, the muffled beat of music throbbed out into the night, sounding almost tribal with its heavy, insistent beat. Ignoring it, Antonia struggled painfully up the steps and rang the bell. It echoed from deep within the house, and for a long moment nothing happened. Antonia was used to this. Although there were at least ten bedsits in the house, she knew from past experience that the lodgers would steadfastly refuse to answer unless they either knew that the caller was for them or the person at the door made such a nuisance of themselves that in desperation someone would at last come. Antonia continued to ring the bell, and at last a window above her head was flung open and the dark shape of a head appeared. 'Yeah,' said a female voice. 'Wot?'

'Hello,' Antonia called back up. 'I want to see Jude.' The rain, by now heavy, lashed at her face, and she was conscious that with her sodden hair and muddied coat that she must look the most terrible sight.

This seemed, however, to make no impression on the woman above. The window slammed abruptly shut, and from within she heard a voice bellow down the stairs, 'Jude! Jude! Get the bleedin' door, will you! It's for you!'

More banging, then footsteps, and then at last the door was flung wide. But it was not Jude who stood there. Instead, Antonia was surprised to see the brawny figure of a man silhouetted against the light. He had long straggly hair and she could make out the shadow of a small moustache. He wore a T-shirt and frayed jeans. For one heart-stopping moment she wondered if it was the dreadful Cy, but then she realised that it could not be – this man was white.

'Who is it, Dave?' called Jude's voice from behind.

'I don't know. Will ye give me a minute? I'm finding out.' His voice was slightly husky, with a Scottish accent. 'Yes?' he said, turning back to Antonia.

'My name's Antonia,' said Antonia. 'I' m the curate over at St Godric's. I've just called to see how Jude is.'

The man looked sceptical, and an odd expression she could not define flitted across his face. 'Ye don't look very clerical,' he remarked. 'In fact ye look a bit o' a mess.'

'Yes, I know,' she replied. 'I had an accident with my bike. I came off.'

She let her coat slip open to reveal the collar about her neck, and the man gave a small exclamation. 'Aye,' he said, 'I suppose yer who you say you are. Ye'd better come in.' He stood back to allow her past, and she was aware of him scrutinising her carefully. She felt he was not entirely happy that she was here.

Jude, however, rushed at her as she came in and flung her arms about her neck, giving her an excited hug. 'I've got a new feller,' she whispered. 'Wot do you fink of 'im?' And without pause, she added breathlessly, 'We're getting married!' The next moment she became aware of the state Antonia was in. 'Blimey,' she said, standing back to survey her, everything else forgotten. 'Wot 'appened to you then?'

By the time Antonia had explained, Dave had taken her coat and hung it across the radiator and had made her a cup of coffee, and from somewhere deep in a drawer Jude had unearthed a small piece of rather grey-looking cotton wool and had cleaned up her leg. Despite the music still throbbing down from above, they spoke in half whispers so as not to disturb the two children, asleep on the camp bed in the far corner of the room. 'Did I hear you right?' demanded Antonia, as soon as the opportunity presented itself. 'Did you say you were getting married?'

Jude nodded, her eyes once again sparkling with suppressed excitement. 'Yeah,' she said, 'we've already been down the registry offfice. Dave said we 'ad to do it right.'

'But where did you meet?' asked Antonia, bewildered. 'And when?' Her eyes flicked over the room. From the general state, it was clear that Dave had already moved in, and Jude flushed slightly, her eyelids fluttering down, an oddly defensive expression on her face. For all her outward toughness, she looked very young and Antonia's heart went out to her. She realised Jude was frightened she would disapprove and that, for some indefinable reason, her opinion mattered.

'Dave was at the pub the other night,' Jude said. 'We got talkin'. I dunno, somefin' clicked. We both of us just knew it was right.'

'Aye, that's right,' Dave broke in. 'I'm the seventh son of a seventh son, I get feelin's, see. I knew Jude was right for me as soon as I saw 'er. Somethin' told me. I knew we were meant. An' I knew we 'ad to get it legal, because it was important. We're goin' t' last!' A small silence fell on the room as they all digested this, and then he suddenly blurted out, 'I knew you were comin' 'ere tonight too! I felt you!'

The words, delivered with such utter conviction and perfect seriousness, made Antonia jump. She had been in the act of taking a sip of coffee, trying manfully to digest their first pronouncement, and she was so surprised now that she took a gulp of air, making herself choke. 'Pardon?' she gasped, when she had finished coughing, wiping the tears from her eyes.

He regarded her gravely. 'You're powerful, you are. I felt your spirit approaching. You can ask Jude.'

Jude nodded. 'It's true,' she said, her eyes round. 'About 'alf past six tonight 'e said, "She's comin' tonight. I dunno who she is, but I can feel 'er. We're at a crossroads."'

'Yeah,' Dave nodded. 'I was told, an' now you're 'ere.'

Antonia felt there was some vital linking clue that she was missing, but it was obvious that both were deadly serious, their eyes fixed on her in eager anticipation. In Jude's eyes she saw a trace of puzzlement, as if she was unsure what was to happen but was convinced something was. It was Dave, however, who riveted her attention. He was sitting forward on the edge of his seat, shaking slightly with suppressed excitement, and with his big hands clasped so tightly round the mug he held, she wondered if it would break.

'Do you often get these sensations?' she asked, unsure how to react.

He shook his head. 'Not like this,' he replied. 'I know things, I've the gift of sight, and I'm a bit of a healer – mae grandma taught me. But tonight, this was different. I just knew.'

Somewhere up above, as if in response to some prearranged signal, the music was turned abruptly off and a silence almost tangible fell on the darkened room. The very air seemed to breathe with suppressed power. From her bed in the corner, Willow gave a little whimper in her sleep, and then rolled over, and out of the corner of her eye Antonia saw Jude looking at Dave with puzzled concern. Suddenly she knew exactly what she had to do. 'Are you a Christian?' she asked. 'Do you know Jesus?'

He shook his head almost painfully. 'Not really,' he whispered back. 'I know who Jesus is, of course, and I've great respect for him. Mae grandma told me about him, but I don't know him, not the way you mean.'

Antonia nodded, and suddenly words seemed to form in her mind. In the quiet of the dark, smoke-filled little room, she told Dave all about God and the Holy Spirit who was sent by the Son to all who believed. The effect on Dave was electric. He seemed literally to hang on her every word, drinking it in greedily. It was as if he had been waiting, agonising for this moment with every second of his life, and Antonia realised with a shock that he had. A feeling of awe swept over her. She felt she was not really important in any of this. God had simply brought her along for the ride, while he set about saving a soul. She had the feeling that throughout all eternity God had ordained that this was the moment Dave should be redeemed. He had planned it. He had brought this rather frightening, wild-looking man, who had clearly lived a life in which whole fields of wild oats had been sown, to this precise point so that he could meet his God. And yet he was such an unlikely candidate, she thought, the type of man people crossed the road to avoid. It occurred to her that he was a sheep in wolf's clothing.

'I've bin a bad man,' said Dave suddenly. 'I've taken drugs. I've bin promiscuous. I've dun a lot o' what yu'd call bad things.'

She nodded, and at the same time her eyes fell on a pendant hanging about his neck. It was an odd sort of thing, star-shaped, with a strange knife design stamped on the front. 'What's that?' she asked curiously.

Dave's hand flew to his neck. 'This?' he said defensively. 'It's nothing. It's just ma pentangle.' She stared at him and immediately he began to say, 'It's nothing. Really. It's Wicca – mae grandma was in it, that's all. She taught me. It's good.'

An odd little silence fell, during which Antonia continued to stare at him.

'Why are are ye lookin' at me like that?' Dave suddenly broke out. 'I've told ye, it's not black. That 'ud be evil. I'd 'ave nae to do with that. I'm not daft.'

Another silence. Finally Antonia said, 'You can't serve two masters, Dave.'

Their gazes locked. Eventually Dave lowered his eyes. 'I dunna understand,' he said. 'I've only ever used it for good. It's 'ealin'. An' there are spiritual powers that we can all get in touch with.'

With his words the tension broke. 'I know,' Antonia said quietly, 'but powers not submitted to God are in rebellion, and when we open ourselves up without his protection, then we open ourselves up to harm.'

He digested this. 'What are ye sayin' then?'

'I'm saying,' she began, 'that you have to choose. And if you choose God, you have to give these things up and repent.' It was as if, in the silence that now fell, the entire room was hanging on her words. They seemed filled with power. 'When we really come to know God,' she said, very softly, 'and give ourselves to him, then he gives us his Spirit in return. We come under his protection, and he begins to heal us and make us what he knows we can be.

But if we've got any kind of allegiance anywhere else, then a real battle begins, because those other powers fight to assert a claim too.' She hesitated and then fell silent, wondering if she had said too much.

For another minute Dave sat with his eyes dropped, absently gnawing at his moustache and staring at the carpet. He appeared to be weighing something in his mind. Jude stared at him. She looked frightened. At last he raised his head and said quietly, 'There are a lot of things that'll have to go, aren't there?'

Antonia nodded, and he seemed to come to a decision.

'All right,' he said. 'If you'd said this to me a week ago I would nae have believed you, but a few things have happened this week. I could nae understand them before, but I do now. You're right. I want to know Jesus. I want to give him it all!'

Chapter Seven

Father Trumpington scowled. 'What do you mean you've got someone else for baptism?' he asked.

Antonia swallowed, aware that this was not going to be easy. 'I met a young man last night,' she said, choosing her words with care, 'in Greystoke Road. We talked and he says he wants to be baptised.'

'Why?' demanded Father Trumpington. He glared at her belligerently, as if suspicious that he was the victim of a practical joke.

'Well,' said Antonia, 'for the usual reason. He wants to become a Christian.' Her tone was a shade too acid and she regretted it immediately.

'What do you mean? That you converted him?' snapped Father Trumpington, in tones of the greatest disbelief.

'Umm, well . . .' Antonia struggled for words, anxious not to antagonise the priest any further. 'I suppose you could say that,' she ended lamely.

But this was not the right thing to say. Father Trumpington went purple, and his eyes blazed. 'Look here,' he exploded, 'you can't just go around converting people like that. This isn't the New Testament! I mean, what sort of a chap is he? We don't just want any Tom, Dick or Harry, you know. We're not running a social club for down-and-outs.'

'He's not a down-and-out!' snapped Antonia.

'But you said you met him in Greystoke Road.'

This was too much. 'You told me to go visiting in Greystoke Road,' she retorted hotly.

They eyed each other malevolently and Father Trumpington ground his teeth. 'Visiting, yes,' he snarled quietly. 'But I didn't tell you to bring them along to church.'

Antonia could have wept with frustration. But so, too, it appeared, could Father Trumpington. He had the uneasy feeling he had been backed into a corner, and that it was a corner of his own making. He had told Antonia to go visiting down Greystoke Road. He had even told her to try converting a few. The fact that he had issued this instruction as a kind of malicious punishment did not make what had now happened any easier to bear. Like it or not, he appeared to have acquired an addition to his flock. He comforted himself with the reflection that this particular sheep would probably not last very long. Nevertheless, the fact the young man was demanding baptism was a problem. He could not exactly refuse. He gnawed at his lip, trying uneasily to think what to do. 'We must test this young man's commitment, Antonia,' he announced at last, sententiously. He restrained himself with difficulty from adding that nothing on earth would persuade him to accept an erk from Greystoke Road into his congregation.

Antonia beamed. 'Oh, I understand completely,' she said, relieved. 'But I'm sure you'll be impressed with his commitment when you do talk to him. He's really serious. He wants to put all his past life behind. In fact, he's asked for total immersion as a sign of everything before being washed away.'

This was too much. 'Total immersion!' spluttered Father Trumpington, his fragile control disintegrating. 'I'm not totally immersing somebody! We haven't got a baptistry, for a start.'

'I've thought of that,' said Antonia quickly. 'We could use the river. There is actually a kind of jetty down at the bottom of the church yard, if we cleared away the weeds—'

'No!' said Father Trumpington. But he had not yet met Dave. Dave was absolutely determined to throw himself body and soul into his new-found faith, and the river too if necessary. Not for him a modest sprinkling on the forehead. He wanted to pass through the waters and emerge into new life. It was he himself who had suggested the river, because he had seen the church from it one day, weeks before, as he was walking past along the towpath on his way into the city, to his job as a bouncer at a local pub. He had noticed, too, the jetty Antonia had mentioned, almost completely hidden by the weeds and reeds, and he had been intrigued. When he had idly mentioned it to some mates, he had learnt that years before there had been a bathing place there, and that the church had used it for baptisms too. And Dave was of a symbolic turn of mind; he thought the idea of plunging into the still, green waters of the river and emerging a new man rather splendid.

Father Trumpington discovered all this the following Sunday morning when, true to his word, Dave and Jude arrived at church, resolutely dragging Eagle and Willow along in their wake. The children had been imaginatively, if rather unusually, dressed in what Antonia could only assume was their best festive attire. Eagle had feathers laced through his hair, and with his dark skin, looked like some fierce little native warrior all set to go to war. His sister was far more delicately dressed, in an ankle-skimming rural smock, with a huge cross hung round her neck. A mass of mahogany corkscrew curls radiated out from her head like a dark and gleaming halo. She looked unbelievably pretty, but also very alien and strange, as indeed did Dave and Jude. Gloria Sunnington, standing guard on the door like some malevolent gargoyle, blanched at their approach.

'How ya doin'? Thanks,' said Dave, taking the hymn books from her inert hand.

Gloria gurgled inarticulately, and the little group swept by, for all the world as if the church was their second home. Father Trumpington saw their approach from up by the altar, whither he had repaired to do a last-minute check of the books. With a sinking heart, he knew instantly who they were.

As if divining his thoughts, Dave raised a cheery hand. 'Hiya!' he yelled down the length of the church. 'How ya doin'?' He appeared to see nothing incongruous in this greeting, nor to expect any form of reply, but the effect on the rest of the church was electric. Eighteen grey heads jerked up and round as if they had been shot. At the same moment the organ swelled out in a pure blast of what sounded like overloud triumph: Norman had pulled out the wrong stop.

Taking advantage of the momentary sense of dislocation that seemed to strike everyone, Father Trumpington scuttled down the church, intent on telling Dave, in no uncertain terms, to be quiet. But Dave misinterpreted the manoeuvre.

'Nice of ye to come down and say hello,' he said genially to the startled priest, seizing the hand Father Trumpington waved under his nose. 'I call that real friendly! I'm Dave, and this is mae *wife*, Jude.' He emphasised this last proudly and Jude obligingly wiggled her beringed left hand under the priest's nose, for all the world like a child showing off her latest trophy.

Father Trumpington blinked. He had no idea, of course, that they had just got married, but in face of such obvious goodwill he found it difficult to know how to proceed. 'Please be quiet,' he said waspishly, sniffing loudly.

But Dave, having once got hold of his hand, seemed reluctant to let go. 'It's a right bonny church ye've got here,' he said.

Conflicting emotions were aroused in Father Trumpington's breast. Pride in face of Dave's obvious admiration and pleasure, and intense irritation at his ready familiarity. The irritation won. 'Thank you. Could you please sit down and lower your voice. People are trying to pray.' For some obscure reason known only to himself, Eagle chose this precise moment to let out a sound like an express train and scrambled up on to the seat of the nearest pew, where he sat in triumph, drumming his tiny heels noisily against the wooden side. Father Trumpington glared at the child balefully. 'And please keep your children under control,' he snapped. 'This is a house of God, not McDonald's!'

Dave's jaw dropped in astonishment, and Father Trumpington seized the opportunity to yank back his hand, then turned on his heel and marched away. Behind him the huge bouncer pulled a face and then meekly sat down, at the same time gathering the children protectively into his arms like some shaggy and unkempt father bear, while Jude shrank up to his side and slipped a hand through his arm. And there they remained, like a forlorn little group of immigrants, for the first time realising they were unwelcome in the promised land. Ken, who had come into the church with his wife, Marjorie, in time to witness all that had happened, went over, and he and Marjorie sat down beside the little group. 'Welcome,' he said, leaning across and stretching out his hand, a huge beam on his face. 'It's really nice to see new faces in the church.'

Father Trumpington, however, was unrepentant. He felt indeed that he had won a small victory, but it occurred to him that he really must have a word with Norman. They could not have the organ going off like that. He could not imagine what had got into the young man. Accordingly he veered off to the right towards the organ console, and was brought up short to see Jackie at that precise moment whispering something into the organist's ear. Norman played another wrong note.

'Oh, good heavens!' snapped Father Trumpington under his breath. Really, the whole world had gone mad. What in heaven's name did Jackie think she was doing?

'Jackie, Jackie,' he bleated, scuttling up before something even more disastrous could happen, 'leave Norman alone. What on earth are you doing? He keeps getting it wrong!'

Jackie turned injured eyes on him. 'He said he needed help,' she said self-righteously.

Father Trumpington gaped at her. 'Said he needed help?' he repeated. He appeared stunned. 'What on earth are you talking about? He's a professional organist! What possible help could he need?'

Norman played on as if his life depended on it and, with immense dignity, Jackie gave a small sniff and turned away her head. 'He said he needed someone to turn the music, and I volunteered.' Her tone implied that Father Trumpington was being totally unreasonable, and he looked at her with the tiniest shade of suspicion beginning to form at the back of his mind. But she looked so virtuous standing there that he dismissed the thought.

'That's very kind of you, Jackie,' he said, restraining himself with an effort and at the same time trying to put warmth and affection into his expression, 'but you musn't talk to Norman while he's playing. It distracts him.'

'I'm so sorry,' she said, immediately repentant. 'I was just pointing out to Norman that his wife had just come in.'

Light dawned for Father Trumpington. 'Ah, you mean you were telling him you were about to go because Gudrun could take over!'

Jackie smiled ambiguously. 'Um,' she said. But this was lost on Father Trumpington. He turned round to peer for the organist's wife. He was becoming acutely conscious that he ought to start the service soon, and that both he and Jackie should by now be in the vestry, assembling with the choir ready to process out. Ah yes, there she was, coming up now with the children in tow. He shuddered at sight of the children. 'Gudrun,' he hissed testily as the young woman drew near, 'you must make an effort to get here earlier if Norman needs you like this to turn the music for him! Poor Jackie has been kept from the vestry because of this.' Gudrun gaped at him in amazement, but Father Trumpington had made up his mind to waste no more time. 'Come along, Jackie,' he said peremptorily, 'come and get ready!'

As they walked together towards the vestry he took the opportunity to whisper to her, 'Are you all right for the choir again tomorrow night? I could pick you up about seven, and we could go and have a drink first.'

'That would be wonderful,' Jackie whispered back. 'Is Norman going too?'

If Father Trumpington had thought there was nothing else that could go wrong that morning he was sadly mistaken – depending, of course, on how you looked at it. Antonia, he was glad to see, when he finally caught up with her in the vestry, appeared subdued, and took his command to her to lead the prayers like a lamb. Once the service had started, he fully anticipated a clear run. He had reckoned, however, without Dave. Halfway through the sermon Father Trumpington made what he felt to be the innocuous observation that throughout his life many had failed to recognise Jesus for who he was. At this point, Dave leapt to his feet and, as if unable to restrain himself any longer, yelled out, 'Alleluia! I recognise him! I didnae once, but I do now! Praise the Lord!'

As if this was not bad enough, Ken joined in. 'Alleluia!' he cried in an equally loud voice, and there was a little chorus from behind him as if in support.

Father Trumpington had the dreadful sensation that some invisible floodgates had been opened, and for a moment there was nothing he could do. It felt to him as if for several seconds pandemonium reigned, and he even saw towards the back of the church a pair of hands upraised. He was not quite sure whose they were, but he was determined to have a word with that person later! As it was, having futilely banged the pulpit several times, he at last resorted to yelling, 'Order! Order!' as if he was the

Speaker of the House of Commons. In the sudden and abrupt silence that fell, he heard a laugh.

It was all quite unnerving. Father Trumpington had never known anything like it before. He had heard of course about churches where this sort of thing went on all the time, but he had never before, thank God, come across it personally – and he did not like it now he had. It was all most unsettling. In fact, it completely threw him off his stride and, try as he might, after that he could not quite get the service back on course. As he said the prayer of consecration for the bread and wine at Communion, he was aware of little rumblings coming up from the congregation, as if he was sitting on top of a particularly turbulent volcano that was about to explode. As he gave out the bread to the communicants, one or two began to sway alarmingly and refused to move, so that he had to nod to Gloria Sunnington to come up and steer them aside, which she did none too gently. The only shred of comfort was that Dave did not try to join their number; heaven knew what might have happened then!

Afterwards Alan Gunningham looked at him sympathetically and said, 'This won't do, will it? Who is that character who was making all the noise?'

Father Trumpington looked at him gratefully and said, 'One of Antonia's protegés. She found them on the Greystoke estate.'

'Ah.' Alan nodded sagely. 'Might have known she'd be behind it. You know, Dick,' he looked at Father Trumpington narrowly, 'I'd get rid of her if I were you.'

Father Trumpington looked gloomy. 'Easier said than done, Alan,' he confided. 'Now she's here, it'll be at least another couple of years before she goes.'

The Treasurer looked at him for a long moment. 'I don't see why,' he said softly. 'I think we should do something before this whole thing blows out of control. She's not suitable.'

Father Trumpington stared at him. 'What do you mean?' he asked.

But the Treasurer merely looked knowing. 'These things can be arranged,' he said. 'You're on the square, after all. What do you think we mean when we vow to help each other?'

Antonia, of course, was oblivious to this. She thought the whole

service had been absolutely wonderful. She had no odea what
had happened but, for the first time in that rather austere and
gloomy church, she had felt real life. It was as if something deep
and wonderful was stirring, which had given off what seemed to
her a quality of joy. That others had felt it too was clear. People's
eyes were shining as they came up to her after the service, and
one or two of them hugged her excitedly. 'That was so marvellous,
dear,' twittered Phoebe as she surged out of the church with Ken.
'Ooh, more! More!' And then she slipped a confiding hand through
Antonia's arm. 'You know, we're really excited by your proposal
for a fellowship group. We've been trying to get one going for
years, but we never could. Perhaps he'll listen to you.' She
indicated Father Trumpington with a jerk of her head, and then
she whispered, 'Do you think you could come and meet our prayer
group and tell us some more about it? I know we'll all want to
join. We meet every Thursday in my house at eight. Do say you'll
come. There are quite a few of us, and Gudrun Pilkington said
this morning she'd like to join too.'

Never for one moment did it occur to Antonia that to accept
the invitation would be wrong. Ken had already told her about
the prayer group, and even Father Trumpington himself had
mentioned it – disparagingly, it was true, but he had spoken of it
as an established fact. And he had encouraged her to get involved
in the activities of the church. She did not give the matter a second
thought. 'I'd love to,' she said, and Phoebe looked delighted.

'What was all that about?' Henry asked, coming up after the
little woman had gone. Antonia told him and he looked pleased.
'There you are,' he said. 'Things are happening! There is a reason
why you're here.' He squeezed her hand. 'That was great today,
but not everyone's too pleased.' He nodded in the direction of
Gloria Sunnington. 'If looks could kill, your Greystoke man would
have been incinerated by now.' He laughed softly. 'You should
have seen her face when he leapt to his feet and shouted Alleluia.
I thought she was going to have a fit.'

'You should have been close to Father Trumpington afterwards,'
she muttered back. 'He was so angry he was shaking. I was sure
he was going to say something.'

Henry shrugged. 'Not a lot he could say, really, was there? But it'll do him good. Shake him up. Who knows, he might even end up converted.'

At that moment Dave and Jude emerged from the church. The children were nowhere in sight, but from inside the building could be heard loud shrieks and wild laughter, and the sound of feet racing up and down. The big man, however, seemed oblivious. His jaw set, he was making a beeline for Father Trumpington. He had been feeling bad ever since the beginning of the service, when it had been borne in upon him that the priest was displeased. Dimly, he felt that they had got off to a bad start, and now he wanted to make amends so that the atmosphere between them would be all right. He was going to say sorry.

Determinedly, he strode over and clapped a huge hand on to Father Trumpington's shoulder, at the same time saying in a loud voice, 'A wee word with you, Reverend!'

Father Trumpington, who was still deep in conversation with Alan, had had not the slightest idea he was there. Startled, he let out a yelp and leapt into the air.

'That's a guilty conscience ye must have there!' said Dave matily.

Father Trumpington glowered, his ears turning scarlet, and Alan scrutinised the bouncer with interest. 'I don't think we've met before,' he said urbanely. 'My name's Alan Gunningham. I'm the Treasurer.'

'Pleased tae meet ye,' said Dave. 'Dave Jackson. We're new.'

'So I understand,' said Alan smoothly. 'Father Trumpington was just filling me in. We don't often get new faces in church. From Greystoke Road, I believe.'

'Aye, that's right. Listen,' said Dave, turning again to Father Trumpington and taking the bull by the horns, 'I'm sorry, we didnae ken the form this morning. We didnae mean to cause a disturbance when we came in.'

Alan laughed soundlessly. 'It just ensured we all knew you were there, old chap.'

But Dave was not to be deflected. 'Is it all right?' he said earnestly to Father Trumpington.

It was of course not all right, but after his conversation with Alan Gunningham Father Trumpington had no intention of revealing that fact. 'Give him some rope,' Alan had advised, 'let everyone else kick up a fuss. Let him be seen as one of Antonia's little mistakes. People will soon start realising she's behind all this, and once they do, they'll jolly soon start making noises that she's got to go. And meantime we'll start lodging a few complaints ourselves. There are always things you can find fault with. You could say you've had a complaint from one of the congregation because she didn't use the right form of words when she introduced the lesson, for a start.'

Father Trumpington had scowled. 'I'd been going to have a word with her about that anyway,' he had said. 'I'm not going to have her dropping all the thous like that, and she said Holy Spirit instead of Holy Ghost.' His tone had implied that this was tantamount to heresy.

'Well, now you can make it official,' Alan had said smoothly, 'and meanwhile I'll have a word with one or two others. I'll have a chat with George Bullen too – isn't she doing the Christmas show this year up at St Thomas's?' He smiled evilly. 'A complaint, I think, from George to the Bishop!'

Now, with a supreme effort of will and mindful of the Treasurer's advice, Father Trumpington schooled his features into a mask of jocularity. 'Of course it's all right,' he said to Dave through clenched teeth. 'Think no more about it.'

Dave looked relieved. 'That's greet,' he said. 'I sometimes think I've got two left feet, but we want tae get this right.' Having successfully negotiated this hurdle, the big man appeared to make up his mind to unburden himself completely before his nerve failed. 'I met yon lassie the other night,' he ploughed on, indicating Antonia. 'She told me about Jesus. She told me where I'd been goin' wrong. And I,' he smiled down at Jude before repeating firmly, '*I* want tae be baptised. Did she tell you?'

'Er, she did mention something,' mumbled Father Trumpington. He felt they were moving on to dangerous ground and that at any moment he was going to be forced to commit himself to something he would dislike intensely. A glance at Alan Gunningham warned him to take care. Agree to everything, Alan had said emphatically when he had explained the dilemma; you won't have to do it anyway. You be Mr Nice Guy, and let them put themselves in the wrong. It was hard, but Father Trumpington reminded himself that in matters of theology he was a liberal. 'Yes, she did mention it,' he said more firmly, 'and I said I felt we needed to test your commitment and that you should receive instruction.'

Dave looked as if he could hardly believe his ears. 'That's greet,' he said again. 'We're quite sure. We want instruction – both of us.' Father Trumpington prepared to turn away, but Dave had not finished. 'And did she tell ye,' he inquired loudly, 'that I want tae be baptised in the river? I want total immersion. I want tae be washed and pass into new life.'

Unfortunately for Father Trumpington, Dave said this loudly enough for those standing around to overhear, and several heads immediately turned curiously. Perhaps even more unfortunately, one of those heads belonged to Ken. 'Total immersion,' he repeated with interest. 'That sounds a good idea. We used to have baptism by immersion when Neville Coddington was here. He used the river too. He said we needed the symbol of being washed from sin and made clean by Jesus.'

But this reminder of what his much-loved predecessor had done did not make Father Trumpington any more kindly disposed to the suggestion. In fact, if anything it had the reverse effect. 'Now look here,' he began. Alan Gunningham looked at him. 'I . . . I . . .' stuttered Father Trumpington. The little group that had now gathered round them looked at him with interest.

'I think you mean you'll have to see if the river's still suitable,' broke in Alan, coming to his rescue. 'It's grown very weedy since Neville Coddington's day, and it's deep here. We used to dive from that old jetty when I was a lad. But I'm not sure the council would allow it any more. They had to stop the swimming after there was a case of Weil's disease.'

'I dunna think that'ud be a problem,' broke in Dave. 'After all, they still swim further up, and I'm more than happy tae test how deep the water is – and clear it if need be,' he added.

Father Trumpington looked at him with loathing.

'Oi've got a little dinghy you cud use if it 'ud be of any 'elp,' said Slynne, who had joined the group in time to overhear Dave's last suggestion. 'Oi cud even help you. Oi've done some river clearance afore, an' it's not too bad down there. The weed wus cut back only five years ago. They 'ave to keep it safe in case people fall in. Oi don't think the jetty's in too bad a state either.'

'There you are then,' said Ken. 'The Lord's already got it in hand, if you ask me.'

'We didn't,' retorted Father Trumpington through gritted teeth. He turned back to Dave. 'I applaud your enthusiasm, young man, but as Alan has already said, we need to make absolutely sure the water is safe before we get carried away with all these plans. And especially we need to ensure that there's no danger of disease.'

'Oh, I'm sure there's not,' said Dave quickly. 'Honest, I swim in the river often. I've never caught anything.'

Father Trumpington unkindly reflected that weeds were resilient. He did not, however, voice this thought. Instead he said deliberately, 'Nevertheless, we must go through the proper channels. It's an exciting possibility, I admit, but so far that's all it is, a possibility. I have to be convinced it's safe.'

'Well, there's no 'arm taking a look at least,' broke in Slynne. 'We're not goin' to know if it's safe or not if we don't 'ave a look!'

'I agree, and I'll volunteer to follow up with the council,' said Ken. He turned to the Treasurer. 'I remember that case of Weil's disease you're talking about, Alan. It was just after Dick came. We were inundated with rats that year. Terrible it was. I've never known anything like it. Began the week Dick was licensed, as I remember. But I agree with Dave, I don't think it's particularly dangerous now, though you're quite right, we need to check.'

Father Trumpington mentally cursed the spirit of generosity that had put it into the minds of so many to help, but short of absolutely refusing to consider the idea there was nothing he could do. Dave looked over the moon and was busily taking up Slynne's offer of help, and everyone else seemed to be chattering to each other excitedly, as if they were only amazed that none of them had ever thought of it before. 'I wouldn't mind being baptised in the river too,' he heard someone say. 'It's sort of New Testament, isn't it!'

Heaven forbid, Father Trumpington thought. Heaven forbid!

Chapter Eight

When she knew that Norman was going to be practising, Jackie had formed the habit of stealing into church and pretending to be at prayer. She could do this fairly easily because she lived only a few doors down from the organist and his wife and she had quickly got to know their routine. During the day Norman would take his pupils, either for the piano, at their house, or on the organ, in church. But at four he would break for a cup of tea with Gudrun and the children, and then at five he would take himself back across to the church, to practise alone. Jackie would see him every evening walking past her window, his coat collar turned up against the cold, a woollen scarf wrapped round his neck. And so she had begun to slip ahead of him, installing herself a good five minutes before he was due to arrive, leaving Elspeth tucked up in front of the telly with a mug of cocoa and a bun.

The first couple of times she had done this the organist had merely nodded at her. But then one day she had deliberately waylaid him, and to her intense delight he had sat down to talk. She had discovered that he was a mere twenty-six, and that his wife was thirty-one, and that they had had to get married after Gudrun had become pregnant. She had discovered, too, that he was bored with his life, that he hated all the trappings of fatherhood and longed to be free. Gudrun was mad, he said, she was clingy, she stifled him, she could not understand. And now there was another baby on the way! The woman was like a battery hen!

Jackie had been hardly able to believe her ears. To her, Norman was already the great artist Father Trumpington had assured her he would one day become. The first time she had seen him she had known that she wanted to be his muse, his inspiration. There was something heroic in the thought of being the mistress of such a man, and she wanted for herself that little bit of immortality that would come from his reflected glory. She had begun to plot her campaign on the same night as the welcome, from the very moment, indeed, when she had been formally introduced to him. She had seen his conquest then as a challenge. She had registered at a glance that Gudrun was clingy. To Jackie's disgust, the woman had hardly let Norman out of her sight the entire evening and, quite apart from that, in her own solemn way Jackie had to acknowledge that her rival was pretty, despite the fact that she was seven months pregnant. All in all, Jackie had rather thought it might be difficult to wean his interest away from her, and yet here was the organist now metaphorically presenting himself to her on a plate.

Jackie did not delude herself. She knew that she was no spring chicken, although she prided herself that she was well preserved. But she knew that time was not on her side and that she must seize her opportunities when she could. So now she pounced. As he had told her all about his marital problems, so she in turn told him all about hers – the selfsame story, indeed, that she had spilled out to Father Trumpington, only she embellished it even further this time, so that Malcolm became not only selfish, neglectful and demanding but, even worse, a brutish lout who physically assaulted her. She had read an article the week before about marital rape, and somehow this too became woven into her tale; after all, she did sometimes suffer from headaches and Malcolm, when they had still had sex, had not always been quite as considerate as he ought to have been.

Norman was appalled. He had poured out his troubles to Jackie because he had ended up that evening having words with Gudrun and he had rather spitefully wanted to avenge himself on her. Moaning about her to someone else had seemed to fit the bill nicely, even if it had involved bending the truth a little. But he had not envisaged that his self-pitying complaints might elicit a parallel response from someone else. Nor in his wildest dreams could he have envisaged such a lurid tale of wronged woe. He looked at Jackie with renewed interest. He saw a woman whom he judged to be in her thirties – about the same age, he thought, as his wife, though probably a couple of years older. Only where Gudrun eschewed all make-up and adopted a rather severe style, Jackie, he felt, had a certain racy and highly covetable stylishness.

Her clothes were obviously expensive, her make-up flawless, and there was a kind of dewy elegance about her that to him, in the dim light of the church, looked very appealing.

Norman liked older women. That indeed had been what first attracted him to Gudrun. There was also, however, a rather petulant strain to his character that made him feel he deserved whatever his inclination might suggest. This, combined with an unfortunate lack of moral restraint, had in the past led him into some difficult situations from which Gudrun had had to extricate him. Not many women would have put up with this; in fact many would have either left or castrated Norman long ago. But not Gudrun. Gudrun truly and passionately loved him. She loved his talent. She adored his unpredictability. And she had made up her mind long ago to put up with his straying – because she knew that he would always come back. Not that she liked it when he went off after other women. In fact all hell was likely to break loose in the Pilkington household when Norman was starting out on one of his little affairs. Then Gudrun would become heavily tragic and there would be hysterics and tears, but it was a game that both of them, in a rather perverted way, enjoyed. Gudrun imagined this was the way artists ought to behave, and so it confirmed her in her appreciation of his talent, and Norman . . . well, Norman just liked a bit of variety.

He scrutinised Jackie carefully, and decided that he liked what he saw. So Jackie had come over with him to the organ console, and she had begun to turn the music as he played. Two evenings later, when her hair had lightly brushed his cheek as she leant across, neither of them had been surprised when his hands had suddenly transferred themselves from the keyboard to her breasts. And somehow, before she knew it, he had managed to undo her blouse and had buried his face against her nipples. Then she was beside herself with ecstasy as he ran his lips up her neck and locked them on to her open, straining mouth. Jackie was a highly passionate woman. She had not had sex for a good ten months. She had not realised how much she had missed it. But as Norman's hands ran over her aching body, it suddenly hit her. She began to pant, in turn beginning to tear at his clothes. In a moment all Norman's thoughts of continuing with his organ practice went completely out of the window, and they slid down on to the floor. And there, under the disapproving glance of the angel who stared down at them from the stained-glass window above, in a frenzy of lust, they consummated their passion.

There was no stopping Jackie after that. She had known for some time that the situation with Malcolm could not continue for much longer the way it was. He would not, she knew, wear it. But she was determined to stave off divorce until she should be financially secure and have a suitable alternative to hand. Now fate seemed to have dealt her the possibility of two: Father Trumpington and Norman. Father Trumpington was of course much older, and if he left Dorothy his career would most certainly be at an end. But he was near retirement age, so would that really matter? Jackie was sure he was financially secure, and if he did lose his job, so what? He would simply have more time to devote to her.

Against that, however, was the fact that he was undeniably rather dull, and he lacked the lustre of his far younger and more volatile rival. Norman not only had age on his side, there was every possibility that one day he would achieve real fame. Jackie liked that. She felt that as his consort she might have a lot of fun. Who knew what worlds might open up before her if she attached herself to his star? However, it had to be acknowledged that for the present his circumstances seemed somewhat straitened. He was clearly living hand to mouth, and she had already overheard Gudrun talking about child-minding as a way of raising money, once the baby was born. Jackie liked the idea of a toy boy, but she was not sure that she wanted to foot the bill. Yet now that she had so decisively won the opening battle of her campaign, her outlook began subtly to change.

Jackie had enjoyed their union. Norman was imaginative when it came to sex and he seemed, too, to know exactly what she wanted. She discovered, somewhat to her surprise, that she could not get enough of it, and she found herself beginning to daydream about the possibility of being not just Norman's mistress, but his wife.

However, she was not prepared to jeopardise everything just for passion – Norman's prospects were not yet sufficiently secure.

Also a lot could go wrong, she knew, in a love affair, especially when it was illicit; and there might be two birds in the proverbial bush, but neither was yet firmly in her hand. She determined to carry on with both. Time, she felt, would prove which was the better course to take and meanwhile she would have a little fun.

If things were going well for Jackie, they were not progressing quite so easily for Father Trumpington. On the Monday morning after the disastrous Sunday, he casually mentioned to Dorothy over breakfast that, as part of his pastoral duty, he had agreed to take Jackie with him again that night to the Carberry choir. Dorothy looked up at him over the toast, stricken, and Father Trumpington had the grace to shift uneasily and run a sticky finger round the inside of his clerical collar which had suddenly, inexplicably, become too tight. 'Uu . . . hum, yes . . . well,' he said, clearing his throat. 'The poor woman seems to be so miserable these days, what with her husband being away for so long. And she loves music. It seems the least I can do.'

Dorothy had not noticed that Jackie had seemed particularly miserable. On the contrary, the woman had seemed to her to be positively glowing whenever their paths crossed. And it had worried her, because for some months now she had been conscious both of Jackie's determined pursuit and of the long, unaccounted for disappearances of her husband. She also knew, painfully, that her husband did not love her, and she dreaded what would happen if the silly idiot took it into his head to go off now.

'Are you taking anyone else along as well, dear?' she inquired, striving to keep her voice neutral.

'Er . . . no, actually,' said Father Trumpington. He became excessively busy with the paper, rustling it and pulling it up so that it obscured his face as he turned the page.

Dorothy looked at him, but she could think of nothing to say. At least, nothing that would not result in a row; and, above all, she dreaded that. Dick became very bombastic when he was roused; he stormed and he shouted, and then he sulked. And he always blamed everybody else, so that in the end she always gave in and acknowledged that she was wrong, just so that there could be a return to peace. But this time it seemed far worse; she had the feeling that something dark and terrible was looming over her, something against which she was powerless to fight.

Father Trumpington finished adjusting the paper and stole a glance at her, but by now Dorothy was staring woodenly down at her cornflakes, mechanically chewing. She did not look as if she was enjoying them. 'Well, it is part of my job,' he said defensively, 'to take care of people.'

'But does that really involve taking them along with you to the choir?' ventured Dorothy in a small voice. She instantly regretted it.

'Of course it does, woman,' exploded Father Trumpington at his most majestic, 'if that's what they need. My job is to help people in whatever form seems most appropriate.' And he went on to tell her in no uncertain terms that jealousy had no place in a priest's family life, and that she must learn to be more caring and to see people's needs more clearly. After that he felt rather better, because it seemed to him that he had justified himself and effectively quelled the demon of guilt. And thankfully Dorothy did not this time respond, so that they finished the rest of their breakfast in silence, after which he retreated to the sanctuary of his study.

Left alone, poor Dorothy had a little weep. Then she phoned up Amelia, her married daughter in Hastings, and poured out to her that Dick did not love her any more. Her husband, she knew, would be furious if he ever found out about this, but Dorothy had reached a state where she no longer knew what to do, and she did not really care. She had to tell someone. She had to have advice, and she had no friend to whom she could spill out her heart. Amelia, when she heard all that had happened, was robust. 'Don't be silly, Mummy,' she advised. 'He is a priest, after all. Why don't you just believe what he says? I mean, Daddy, really! You can't honestly believe that he'd carry on at his age. Of course he loves you. He's just not very demonstrative, that's all.' Amelia at thirty found it difficult to believe that someone in their sixties could fall prey to passion. She began seriously to consider whether or not her mother was having a breakdown. After all, it seemed so irrational to get upset over something as trivial as this. 'Look,' she went on, remembering all the advice columns in every woman's magazine that she had ever read, 'why don't you do something to make yourself more attractive? You know, put a bit of zest back into your marriage. Go and have your hair done. Buy a couple of new outfits. Make Daddy take you out to dinner!'

'Do you really think I'm being stupid?' sniffed Dorothy, wiping away a tear.

'Of course you are, Mummy,' bounced back Amelia.

'And do you really think it would help? If I did what you said? You know, going and getting my hair done and things?'

'Absolutely! Make yourself beautiful for him. You're not that old. Have a make-over.' And then as an afterthought she added, 'Maybe that's what you need to make *yourself* feel better.'

Dorothy was not convinced. Nevertheless, what her daughter said did make a lot of sense. Perhaps she had been a doormat for too long, and perhaps she did need to fight fire with fire. She took a long hard look at herself in the mirror and saw an elderly woman, overweight and with grey hair. She phoned up the hairdresser and made an appointment for the next day, which was the earliest they could fit her in. Then she went and withdrew some money from the bank.

True to his word Father Trumpington picked up Jackie at seven that same night. She was ready and waiting, having previously arranged for Elspeth to spend the night at a friend's. She was wearing a long grey skirt and clingy white top, and Father Trumpington thought she looked ravishing. 'I thought we could go and have a drink first,' he growled, helping her into his car.

'Lovely,' breathed Jackie. Her thoughts were on Norman, whom she had seen again only a couple of hours before. He, too, had suggested they go out, and Jackie had agreed to go with him in a couple of days' time to a little pub a long way out of town.

Father Trumpington also took her to a little pub outside town. Like Norman, he wanted to ensure that they were not seen. Jackie felt deliciously naughty, and after two vodkas she also felt ready to be deliciously indiscreet. As they got back into the car, she leant across and slipped her hand inside Father Trumpington's jacket, gently sliding it down his rather portly stomach until her fingers found the top of the zip on his trousers. Father Trumpington leapt about three feet into the air, but it was a leap of pure joy, all the more intense because so unexpected. His manhood reared itself, and with bated breath he waited to see what Jackie would do next. He was not disappointed.

Ten minutes later, when it was all over, she turned and smiled at him sweetly. 'Shall we go to the choir now?' she asked.

Father Trumpington did not notice the next morning how strained Dorothy seemed. In fact he hardly noticed her at all. His thoughts were too full of Jackie, about whom he had managed to have a wonderfully erotic dream. He felt like a boy again, sixteen and in love. Dreary Dorothy was the last person he wanted to be bothered about. He had arrived back the preceding night at about eleven o'clock. Dorothy was already in bed, pretending to be asleep, and as he clambered heavily in beside her, she smelt on him the last traces of his little frolic. Her worst fears were confirmed, but she said nothing. There did not seem to be any point. But long after he was gently snoring, she lay awake, alternately raging at the injustice of it all, and plotting improbable schemes to win him back – and be avenged!

The result was, the next morning she looked even more unattractive than ever and, to console herself, had three extra pieces of toast and a vast amount of jam. Yesterday, following Amelia's advice, she had, it was true, taken some money from the bank but then, when it actually came to spending it, she had drawn back, the puritan in her re-emerging and castigating her intention to buy clothes as mindless vanity. Instead, she had gone as usual into work. Now, however, staring at her husband's florid and indifferent face across the breakfast table, her resolve hardened. If she did not do something now, and fast, she knew she was going to lose everything she had ever had. Dorothy did not really know much about fashion and clothes, but deep within her there lurked a hardy spirit and, after all she had endured, she was more than ready to go to war. It was not that she loved him. She did not. But she wanted to preserve her life. She phoned the bank and told them she would not be in because she was ill, and then took herself off down to the shops.

She had already worked out that in this case her usual shopping haunts would not do and, with gritted teeth, she headed straight for the most fashionable shop she knew, in the centre of the town. She had never been inside it before and now, in her homemade knitted woolly, felt distinctly out of place. The sales assistant evidently thought so too, but she appeared to sense a killing. Seeing Dorothy hesitate on the threshold, she undulated over towards her and pounced before she could withdraw. 'What exactly is Madame looking for?' she inquired. Dorothy was tempted to say the way out but, faced by this gorgeous and exotic creature (could her hair really be that purple colour?), she lacked the courage.

The assistant gave her the faintest of chilly smiles and, seeing that she was struck dumb, propelled her in the direction of the rails. 'Is it a wedding?' she inquired. 'Or a party?' Dorothy managed to gurgle something about it being neither of those things, simply that she wanted a change of image. The assistant gave her a pitying look and then randomly began to twitch different outfits off the rails. Could she suggest this season's layered look, she murmured, and perhaps a pyjama suit? Very forgiving, she added, eyeing Dorothy's ample curves.

Two hours later (which, extraordinarily, was how long it had taken) Dorothy emerged with a skirt that came down to her ankles and a rust-coloured top that made her look like a sack. But they were, the sales assistant had assured her, very 'in'. She had also been persuaded to buy the pyjama suit, which the assistant had insisted no woman of fashion could be without, and what was supposed to be a slinky little number in black. She also had a couple of long tunic sweaters and a pair of leggings, though she had retained enough common sense to stand firm against the tartan mini skirt.

Next she headed for a shoe shop because the assistant had been adamant that her sensible brogues would not do. In there she was stunned by the teetering heels that seemed to be the rage, but a kinder assistant this time directed her to a more muted and elegant court – Dorothy was surprised, they really looked quite nice. Next, at long last, it was the hairdresser's. It had been at least eight years since Dorothy had last set foot inside a hairdresser's shop. She had worn her hair in an unfashionable bun for years, and every once in a while had simply snipped an inch off the ends to keep it strong. It was quite difficult going in, but once seated she took a deep breath and announced, 'I want it cut. I want it coloured. And I think I want it permed!'

The stylist was a young man named Michael who prided himself on his artistic sensibility. Now he went slightly pale. 'Have you thought about this?' he asked nervously.

Dorothy had thought about it. Indeed, she had thought about nothing else ever since the conversation with Amelia, and she was not about to turn tail at this point. 'Yes, I have,' she said with determination. 'I want the most fashionable style you can give me, and I want lots and lots of highlights.' She thought of the sales assistant in the shop. 'I'd like some purple and some red.'

Michael went and conferred with a colleague and then they both came back and talked to each other in low tones, tweaking her hair and pulling it this way and that.

'Nice condition,' said the other young man, 'and it's very thick – surprising really.' Dorothy began to feel like a plate of meat, but they were ignoring her now.

'It depends how short we want to go,' said Michael.

'Umm,' responded the other. 'Needs a bit of height here, I think.'

'Ye-es, and a streak here over the eye. Not too much aubergine though. No.'

'No, I don't think so either... copper and silver, I think, with just a touch of mahogany.'

They fetched the colourist, who came over and largely agreed with them, but could he suggest a background of ash brown, just to integrate and warm things up?

Before she knew it, Dorothy was sitting in front of a mirror with a plastic bag over her head and little bits of foil sprouting in every direction. It looked distinctly odd, but an hour and a half later she was astounded to see a different face stare back at her out of the mirror. Gone was the homely, silver-haired reflection that had gazed back at her for at least the last ten years. In its place was this rather startling lady with dark, multi-coloured hair and a surprised expression. Michael and his colleague thought it looked wonderful. 'Absolutely marvellous!' they said to each other. It transformed her. Dorothy vainly searched the mirror for herself, but could only find this rather hard-faced stranger. 'You'll love it,' Michael assured her, seeing her unease. He did not consult her again, but instead began to snip and shape. With a feeling of desecration Dorothy saw her hair falling all round her on to the floor. She hardly dared look at this stranger who was emerging before her in the mirror now, this stranger who looked as if she might actually wear the clothes she had bought.

Forty minutes later it was done. Her hair was very short and swept elegantly up at the sides over her ears, while a deep and amazingly coloured wave fell across her brow. She certainly looked different. She was not sure if she liked it. And then, as she tried to fit herself to this new image, Michael (who appeared to be feeling very pleased with himself) said, 'We ought to do something about the face now.' Other stylists gathered round to admire, and then the beautician appeared. 'We need to match the face tones to the hair,' murmured Michael confidentially. And then even more softly, 'It doesn't quite fit at the moment.'

When Dorothy emerged, crimped and painted, she felt that her head now sat like a stranger on her body. In fact her body felt all wrong, lumpy and bulgy like a well-worn futon. And then inspiration struck – she would do for her body what she had done to her hair. She would take up aerobics! Clutching all her carrier bags, she headed for the health club in the High Street and recklessly signed on for a beginner's class. Her new self also bought a skimpy grey and pink spotted leotard, matching leggings, and trainers that made her feel faint when the assistant told her the price. But she had come too far to turn back now. Swallowing, she took out the cheque book for her joint account with her husband, and defiantly wrote out a cheque for what seemed the most enormous amount of money. A little voice whispered to her that it was right that he should pay.

After that she could not wait to get home and put on some of the clothes that she had bought and get to know her new self in her own mirror.

Her husband returned home just as she was trying on the leotard. He had no idea that she was in the house and, as he came marching up the stairs intent on going to the lavatory and getting himself a clean handkerchief before going out again to see Jackie, he was confronted by this strange and terrible figure stretching and gavotting in front of the mirror in his bedroom. He had not the slightest idea who it was but the woman (for woman it unquestionably was) looked dreadful, her wobbling curves under the straining lycra seeming to carry the most terrible threat.

For one deranged moment Father Trumpington wondered if he was hallucinating, and if this terrible banshee figure had not been sent to him by the devil as retribution for his exploits of the last few days. Then he reminded himself he did not believe in the devil. He looked at the figure more closely, outrage beginning to oust the fright he had felt. They were being burgled, that was the explanation. He would soon settle this! But as he prepared to wade in and do battle to turn the intruder out, something in the figure struck him as familiar. Something about the shape of the breasts . . . and the stomach. He stared in paralysed and fascinated horror as the terrible truth dawned. Slowly he raised his eyes, and found himself staring straight into the apprehensive gaze of his wife. 'Good God!' he said.

Chapter Nine

Father Trumpington did not spend a happy evening. In face of his shock Dorothy was totally unrepentant. To prepare their dinner of cold beef and Russian salad (she had not, she said, had time to cook) she removed the leotard and put on in its place the leggings she had bought and a tunic top. Father Trumpington had never been an admirer of his wife's legs, and he found himself staring at them in fascinated horror as she wobbled her way back and forth across the kitchen. But to make matters worse, to his intense chagrin she seemed utterly oblivious of the spectacle she presented. He thought with terror of what would happen if she appeared like this before his parishioners or – even worse – the Bishop. And as he grappled with this awful prospect, all thoughts of seeing Jackie were temporarily forgotten.

When Dorothy saw his shock, she discovered she rather liked her new persona. She had had doubts up to that point, but when she saw his stunned expression reflected in the mirror as he came up the stairs, they disappeared. She had at last caught his attention! The realisation gave her a feeling of power, the first such feeling she had had in years, and something in her awoke. She opened a bottle of wine. She became positively skittish. As she wafted her way past her husband carrying the dirty plates, adopting the same kind of walk that she had seen the sales assistant in the shop use, she chucked him under the chin. Father Trumpington went rigid, and a glassy sheen came to his eyes. Dorothy was not deterred. Indeed, she felt that things were going exactly as she had planned. Without more ado, she sat herself on his knee and began to nestle up close. Father Trumpington was revolted. He could not believe that Dorothy was acting like this. But she was. 'Why don't you and I take our wine upstairs?' she breathed, panting slightly.

Father Trumpington could take no more. With a strangled cry he leapt to his feet, at the same time shoving her violently from

113

him. With a dull thud, she landed none too gently on the floor, and the dirty plates that had still been clutched in her hand ricocheted across the room. Father Trumpington found his voice at last. 'Pull yourself together, woman!' he thundered. 'Why on earth should I want to go upstairs with you?'

Dorothy's face crumpled as if she had been struck. 'But . . . but . . .'

'Have you no sense of decorum? Look at you! Oversized mutton pretending to be lamb!'

For one dumbfounded moment Dorothy stared up at him, as if incapable of understanding what he was saying. Then she gave a single, mewling cry and, without waiting to hear any more, scrambled to her feet and rushed from the room. The bubble had been burst.

It was in a belligerent mood and determined to vent his anger on someone that Father Trumpington went down to church to say the daily office with Antonia the next morning. As he had plotted with Alan, he had been planning ever since the Sunday to take her to task but the opportunity had so far eluded him. Monday had been her day off, and Tuesday they had both been caught up in Chapter, the combined meeting of clergy within the deanery. However, this morning, he decided, remembering his wife's ardour of the night before with a shudder, was it! She was going to pay.

He waited until after they had finished the office and then, as they stood on the pavement outside, he said frostily, 'By the way, Antonia, there have been some more complaints.'

She eyed him warily. 'About what?'

'About you, my dear.' Her expression of startled surprise reminded him of Dorothy the night before. It fuelled his wrath. 'Yes,' he said savagely, 'people are objecting yet again to your preaching style, and to the way you don't stick to the accepted form of words. In particular, there has been a complaint that you used the term Holy Spirit instead of referring to the Holy Ghost.'

Antonia stared at him dumbfounded. 'I'm sorry,' she said, 'I didn't realise there was any difference. I just usually think of the Holy Ghost as . . . the Holy Spirit.'

'Didn't realise there was any difference!' screeched Father

114

Trumpington. 'Of course there's a difference. We've been talking about the Holy Ghost for years, we don't want any of this modern new-fangled Spirit stuff. And while we're on the subject, please stick to thou and thee. You're far too familiar with God, you know! You make it sound as if he's a personal friend. It really won't do. We'll have a bit more reverence from you, my girl. In future you'll stick exactly to the wording of the 1662 prayer book. That way perhaps you won't cause quite so much offence.'

She looked at him stiffly. 'May I know who's complained?'

'No, you may not,' snapped Father Trumpington. 'What business is it of yours? Just take it from me that people are not happy, and it's not up to you to go changing things willy-nilly. Or,' he added as an afterthought, 'picking on people if you think they disapprove!'

Antonia was stung. 'I have absolutely no intention of picking on anyone,' she retorted. 'But I thought perhaps it might help if I could talk to them, maybe even apologise and explain my view.'

Father Trumpington smirked. 'Ah yes, of course,' he said. 'Well, let me give you two names for starters: Alan Gunningham and Gloria Sunnington. They are both extremely upset by what they see as your highly inappropriate conduct. Alan himself asked me to have a word with you. He says your manner during the services entirely disturbs his spirit of prayerful recollection. Perhaps you should go and apologise to him. I'll give him a ring and let him know you're coming.'

All of this, unbeknown to them both, was being observed by Gudrun from the confines of her house. She was feeling wretched this morning and, in an intensity of anguish, had flung herself bodily up against the net curtains that screened the living room from view. There, effectively hidden, she had watched Father Trumpington and Antonia emerge from the church on to the pavement and begin to talk. It had soon become obvious that all was far from well and, taking some comfort from the distress of others, she had stayed to watch. She saw Father Trumpington wave his hands in obvious anger, and Antonia start back. She observed the look of anger and stunned disbelief on the curate's face, and the unpleasant aura of triumph that oozed from the priest. And she felt inexplicably comforted.

The reason for her distress was not hard to find. She had discovered her husband's involvement with Jackie. The night before, he had left some music behind at home, which she knew he wanted to practise in readiness for a radio recital he was to give the following week. Dutifully she had settled the children down to tea and had then picked it up and scuttled after him over to the church. But even as her footsteps drew near she had sensed something wrong. She had no idea what it was, but as she drew near to the door, it was as if something dark and cold fell upon her, filling her with dread. Hardly knowing what to do, she pushed open the door and crept in. Through the gloom the single light over the organ console made the figures there stand out in relief. Gudrun recognised Jackie with her husband instantly. In a paroxysm of preternatural, frozen dread, she saw the other woman laugh, and then stoop down and fleetingly kiss Norman on the cheek. For one petrified second Gudrun stared at them both in horror and then, as silently as she had come in, she spun on her heel and fled.

The two children were surprised when she came back so soon, and their curiosity was aroused by the fact she was still clutching the music in her hand. 'Where's Daddy?' they wanted to know. 'Couldn't you find him?'

Gudrun found she was shaking convulsively and in an effort to calm herself she wiped a hand across her eyes. 'Yes . . . no . . . I felt unwell. I came home.'

They were immediately frightened. Their mother, they knew, was not physically strong, and she had been finding the weight of the baby hard. 'Shall I go and get Daddy?' the eldest asked.

Gudrun shook her head. 'No, it's nothing . . . I'm all right. I'm quite well. Just let me sit down.' And with that she collapsed at the kitchen table and began to sob, her head sunk upon her hands, while the terrified children either side of her exchanged bewildered glances and clung dumbly to her skirts. But after five minutes of that she began to get a grip on herself. There was the baby to think about, she chided herself. She had faced this problem before. She knew exactly what to do. And at all costs some outward trace of normality had to be preserved – for the children's sake.

She looked then at their tiny, ashen faces turned up to her with dread, and she clutched them to her, her mind reeling. But a plan was already forming. She would let Norman know that she knew, she decided, but at the same time she would allow him to carry on for a while; he would soon become bored. Jackie could not pose a serious threat. This was just a minor dalliance, indulged in while she herself was of necessity less available. Unlike her husband, Gudrun had long since guessed Jackie's age. He could not long stay besotted, she reasoned cruelly, not with someone old enough to be his mother. Let him have his head; he would come back, she knew it. But still it caused her pain, a physical pain down her right side, and she forced herself to take long deep breaths, willing peace into the disturbed and kicking child.

When Norman returned later, the children were in bed. Wooden-faced, Gudrun had given them supper, bathed them and even read to them the story of *Peter and the Wolf.* Then she had settled down to wait. When he came in he had been entirely oblivious to anything untoward and gave her a quick kiss on the head, at the same time humming softly. Gudrun looked at him angrily. 'So. You have someone to help you now?'

Norman froze, in the act of buttering himself a piece of bread. 'What do you mean?' he asked guiltily.

Gudrun was quietly and rationally relentless. 'It's no good,' she said, 'I saw you with her. I came over to the church.'

He turned to look at her, stricken, the colour draining from his face. 'When?'

'Just now. You left your music behind. I thought I would be kind. I took it over for you.'

'What did you see?'

'I saw her kiss you.'

They stared at each other in silence. It was as if a graveyard had opened up between them. Norman swallowed – afterwards she remembered it distinctly – and after a second she said, 'You promised it wouldn't happen again.'

He shut his eyes in a spasm of pain. 'It's nothing,' he said. 'She was just there. It's all right.'

Gudrun sighed. 'Do you love me?' she asked heavily.

But this kind of questioning always embarrassed him, and he

wriggled uncomfortably. 'Of course I do,' he mumbled, turning away, 'but you know how it is. It's nothing.'

From that moment a bitter and potentially explosive calm had descended on the house. When she spoke to him, Gudrun was icily polite and he, feeling guilty, was irritable in return. When the children got up the next morning, they did not understand it at all. Later, when they had all left the house, Gudrun finally broke down, as she had been aching to do, and howled into the unyielding sofa. It was after this that she saw Antonia and Father Trumpington and, feeling drained of all life, she stood to watch.

When Henry heard what had taken place, he was enraged. 'He's got no right to treat you like that!' he exploded. 'Ever since you've got here he's been down on you. It's ridiculous. What difference can a few thous and thees make? Stupid, vicious old fossil! I've got a good mind to go round and tell him what I think of him!'

But this frightened Antonia. 'No, you can't,' she said. 'It hasn't really got anything to do with you. You'll just make matters worse.'

Henry eyed her truculently. 'Of course it's got something to do with me,' he said. 'It's got everything to do with me. We're engaged. We're going to be married soon. I'm supposed to take care of you.'

'Oh, don't be so prehistoric!' snapped back Antonia, her patience breaking. 'Husbands don't look after wives these days. It's supposed to be a partnership. I can't come crying to you every time I've got a battle to fight. And it's *my* battle, not yours!'

Henry glowered. 'What affects you, affects me,' he stated, 'and I have not only a right, but the duty to defend you. And I'm not just going to stand by while that *bastard* treats you like this!'

'But you'll make matters worse,' screeched Antonia. 'How do you think it will look if it's known you went and had a row with him? What effect do you think it's going to have on me? The Bishop will imagine I'm a complete wimp! I'm sorry I told you!'

They were arguing in Kathleen's front room, and at this point she came in bearing a tray, a worried expression on her face. She knew what had taken place with Father Trumpington, because Antonia had been upset and had told her. And, indeed, it had been she who had advised Antonia to tell Henry, but she had not been at all prepared for the row that had erupted between them. Now she could think of nothing to do that might help; except, that is, bring them a cup of tea.

Coming through the door, it caused her real pain to see their angry faces, and yet she could understand how both of them were feeling. Antonia, she knew, felt she had to prove herself, and so it was vital for her that Henry should not interfere. Kathleen could well see the common sense of this position, because in the few short weeks that she had really come to know the girl, she had witnessed time and again the strength of feeling that there was against women in the church. Hardly a day passed without her being aware of some subtle put-down that Antonia had to bear. She had seen, too, the outright hostility and the rudeness with which some people treated her, as if it was their right. And on top of all that, she had seen the attempts constantly made by some to undermine whatever slender authority Antonia might have – and all, it appeared to her, because Antonia was not a man. Now she herself felt angry. Of course the girl was sensitive, she thought. Who would not be if they had to contend with all of that?

Yet Kathleen could understand Henry's position too because, whatever she had seen, he had witnessed far more, and she understood the pain it could produce to see someone you loved treated in that way. She could understand how he raged internally and longed to leap to her defence. And yet here they were, rowing with each other!

'Sit down,' Kathleen commanded gently. 'This won't do. You musn't fight each other. He's won if you do that.'

They both looked at her, anger still flaring in Antonia's eyes, abject misery shining from Henry's. Then they both sat down meekly, like two naughty children who were unsure how to make amends. Kathleen eyed them measuringly. 'I remember Jesus had a little bit of opposition to contend with,' she said firmly, 'but he certainly didn't act like this. Come along, both of you, and let's be sensible. Apologise to each other and make up.' She poured out the tea, and when she looked round again she was relieved to see them smile at each other.

'Sorry,' said Antonia awkwardly to Henry. 'I know you're trying to help. I'm just really worried that, if you do that, it won't.'

Henry looked rueful. 'I don't want to hurt you,' he said. 'I just don't know what to do. And the thought of him and what he keeps saying to you, and the things he insists you do, it makes me so angry. I feel like hitting him.'

'That's better,' said Kathleen approvingly. Antonia and Henry looked at each other and then burst out laughing. 'Oh no, I don't mean you should hit him,' said Kathleen, turning pink, 'I simply meant . . .'

'We know exactly what you meant,' said Henry. 'Thank you.'

But though good relations were restored and Kathleen could look at them both with some measure of reassurance, it did not solve the problem, because Henry still remained filled with rage. Though he said nothing, he began earnestly to wish that Antonia had some other sort of job. He was beginning to feel that he could no longer continue to stand dumbly by while people who should have known a lot better mistreated and abused her.

By the evening, however, a measure of calm seemed to have returned to them both, so much so that Antonia felt she could face the prospect of Phoebe's prayer group, if not with enthusiasm, at least with equanimity, and Henry felt that he could bear to let her go. This last had almost precipitated another row, because Henry had been summoned by his senior partner to dinner with a client that evening, and he had at first tried to persuade Antonia not to go along to her own meeting until he could be there to accompany her. This had provoked from Antonia the response that he was not her minder, and that she did not need someone to hold her hand. But Henry had been worried. He did not want her to suffer any more verbal assaults, and it was only when he had been reassured that everyone who was going to be there that night was friendly that he had finally and grudgingly agreed. Accordingly, they had parted from each other at seven thirty, and Antonia set off.

Phoebe lived in a small inter-war semi, down a little cul-de-sac that faced St Thomas's hospital. As if a living embodiment of the maxim that opposites attract, the little woman was married to an extremely large and brawny mechanic named Don, who had had to take early retirement because of an injury to his knee, and who now spent most of his time either in the garden or taking to bits cars that somehow never seemed to get re-assembled. In this latter occupation he was enthusiastically helped by his two sons, both of whom still lived at home, and both of whom had inherited his passion for things mechanical. It was an untidy kind of a house, with the air of having been much and none too gently lived in.

'Come in, luv,' said Don answering the door in response to Antonia's ring, some unidentifiable piece of car machinery in his hand.

Behind him there was a screech from his wife. 'Donald Protheroe, get that oily thing out of my house at once!'

He gave Antonia a conspiratorial wink. 'Phoebe!' he said, as if this explained everything. 'Gets a bit upset sometimes. Take no notice, I don't.'

All this was delivered with the greatest good humour and Antonia found herself ushered into a small and overcrowded front room – overcrowded not because all the others were there yet but because Phoebe seemed to have crammed small and highly coloured ornaments on to every available surface. There were donkeys from Spain, pixies from Cornwall, gaudy little figures in different kinds of national dress, and hundreds of little Toby jugs and ornamental jars, all with names of various places stamped upon their sides. They were a riot of gaudy colour and, set against a background of patterned wallpaper, they made Antonia's head swim. Any space that was left seemed to have been stuffed untidily with car magazines and greasy books. They were piled on the small table, stuffed under the chairs, and there were even some scattered over the floor. The effect was like a declaration of war, as if the feminine strivings after fussy prettiness on the one hand had been overwhelmingly met by masculine no-nonsense untidiness on the other. On balance, Antonia rather thought that, surrounded by men as she was, Phoebe appeared to have lost, but it felt a happy house for all that.

Carefully negotiating her way round a pile of *Exchange and Marts* that looked as if they had been flung in defiance into the centre of the floor, she settled herself into an easy chair and prepared to wait. Phoebe, meanwhile, was bustling around like a mad thing. She swept into the room, gathered up papers and tipped them wholesale into a cupboard at the side of the fire. Then she bustled out as if her life depended on it – to put on the kettle, she explained – and returned a moment later, bearing two plates piled high with freshly baked biscuits that gave off the most wonderful smell. Antonia, who had been unable to eat much dinner, felt her mouth begin to water and realised suddenly that she was really very hungry. She offered to help, but Phoebe shooed her down, clucking like a benign mother hen. 'No, no, dear,' she said, 'you just stay where you are. We'll be straight in a jiffy now.' She disappeared again, only to trot back a second later with teaspoons and a sugar bowl. There were several of these scuttling little trips, papers out, civilisation in, and gradually the room re-emerged from its masculine chaos into what evidently approximated for Phoebe to feminine calm.

'You've met Don then,' Phoebe said, on one of these forays. 'He won't come along to St Godric's. Says he can't stand Father Trumpington. Not that I blame him, I suppose. It was the organ that did for him, and all that fuss about money.' Bang went a milk jug down on to the table. 'But I suppose if the truth be told, he prefers his cars anyway. He's not much of a one for any kind of show.'

By the time the others had arrived, there was no trace left of the chaos and Phoebe at last sat down herself, looking triumphant and pleased. She oozed kindliness and it seemed to infect everyone else. Antonia discovered it was a larger group than she had anticipated. There were fifteen of them in all, though as they were at pains to point out, their numbers had been swelled that night by the addition of herself, Dave and Jude, and Gudrun who arrived pale and panting, five minutes late.

Ken led the meeting, and they quickly settled down to pray. They prayed for the state of the world, and especially their own little corner of it at St Godric's, and they prayed for God's grace to Father Trumpington and Antonia that they might be enabled to work together – at which point Antonia almost choked – and they prayed for the coming of God's spirt in power. After that they moved to more specific concerns, and thanks were given in particular for Donald's knees, and Mrs Eldridge's cat which had mysteriously gone missing the previous week but which had now miraculously returned, to her evident joy. This last was obviously news to some in the group and there were 'Aahs' of satisfaction and a chorus of 'Thank you, Lord'. And then Ken looked up and asked, 'Anyone got anything specific they'd like us to pray for?'

Silence fell on the group. Gudrun looked down at her hands tightly clenched in her lap and, unnoticed by everyone, silently began to cry. Antonia pulled a face but knew she could say nothing about Father Trumpington's criticisms, and then Dave suddenly said, 'I've got something!'

They all turned and looked at him expectantly and he went on, 'It's two things actually. I'm not sure the Lord wants me tae be a bouncer. It's violent, I hurt people, I know, but I dunna know what else tae do, and t'other things is, I'd like a prayer for that wee jetty down by the river. It's pretty rotten at the moment and Edgar Slynne and I are goin' to try and fix it, but we're not sure if Father Trumpington'll approve.'

They digested this and then Ken said, 'Yes, I can see both those things need prayer, especially the question of what you're going to do.' He looked round at them all seriously, and Gudrun surreptitiously wiped her eyes on the back of her hand, but no one noticed – they were all still staring as if hypnotised at Dave. 'That's a big one, folks,' Ken went on after a second. 'Let's ask the Lord.'

Protected by their closed eyes, Gudrun now began openly to cry. Halfway through a long and very earnest prayer by a spotty young man with glasses, they were interrupted by a loud sob. Everyone's eyes flew open and became riveted by the spectacle of Gudrun sliding gently to the floor, heaving sobs now racking her shaking frame. 'Oh,' said Ken. They all stared at her transfixed, momentarily at a total loss what to do, and then Gudrun, discovering she had gone this far, seemed to come to a sudden decision to abandon every last remnant of control. She began to drum her heels angrily on the floor, at the same time clasping her hands either side of her head and beginning to rock agitatedly back and forth. Painful sobs continued to tear at her.

'It's not fair,' she hiccupped. 'It's not fair. Nobody knows! Nobody knows the pain I have to bear!'

At this point Antonia suddenly came to her senses and,

struggling to her feet, swiftly crossed to Gudrun. She stooped down and cradled her tightly in her arms, clasping her fiercely to her as she would have a distressed child. For a second Gudrun fought her, straining away, and then, just as suddenly, she collapsed listlessly, all the fight seeming to go out of her. Instead she wriggled slightly and then buried her face against Antonia's shoulder, her body sprawled crookedly like that of a broken doll. In the abrupt silence that now fell, she seemed suddenly almost unnaturally still.

'It's all right,' Antonia began to croon softly. 'It's OK.' She continued to hold her tight and, after a moment, was rewarded by feeling the other woman's body relax. Then, just as suddenly, Gudrun twitched with a violent spasm and clutched at her stomach. A look of intense surprise settled on her face she now turned up to Antonia. 'Oh my God,' she whispered, 'the baby!'

Gudrun's baby was born, seven weeks premature, in the early hours of the next day. It was a little boy, Otto, and he weighed 7lbs 2ozs; a good size, the nurses said, for a child born so soon. But they said it with a kind of forlorn hopelessness. Gudrun had had a terrible time. She had torn herself internally, and the cord had become twisted round the baby's neck. When the medical staff had finally delivered him, by Caesarean section, it was clear that all was not well, with either mother or child.

Norman, the previous night, had been nowhere to be found and so, by nine the next day, he still did not know. The children were safe with Phoebe. She had volunteered to have them the previous night after it became clear what was happening and once the babysitter had been sent home. But still no one knew where Norman was.

Antonia left him a note. Then she went with Gudrun to the hospital and stayed with her during the labour – until, that is, she was bundled unceremoniously out of the room. After that she had waited in the hospital corridor, sick with dread and desperately wishing that Norman could be found, so that her vigil might be relieved. He ought to be here, she told herself, it was his right. More than that, it was his duty. She wondered if he was away but, whenever she had asked, Gudrun had seemed in no fit state to say. In fact, whenever Antonia had mentioned his name Gudrun had turned away with a groan. Antonia could only suppose it was because she so desperately wanted him to be there. For herself, the sight of so much suffering and pain was a shock. She had never before seen so much agony and it frightened her because there seemed to be nothing she could do.

When she finally saw the baby – being trundled past her in an incubator, what seemed to be hours later – her heart twisted with grief. He seemed so small and so vulnerable lying there and already, with the wires taped to his tiny and perfect limbs, it felt as if his body had been desecrated. But what really upset her was the fear she saw on one of the nurses' faces. Up until then she had somehow imagined that nurses and doctors did not actually feel any kind of immediate involvement with their patients; it was, after all, their job. But she saw such distress on the young student nurse's face that it filled her with dread – which deepened when the girl, seeing her collar, asked if she could have a word. It transpired that this was the first such case she had ever seen, and she was frightened too. Gudrun was so badly ripped, she confided to Antonia. It was so different from the textbooks. And the baby . . . It was then that Antonia first heard voiced the doctors' fears for his survival. Somehow, up until that point, it had not seemed so bad. She had told herself that this kind of thing happened all the time. Now she knew it didn't.

Still Norman did not come. She tried phoning the house, but there was no reply. And then, at ten past ten, he finally arrived. He had got back to the house, he said, and found her note. He seemed so calm when she poured out all that had taken place. Antonia bristled; it was as if he did not care. Up till that point she had been trying to shield him from the full horror of all that had happened, but she felt so angry by his casual acceptance that she was stung into saying, 'She might have died! She still might! And . . .' She had been on the point of saying that it did not look too good for the baby either, but she found she could not, tears welling up in her eyes. Instead she said, 'Where were you? Gudrun really wanted you, you know!'

He flushed and then stammered defensively, 'I got caught up, I couldn't help it. I came as soon as I knew.'

And with that she had to be satisfied, because he turned abruptly away and marched off in the direction of the ward. Antonia went home.

Chapter Ten

Christmas was drawing on apace and the church was now a hive of activity. The Christmas bazaar was only ten days away, and after that loomed the party. Antonia discovered she was expected to organise not just games and music but also a little show drawing on the talents of the parish. 'Phoebe recites,' Slynne informed her, 'Gloria sings. An' I expect the new organist moight play somethin'. An' the young people loike t' put on a bit of a review. An' there's the Barber's Shop group. Ooh, there's lots a things. Great fun, it is!'

Antonia felt herself grow pale. A lot of descriptions were passing through her mind, but at that precise moment 'fun' was not one of them. Nevertheless, she buckled to, and with Slynne's help began valiantly to draw together her cast. A notice given out in church on Sunday morning brought forth further offers of help, and gradually the evening began to take shape. Food was arranged, decorations organised, an 'entertainments manager' appointed to supervise the games, and the cast list for the show grew... and grew, and grew.

Throughout all of this Gudrun had to stay in hospital. Her body was proving slow to heal, but also she could not bear to leave Otto who, against all the odds, was still tenaciously clinging to life, locked inside his incubator.

Phoebe offered to keep the children until Gudrun could go home. She said that this would lighten the load for poor Norman and make it easier for him to visit. Jackie rallied to help too. She offered to have Norman round, with her and Elspeth, for all his meals. The little girl had a tantrum the fifth day he arrived and said she didn't want him there any more, and where was Daddy? Why didn't *he* come and eat with them any more? Jackie told her to be quiet and then, when that did not work, sent her to her room. 'You mustn't be so selfish, Elspeth,' she admonished. 'We must share what we have with others. Poor Norman's going through a very difficult time.' The little girl promptly burst into tears. She was tired of being shunted around the way she seemed to be these days, and she could not understand where her daddy had gone, and why he never got in touch with them any more. She thought perhaps he did not love her.

Father Trumpington thought Jackie's offer very generous, and he spoke warmly of her caring concern to Dorothy, who felt she could have hit him. He paid one visit to the hospital and aroused the ire of the nurses when he rather callously remarked that it might be better for little Otto to die. He was actually expressing an honestly held view; he could see no point at all in striving to keep alive children – or adults for that matter – who might be permanently impaired. But the nurses, who all made a tremendous fuss of the tiny little scrap, looked at him from then on with loathing.

Antonia, busy though she was, went up often, and a friendship began to develop between the two women, so much so that, very cautiously, Gudrun began to entrust to her little scraps and details about her rather forlorn life. Finally, one bleak night in early December, having sworn her to the utmost secrecy, Gudrun told her all about Norman and Jackie.

The trauma of little Otto's birth had done nothing to heal Gudrun's relationship with her husband. In fact, if anything it seemed almost to have made matters worse, because in some obscure way Norman made it clear that he thought the whole sorry affair was entirely her own fault, as if she had somehow engineered Otto's premature and traumatic birth out of revenge. Of the child himself, Norman took hardly any notice. He appeared to be indifferent to this latest addition to his family and made every excuse he could to avoid having to go and see him. If he knew he was behaving badly, he gave no sign. When he visited Gudrun, which he did each evening for appearance's sake, he sat beside her bed in silence, sulkily refusing to talk to her and making it clear he would far rather be somewhere else. Chilled by his presence, Gudrun seemed to be increasingly and relentlessly swallowed up by the shadows that had first stretched out their icy hands over her that night when she had seen her husband and Jackie together in the church.

She cried a lot those first days and the medical staff, who were beginning to get worried, moved her into a side ward on her own so that she would not upset the other mothers. Depression was settling in, they whispered. They said as much to Norman, but he only shrugged. 'She'll be all right,' he said indifferently. 'No she won't,' they responded acidly. A psychiatrist was sent for to prescribe some short-term medication and see what he could do to help her get over the problem. He was met by a blank wall of tearful misery. Gudrun refused both to talk to him and to take the pills he prescribed. 'No,' she said stoically, when the nurses chided her at night. 'I do not need them. I am not ill, only unhappy. I do not need pills. I will put the situation right.'

'You can't,' said the nurses sadly, misunderstanding her and thinking she was referring to baby Otto. 'That's in the hands of God.'

'In my hands too,' said Gudrun flatly. And from that position she would not be moved, so that the doctors and nurses began to talk admiringly of her courage, and to mutter sadly to each other that not even her will could keep poor baby Otto alive, no matter what she believed. Gudrun, however, was not talking about Otto, although she did believe that if she could snatch back Norman from the stupidity upon which he had embarked, the baby would live too. For Gudrun truly believed that she was in a battle now for the life of everything she held dear. Hers was the fight – she knew – and her foes were the powers of darkness, all concentrated as she now believed in the person of Jackie. Defeat the dragon lady (as she mentally named her) and her family would survive.

As she reasoned it, Norman had fallen prey, but he was a man and therefore weak. He had not betrayed her – only an equal could betray – he was merely a casualty. Her task now was to rescue him, in combat if need be, and set him free. Once her foe was vanquished, he would soon come back to heel. But could she defeat her enemy? Was she strong enough? This was the question that preyed upon her mind and haunted her days and nights. Before, when this had happened, she had always known the power of her hold over her husband, but something about Jackie and this new situation frightened her. She had never known

Norman like this before. And an icy presentiment of dread that nothing could break through seemed to wrap itself round her as she lay in her hospital bed.

It was into these frozen wastes of loneliness that Antonia came. Each day, while Gudrun was in hospital, Antonia ploughed her way into the ward like some sturdy and relentless little pilot's tug, stolidly picking its way through the ice floes of Gudrun's Antarctica, as if intent on working her ice-bound ship free and guiding it back to the clear waters of the sea. Gudrun could never understand it but somehow, throughout that terrible time, Antonia was the only person who was real to her. She seemed to be the only person whose voice Gudrun could hear. Somehow, when Antonia came, Gudrun knew she was no longer alone, and a glimmer of hope began to dawn in her that there was still a chance; she could still break free.

One day Antonia suggested to her that they anoint baby Otto, and the next day she arrived bearing a tiny phial of oil. Together they went to the incubator where the baby lay, so still he looked as if he was no longer breathing, and then Antonia prayed over him, and very gently made the sign of the cross on his forehead with the oil. 'In the name of Jesus Christ,' she said softly, 'son of the Sovereign Lord God, we claim for this child the life and wholeness of the Spirit. As Christ on the cross became a curse for our sakes, so now in his name we break the curse of death over this baby and his family, and claim for them all the freedom of the Kingdom of God.' Under her touch the baby stirred slightly and puckered its lips, and then Antonia stood back.

'Is he going to be all right?' Gudrun asked plaintively, and a tear slid down her face, followed by another and then another.

'I don't know,' said Antonia.

The oil glistened slightly in the light and suddenly, unexpectedly, the baby whimpered. 'Ooh!' said a nurse standing there at their side – she was a Christian and had asked if she might join them – 'Ooh, did you feel that? I felt something brush past me! It felt all warm and light. Look! Otto's smiling!'

'Newborn babies can't smile,' sniffled Gudrun.

'But he is,' insisted the nurse. And it was true, over the baby's tiny little bruised face had come a strange expression that looked peculiarly like joy. 'Gosh,' said the nurse, awed, 'can you see that too?'

'Yes,' said Antonia softly.

'It's wind,' hiccupped Gudrun through her tears, but nevertheless she looked.

The expression on Otto's face stayed for perhaps thirty seconds, and then he seemed gradually to relax. Outwardly he looked just as he had before, but all three of them felt that something inexplicable had taken place. 'Did we really see that?' asked the nurse at last.

'I don't know,' said Antonia hesitantly. She felt terrified of raising Gudrun's hopes too far. 'Maybe it was just one of those things,' she said at last. 'A coincidence.'

The nurse gave her a pitying look. 'Do you really believe that?' she asked. 'I've been nursing him since he came in here. He's never done that before.'

They both looked at Gudrun, but she was still staring at the child, her hands clasped in front of her until the knuckles shone white, an expression of such intensity on her face that it was akin to pain. She seemed totally oblivious of them. 'Oh God,' she whispered, 'please, please, please . . . Please help my child. Please give him back life. Please smash the hold of the dragon lady. Please free my family . . .' And then without a word she turned and walked stiffly back to the ward.

Antonia and the nurse stared at each other. 'Oh God, I hope it is a miracle,' said the nurse. 'I don't think she's going to survive if it's not.'

Three days later they removed the tubes, and Gudrun was allowed for a short while to have Otto beside her bed, but the doctors were still not optimistic. 'We're very sorry,' they told her and Norman when he came in that night for his daily visit, ' but we've discovered a heart defect. It's miraculous the way he seems to be holding his own, but if he does get through this, he's going to need surgery.'

Gudrun nodded dumbly, the expression on her face inscrutable, and the doctor looked at her with concern. He looked at Norman, but Norman seemed bored. 'Oh, I expect he'll pull through,' he said bitterly. 'This is the way we seem to live. Perpetual crisis!'

He seemed on the point of adding something but then changed his mind, and an uneasy silence fell.

'I'm very sorry,' repeated the doctor lamely. 'We'll do our best.'

After he had gone, Gudrun sat wrapped in silence, refusing to speak. She seemed to be hardly aware that Norman was even there any more, and after a couple of desultory comments, peeved, he got up to go. 'Well, it's not my fault,' he said bitterly, pausing at the foot of the bed. 'This would probably have happened anyway.' Still she said nothing and, enraged, he exploded, 'It's about bloody time you pulled yourself together! You've got two other children, you know! When are you going to come home and start looking after them? This is difficult for me too, you know!'

That caught her attention. 'Oh, I'm sorry,' she said sarcastically, her eyes flashing as she looked up. 'Having to do something for a change is getting in the way of your little dalliance, is it?'

'No!' snapped Norman. 'Yes . . . my work . . . It's your job!' He stormed out and Gudrun watched him go. The ice floes had receded a little, she discovered, but they were still there. Nevertheless, she felt she had been granted a reprieve. Against all the odds, she could feel traces of warmth. There was, she decided, hope.

Norman felt there was hope too, but at that moment he was locating it a long way from his wife.

'Hi,' Jackie called cheerily as he let himself in through her front door, using the key she had given him only a couple of nights before. 'Elspeth is round at Caroline's tonight.' She appeared momentarily in the doorway of the kitchen, her body silhouetted darkly against the light. For a second she looked wreathed in inky black, terrible with a kind of dark beauty and, in spite of himself, Norman shuddered. But the effect lasted only a second, and the next moment Jackie glided out into the hall, her face upturned for a kiss as she came forward to greet him, a food-splattered spatula still clutched in her hand. Behind her, wonderful smells emanated out into the rest of the house. Norman identified garlic and tomato, and a delicious aroma of wine. 'That smells good,' he said appreciatively, obediently bending and kissing her full on the mouth.

She returned his kiss with ardour and then stood back to peer intently up into his face, her expression inscrutable. 'I've done something special,' she announced.

'You always do something special,' he teased, and it was true. Jackie's cooking, like herself, was exotic and slightly frivolous, as far removed from Gudrun's no-nonsense country fare as chalk from cheese. Norman revelled in it.

'No, really special,' she chided him. 'Elspeth's away all night . . .' She paused. 'You can stay, if you like.'

He let her draw him behind her into the kitchen, pulling him by the tie. Beyond her he saw the dining room, the table already laid, flowers spilling out across the centre in the gently flickering glow of two enormous candles. He thought of the family table at home, littered as it always seemed to be with bits of paper, crayons, glue pots, half-finished models made by the children – all hastily pushed aside when it came time to eat. He thought of the children whining and arguing, eternally arguing. He thought of Gudrun shouting. Right now he could think of nowhere he would rather be than here with Jackie.

Afterwards, much later as they lay in bed, their passion spent, he told her about Gudrun. 'I don't know what's wrong with her,' he complained. 'The doctors say she's depressed, but she keeps looking at me as if it's all my fault.' His hand felt between Jackie's legs, gently rubbing. 'She's just totally neurotic,' he said bitterly. 'I don't think I can stand it any more.'

Jackie was not really listening. 'Mm, that feels good,' she breathed. She stretched luxuriously, like a cat. His hand made her feel all prickly. 'Don't think about her,' she murmured absently.

But Norman, having begun to speak about Gudrun, found he was unable to stop. It was as if something was goading him. 'She accused me of not pulling my weight,' he said petulantly. 'There she is, lying in bed all day like a bloody prima donna, and she accuses me of doing nothing. And she acts like the baby's hers! Like she's the only one that cares! The only one who's allowed to care.' Jackie nuzzled his neck, but he ignored her. 'She never thinks about the strain I'm under. That's irrelevant. She never thinks that I've got to look after the kids while she's in there *and* hold down a job!'

Jackie forbore to point out that Norman had not actually had to do very much in the way of looking after the kids, but she stirred uneasily. Dimly she realised that he had forgotten her. Jackie was not used to being ignored, and she was certainly not prepared to play second fiddle to Gudrun. She frowned into the dark and then rolled closer, again nuzzling Norman's neck and biting him playfully. But it was no good. She could feel in his total lack of response that he was slipping even further away. 'Forget about her,' she urged, fighting desperately to regain control. 'Leave it all behind.'

It was too late. 'I can't forget about her,' said Norman savagely. 'She makes me feel so bloody guilty, as if I've done wrong.' He sat up abruptly, all thoughts of Jackie suddenly exploded from his mind as, for the first time in days, he allowed Gudrun full entry into his thoughts. Up until then he had been rigorously excluding her, along with all thoughts of the new child, but Jackie's urging to forget her had, paradoxically, opened the floodgates against a swelling tide of inarticulate grief. Without understanding, he suddenly felt that something indescribably precious was passing beyond his reach, and the feeling made him blind with rage. 'It's not fair!' he raged.

Jackie jumped, gazing at his unyielding back in surprised dismay.

'I'm going home!' said Norman. And the next moment he had stumbled out of bed and was groping blindly for his clothes.

'But you're staying the night,' Jackie wailed.

Norman shook his head. He felt suffocated, choking. He struggled to put on a sock that, against all reason, seemed to have taken on a life of its own, in the dark knotting itself round his toes so that he was unable to pull it up. 'Oh shit!' he said. In desperation he wrenched it off and flung it against the wall, pulling on his pants instead, and then his shirt and jeans.

Jackie had had enough. Angrily she sat up and flicked on the bedside light. 'What on earth are you doing?' she demanded.

'I've got to go,' said Norman. 'I've got to see Gudrun.'

In the dim light he looked ridiculous, standing with one leg in and one leg out of his trousers, hair tousled, his shirt hanging undone. At mention of her rival's name, Jackie felt even more enraged but, far worse even than that, she had a terrible suspicion from the expression on Norman's face that he was about to cry. She looked beyond him to the clock. 'It's two o'clock in the morning,' she said, striving to keep her voice reasonable. 'You can't go to the hospital now. It'll be all locked up.'

'I've got to see Gudrun,' Norman said again. 'Oh God, what have I done?'

He sounded like a child, and in a trice Jackie was out of bed and at his side. This was a challenge she was going to meet head on. 'Nothing. Nothing,' she soothed, wrapping her arms round his neck and pulling his face down on to her chest. 'It's not your fault.'

'But what have I done?' said Norman. 'She'll never forgive me.'

A steely glint came into Jackie's eye. 'Don't be silly,' she said robustly, 'you've got me now. Don't let what's happened get in the way of our love.'

'But I've hurt her,' said Norman hoarsely. 'I've hurt Otto.'

'No, no,' chided Jackie, 'this would have happened anyway. You said so yourself. Gudrun's not strong. She hasn't been well. You can't feel guilty about this.'

'But I do,' moaned Norman.

'You mustn't,' said Jackie. Firmly she drew him back towards the bed. 'It's perfectly natural for you to feel like this, and a real tribute to how sweet you are.' She slid the shirt off his shoulders. 'Gudrun's not right for you. You know that. You married too young. She stifles you.' She pulled him back down so that his head rested on the pillow, and then expertly slid herself down on top of him. He made a half move of protest, attempting to rise, but quickly she lunged forward and pressed her body on to his, pinning him to the bed. 'Stay,' she whispered firmly, putting the whole force of her personality behind the words. 'You'll feel better in the morning.' In that moment she made up her mind. No matter what it cost, she was going to get Norman for her own, completely. She would marry him, and both Gudrun and Father Trumpington could go hang!

* * *

135

Antonia was beginning to feel that, although the Christmas party might not be quite the disaster she had feared, the spirit of the approaching season was markedly absent. She did not know what to do with Gudrun's revelation of the relationship between her husband and Jackie. It had been given in confidence and Gudrun had sworn her to secrecy, but if the affair really was going on, Antonia knew full well that Father Trumpington ought to be informed. He had a right to know. Such things could not be condoned in a church, and equally neither party ought to be taking Communion until matters had been put right. Yet she could not betray the confidence because, if she did, Gudrun would rightly never trust her again. So Antonia found herself in a dilemma that she was unable to share even with Henry, which in turn put a strain on her own relationship, because Henry could see that something was wrong and felt that she was just refusing to say. Henry, indeed, seemed unable to comprehend that confidentiality meant there were certain things she could never share with him. 'We're going to be married,' he protested in one of the endless discussions they seemed to have on the topic. 'That means we simply shouldn't have secrets from one another.'

'But they're not secrets,' retorted Antonia. 'At least, not mine. I don't have the right to share them. People have got to know that whatever they tell me won't go any further.'

'But it wouldn't be going any further,' objected Henry.

'Of course it would,' said Antonia.

'In the Bible,' said Henry obstinately, 'it says that a man shall cleave to his wife and that they shall become one flesh.'

Antonia breathed heavily. 'It doesn't mean that,' she said.

But for all her arguments Henry remained unconvinced, and the fact that she would not tell him became a bone of contention between them.

Between Antonia and Father Trumpington, however, an uneasy truce seemed to have been called. The good Father was actually too busy preparing for his initiation into the Royal Arch to be too much bothered by Antonia and, when not thinking about that, his thoughts were increasingly taken up with Jackie, whom he now haunted almost daily, dropping round at odd times for, as he said, tea and a chat. His overriding wish now was to put their relationship on a more permanent footing.

Some years previously he had bought two small but rather pretty cottages, one in Devon, the other on the Sussex coast, and it had occurred to him that retirement to one with Jackie and banishment to the other for Dorothy presented a rather satisfactory prospect for his twilight years. Not that he had as yet shared these plans with anyone else, but in leisure moments his mind now tended to be occupied with the knotty problem of how best to bring them into being with the least disruption to himself. Dorothy, he knew, might justifiably raise some objections when she learnt what he had in mind and, while in terms of sentiment this did not bother him unduly, there was a more practical problem, in that the titles to both houses were in their joint names. If Dorothy proved difficult, all could be lost; matters therefore had to be handled with tremendous care.

Accordingly, Father Trumpington had not had much time to spare to worry about what Antonia was or was not doing, and to every one of her requests he had tended to say testily, 'Yes, yes! Just do it.' So she had, but the opportunity of even alluding, albeit ever so obliquely, to what was going on between Jackie and Norman had never arisen. She arranged one last meeting with Slynne to go over final arrangements for the party, and then decided that she would try and do something about the problem presented by Norman and 'the seductress' (as she mentally called Jackie) herself.

She arranged to meet Slynne the Tuesday before the party at five o'clock at his house. 'We can 'ave a cup of tea,' he said when she spoke to him on the phone the day before. 'Oi'll 'ave finished moi bit o' gardenin' by then.' He had sounded cheerful, but when she got there, she found him morose. 'Oi'm fed up,' he complained when she asked him what was wrong.

'Why?' she asked apprehensively, wondering if he was about to tell her that the entire parish was boycotting the party. But it was nothing like that.

Slynne stared glumly into his tea and then, after what felt like an age, he muttered gruffly, 'Oi'm in love, see!'

Antonia felt her jaw drop. At a conservative estimate she would have put Slynne in his early seventies, robust, it was true, but far from being in the full bloom of virile manhood. She had rather imagined that sort of thing would not bother people of his age. 'Do I know the lady?' she inquired.

'Ooh arh!' said Slynne. 'You know 'er all roight. It's Jackie.'

A kind of suspended silence seemed to hang around this announcement, as if the whole room was waiting for her reply. Antonia blinked, abashed, and then looked up to find Slynne staring at her shyly, for all the world like a teenager who has just announced his first love.

'I see,' she said carefully, wondering what on earth to say. But she need not have worried, because having dropped his bombshell, Slynne was off.

'Oi've loved 'er this last year,' he said breathlessly, 'ever since the 'arvest last autumn. She cum back for a cup o' tea, see. She told me all about 'er and 'er 'usband. That Malcolm!' He pronounced the name with loathing. 'Ooh, treats 'er somethin' rotten, 'e does! Should be 'anged!' But this Christian sentiment once expressed, Slynne abandoned the topic of Jackie's husband. 'She's wunnerrful,' he breathed, 'an angel! Oi want t' marry 'er, see?' He pronounced this last as if the vision of loveliness herself stood before him in the room, staring at a fixed point some two feet below the light fitting, a look of ineffable tenderness on his face. His gaze was so fixed that Antonia stirred uneasily, momentarily wondering if he was actually staring at something, but the next instant Slynne shook himself, a look of anger flooding his face. 'Trouble is, oi don't seem to be gettin' nowhere!'

Antonia groped for words. The idea seemed so ridiculous that she felt lost. A picture of Jackie, chic and expensive, came unbidden to her mind. Then she looked at Slynne. He had on an old grandad shirt that was frayed at the cuffs, and a grey woolly sweater with holes in it. On his chin was a three-day stubble that made him look, she thought, like an ex-con. Then, almost unconsciously, her gaze slid down to his carpet slippers. They must once, she felt, have been a maroon check, but now they were so dirty and frayed that it was difficult to tell with any certainty what colour they had been, while the big toe of his left foot poked through an untidy, gaping hole. She swallowed. 'Er, are you quite sure about this?' she asked tentatively.

Something in her tone made Slynne's head jerk round, and he glared at her suspiciously. 'What do you mean?' he demanded.

'Nothing,' said Antonia hastily. 'It's just that, well, I mean . . . she's so much younger than you are.'

Slynne grunted. 'It's not so big a difference,' he said defensively. 'She's forty-eight. Oi'm sixty-eight. It's only twenty years. That's nothin' when as you're in love!'

'Ah, I see.'

'An' she's interested. Oi know that. We talked. Got the same interests, see? The church, music, an' oi've got a bit put by.'

'Yes, but . . .'

Slynne ignored her. 'She needs someone to look after 'er,' he insisted. 'Oi could do that. Oi want to tell 'er. But just recently oi don't seem to be able to get near 'er.'

Antonia stared. 'What do you mean?' she asked.

'Eh, what? Well, every time oi go round, she's busy. There's that there organist allays seems to be there, fur a start. Oi know it's very sad an all that, wot's 'appened to 'is woife and the baby, but oi can't see no reason why he allus 'as t' be there. An' when 'e's not there, it's 'Itler! Three times oi've bin round there, and each time 'e's bin there. Mowing 'er lawn, 'e wus, last time. Oi said to 'er, oi can do that fur you. But 'e won't 'ave none of that. My pastoral duty it is, Edgar, he ses. And then Jackie sent me off with a flea in moi ear . . .'

He rambled on, but Antonia was lost in thought. It occurred to her that maybe Father Trumpington knew about the situation between Norman and Jackie after all, and that she had been worrying herself unnecessarily. Maybe this was his way of keeping an eye on the situation, and maybe she would not have to do anything after all. How foolish she had been, she thought, to have imagined the problem was wholly her own. Father Trumpington was an experienced priest, after all. She turned upon Slynne such a look of radiant and relieved sweetness that the latter blinked. 'So you think it is a good idea then?' he said, puzzled.

'I'm sorry,' said Antonia, realising she had not heard a word of what he had just said. 'What did you say?'

Slynne breathed heavily. 'Dang me!' he muttered. 'Oi said, do you think as oi oughta to tell 'er 'ow oi feel at the Christmas party?'

Antonia gaped at him. He had her full attention now and, gratified, he went on, 'Oi could pop the question, couldn't oi? And then, if as she said yes, we could announce it. Oi could get in some champagne!'

This, Antonia knew, was not a good idea. 'But Edgar,' she stammered, 'Jackie's still married.'

This, however, did not seem to cut much ice with Slynne. He knew the *theory* that marriage was for life, but he had worshipped long enough at St Godric's to feel that this was one of the more dispensable Christian truths. 'Oi know that,' he asserted now. 'But not fer long!' He rubbed his hands with glee. 'Oi think as oi need t' get in there quick.'

Antonia could only gaze at him. 'Pop the question,' she repeated vaguely, 'at the party.' She bit her lip, all too clearly envisaging Jackie's likely response. But how could she put this to Slynne without mortally wounding his feelings? The little man seemed so intent. 'Well . . .' she began, looking at him apprehensively. Slynne looked at her eagerly and her nerve failed. She could not do it. She simply could not be responsible for the hurt she felt sure he was going to feel, and he would not believe her anyway, she was sure of that. The only person he would listen to now was Jackie herself. At the same time another thought occurred to her – rather a spiteful, malicious little thought. Jackie had led Slynne on, she had no doubt. She had seen her in operation too often to imagine it was all fantasy on the old man's part. Why, she had even seen Jackie try it on with Henry, and had felt furious with her, mollified only by Henry's complete lack of interest. So why not let her sort this out herself, she thought spitefully. Serve her right! Antonia made up her mind. 'You talk to her, Edgar,' she said decisively. 'I'm sure that's the thing to do.'

A look of pure joy exploded over Slynne's face and Antonia felt a quick stab of guilt. 'Dang me, oi will then!' said Slynne.

Chapter Eleven

The day that was to mark Father Trumpington's initiation into the Royal Arch of Jerusalem dawned fair and clear. Father Trumpington awoke with a sense of excitement. Beside him Dorothy stirred and then rolled over, a faint snore gently issuing from her half-open mouth. She was not a pretty sight in her curlers and pink hairnet and, looking at her, Father Trumpington shuddered. It was a cruel fate, he reflected, that had given him Dorothy for a wife. But not for much longer! He leapt out of bed, humming softly, inadvertently kicking his wife as he heaved his legs over the side. The bed springs groaned protestingly, and so did Dorothy. 'Ow!' she said. 'That hurt!'

Father Trumpington ignored her. He spread his arms wide with the sheer joy of the day and then, feeling even more exhilarated, leant down and touched his toes.

'What on earth are you doing?' demanded Dorothy, sitting up.

'Exercise, my dear,' he boomed. And then he gave a little half skip. 'Today's the day!'

'What day?' demanded Dorothy suspiciously.

'The day I get initiated into the Royal Arch!'

'Oh that,' she said. Her tone expressed complete uninterest and, without more ado, she heaved herself back down on to the pillow and closed her eyes. Father Trumpington regarded her sourly; she had got to go. But not even Dorothy could dent his mood of happy optimism today. He resumed his hum and headed off towards the bathroom.

His mood persisted throughout breakfast and the morning office, and then he returned to his study to begin work on his sermon for Sunday – he rather thought he might say something on Handel this week. However, hardly had he started when the doorbell rang. It was one of Dorothy's mornings at the bank and so, muttering disgruntledly to himself, he got up and went to see who was there. When he opened the door, he rather wished he had left it, because he found himself confronted by Dave.

The big man had made a serious effort over the last few weeks and was at a loss to understand why Father Trumpington seemed to dislike him so much, but that he did was obvious. Whenever the priest saw him his face seemed to cloud over and a glazed expression came into his eyes. Dave was bewildered and tried harder and harder, but whatever he did only seemed to make matters worse. Now he tried to smile with what he hoped was an ingratiating air, but he unaccountably felt so nervous that he ended up with a leer. Father Trumpington glared at him, his suspicions that Dave was trying to irritate him confirmed. 'Yes?' he said ominously.

This was not a good beginning. Even Dave could tell. He swallowed nervously. 'I just wanted tae tell ye,' he blurted, 'me an' Ed, we've fixed the jetty!'

Father Trumpington stared at him blankly. By resolutely refusing to think about Dave, he had managed to erase from his mind the unwelcome and unusual request for baptism that the man had made. With rather misplaced optimism, he had thought that if he himself said nothing, Dave would forget, or lose interest, or even that the jetty might collapse – preferably with Dave on it, and that he would never be heard of again. But now here he was with a great big beam on his face, like some untidy puppy who has just found a bone. Father Trumpington looked at him with distaste, and said nothing. The silence extended.

'Er, could I come in?' said Dave, uncomfortably. 'Antonia said the confirmations were in March. So I wondered if we cud fix a date now?'

It was on the point of Father Trumpington's tongue to say no, and slam the door, but Alan's words floated back into his mind: 'Give them enough rope, Dick . . .' He forced himself to smile. 'Certainly,' he said through clenched teeth. 'I'm in the middle of a sermon, but don't worry . . .'

Dave clumped his way into the study. Father Trumpington, bringing up the rear, could not help but notice that wherever Dave trod he left a spatter of mud on the carpet. He tutted fussily, but Dave seemed oblivious. 'Well,' he said as he sat down, 'I'd like tae be done as soon as possible!'

'Done?' Father Trumpington inquired icily.

'Yeah. Ye know, I want tae be official. An' I wondered if we could maybe have a bonfire at the same time?'

Father Trumpington stared at him uncomprehendingly. Was the man worried about the cold? Or did he perhaps want a barbecue and fireworks as well? 'Baptism is not simply an excuse for a knees-up,' he said frostily. 'And if you're worried about the cold, we should perhaps defer the *ceremony* till the summer, or even,' he added hopefully, 'drop the idea of the river altogether.'

It was Dave's turn to stare at him blankly, and then light dawned. 'Oh no, I dunna mean that,' he said hastily. 'It's not the cold, and I'm not suggesting a rave.' He flushed. 'It's just that Antonia's been teaching mae what it means ta follow Jesus, an' I've a lot of stuff that I know is wrong. Tarot an' stuff, crystals, books – you know the sort of thing. She says I've got tae destroy it all, an' I want to, but I wanted it tae be significant. Public. So I thought maybe we cud burn everything an' I could publicly renounce it all, and then be baptised.'

The tendency that Dave had noted before for Father Trumpington's face to freeze whenever they were talking became even more marked, added to which he seemed to be having difficulty breathing. Dave looked at him uncertainly. 'Are ye all right?' he asked.

Father Trumpington exhaled noisily and, placing the tips of his fingers together across his chest, regarded Dave stonily. 'Don't you think perhaps that's a shade ostentatious?' he asked.

'Er, no, I don't think so,' said Dave. He was not sure what the word meant, but he thought it sounded vaguely official. 'I dunna think the council mind what ye do.'

Father Trumpington's suspicion that Dave was deliberately obtuse increased. 'I meant,' he said with emphasis, 'that it would perhaps be going a bit far.'

Dave looked crestfallen. 'How do ya' mean?'

'I mean that a public burning is not the usual mode of procedure.' Father Trumpington thought of all the babies he had baptised over the years, and of their parents in their smart suits and big hats. As often as not such occasions were the only time he saw most of these families in church. And recently some of the couples he had performed this particular office for had not even been married, while a few had said that they would rather not make the vows because they did not believe, but would he like to come to the party afterwards? Father Trumpington saw nothing wrong with this. Indeed he thought it was a civilised way to behave, but what Dave was suggesting most definitely was not.

Dave's lower lip jutted. 'It's important tae me,' he insisted. 'I've been a bad man. I want tae put it right. I want him up there tae know.'

'Then tell him,' said Father Trumpington acidly, 'but I will not have the churchyard made into a bear garden!'

Dave looked at him. He was beaten on this one, he knew. 'Well, I'm going tae burn them somewhere,' he said.

'How about Guy Fawkes' night,' suggested Father Trumpington sweetly, 'next year?'

Dave looked at him with immense dignity. 'I dunna think you're being very nice,' he said. They looked at each other measuringly, and then he went on, 'Can we fix a date for the baptism at any rate? You can't refuse me that!'

Father Trumpington glared, but on this particular point he was cornered. Half the church had already heard him agree. With immense effort of will, and not a little internal rage, he reached for his diary.

After some wrangling they finally agreed on 3 January, because it had suddenly occurred to Dave that this would be the most splendid start to the new year, and from this point he refused to be budged despite Father Trumpington's forcibly pointing out to him that they might at that time have to contend with ice and snow. 'No, it's all right,' Dave insisted. 'Ye don't have tae come in the water, ye can just lean over. I dunna mind. And I'd even quite like it if there was snow, it'ud make it more, kinduv, meaningful!'

Father Trumpington looked at him as if he was mad, but he had the feeling that trying to stop Dave was like trying to stop a runaway lorry by standing in front of it with a flag. The big man was deaf to all reason. He had got it fixed into his head that he wanted to make a grand gesture for the Lord. Father Trumpington hated fanatics, which was what he suspected Dave was. It was all Antonia's fault, he decided, as he stared inscrutably at Dave across the wide expanse of his desk. She was responsible for this dreadful man coming into the church, and it was she who had put all these crackpot ideas into his head. Things had been quiet before she arrived but ever since her first Sunday, it was as if the whole church had gone mad. Not for the first time he thought with longing of her departure, but meantime here was Dave, still staring at him expectantly, and because Father Trumpington wanted him to go away and because he could no longer be bothered to carry on the argument, he said yes.

The memory rankled all day, casting a shadow over everything he did. As he changed his suit in the early evening in readiness to go to his initiation, he felt as if something bright had been snatched from him. He left Dorothy sitting in front of the telly, with a plate of baked beans on toast perched on her knees on a tray. She had had a heavy day at work and looked tired, but he did not notice. Every time he looked at her aubergine-streaked hair these days, he felt himself cringe, but she had proved un-expectedly obdurate when he had attempted to remonstrate with her. Now, clad in her exorbitantly expensive pyjama suit, she glared at him defiantly, knowing what was passing through his mind. 'Off to play your silly games, are you?' she inquired disdainfully.

'That's right, dear,' he replied, equally disdainfully, and managing to make the endearment sound like a term of abuse. 'Don't wait up.'

He picked up Alan from his house, as they had arranged before, and off they went. It was a clear, frosty night, with the stars overhead brilliant in an inky sky, but there was an uneasy feel to the air, as if bad weather was coming, and Father Trumpington found himself wondering if they were going to have snow. A white Christmas might be rather nice he thought, though Dorothy would be sure to complain. The next moment, however, all such thoughts went from his mind as the gates of the Lodge loomed out of the darkness before them. They had arrived.

In the car park, stamping his feet and flailing his arms to keep out the cold, they found the Archdeacon, who was also a Mason and who, with Alan, was going to act as one of his sponsors. 'Big night tonight, Dick,' he said, as they drew up, his breath coming in a long frosty stream.

Father Trumpington nodded dumbly. Now it was all about to happen, he found it almost impossible to speak; he had been looking forward to this evening for so long. 'Ye-es,' he responded.

Together they walked into the Lodge, and Father Trumpington found himself being conducted into a small, bare anteroom at the back of the main hall. It reminded him rather of his vestry. There were three straight-backed chairs, and a clothes rail with some half-dozen metal hangers. He felt a sudden surge of excitement and glanced quickly at Alan and the Archdeacon. They were shrugging off their coats, the Archdeacon puffing slightly with the effort, but there was an air of repressed excitement about them too. 'Come along, Dick,' chided the Archdeacon, glancing up at the same moment and catching his eye. 'Get ready. We've got to blindfold you, you know.'

They put on their regalia, and then Father Trumpington stood meekly while they blindfolded him. One of them took him by the hand, he was not sure who, and he heard the sound of the door ahead being opened. Immediately it was as if a current of electricity flowed through the air. Clammy warmth mixed with cigar smoke seemed to billow out and engulf him, and then they were processing slowly forwards, their feet noiseless on the thick pile of the carpet. He heard the sound of chairs being pushed back. Somewhere to his left someone coughed, and a voice muttered something, but he could not tell what was said. The darkness was absolute. He could feel people all around, but he had no idea how many were there. It was as if he was going into the Holy of Holies, in the presence of a god.

He felt himself being guided slowly forwards, and then a hand was laid briefly on his shoulder, to restrain him from going any further. 'Who seeks admittance?' intoned a voice. He heard the Archdeacon answer on his behalf, and tensed himself, his mind going over the responses he knew he was now going to be required to make. Panic! He could not remember a word. And then the voice was addressing him, and almost without thought, he heard himself responding, the ancient formulas that he had so painfully learned spilling from his lips. Question. Answer. Question. Answer. Promise . . . Penalty. It seemed to go on and on, though in reality he knew the whole thing could have lasted only a minute or so. Then he felt a movement at his side, a hand brushed his bald head, and the blindfold fell away.

The sudden restoration of light made him blink and for a second he was unable to see, but then his eyes adjusted. He found himself standing facing the chapter, decorated with what he knew instantly were standards of the twelve tribes of Israel. He had expected to find in front of him the Worshipful Master, and the Senior and Junior Wardens of the Lodge, but instead, across the dais and seated at the eastern end, he saw three men, with the titles Zerubbabel, Haggai and Joshua before them. The man seated behind the title Zerubbabel rose to his feet, and Father Trumpington recognised his bank manager, and Dorothy's boss. 'Brother,' he began, 'you have entered into the secret. You have passed from death to life . . .'

The words flowed over him. In an uncomprehending daze he heard all about the loss of the secrets hidden by the master builder of Solomon's temple, Hiram Abiff, long ages before. He had placed them in a subterranean room, the voice said, beneath the temple, and there they had been lost. Father Trumpington heard the passwords, never to be uttered outside this room, and he heard himself enjoined to seek, in company with his fellow Masons, to rediscover the secrets and repair the loss. Father Trumpington felt himself in the presence of real power. He looked around at his fellow Masons and a warm glow of brotherhood swelled in his chest. He felt he had come home.

Towards the end he was led to what he was told was the 'altar of incense'. He found himself standing before a sort of double cube that he had not noticed before. On the top was a square metal plate, and placed upon it a circle and an inscribed triangle made of the same metal. On the circle he made out the words JE-HO-VAH, and on the triangle JAH-BUL-ON.

Zerubbabel was speaking again. JE-HO-VAH, he explained, meant Father Lord, Word Lord, and Spirit Lord. Father Trumpington stared at it fascinated as the principal's voice went on. The 'real' name for the true and living God, he intoned, is not Jehovah, but Jahbulon, 'True and Living God Most High'. Father Trumpington caught his breath. He knew exactly what was to come and he agreed with it wholeheartedly. He was sick of all this sectarian rubbish about there being only one God. People worshipped God in their own way, but it was all the same. The Masons really had rediscovered a secret! And now he was privileged to partake of that. Jah, the god of the Israelites, said the voice, Bul, the god of the Syrians, and On, one of the hierarchy of the gods of Egypt. So sacred was the name of Jahbulon, he was told, that he must never utter it by himself, but only with the help of two other Royal Arch Companions.

While he was being instructed in how to do this, something very strange happened. He had been aware for a while of a faint smell of burning coming from somewhere to his right. He had thought at first that he was imagining it, and then perhaps that someone had dropped some ash from a cigar, but, as the ceremony drew to a close, the smell became more and more pronounced. Suddenly, just as it was his turn to say 'Bul', a long finger of flame snaked up into the air from one of the drapes at the side of the dais. From all around there were startled sounds of consternation and then the next moment the whole curtain went up in noisy, crackling flames. The heat was amazing. One moment there had been nothing, the next it was blasting out like a furnace, with black smoke billowing into the air.

'Get a fire extinguisher!' yelled the bank manager. Father Trumpington could only stand and stare with fascinated horror as all around him people rushed to put out the blaze.

'Bul,' he said miserably to himself.

The next day the blaze was all over the local papers. 'Unexplained Fire Devastates Masonic Hall' ran one headline, 'Masons Go Up In Flames!' said another. The reports told how, in the middle of a routine meeting, a fire had suddenly broken out causing thousands of pounds worth of damage. The main hall had, in fact, said the articles, been gutted, because the one extinguisher that worked had proved inadequate and though the bank manager had quickly organised everyone there into a chain to try and fight the fire with water, that too had proved inadequate. On top of that, the articles ran on, the fire service had taken forty-five minutes to reach them, by which time the whole of one end of the building had been ablaze.

148

Various theories were put forward as to why it had started, from an electricity short in old wiring to spontaneous combustion – this from a wag on one of the freebies, who appeared to find the whole incident rather amusing. Father Trumpington felt miserable; his initiation had ended in chaos, his dinner suit had been ruined and Dorothy, when he had finally come home, had almost had a heart attack laughing. Father Trumpington had been deeply offended. But as if all of this was not enough, he discovered on the front of one of the papers a photograph of himself. It was not a very flattering photograph. He looked rather dazed, and his bow tie had somehow ended up under one ear. Even more unflattering, the photographer had caught him with his face grimed with soot, so that he looked like one of the old-time Black and White Minstrels. Bad though the photograph was, however, he was still recognisable, and Father Trumpington ground his teeth when he saw it. There might be trouble, he thought, from all of this.

It arrived in the middle of the following afternoon. He was sitting in his study drinking a cup of tea when the telephone rang. The voice of the Bishop's chaplain boomed down the line. 'Richard!' he bellowed. He did not sound overly well-disposed and Father Trumpington winced. He disliked the Bishop's chaplain at the best of times, but now he thought the young man sounded positively offensive. 'The Bishop wishes to know if that is you on the front of this afternoon's paper.'

Father Trumpington swallowed. He wondered whether or not he ought to deny it – he knew the Bishop's views on Freemasonry – but then he reflected that the Archdeacon had been there too, along with at least two other senior clergy from the diocese. 'Yes,' he said defiantly. 'As it happens, it is.'

The Bishop's chaplain was made of rather sterner stuff than the Bishop. Father Trumpington knew that if he had used that tone of voice with the latter, he would instantly have given way and maybe even apologised. Not so the chaplain. There was a silence, and then his voice said coldly, 'The Bishop would like you to come in and see him at ten tomorrow morning.'

'I can't come in at such short notice,' spluttered Father Trumpington, outraged. 'I have an appointment.'

'Cancel it,' said the chaplain briefly, and hung up.

An agonised phone call to the Archdeacon brought him no comfort. 'Whatever you do,' said that worthy, 'don't tell the Bishop that I'm a Mason too. I'll stand by you, and I'll do all I can to help. We all will, but you are *not* to say that I was there.' And then he relented. 'Don't worry,' he said comfortingly, 'there's nothing he can do. You haven't done anything wrong, after all.'

It occurred to Father Trumpington to wonder why, if he had done nothing wrong, he should say nothing, but then he castigated himself for being naive. He knew perfectly well that the Church was publicly opposed to Freemasonry, even if there were many priests in its ranks. And he knew that in career terms discretion was the word. 'Secrecy,' admonished the Archdeacon. 'We cover each others' backs!'

Nevertheless, it was with a slight twinge of apprehension that Father Trumpington went along to Church House the next day. As a tiny expression of defiance he arrived five minutes late, and found the Bishop's chaplain waiting for him at the door. The chaplain, who was called Nigel, eyed him coldly but forbore to say anything and ushered him straight up to the Bishop's office. Father Trumpington had been hoping that Nigel would then withdraw, but his hopes were dashed when Nigel firmly closed the door, with himself on the inside. He saw a look pass between the Bishop and his aide and then he was told to sit down.

There followed one of the most uncomfortable half-hours in all of Father Trumpington's life. The chaplain and the Bishop sat side by side on the far side of the Bishop's huge expanse of mahogany desk. The Bishop reclined in a thickly padded, leather swivel desk chair, while Nigel sat some two feet away on a far more modest upright. Nigel's manner was quietly deferential – until, that is, he turned his steely gaze on Father Trumpington. Under his eye, Father Trumpington squirmed uncomfortably. Father Trumpington found himself sitting in the middle of the room facing them. The Bishop himself did not say very much, leaving the questioning instead to his chaplain, who couched every remark with, 'The Bishop was wondering . . .' or 'The Bishop feels . . .' He seemed to have an uncanny knack for knowing exactly what it was the Bishop wanted to say.

Now he began, 'The Bishop was wondering if, from the photograph, we may gather that your presence at the hall was not simply fortuitous, and that you are in fact a practising Mason?'

Father Trumpington's chin went up. 'What if I am?' he inquired. 'There is absolutely no incompatibility between Freemasonry and the Church.'

The Bishop cleared his throat in protest, and Nigel said smoothly, 'I need hardly remind you that the report of Synod disagrees with that.'

A steely glint came in turn into Father Trumpington's eye. 'And I need hardly remind you,' he snapped back, 'that though the Church has said it cannot endorse Masonic teachings, it has not felt moved to forbid membership, and that several of the churchmen involved in compiling that report were in fact themselves Masons.'

The Bishop interjected in a small voice, 'That can only be deplored.'

It was Nigel, however, who moved in to the attack. Father Trumpington had long suspected him of being an evangelical of the worst kind; now his suspicions were confirmed. With a complete lack of emotion, the young man began to go through Masonic doctrine. Father Trumpington was amazed that he knew so much.

'Jahbulon,' he stated, 'is a composite name that Freemasons claim to be the inclusive name of the supreme deity. It is in fact a combination of Jehovah, Baal and Osiris. In Scripture both these deities are identified with Satan. Time and again the Jews were told they could not combine worship of these deities with Jehovah. When they persisted, they came under God's judgement. Christ himself endorsed that teaching. You cannot be a Christian and at the same time purport to worship a supreme deity that denies the sovereignty of God, or that refuses to acknowledge Jesus Christ. The Bishop is determined to oppose the practice of Freemasonry by his clergy in this diocese.'

'But that's preposterous,' spluttered Father Trumpington. 'One of the main and, if I may say, most highly valued strengths of the Church of England is its diversity of worship. We are strong simply because we do not insist that everyone has to believe or envisage God in the same way.'

'No,' said Nigel firmly. 'The Bishop feels there is a world of difference between worshipping the same God in different ways, and worshipping different gods in what is ostensibly the same way.' He looked at Father Trumpington and then demanded, 'Are you prepared to give up your membership of this group?'

Father Trumpington did not even think about his reply. 'No,' he snarled back. 'I am not.'

There was a silence, and the Bishop looked down at the open file on his desk. Father Trumpington wished he could see what was in it, but it was too far away. The Bishop looked at Nigel, and very slightly inclined his head.

'Richard,' said the chaplain, 'we believe you are going to be sixty-four in two years' time.'

This was a different tack and, disconcerted, Father Trumpington nodded.

'Have you thought about your retirement?' asked Nigel.

Father Trumpington blinked, and then swallowed. He could think of absolutely nothing to say. It was true that his retirement had been very much in his thoughts over the past few days – and a picture of that wonderful little seaside idyll with Jackie floated again into his mind. But at this precise moment he was not sure he liked the turn the conversation seemed to be taking; there was no way he was going to allow himself to be pushed out before he chose. 'I . . .'

Nigel did not wait for him to go on. 'The Bishop would like to suggest that you do think about it.' He paused. 'Seriously. And that you do not take too long. He is unwilling to reprimand you publicly – there has already been too much publicity given to Freemasonry. But he thinks, if you feel you cannot give up this practice, that it would be better for you to go and enjoy your retirement.'

Father Trumpington could only stare at him stupefied. He was one of that dying breed within the Church of England that had tenure, which meant he could stay on in his parish till they carried him out of the vicarage feet first, if he so chose. The Bishop, he knew, was well aware of this, so there was no way that he could enforce what his chaplain was now suggesting.

There was a silence, and the Bishop shifted uncomfortably. He seemed to have discovered something of inordinate interest outside the window. Father Trumpington looked at him furiously, but it was Nigel who once again spoke.

'A man of your age,' he suggested, 'hardly wants the strain of a scandal caused by a row with his Bishop over something like this, surely? I mean, could your health stand it?'

Father Trumpington knew that war had been declared. 'You can't force me to retire,' he snarled. 'I have tenure, after all, and my health is very good, thank you.'

The two men looked at each other measuringly. Eventually Nigel said, 'You are of course quite right. In the circumstances you do have the choice. But perhaps you may care to reflect that from now on we shall be watching you very closely. Very closely indeed.'

It was a threat and Father Trumpington knew it. He left with a hard knot of impotent rage that made him feel sick curled in the pit of his stomach. In fact, he was so angry that his hands were shaking and he could hardly unlock the door to his car. Somehow, however, he managed it and stumbled in, breathing heavily. He would not be bested by that pipsqueak of a chaplain, he thought furiously, viciously jamming the key into the starter and revving far too much. They could not force him to retire, whatever they did. He must speak to the Archdeacon!

Chapter Twelve

Gloria was looking forward to the Christmas party. She bought a new dress. It was deep red with a daringly low neckline, and when she put it on with her three-inch black stilettos, making her all of five feet one, she felt absolutely irresistible. Griff thought so too, for when she tried it on when she got back home, he attempted to wrestle her down to the bed, planting wet sloppy kisses on her ears (he was aiming for her mouth) and fumbling with the zip at the back. 'Gerroff!' Gloria shouted out, enraged. 'You'll get me all creased.'

'Take it orf then,' panted Griff. And because it was coming up to Christmas, and because Gloria was in an exceedingly good mood, she relented. Consequently, for some days after, there was a measure of unusual goodwill in the Sunnington household, so much so that Griff was emboldened to ask if he might accompany Gloria to the party. This was pushing it, he knew, and the scowl on her face made him quail. But then, unexpectedly, she said yes and so, to his intense surprise, Griff found himself on the Saturday evening dressed in his best suit and with a carefully knotted tie, all ready to go. It should perhaps be pointed out that Gloria had agreed only because she had not really wanted to go alone, and because at the back of her mind was the vague idea that if Father Trumpington saw her with another man, albeit her husband, he might be jealous. Griff, however, did not know any of this, and so it was in a mood of happy ignorance on his part that they set out.

Slynne had dressed carefully for the big event too. Like Gloria, he had been out buying, but in his case it was a rather alarming multi-coloured velvet jacket with an upright leather collar. It was not very comfortable, but he had seen it in the window of a rather bizarre clothes shop a few days before and had known instantly that Jackie (who was herself so stylish) would appreciate it. What he had failed to take into account was that he had made his purchase from a shop usually frequented by seventeen-year-olds, and that a style that looks good on teenagers is not always appropriate to someone of rather more mature years. In fact he looked a complete idiot but, as he surveyed himself in his hall mirror, all he could see was the gaudy splendour of the coat. Jackie, he hoped, would be totally unable to resist. So he, too, set out in a mood of profound optimism.

Not everyone was so blessed. Gudrun had thought about the question of the party for a long time. She did not like parties, in fact she hated them, and baby Otto was still not strong enough for the hospital to allow him to go home, but she was mindful of the fact that the other children needed her too, and she felt more ready now to go to war. Something profound *had* happened the night Antonia had prayed with her for Otto. She had been given hope, and she was absolutely determined that she would not simply stand back and allow her rival to usurp her place. Norman, she knew, was looking forward to the party; he had let drop that he was going to play. She felt, however, that his air of furtive excitement had more to do with Jackie than with the fact he was going to play a jolly Christmas piece which, as he had informed her, was a 'musical joke'. Accordingly she made up her mind that she would go too. She did not tell Norman this, but the day before she suddenly announced that she was at long last coming home. From now on, she said, she would come in each day to spend time with Otto, but for the rest, she would resume her proper place in the house. Norman had looked appalled. 'B-but you can't!' he stuttered, and then desperately, 'Otto still needs you here.'

She looked him in the eye with disdain. 'No,' she said, 'there's nothing more I can do by being here all the time. The nurses take care of him at night anyway. Bethany and Iwan need me more now. I have neglected them. It's time for me to come home.'

She did not reveal to him her plan of accompanying him to the party. She knew he would assume that she would stay at home like she usually did, and she had no intention of alerting him now to what she was planning to do. Better, she thought, if Jackie was not forewarned. Besides which, she suspected that things were not quite as idyllic between the lovers as Norman had previously made them appear. Perhaps now he would even be grateful to be rescued. He would rage and storm, of course – there was, after all, his pride – but maybe, deep down, he was beginning to feel a little regret. Gudrun hoped so. Ever since their row after the doctor had broken the news to them of baby Otto's heart condition, she thought he had seemed rather subdued. He still behaved appallingly, of course, brusquely making it obvious at nights where he was going, but she thought she detected a touch of guilt, and a shade more consideration in his attitude towards her than was usual.

She planned her campaign with military precision. All through the next day she said nothing. She had asked Phoebe a few days before if she would mind caring for the children a while longer. She needed to adjust, she said, and get used to being at home again. Phoebe had agreed willingly. She could fully see the sense of Gudrun's suggestion, and would indeed have suggested it herself, but more than that she was worried by the way Gudrun looked. 'There's something wrong,' she confided to her husband when she got back home. 'It's not just the baby. She looks terrible. Her skin's all waxy, and she doesn't seem to be there. And she's so thin. It's odd. New mums are usually a bit plump, but she looks like something out of Belsen!' She thought for a while, her kindly brow furrowed with concern, and then said pensively, 'You know, I wouldn't be a bit surprised if she didn't have a nervous breakdown.'

But Gudrun was far from a nervous breakdown. With ill-concealed irritation Norman picked her up on the Saturday morning and brought her home, grumbling all the way. He saw her safely installed in the house and then, without even offering to make her a cup of coffee, flung off over to the church – to practise, he said. Gudrun was quite glad to see him go; she hated his moods. As soon as she was alone, she went upstairs and opened the doors to her wardrobe, and then very carefully began to go through her meagre stock of clothes.

She had rather thought that for the party she would put on an old Indian print smock that she had always loved and felt comfortable in, but when she took it out now she realised with a sinking heart just how dowdy it was. The colours, which from her hospital bed she had remembered as glorious and vibrant, looked faded and dull, while the material had been washed so much it no longer seemed to have any body. In this dress she had always felt herself to be arty and exotic, but with painful clarity she suddenly caught a glimpse of herself as seen through the eyes of others. Boring, dull, hopelessly out of date! Jackie, she felt, woud despise her in this. It would be no contest.

Despairingly she twitched it aside and looked at her other two dresses, but it was exactly the same with them. All of them, like herself, looked old and homely and worn. She burst into tears.

It was in this sorry state that Antonia found her some ten minutes later. 'Whatever's the matter?' she asked when she had finally persuaded Gudrun to sit down in the kitchen, and had placed in front of her a cup of hot tea. 'Why are you so upset? Is it Norman again?'

Gudrun blubbered into the tiny scrap of rag that she insisted was a hankie. 'No,' she sniffed, 'it's me!' And then she poured out her plan to Antonia, how she had intended to go along to the party tonight, how she had planned to look effortlessly gorgeous so that Norman would realise just how silly he was being, how she had been going to triumph over Jackie. 'But it's useless,' she ended up, snivelling afresh into the hankie. 'I look such a fright. Everything I've got seems so dowdy!'

Antonia surveyed her. 'Stand up,' she commanded. The order was so abrupt and strange that Gudrun rose to her feet before it occurred to her to ask why. 'Hmm,' said Antonia measuringly. 'Turn round.' Obediently Gudrun slowly spun round, glancing back at Antonia with an air of puzzled inquiry. Perhaps ten seconds elapsed and then Antonia said consideringly, 'You know, we're about the same size. Maybe you're an inch taller. But it's not much.'

Gudrun stared at her uncomprehendingly and suddenly Antonia smiled. 'Wash your face,' she ordered, and put your coat on. Then come with me.'

'But why?' asked Gudrun.

'Because you're going to borrow something of mine.'

Half an hour later Kathleen heard them giggling up in Antonia's room – at least, she heard Antonia giggling. She was not sure whether she heard Gudrun join in or not. Reason told her that from the state the young woman appeared to be in this was unlikely, but she hoped profoundly that that was not the case. Kathleen was a great believer in the curative effects of laughter and, having suffered so much herself, she recognised instantly the pain being endured by someone else. She did not know much about Gudrun, and she certainly knew nothing about the state of her marriage, but from what she had seen of her, she liked and felt sorry for her. And so, without understanding why, she began to pray that Gudrun might receive the help and healing she needed. It was not easy, the noise coming from upstairs made it hard to concentrate. 'Try this on,' she heard Antonia say, 'and these shoes.' And then encouragingly, 'Your hair looks great, honestly. Maybe some make-up would help.'

There were more murmurings and bumps, and then the sound of something being dragged across the floor. Gudrun saying, 'No, I can't!' And Antonia saying, 'Of course you can!' Finally they came down to the lounge where Kathleen was rather nervously drinking her tea, in between attempting to pray. Antonia came in first.

'We want your honest opinion,' she said. 'I think Gudrun looks terrific, but she's a bit nervous. She says it makes her look too young and it's too suggestive, so we want to know what you think.' Then she threw open the door and stood back.

Gudrun stood framed against the light. She had on a long natural-coloured raw silk dress that reached down to her ankles. It looked deceptively simple, cut narrow and straight, but it showed off every angle and curve of her body. Kathleen gazed at her in surprise. She had seen Antonia wearing the same dress only a couple of nights before, when she had been going out to the theatre with Henry, but whereas on Antonia it had appeared demure, somehow on Gudrun, with the look of intense fragility that the experience of the last few weeks had stamped upon her, it gave her the air of some passing and insubstantial sprite. Kathleen's eyes travelled slowly up. Gudrun's hair was coiled on top of her head, with wispy curls escaping over her ears, so that her face, in keeping with the dress, had taken on a kind of angular, waif-like beauty.

Kathleen could only stare at her. 'My goodness,' she said softly, with a dim feeling that somehow, somewhere, her prayers were being heard, 'you look beautiful!'

Antonia was delighted. 'There!' she said. 'What did I tell you?'

So Gudrun, too, had something to wear, but still she did not tell Norman that she was going to the party. She had intended to, but when it came to it her nerve failed. He had looked so angry when he had returned home, and they had barely exchanged half a dozen words while he had a bath and changed in readiness to go. As she had suspected, it had not occurred to him that she might like to go along too. The possibility had not even been raised, and when the phone rang at about half past six, she heard his voice saying, 'Yes, that's right, she is home . . . No, she won't be coming, Gudrun doesn't like parties . . . She'll be much happier here, and she can rest too . . . Yep. OK . . . See you there. 'Bye!'

She had no idea who he was talking to. She rather thought from his tone that it might have been Father Trumpington, but when he poked his head through the door some two minutes later he only said, 'I'm off now then. Don't worry if I'm late.'

'Aren't you a bit early?' she asked. 'I thought it didn't start till eight.'

'Oh . . . yes, that's right,' he said vaguely, 'but I said I'd help get things ready. You know how it is.'

Liar, she thought, but she merely inclined her head. 'Yes,' she said, 'I know how it is.'

The door slammed behind him and a deep silence fell. She waited motionless for perhaps five minutes, till she was sure he would not return, and then she crept upstairs to retrieve the dress from under the bed where she had hidden it. The butterflies in her stomach felt as if they were turning cartwheels, and for two pins now she would have abandoned the plan altogether. In the sickly electric light given off by the sixty-watt bulb over their bed, the whole idea seemed ridiculous. How could she ever have contemplated this? Even worse, how on earth could she go into that bleak church hall by herself? Downstairs the clock struck seven. The sound echoed through the empty rooms. That decided her. With trembling fingers she picked up the phone beside the bed and dialled Antonia's number. 'Hello,' she said, when Antonia answered. 'Norman's already gone. He doesn't know I'm coming . . . Can I come with you?'

* * *

She was sitting waiting, dressed and ready to go, when Antonia and Henry arrived some three-quarters of an hour later. Henry gave a low whistle. 'I say,' he said, 'you look great!'

Antonia winked. 'See!' she said.

Gudrun nodded, but it was with a trembling heart that she shuffled on her duffel coat and prepared to follow them out of the house and across the road. The night air, when they finally emerged, was bitter, while overhead the stars twinkled brilliantly in a cloudless sky. Christmas, she thought, the season of goodwill, but inside her was an empty, terrified vacuum. She could almost sense the nearness of her foe.

At that moment a cheery voice shouted 'Hiya!' and Dave and Jude seemed almost to bound along the pavement, with Eagle and Willow scuttering around their feet like over-excited, noisy puppies. There was laughter and greetings, and Gudrun found herself in turn hugged and fussed over, and then, in a tight little band, they erupted into the hall. Gudrun found herself catapulted forward. Heat hit her, and light, and the noisy beat of some Christmassy pop tune from a cassette. 'Gudrun!' said a voice. 'You've come after all! How lovely...' But Gudrun did not hear the rest. Instead she was transfixed by the sight of her husband standing some ten yards away. His back was towards her as she came through the door and he was leaning nonchalantly up against the wall. Beside him was Jackie, and they were talking to the Sunningtons and Father Trumpington. At that precise moment Jackie gave a loud bray of laughter, throwing back her head, and at the same time laid her hand proprietorially on Norman's arm. She did it as if she had a perfect right, as if, indeed, they were a couple – and then, in what to Gudrun felt like slow motion, she saw her husband's hand reach up and grip Jackie's, his face contracting in a spasm of laughter. At the same moment he looked up, and their eyes met.

The sudden change was almost comical. Norman's face froze in disbelief, and then he leapt away from Jackie as if he had been shot. The effect on the group was equally electrifying. As if on cue they all turned at the same moment and stared, and Gudrun had the satisfaction of seeing Jackie flush guiltily and snatch back her hand. But then Jackie's eyes hardened, and she glared at Gudrun angrily.

It was Gloria, however, sensing something scandalous in the wind and dying to find out more, who now came forward. 'Gudrun,' she said, her voice oozing insincere concern, 'we thought you weren't coming. Norman said you weren't well enough, dear!' She looked Gudrun up and down appraisingly, but the expression in her eyes was not kind and, unable to help herself, Gudrun flinched.

It was not an auspicious beginning. She was conscious of Norman staring at her with cold rage and, before his anger, she took a faltering step back, her eyes darting despairingly round for a way of escape. But at that moment Antonia came up to her side, and she felt her hand slip through her arm, steadying her.

'That's right, Gloria,' Antonia said smoothly, 'Gudrun is still very weak, and we all thought at first she wouldn't be able to manage it. But she really wanted to come because she wanted to see everyone, say thank you for all the cards and everything. Earlier on she was a bit shattered, it's true, but this evening, after Norman had left, she thought perhaps she could manage it after all, with a little help. But it was too late to get hold of Norman, so she rang me. And hey presto, here she is!'

Henry joined in. 'Yes,' he said, coming up on Gudrun's other side so that they formed a phalanx around her, 'and if she doesn't sit down in a minute, I think she might fall down!'

Cushioned by their protection, Gudrun found herself lifted almost bodily into a chair. A low ripple of admiration ran round the room and, as if released from some powerful spell, people suddenly rushed up and began to throng round. 'How are you, my dear?' Gudrun heard people say. 'How wonderful to see you! How's the baby?'

Father Trumpington himself scuttled off and brought her a glass of punch. 'Plucky little thing,' he said, placing it into her hands. 'How very thoughtful of you to come along tonight. But you must be careful not to overdo it, my dear. Norman,' he commanded peremptorily, 'come over here and take care of your wife!'

Norman scowled, but there was nothing he could do except comply.

Seeing his expression, Father Trumpington beamed. He had been feeling rather irritated by the attention Jackie had been lavishing on the organist but, try as he might, up till then, he had been unable to draw her away.

At the same moment Dorothy, who had been busy warming jacket patotoes, emerged from the kitchen to see what all the commotion was about. Like Gudrun she took instant note of Jackie's proximity to her husband, and a grim look came over her face; unlike Gudrun she had no desire to turn tail and flee. A sea change had come over Dorothy in the past few weeks. She had passed from downtrodden to bold, to depressed; but now that too had gone, replaced by angry bitterness that had given birth to a certain waspishness in her demeanour. Glaring, she came forward, a tea towel clutched in her hand, intent on separating her husband from Jackie as effectively and quickly as she could.

'Dick!' she bellowed. 'Come and help me in the kitchen and give the poor girl some air.' Because there were so many people around, Father Trumpington, like Norman before, could only obey. But the smile he pinned on his face was one of pure dislike and, as he followed his wife into the kitchen, it was with difficulty that he restrained himself from placing his hands round her fat throat and throttling her.

Gloria, who had taken in the whole scene with interest, smiled thinly at Antonia and moved away. Father Trumpington she did not suspect, but she felt sure that there was something going on here, something that definitely concerned Norman and Gudrun and, unless she was much mistaken, Ms La-de-da Jackie Newberg too. She glanced sharply at Jackie as she sailed past, and was rewarded by catching a most bizarre expression on her face. Jackie was still staring at Gudrun, like almost everyone else in the room. But unlike everyone else, there was nothing gentle or concerned in her manner. On the contrary, her face had taken on a kind of malign calculation, while there was something feline and cruel in the narrowed eyes that she fixed upon Gudrun. She looked evil, thought Gloria and, in spite of herself, she shivered. She would not, she thought, like to be in Gudrun's shoes – but of course she was not. With quiet satisfaction she now abandoned Griff, with a muttered explanation that she must go and help

163

Dorothy with the sausage rolls, and headed off in Father Trumpington's wake.

Norman, meanwhile, had finally registered his wife's attire, and was staring at her in amazement. 'Where on earth did you get that dress?' he hissed.

'It's Antonia's,' muttered Gudrun, glad of anything that seemed to divert him from his obvious rage.

'Doesn't she look nice?' said Antonia, who had caught the exchange.

'Hmm,' said Norman. But he looked at his wife more closely and, safe in the knowledge that Antonia's explanation had saved him from looking a complete fool, he allowed himself a thin smile.

'I'm glad things are lookin' up, pal!' said Dave, clapping him in a friendly fashion on the shoulder.

To his intense surprise, Norman suddenly discovered that he was not so very displeased by the attention Gudrun's appearance had provoked after all. In fact, if anything, he felt almost proud, as if he himself had done something rather splendid. It occurred to him that they really had been through a rough time, what with baby Otto and everything. It was right that people should be concerned. Besides which, he had forgotten just how pretty his wife could be. And he looked at her more closely.

Across the room Jackie glared. She knew exactly what was passing through his mind. With difficulty she forced a smile on to her face and turned with the greatest sweetness to Slynne, who had just come in. Slynne could not believe his luck. All through the afternoon he had been planning how best to approach Jackie, plotting devious and ever more elaborate schemes to win her attention away from the crowd that always seemed to be around her, and untimately get her on her own – and now here she was practically throwing herself at him! Slynne, not by nature an overly religious man, thanked the Lord, and prepared to be charming.

'Evenin', Jackie,' he said, in response to her breathless hello. 'You're lookin' very noice t'noight, moi dear. If oi may say so.' His face was on a level with her chest, from which indeed he was unable to tear his eyes. Her lycra top, he felt, promised untold delights.

Jackie glared at him indignantly, and the next instant took in the full glory of his jacket. Her jaw dropped.

'Oh, oi see you're admirin' my jacket,' said Slynne, catching her expression.

'Aa . . . h,' said Jackie faintly.

'Quite somethin', isn't it? Oi thought oi'd splash out a bit this year. Only live once, atter all. Know what oi mean!' He nudged her in the ribs, something he would never before have dared do, but what he felt to be her admiration for his finery was making him bold. Jackie was speechless with rage and, taking her silence to be heartfelt assent, Slynne now gripped her hand in his own sweaty paw and announced, 'Let's dance!'

The next hour for Jackie was pure nightmare. Wherever she turned, there was Slynne. She could not get away from the obnoxious little man. First he danced with her. Then he fetched her food. Then he sat her down in a corner and talked at her. Finally, when she made a determined effort to escape, he followed her to the Ladies where she had taken refuge, hoping he would grow tired and attach himself to someone else. Slynne, however, was made of sterner stuff than that. 'You alroight, Jackie?' he called through the door after she had been in there some five minutes. ''Urry up, we're goin' ta dance a reel!'

'Oh God!' said Jackie. But there was no escape. He was already pushing open the door with his foot, and she felt that at any moment he would burst in. She arranged her face carefully and slid out. 'Oh Edgar,' she breathed, 'you really must excuse me for this one. I feel quite tired.' She smiled brightly. 'Why not go and ask someone else? Why not try Gudrun?'

His face clouded. 'She's not up to a reel,' he said. 'She's only just come outta the 'ospital. Besides, oi want to dance with you.' Then his face brightened. 'We could go an' sit somewhere quiet.'

Jackie was spared this suggestion by Father Trumpington's approach. He had at last escaped Dorothy, who had been asked to dance by Dave. He felt there was something of poetic justice in this, and while his wife was otherwise engaged, he was determined to snatch a moment alone with Jackie. Accordingly he laid a large hand on her arm and said, 'My dance I think, Jackie.'

'Oh Dick,' simpered Jackie, relief flooding over her. 'Yes. Of course.'

''Ere, you said you wus too tired!' said Slynne furiously.

But Jackie was already moving away as fast as she could. 'Never too tired for Father,' floated back over her shoulder.

Slynne stared at her retreating back in dismay, but he comforted himself with the thought that perhaps Jackie was enjoying the pursuit and wished to prolong it a little longer. And as he stood there looking after them, feeling outrage at Hitler's intrusion, it suddenly occurred to him that he was actually rather enjoying the game too. 'Aar,' he muttered to himself reflectively, stroking his stubbly chin with his hand, 'if that's the way she wants t' play it!' And, not displeased, he went and sat down where he could keep an eye on her – and catch her as soon as the dance was over.

'I've been wanting to talk to you all night, Jackie,' said Father Trumpington as soon as they were on the floor. 'I'm sure Dorothy knows.'

Jackie, in the act of swinging round, stared at him blankly. 'Knows what?" she asked.

'About us!'

The dance took them away from each other down the lines of the set. 'She's been behaving most oddly,' he panted when they again met up at the far end. 'I'm sure she knows what's happened.'

Jackie smiled vaguely. Her eyes were fixed somewhere on the far corner of the room, a dreamy expression in them. 'I really don't know what you mean,' she said.

Father Trumpington twirled round. 'What do you mean, you don't know what I mean?' he spluttered. 'I think she knows what's going on – what we did!'

Jackie was having none of this. After one and a half hours of Slynne, she felt totally unable to cope with the unwanted attentions of anyone else. All she wanted to do now was to get hold of Norman. She looked Father Trumpington in the eye and stated coldly, 'There's nothing going on. We did nothing!'

The next couple joined them on the end and the set moved up. Jackie and Father Trumpington clasped hands and spun round in a circle, and then made an arch with their arms under which the other couples could dance. Father Trumpington felt as if his world was disintegrating. 'The other night,' he hissed. 'The choir!'

Jackie smiled obtusely. 'Yes,' she said, 'I enjoyed the choir.'

'But the other . . . you know.' Father Trumpington became aware that from the other set Dorothy was glaring at him. He looked away hastily. 'Look, Jackie,' he hissed, the next opportunity he had, 'we've got to talk. We've got to plan. Can I come round?'

It was a good two minutes before they again met up in the dance, and when they did Jackie smiled at him coolly and said, 'I'm busy over Christmas. Maybe after. Give me a ring.'

All around them clapping broke out as the dance finished. 'But,' began Father Trumpington desperately.

At that moment Dorothy came up. The dance had lent a high colour to her cheeks that clashed violently with her aubergine hair. 'Come on, Dick,' she said grimly. 'It's about time you danced with me.'

Taking advantage of the general confusion as people changed partners, Jackie detached herself and began to head purposefully towards Norman, now sitting in a small group with Gudrun on the far side of the hall. But Slynne was ahead of her.

'Jackie,' he panted, catching hold of her elbow just as she reached the edge of the floor. 'Dang cheek 'e's got! Oi thought that dance 'ud never end. Come an' sit down. There's somethin' oi want to say.' And, holding her in a grip of steel, he began to propel her remorselessly towards a small shadowed table that was about as far away from Norman as it was possible to get. Jackie could have cried with rage, but short of kicking Slynne on the shins there seemed nothing she could do.

Father Trumpington was having the selfsame difficulty with Dorothy, because she had wrapped her pudgy hand round his and now refused to let him go. 'Come on,' she repeated, 'I want to dance.'

'I don't dance,' he said, through clenched teeth.

But Dorothy would have none of this. 'You just did,' she pointed out. 'And you don't want people saying you're more considerate towards your parishioners than you are to your wife!'

A few weeks back and she might have tried looking coy, but

now she stared at him menacingly and Father Trumpington swallowed. He had discovered he was rather frightened of this purple-haired Valkyrie that Dorothy had become. There was an element of unpredictability about her that he did not like. 'But I don't like the Gay Gordons,' he said weakly.

'You surprise me,' snarled Dorothy. Her aerobic exercises of the past few weeks had not been without result. She was not visibly any thinner, but she had developed considerable strength. Now she hoisted his arm over her shoulder and Father Trumpington was surprised to find his hand clamped by what felt like iron pincers. He wriggled, but short of an unseemly scuffle there was nothing he could do.

'Hello,' trilled Gloria as they took their places on the floor. She had been watching him like a hawk all evening, but so far had been frustrated in her every attempt to get him alone. It had not escaped her notice that Dorothy had stuck to him throughout the evening like glue, nor had she failed to remark over the past few weeks Dorothy's rather startling change of appearance. Indeed the whole church had noticed it, and it had provided, just as Father Trumpington had feared, a fascinating topic of conversation. Opinion was divided. Some said a vicar's wife ought not to dress like that – ever! But others, mainly the men, said it was about time poor Dorothy did something, she had been looking so dowdy, and it was encouraging to think that such a mouse of a woman should have some life in her after all. She might have gone a bit overboard, (no one was entirely sure about the aubergine hair), but, all in all, they thought it was a good thing.

Gloria, however, had observed the changes from a rather different perspective. It had occurred to her to wonder what had driven Dorothy to such excess, and her fertile imagination had quickly provided a cause. Dorothy, she thought, was in a panic because she had realised she might lose her man. It had been but a short step from this deduction for Gloria to pinpoint the temptress who might be the originator of these fears – herself. She had concluded that Dorothy was frightened of her – Gloria's – powers. So now she smiled archly, an effect spoiled somewhat by Griff choosing that moment to stand on her toe. 'Ouch!' she said, and thrust him away.

Griff shuffled uneasily. He was not very keen on all this dancing lark, he kept on getting it wrong. He was convinced he had two left feet, and he especially loathed the Gay Gordons. He thought it was a pansy dance. But for some reason Gloria had insisted that they join in. 'Sorry,' he mumbled.

Gloria had a brainwave. 'Tell you what,' she said brightly, 'why don't we change partners? I've been dancing with Griff all night, and I'm sure you don't want to stick with your husband, Dorothy. You must see enough of him during the day.' She giggled, and then very adroitly slipped out from under Griff's arm and into Father Trumpington's nerveless embrace, at the same time substituting Dorothy for herself with Griff.

Dorothy looked dumbfounded, but the little band chose that moment to strike up the tune and the next second they were off.

'You seem to have been busy all night,' shouted Gloria to Father Trumpington as they walked forward in time to the music.

'Oh . . . er, yes,' responded Father Trumpington vaguely, his eyes searching for Jackie.

Gloria interpreted his look as unease due to his wife's proximity, and felt pleased. It must be true. The nearness of her presence was disturbing him, and he did not want Dorothy to know. 'You naughty boy,' she said playfully. 'I think you've been trying to avoid me!'

In the act of turning, Father Trumpington froze. 'Pardon?'

Gloria had succeeded in gaining his complete attention, but somehow the effect was not quite what she had anticipated. 'I said, I think you've been trying to avoid me,' she repeated, a little less certainly.

Father Trumpington looked down at her as if she was mad, and suddenly realised that he was staring down her cleavage. Good heavens, what was the woman wearing? He had not realised how low her dress was before, nor how large she was! His eyes took on a glassy sheen; he really must preach on modesty some time, this was embarrassing. He became aware that Gloria was staring up at him belligerently, as if expecting some kind of answer.

'Ha, ha! Very good,' he laughed uneasily. 'Very funny. Avoiding you! Yes!' The ladies all began to spin round, and Father

Trumpington took advantage of the temporary respite to exhale heavily.

Gloria gave one last twirl and planted herself firmly in his arms. She decided to try another tack. 'Dorothy's looking . . . different.'

Father Trumpington shuddered and closed his eyes. 'Yes,' he agreed.

'Bit sudden,' persisted Gloria.

'Umm.'

'People do change suddenly sometimes . . . when something happens.'

He looked at her narrowly, but Gloria merely smiled up at him innocently. Once again Father Trumpington felt his eyes drawn towards her breasts and hastily looked away. Really, this was too bad, the woman ought to be more considerate; the last thing he wanted was for her to think he was staring at her chest. But that was precisely what Gloria did think and, despite his rather strange behaviour, she again felt encouraged. He was a wonderful man, she thought, so upright. That he was attracted to her, she was certain, but he was obviously fighting a terrible battle with guilt. Religion had a lot to answer for! She herself did not feel any such constraint. He needed, she felt, to be helped now. He needed her to take the lead. Under cover of the music, she slid her hand down inside his jacket until it rested lightly on the inside of his waistband, and then began to knead her fingers gently, suggestively, into his skin. 'I sometimes feel I'd like a change too,' she murmured.

Father Trumpington leapt into the air. Fortunately, at that moment so did all the other men, so it simply looked as if he was joining in the dance with zeal. That at least was what Griff appeared to think, because he winked at him broadly.

'Gloria, please! Restrain yourself!' Father Trumpington snapped under cover of the music. He shoved her none too gently and she withdrew her hand as if she had been stung. But then she smiled.

'It's all right,' she murmured, 'nobody'll see. Certainly not Dorothy. Nor Griff.' And to his complete horror she once again insinuated her body up against his, her chest now pressed not far above the same place where moments before her hand had been.

Father Trumpington was not quite sure afterwards how he

managed to survive that dance. He was convinced his blood pressure had soared, and at one point there had been an unpleasant singing in his ears. At every available opportunity Gloria had thrust herself up against him, and she had kept going on about how Dorothy was jealous, and how she understood; that they must be discreet. Father Trumpington felt certain she was drunk. For once in his life, when the music ended, he was actually pleased to see Dorothy and gratefully seized her hand, so that she looked at him suspiciously.

'I enjoyed that,' said Gloria. She smiled seraphically at Dorothy. 'I'll have to borrow your husband again some time.' On the whole she was rather pleased with the progress she had made. She felt they had come to an understanding.

At nine thirty it was time for the entertainment to begin, and Norman escaped from Gudrun to help clear a small space around the stage and take his place at the piano. As well as playing his 'musical joke', he had agreed to accompany the singers, so that it was easier now for him to remain on stage. He was not sorry to escape. Gudrun's appearance had undeniably surprised him, especially how good she looked, but the heavy, reproachful eyes she kept turning on him made him shudder. He knew that they were in for a scene when they got back home.

Jackie would never behave like that, he reflected. She always made him feel good; he did not want Gudrun's tragedy. Earlier on, catching sight of Jackie briskly heading towards the loo, he had actually tried to slide away but Henry, who appeared to have taken it upon himself temporarily to act as warder, had blocked his way and begun to talk loudly about organ recitals he had been to. Norman had had no idea that Henry was such a fan, but it had been a good ten minutes before he could extricate himself and, when he looked again, Jackie was nowhere in sight. However, as he moved chairs around, under cover of the general chaos he managed at long last to snatch a few words with her while she was once again sitting alone, Slynne having felt it his duty to help prepare the stage. 'Jackie,' he hissed, 'I'm sorry. I didn't know she was coming. I never dreamt she'd do this!'

Jackie glared at him angrily. Now Norman was actually in front of her she found she was consumed with jealous rage. All thoughts of being nice flew out of the window. 'How could you?' she snapped. 'You could at least have warned me.'

'I didn't know!'

'What do you mean you didn't know? She came home this morning, for God's sake!'

'But she never normally comes to parties,' said Norman plaintively. 'She never said anything.'

Jackie looked at him consideringly. 'What are we going to do?' she asked at last. 'When shall I see you again?'

'Tomorrow after church,' hissed Norman. 'I'll make some excuse and come round.'

Jackie did not smile. Instead she just looked at him. 'You'd better,' she said meaningfully.

Then Norman had to go, and Jackie found herself once again sitting next to Slynne. She felt she was going to scream if this went on much longer. The first performer got up and recited what was supposed to be an amusing poem about a church mouse. Unfortunately he forgot his words halfway through and had to be prompted loudly, so that the effect was rather spoilt. Under cover of the dark, Slynne took hold of Jackie's hand. She tried gently to move it away but found that, wedged as she was against the wall, there was nothing she could do. During the next item, which was loud and accompanied by a great deal of laughter, Slynne leant across, so that his hot clammy breath wafted against her cheek, and whispered hoarsely, 'Oi luv you!'

Applause broke out and he sat back and joined in loudly. Freed of his restraining grip, Jackie began hastily to rise to her feet, but she had reckoned without the confinement of the chairs created by the row in front and could not even stand fully without first asking them to move. So desperate was she that she was prepared even to attempt that, but a voice behind said crossly, 'Ssh! Sit down.' Her nerve failed.

Slynne did not even notice. As the applause died away and the next trio of performers came on stage, he groped again for her hand, and prepared to resume. 'Oi've allus luved you,' he said. 'Oi think as we oughta get spliced!'

Jackie was rigid. This could not be happening to her. The show went on, and Slynne continued to whisper sweet nothings in her ear, which now felt damp and hot. For the climax of the evening, Norman began to play. It was a spirited little number, with lots of flourishes and twiddly bits, and he kept grinning inanely at everybody as if expecting them to do something The audience was uncertain how to respond. During a pause, a few people clapped uncertainly, but then Norman suddenly launched off again and they stopped, embarrassed.

'So what do ye think then, Jackie?' Slynne panted, oblivious of the music. 'Shall we?'

Jackie swallowed. She felt absolute terror and did not know what to say. Slynne, however, took her silence as assent and quickly leaning across, gripped her hard by both shoulders, and planted a wet, sloppy kiss on her mouth. Jackie's mouth dropped open with shock. It was a mistake, because the next instant his tongue was feeling round her gums. Revolted, no longer caring what anybody thought, she sprang to her feet, thrusting him away and lashing out at the chairs in front in a positive frenzy to escape. 'You revolting little man!' she screamed. 'Get off! Leave me alone!'

Her hand connected sharply with his cheek, and the next second she had somehow vaulted across his knees and was clambering across the other people seated in the row. 'Ow!' said Ken. 'Mind what you're doing with that knee, my girl!'

Jackie did not care. Panting and almost weeping with rage, she finally made it to the gap running down the centre of the chairs and scuttled from the hall. 'Does this mean you don't wan' t' get married then?' came a plaintive voice behind her. She was aware that a stunned silence had fallen in her wake, and felt even more enraged. How dare that repellent little man embarrass her like this! How dare he do that to her?

As she reached the cloakroom and grabbed her coat, she heard a commotion behind her. 'Jackie!' said Father Trumpington's voice.

'Oh, leave me alone!' she shouted, rounding on him. 'I'm fed up with the lot of you!' And she fled from the hall, her heels making an angry staccato on the pavement. She did not stop till she got home, and was rather surprised as she pushed her key in the lock to see a light on in the front room. She wondered vaguely who it could be. Elspeth? But she was supposed to be staying the night at her friend's. A burglar? No, burglars did not put on the lights. She supposed she must just have forgotten to turn it off when she left with Norman earlier.

She pushed open the door and almost fell bodily through it, allowing the tears at long last to spill over on to her cheeks. At the same moment the door to the living room opened and a man stepped into the hall. Half blinded with tears, Jackie looked up, her heart leaping in sudden fear. But the man before her was familiar. He stood tall and dark, dominating the tiny hall, a saturnine expression on his face. 'Malcolm?' she said faintly.

He said nothing, just continued to look at her. Jackie could think of absolutely nothing to do. She remembered with horror all those unopened letters. Letting her coat drop, she slumped on to the floor and burst into noisy, unattractive sobs. It was a perfectly awful ending to a perfectly awful day.

Chapter Thirteen

Jackie did not go to church next morning. She had a difficult time explaining to Malcolm why she had arrived home in such a dishevelled state. She had a difficult time, too, explaining where she had been, and how there came to be a pair of male underpants in the bathroom. He had looked unconvinced when she said she had been to the Christmas party at church, and even more sceptical when she tried to persuade him that the pants were his own, left there two years ago. 'Do you really mean to say,' he asked, 'that they haven't been washed in all that time?'

Jackie attempted an enigmatic smile. 'Well,' she said, 'they remind me of you.'

The underpants, however, were not what Malcolm wanted to talk about. The reason he had come back so unexpectedly, he said, was to get things sorted out. 'I haven't heard from you in months,' he complained, 'I wondered if something was wrong. Even Elspeth hasn't written!' At mention of his daughter, his face darkened, 'She *is* all right, isn't she?' he demanded. 'Where is she?'

'Of course she's all right,' said Jackie hastily. 'She's just staying overnight with a friend, that's all. She often does.'

'Thank God.' Malcolm's face crumpled, and she suddenly realised how frightened he had been. 'I thought maybe you'd gone away when I got here and found the house empty. I didn't know what to think.'

There was a small silence and he suddenly looked up and stared at her critically. Jackie, aware of her mascara running in black rivulets down her cheeks, felt at a distinct disadvantage. But Malcolm seemed not to notice. 'Perhaps it's for the best,' he said pensively, more to himself than to her. 'We do need to talk after all. Maybe it's good she's not here.'

Jackie sniffed and wiped a charcoal tear from the end of her nose with the back of her hand. This, she felt, did not augur well, but she was still trying to think how best to divert his attention from the underpants, so she said nothing. With his next words, however, her blood ran cold. 'Jackie,' he began, 'what I would really like is for you and Elspeth to come out with me to India, and for us to start again. I know it hasn't been easy for you: it hasn't been too good for me either. But I'd like us to be a family again. I miss Elspeth, and for her sake I think we should try and make a go of it. A kid needs both parents.'

Jackie stared at him, goggle-eyed. Somehow, after the events of the evening, she found her brain did not seem to be functioning quite the way it should. She was even uncertain for a moment if she had heard him right, and then the thought occurred to her that she was suffering from some terrible nightmarish delusion, and that nothing that had happened to her over the last few hours was real. She felt an hysterical laugh rise in her throat, but the next second it died. 'You've got to see, Jackie,' Malcolm was saying seriously, 'we can't go on like this any more. We're either married or we're not, but I'm not prepared for us just to go on living apart indefinitely. We've got to get things sorted out.'

With despair she realised that she was not after all suffering from some temporary delusion, and that the man standing before her was all too real. However, she still couldn't understand exactly what he was saying. He seemed to be giving her some kind of ultimatum. India or . . . and then he said it for her. 'If we can't make a go of it, Jackie, then the only thing left is divorce.'

She swallowed. 'No, I don't want that,' she said hoarsely. And it was true. In that one thing alone her mind was absolutely clear. She did not yet want divorce. She was not financially prepared. Also, what would happen to Elspeth? Malcolm had already made it clear he was missing the little girl and wanted her back. If they divorced now, perhaps he would want custody – in India. She froze with horror. She would never agree to that. But it occurred to her that, though the mother was usually given custody, Malcolm could actually make her life very difficult, knowing what he did of her past history. She suspected he would have few qualms about making public her little indiscretions, if he felt it might serve his own ends. She thought rapidly, trying to work out how best to handle the situation. 'Why don't you come back here?' she suggested, playing for time.

Malcolm looked unhappy. 'My life's in India now,' he said. 'I couldn't come back to England.' His face suddenly became animated, 'And besides which, there's this really exciting project I'm working on. We're building a dam. I couldn't leave that now. And it's wonderful out there, Jackie. You've no idea. The atmosphere. The colour. Just give it a chance.'

Malcolm had been twenty-five when they first met; Jackie, twenty-seven. They had made an unlikely couple, even then. He had been the brilliant young scientist all set to go to the top, and she was a secretary in the college where he worked. Even then Jackie had had something of a reputation, but Malcolm had never known anyone like her. He had fallen completely under her spell. And so they had married.

The first three years had been good. Jackie had continued to work at the college, but she had enjoyed her new status as Malcolm's wife and been very much the perfect wife. Eventually, however, she had become bored and had embarked on a rather seedy little affair with a scientific salesman who used to call in at the labs. Malcolm had been devastated. There had been tears and recriminations when it had all come out and Jackie had begged for forgiveness – and Malcolm did forgive her, but he no longer trusted her. There had followed twelve years of uneasy peace, during which time Jackie had continued to tumble in and out of liaisons, and Elspeth had been born.

For Malcolm, Elspeth was the best thing in his whole life. He had wondered once if she was in fact his, but that suspicion had long since been laid to rest because the little girl had his same solemn expression and dark good looks, and her way of reacting to things seemed uncannily like his own. It had almost broken his heart when he had felt compelled to leave, but he had arrived at a point with Jackie where he could no longer stay and hang on to his sanity. She had, he felt, quite literally been driving him mad, and so he had fled. But now, two years on, he felt strong enough to return. Strong enough, in fact, to take Jackie on again, but this time he was determined that it should be on his terms.

He had forgotten quite how obdurate Jackie could be. They argued into the small hours, and then Jackie announced that she was too tired and really had to go to bed. He had retired to the spare room, and had been angry when twenty minutes later she had slid in beside him. But Jackie was very good at capturing and dealing with rogue moods when she wanted and soon they were making love. Truth to tell, he had not needed very much cajoling. He had led a celibate life since he had left Jackie two years before. He had been so angry with her, and so disappointed, but there was still a part of him deep down that loved her, and that wanted nothing more than for her to love him. Easy, then, to persuade himself that he mattered to her, to give himself up to her touch. He had made love like a starving man suddenly presented with food.

When they awoke in the morning it was late – almost lunchtime, in fact – and the sunlight was streaming in through a small chink in the curtains, as if trying vainly to rouse them. Malcolm found Jackie's head cradled against his shoulder, and a deep sense of peace suffused his soul. He had, he felt, in every sense come home, and things were going to be all right; they could work it out. He lay there savouring the soft scent of her perfume – the perfume he had never quite been able to drive from his head – and at that moment she opened her eyes and smiled.

'Good morning,' he said softly.

'Hi,' she breathed back.

'You've missed church,' he said. 'Sorry.' She smiled and nestled closer, and he leant across and gently kissed her head.

The sound of a key turning in the lock downstairs made them both start. Jackie went rigid with sudden fear, but after a second Malcolm laughed. 'It's OK,' he said, 'it'll be Elspeth. Come on, let's go and tell her I'm here.'

He was out of bed and pulling on his pyjamas before Jackie could stop him. He flung open the bedroom door, in the act of buttoning up his pyjama top and there, standing on the landing and looking surprised, was Norman. For perhaps five seconds they all stood there, like some terrible waxwork show, and then Malcolm said, 'Who the hell are you?'

The sound of his voice seemed to release Norman from the spell. He in turn bristled and said, 'What do you mean who the hell am I? Who the hell are you?'

Jackie winced.

'I'm Malcolm,' said Malcolm. And then, because Norman still looked blank, 'Jackie's husband.'

Norman's eyes widened and he took a step back. Jackie thought for one moment that he was going to turn tail and flee, and rather wished he would, but the next instant he appeared to change his mind and instead stood his ground. 'I'm Norman,' he said. 'I'm the church organist.' He said this as if it should somehow have explained everything.

Clutching the sheet, and glancing from one to the other of them, Jackie saw her husband look briefly confused. 'Well, you won't find an organ in here,' he said finally. His face darkened. 'You have your own key, do you?'

Norman nodded dumbly and Malcolm turned and stared at Jackie for a long minute. 'And do I take it,' he inquired, his voice steely, 'that you are also the possessor of the green underpants at this moment lying in *my* bathroom?'

Being the only one of them without any clothes, Jackie felt at a distinct disadvantage as they both now turned and looked at her, as if expecting her to supply some kind of logical answer that would make everything clear and restore peace. Jackie found she was unable to provide it. 'Er, no . . .' she said, her mind working furiously. And then dried up.

'What?' said Malcolm, his voice icily calm, and Jackie realised that he had interpreted her answer as meaning there was someone else as well.

'Oh no,' she said hastily, 'I don't mean that. I'm sure they're yours, Malcolm. And Norman has a key . . .' At this point, unable to think of anything better to do, she paused and batted her eyelashes, hoping to impress upon them both how very noble she was, and then went on, 'because I've been looking after him and cooking his meals while his wife's been in hospital.'

The attempt was wasted. 'How kind!' sneered Malcolm. 'So the fact you're cooking meals for him means he can just walk in whenever he wants, does it? Doesn't have to knock? In fact he can treat this home as his own, which I suppose,' he cast a withering glance at Norman, 'means he has the use of your bedroom as well! What else do you share with him, Jackie? Your hot water bottle? Do you have a joint bank account as well?'

Norman appeared to feel he had to say something. 'No,' he said desperately. 'I didn't know Jackie was still married. At least I knew technically she was still married. But I thought she was separated . . . getting a divorce.'

The look Malcolm turned on him made him start back in fear. 'So that's what she's telling people, is it?' he snarled. And then with a strangled cry of rage he lunged at Norman, who really did turn tail now and bolted like a scared rabbit down the stairs. The sound of the front door slamming after him echoed through the house. 'You bitch!' shouted Malcolm, frustrated of his prey and turning back on Jackie. 'You whore! Just how many people have you slept with since I've been away? Just what kind of lies are you telling everybody?' He raised his hand to hit her, and Jackie screamed and cowered back. Her obvious fear recalled him to himself, and his hand dropped. 'You bitch,' he repeated bitterly, 'you're just not worth it.' He shoved her violently away from him and then turned and rushed into the bathroom, where he threw up noisily down the sink.

So rough was the push that Jackie fell off the bed, banging her nose on the small cupboard that stood at the side. She was as much shocked by this as she would have been if he had actually hit her and, raising her hand to her nose, discovered a small trickle of blood. She stared at it in disbelief, and then abruptly scrambled to her feet and began hastily to pull on clothes. She had, she realised, to do something now, and she had to act quickly. Malcolm, she knew, would never forgive her for this, so she had to make the best of the situation while the chance still remained. Divorce seemed inevitable, but she was determined that he should not get Elspeth. To that end she would use whatever small advantage she had.

Her brain worked quickly. At all costs no one must know that Norman had blundered in and discovered them in bed. No one must know anything about Norman at all, in fact; she could quite easily maintain that Malcolm had come back and that they had had a row. She could say, too, that Malcolm had hit her, as evidence of which she had the bleeding nose. Surely no judge then would give him custody of Elspeth, not if he was known to be violent. But how to ensure that he was known to be violent?

Inspiration came as she pulled on her tights. She needed the independent witness of someone whose word could be trusted. The evidence of a clergyman would be perfect. Jackie knew, however, that she could not possibly phone up Father Trumpington for this. If she did, there was no knowing what might emerge, and besides, she was unsure how he would react. He was already jealous of Malcolm, she knew, and the last thing she wanted was for him to come round and get into a fight with her husband. Jackie thought of possible newspaper headlines with a shudder. No, she must not tell him; but she could tell Antonia. The girl might not be a full priest, but she was in holy orders, and the fact she was a fellow woman, Jackie thought, might well work to her advantage.

Jackie ran her fingers through her hair, staring at her reflection critically in the mirror, and saw with annoyance that the trickle of blood had dried up. She did not flinch. Very deliberately, she picked up the silver-backed hairbrush lying neatly on the dressing-table top and hit herself once, hard, on the nose. The pain was excruciating. For one brief second it was as if a poker had exploded inside her head, and then her nose began to pour with blood. She looked at it with satisfaction, letting it drip on to her top and then, gathering up a handful of tissues, headed for the door. She would phone from the call box on the corner.

Antonia was in the middle of Sunday lunch when Jackie's call came through. 'It's for you,' said Kathleen, handing it to her with an apprehensive air. Jackie had managed to produce a sob.

Antonia listened, her face impassive. 'So where exactly are you now?' she inquired.

'In the telephone box,' burbled Jackie, 'on the corner. I daren't go home. He's a beast. I'm frightened what he'll do.'

'Don't you think you should phone the police?'

But this was the last thing Jackie wanted. 'Oh no,' she said hastily, 'he's not that bad. At least, I mean . . . he is my husband. I don't want him charged or anything.'

'Then what do you want?' asked Antonia patiently.

Jackie thought. 'Well,' she said at last, 'I rather thought you could maybe come here and we could have a talk. I just need a bit of help working out what to do.' She managed to sound quite pathetic, and felt proud of the achievement.

After a moment Antonia said, 'OK, wait there on the corner. I'll be with you in ten minutes.' Then a thought occurred to her. 'I really ought to tell Father Trumpington. Are you sure you wouldn't prefer to talk to him?'

'Oh no,' said Jackie with truly heartfelt sincerity, 'not him. I want to talk to you. I don't want to talk to a man at the moment, but I suppose I don't mind *you* phoning and telling him. If you think you must.'

Antonia put down the phone and looked regretfully at her roast lamb and cauliflower cheese. 'I'm sorry,' she said, 'I've got to go out. Jackie sounds as if she's in trouble.'

'I don't like that woman,' said Kathleen decisively. 'I never feel she's quite honest.'

Antonia phoned Father Trumpington. 'I've just had a call from Jackie Newberg,' she said. 'She sounded pretty upset. Apparently her husband came home unexpectedly last night, and she says he's been knocking her around.'

There was a stunned silence from the other end of the line and then, in a small voice, Father Trumpington said, 'Her husband?'

'Yes. He's been away in India apparently. They've had some differences. He suddenly turned up last night, without warning, and gave her an ultimatum – go back with him to India or divorce. She says they quarrelled, and it ended up this morning with him hitting her.'

Father Trumpington experienced a moment of blinding revelation. He had been in a state of abject misery since the previous night, totally unable to account for Jackie's odd behaviour. Now, however, he thought he began to understand, and with the knowledge his heart soared. Jackie's husband had returned! Of course, that explained why her manner had been so altered towards him. She had not changed. Not deep down. She had simply been frightened that Malcolm might discover what had taken place between them.

It occurred to Father Trumpington to wonder briefly why Malcolm had not accompanied Jackie to the party, but he dismissed that thought. From what Antonia was saying, the man

182

had obviously come back for a reason. He had probably simply not wanted to become involved with people socially till it was all settled. Or maybe he had been tired. There were a hundred and one reasons why he might not have wanted to come, but Jackie had obviously known, and it had been that knowledge that had made her act in such a strange way. With the realisation, Father Trumpington felt jubilant. How brave she was, he thought. She was trying to protect him.

But the next second panic struck. Jackie said they had quarrelled, and that Malcolm had hit her. Obviously he had found out – at least something, even if he did not know it all – and now she had phoned Antonia for help. His brain worked furiously. Did this mean that he himself was about to be exposed? Why had Jackie not phoned him? Was this a good sign, or bad? *Did Malcolm know about them, or not?* And was Jackie still trying to protect him? Would it jeopardise everything if he himself were now to become involved? He bit the tip of his finger in an agony of indecision, and heard Antonia say, 'Do you want to go round?'

'What?' he asked, paralysed.

'I said, do you want to go round? I thought maybe you could have a word with him while I go and see her.'

'Good God!' said Father Trumpington, genuinely shocked. 'I don't think that's a very good idea. I always think with these domestics that you should let people get on with it. I don't think it's going to help him if I turn up. It might be the red rag to the bull.'

There was a silence while Antonia digested this. 'But I thought,' she said at last, 'that we could maybe help them patch it up. It might be easier for them to talk if one of us was there, without things developing into a row. And Jackie has enormous respect for you, I know.'

Father Trumpington felt dangerously cornered. 'No, no, my dear,' he blustered. 'She's phoned you. She obviously wants a woman. We've got to respect that. I really don't think I can do anything to help.' He put down the phone before Antonia could say anything more.

As he stared at the receiver, conflicting emotions warred in his breast. He was at a loss to know how to interpret what had happened, but he felt that things might well be coming to a head. From the sound of it, Jackie, in the not too distant future, would have her freedom, and then . . . what untold delights were in store for him? He felt like singing out aloud the Halleluia chorus from Handel's Messiah, but was restrained by the thought that it might be better for Dorothy not to know what had taken place; he was going to have difficulty enough disguising his excitement as it was.

At that moment, his wife put her head round the door. 'There's someone to see you,' she announced. And then more softly, so as to make sure the someone did not hear, 'He looks in a bit of a state.'

Father Trumpington's face contracted with annoyance. 'Oh, for heaven's sake,' he said, 'it's Sunday! People are so inconsiderate. Do I really have to see him?'

'Yes,' she hissed tartly, 'you do.' And without more ado she threw back the door and ushered the man in.

Father Trumpington saw a man in his mid to late forties, tall, dark, and what might be termed conventionally good-looking. There seemed something oddly familiar about him but, for the life of him, Father Trumpington could not place where he might have seen him before. That he was distressed was obvious, because there was a look on his face of intense pain and his hands, as he sat down, were shaking. 'It's good of you to see me,' he said.

'What's wrong?' said Father Trumpington, curious in spite of himself. 'What's happened?'

The man sat for some moments, his face working. He was clearly finding it almost impossible to speak. At long last he managed, 'It's my wife.' He stopped again and Father Trumpington waited. After a minute he went on, 'I've found out she's having an affair.' And with that he put his head forward on his hands and began to sob.

Father Trumpington regarded him closely. He did not feel any particular sympathy for the man, but there did seem something terribly familiar about him. 'Excuse my asking,' he said, 'but do I know you?'

The man looked up, his face haggard. 'Yes,' he said, 'we've met

. . . a long time ago.' He clenched his lips as his face again contracted in a spasm of grief and then brought out with difficulty, 'My name's Malcolm Newberg . . . my wife's Jackie. She goes to your church.'

Father Trumpington looked at him aghast, his jaw dropping. Of course he looked familiar. He had no recollection of their ever having met, despite what the man said, but he had seen his photograph dozens of times on Jackie's mantelpiece.

'Yes,' said Malcolm bitterly, mistaking his expression, 'you may well look shocked. I was shocked too. My wife, the devout churchgoer!'

Father Trumpington's tongue shrivelled inside his head. He had no idea what to say. All he could think was that his lover's husband was sitting in front of him in his study, and he felt paralysed. Did Malcolm know or not? That was the question that kept hammering through his brain. He knew she was having an affair, that much he had said, but did he know with whom? Father Trumpington began to wonder if at any second he was going to find himself suffering the same fate as Jackie, but on reflection it occurred to him that this was unlikely. Malcolm was clearly deeply distressed and had obviously come looking for help; he would not, Father Trumpington thought, have sought comfort from his wife's lover, even if he was a priest. This thought, however, did not comfort him unduly, because while Malcolm might not yet know, at any moment Dorothy might come back through the door, and if she discovered who it was who was sitting there, and what had happened, she wouldn't need her experience at the bank to put two and two together and come up with a very uncomfortable four.

He looked nervously towards the oaken panels of the study door, but they remained reassuringly shut. 'How do you know this?' he asked carefully, striving to keep his voice low.

'I came back last night,' said Malcolm. Father Trumpington nodded. 'She was out somewhere, so I waited.' Father Trumpington's eyes bulged, this version did not quite accord with his own scenario, but Malcolm appeared not to notice. He twisted his hands together and went on, 'We've had difficulties. Married people do – I expect you've had some yourself. And you may know we've been living apart for a couple of years. But I really wanted us to get back together. That's why I came back. I thought we had a chance.' At this point he stopped again and Father Trumpington had to wait as he struggled to control himself. After a minute he resumed, 'She didn't seem too pleased to see me at first. But we did make it up, and eventually we went to bed.' Father Trumpington looked at him with real jealousy. He had often fantasised about waking up beside Jackie in her bed, but it was a pleasure that had so far been denied him. 'This morning,' Malcolm continued, 'this morning . . . we woke up . . . There was someone coming through the front door . . . This bloke walked in . . .'

Father Trumpington had been staring at him, wondering if there was any possible explanation he could offer that would protect him from being defrocked if he were to attack Malcolm now, when the words suddenly seeped through to his brain. 'I beg your pardon?' he said incredulously. 'A man?'

'Yes, a tall bloke. He said his name was Norman. Had his own key and everything.' And then Malcolm dropped his bombshell, 'He said he was your church organist.'

Malcolm did not notice the effect his words were having, but Father Trumpington had gone pale and his breath was coming in short, shallow gasps. 'The organist?' he repeated, in shocked tones.

'Yes. He made some pathetic comment about not knowing Jackie was still married.'

He was going on, but Father Trumpington had ceased to listen. The organist . . . Jackie was having an affair with Norman! It was beyond belief. He wanted to shout, 'No, you've got it wrong, it's me she's having an affair with,' but he realised how stupid that would sound.

'I say,' said Malcolm suddenly, 'I'm terribly sorry. I hadn't realised . . . this must be an awful shock for you too, going on in your church!'

Father Trumpington looked at him speechlessly. He tried to say something, but found he could not.

Malcolm bit his lip. 'I'm sorry,' he said, 'I didn't mean to bring you all this trouble. I just thought you were someone I could talk to, and that you might be able to help.'

As if from a great distance, Father Trumpington dragged his thoughts back and discovered, somewhat to his surprise, that he still knew how to use his tongue. 'Help?' he asked hoarsely.

'Yes,' said Malcolm. 'There's no way I can stop here now. I couldn't. Not after that. I just want to go back to India. But I've got to arrange things first. I thought I'd go and see a solicitor tomorrow and start things moving for a divorce . . . But it's Elspeth.'

'Elspeth?' repeated Father Trumpington. He had remembered how to speak, but he seemed to be having the most enormous difficulty concentrating.

'Yes,' said Malcolm. 'I'm going to have to leave her here with Jackie – for the time being, at any rate. I can't simply whisk her out of the country, but I'm just so worried about her. I'm worried about the influence Jackie's having on her. I will try and get custody, of course, but meantime,' he looked at Father Trumpington appealingly, 'can I ask a favour? Please, can you keep an eye on her?'

Dazed, Father Trumpington heard himself gurgle inarticulately, which Malcolm took as assent. He rose to his feet. 'He's a real swine, that organist,' he confided. 'He's married too, isn't he? Jackie said his wife was in hospital. Can you imagine what kind of a bastard would do that?'

'His wife's just had a baby,' said Father Trumpington tonelessly.

'Has she? Poor woman. The swine! I wouldn't have him in my church.'

Father Trumpington nodded, here at least was one thing on which they could agree. 'No,' he said.

At the front door Malcolm paused. 'I say,' he said, 'thanks for being so understanding. You've been a real help. I was really knocked for six when I found out what Jackie had been up to. And that organist chap! I could have killed him! He ran away, do you know that? Mind you, I wasn't much better; I was sick.'

There was a small sound behind them in the hall, and Father Trumpington turned to see Dorothy standing there, a dishcloth in her hand.

'Thank you anyway,' said Malcolm again. 'I'll be in touch.' And with that he was gone.

An eerie silence descended on the hall. 'You stupid old fool!' said Dorothy witheringly.

'What do you mean?' asked Father Trumpington.

She was remorseless. 'You,' she said. 'Thought she was in love with you, didn't you? An old goat like you. Well, maybe you've learnt some sense at last!' And then she sniggered. 'But Jackie and Norman – he did mean Norman, didn't he? Who'd have imagined it! I would have thought he was a bit too drippy for that.'

Father Trumpington looked at her and then, utterly defeated, he turned and staggered back into the sanctuary of his study. He felt as if he had aged. It was all too much to take in. His fragile bubble of fantastic joy had been exploded. He needed to hide away now and lick his wounds; he needed to see what was left. Behind him, as he shut the door, he heard Dorothy laugh.

Chapter Fourteen

Antonia found Jackie waiting for her, as she had promised, on the corner by the phone box outside the church. It was a grey day, with a fine drizzle just beginning to fall, and in the quiet of the afternoon there was no one about. From a distance Jackie had achieved the rare feat of looking forlorn, but as she came closer Antonia saw that this was largely the effect of cold, for Jackie, wishing to reinforce the impression that she had fled in haste, had put on only a thin jacket. She was beginning to regret this because twenty minutes standing waiting in the freezing damp had produced a violent fit of shivering that she was totally unable to control.

As she came to a halt in front of her, Antonia saw that she had a blood-stained tissue clamped to her nose. As far as she could make out, the bleeding appeared to have stopped but a trickle that Jackie had been careful not to wipe away still trailed from her right nostril. Apart from that she looked perfectly normal. There were a couple of spots of blood on her sweater, and her nose was rather pink, it was true, but in all other respects she appeared fine.

'Oh, Antonia,' snivelled Jackie, 'thank you so much for coming.'

The curate regarded her drily. In the course of her work she had often had to deal with battered women. One of her placements at college had been at a women's refuge, and Jackie, to her eyes, did not in the flesh present a very convincing picture of abused womanhood. Jackie obviously divined what was passing through her mind because, as if on cue, she said, 'He was terrible. A beast! I had to run away . . . I don't know what would have happened if I'd stayed.'

'So what did happen exactly?' asked Antonia. She dismounted carefully from her bike and propped it against the wall, and then turned and regarded Jackie evenly.

'Well, I've already told you,' said Jackie with a touch of

irritation. 'He came back last night and *demanded* that I go back with him to India. And when I refused, we quarrelled. This morning he was fearfully angry, and when I tried to talk to him, he hit me!' At this point she dissolved into tears and blew her nose loudly. She was rewarded by a tiny circle of pink on the tissue. 'See,' she said triumphantly, 'it's still bleeding! He's a monster!'

Overhead a crow screamed. It sounded disconcertingly like laughter, and Jackie looked at it with dislike.

'Well,' said Antonia eventually, 'if you don't want to make a complaint to the police, what do you want? Would you like me to come back with you to collect some clothes?'

Jackie looked puzzled. 'Clothes?' she said. 'Why should I want clothes?'

'Well, if you feel he's that dangerous,' said Antonia patiently, 'presumably you don't want to go back while he's still there. Or are you hoping that if I come along you might be able to talk and sort things out?'

Jackie looked at her as if she was mad. 'Oh, he's not dangerous,' she said, 'he just got a bit carried away. I'm not frightened to go back.'

'Then you'd like me to come with you so that we can all talk?'

'Oh no!' Jackie looked completely stunned. 'That wouldn't do at all. I'll go back in a while, but I don't want to talk to Malcolm. There isn't really anything left to say.'

In spite of her every intention to be sympathetic, faced by Jackie's apparent absence of concern or fear, Antonia felt her own irritation rising. She felt she was being used and, quite apart from that, she was hungry. She rather resented having had to leave her roast lamb. 'I really don't understand,' she said with some asperity. 'You're not frightened of your husband. You intend to go back in a minute but you don't want to talk to him. So exactly why am I here?'

At that moment Gudrun happened to glance through the window of her front room. She was just getting ready to go up to the hospital and, to her surprise, Norman had offered to drive her. She took this to be a good sign, although she was feeling a little puzzled that he seemed to have come back from church in such a peculiar state. She had very tentatively tried to ask him if he had seen Jackie, wondering if that was the reason for his odd mood. He had at first refused to answer her and then, when she had persisted, had said brusquely that Jackie had not been there. Gudrun felt that this was odd, but with that she had had to content herself, and only seconds after this exchange he had offered to drive her up to the hospital.

She was, however, uneasy and now, as she shrugged on her coat, her eyes fixed upon Jackie talking earnestly to Antonia, and clutching something that looked bloody to her face, it struck Gudrun just how strange the last twenty-four hours had been. It was borne in upon her that Jackie looked angry, and that she appeared to be explaining something at great length and with great vehemence. Behind her there was a small sound as Norman came into the room. 'You ready yet?' he inquired tonelessly.

Gudrun did not answer and he glanced questioningly in the direction she was staring across the street. His eyes fell immediately on Jackie and, unable to help himself, he staggered back. It appeared to Norman, as his disordered brain tried to take in the full import of the scene, that Jackie was looking over towards the house. That she was angry was obvious and she seemed, he thought, to be pointing in the direction of their front room – to be pointing, in fact, straight at him.

Actually, at that precise moment Jackie was insisting vehemently, 'I must go back. It's my home!' And to reinforce the point she was waving a determined hand in the direction of her own house. But to Norman it looked as if she was making some terrible accusation against him and, with a feeling of dread, he imagined that at any moment he was about to be exposed. He took another faltering step back, his heart lurching, and at the same time tried to press himself up against the wall in a vain attempt to hide. So distraught was he, that it did not occur to him that Jackie would be hard pressed to explain how he happened to have a key. The only thing he could come up with to account for her presence across the road was that, in order to disguise her activities from her husband, she was about to accuse him of being some kind of sexual pervert who terrorised women in their own homes.

'Whatever's the matter?' asked Gudrun, at last turning round and taking in the sight of her husband cowering up against the wall. Her face darkened. 'Norman,' she said ominously, 'what have you done?'

Norman swallowed. 'Nothing!' he said, a shade too quickly. 'I just thought we ought to go.' He tried to laugh casually but succeeded in producing only a small bleat and she looked at him narrowly.

'She looks cross,' she remarked, turning back and surveying Jackie. 'Don't you think so, Norman?'

'Who? What? Oh, Jackie!' Norman tried to pretend that that was the first time he had caught sight of her but knew, with a sinking heart, that it was no good. 'It wasn't me,' he said defensively.

Gudrun spun round and glared at him. 'What wasn't you?' she demanded.

Norman quailed. 'Whatever's made her cross.'

This response appeared to please Gudrun. She took a long, hard look at him and then, unexpectedly, smiled. 'Perhaps you're right,' she said consideringly. 'We should go.' And she swept past him, heading for the kitchen and the door that would take them out the back way through the garden.

Jackie meanwhile had finally managed to convince Antonia that she did not need alternative accommodation and that she did not wish her to act as mediator. This had not proved very easy because Antonia, having been summoned out, seemed determined to force on her all the help she could. Jackie, however, had been adamant, and before her obvious anger Antonia had eventually given way. When Jackie did finally manage to tear herself away, the shadows were lengthening and she discovered she felt absolutely exhausted, so that it was with real rage that she directed her footsteps home. When she got there she found a surprise awaited her. The house was totally empty, its windows staring like sightless eyes on to the empty street. 'Malcolm!' she called tentatively, pushing open the front door. No answer. 'Elspeth!' Silence. Feeling relief that she was at least going to be spared another angry confrontation with her husband, she pushed her way into the kitchen – and discovered, on the table, a note. 'You bitch!' it ran. 'It really is over now. I'm going to see my solicitor in the morning. Don't expect a penny from me in the future. You're on your own! Malcolm.'

In another part of the city things, though equally devious, were far less fraught. Alan Gunningham was speaking to Professor George Bullen on the phone. 'Yes, George,' he was saying, 'the Bishop called him in. Gave him a hard time, I believe, and all because he's on the square.'

'Doesn't like us, does he?'

'You could say that. I'm told if they still went in for public burnings, the Bishop would have Freemasons at the top of the list, along with witches and heretics.'

Professor Bullen tutted. 'Such closed minds,' he said gently.

'Yes,' agreed Alan. 'The trouble is he's seen the photograph of Dick in the local rag and he's taken it as hard evidence. Threatened him, I believe. Said he had to give up Freemasonry or he was out.'

Professor Bullen, who knew the Bishop, expressed surprise that he could threaten anyone, but Alan went on, 'Oh no, not himself. He's got some sort of hatchet man apparently, a real hard-liner. Calls himself his chaplain, but he does all the dirty work. Word has it on the grapevine that he absolutely hates Masons. In fact I hear he's writing a book about us or something.'

Professor Bullen laughed gently. 'Perhaps we should give him some help,' he suggested.

But Alan would have none of this. 'Look here, George,' he expostulated, 'this is no laughing matter. This chap could cause a lot of trouble. He's ambitious and he's got connections – you know the sort of thing. I've heard about him before, and it sounds very much like he wants Dick out. The Bishop's putty in his hands.'

There was a silence and then Professor Bullen said, 'I see. The forces of bigotry are lining up against us, are they? You feel we ought to do something actively to support Dick?'

'Yes, I do. It's not going to help any of us if Dick gets thrown out for being one of the Brotherhood. Besides which, it's preposterous. There's nothing wrong with Freemasonry. A lot of churchmen are Masons. Why, at the Lodge the other week we had eight priests – and a lot of us are practising Christians.'

Professor Bullen, who had no faith himself, grunted. He had long since come to the conclusion that man had to work out his own destiny, and the petty wrangling of Christians, or indeed any religious group, seemed to him absurd. Still, he took Alan's point; he was not prepared to allow some fundamentalist bigot of the worst kind to bring Freemasonry into disrepute. 'So what do you suggest we do?' he asked mildly.

This was what Alan had been working towards. 'Well,' he said, 'the Archdeacon is on the square, and so is Canon Johns. I thought maybe we could have a word with them, they've both got clout. And I was wondering, perhaps some nice quiet little appointment could be found for this chaplain chappie elsewhere. You know, something more suited to his talents – youth worker in the Gorbals or something.'

'You really do dislike him, don't you?'

'It's not personal,' Alan assured him, 'I just think he could do a lot of harm, and it could be in all our interests to get him out of the way. I know Dick would appreciate it.'

'Hmm, yes.' The continued reference to Father Trumpington, however, brought another matter to Professor Bullen's mind. 'Talking of Dick,' he said abruptly, 'how is he, apart from this? How's that new curate of his shaping up?'

Alan snorted; this was another subject that raised his ire. 'She's being a real pain in the arse, if you ask me,' he confided. 'She's winding poor Dick in circles with all the trouble she's causing. She's someone else who ought to go!'

'What sort of trouble?' inquired Professor Bullen, genuinely interested. He had rather thought it was a good thing when he had first heard 'old Dickie' was going to get a woman curate, especially when she turned out to be pretty.

'Oh, you know,' said Alan obscurely, 'praying with people. Encouraging all this happy clappy nonsense.'

Professor Bullen did not know. 'Good heavens,' he said. 'Do you mean you've got guitars in St Godric's?'

'No, thank God,' said Alan ominously, 'not yet. But if she's allowed to go on unchecked, who knows what sort of mass insanity we might end up with. She even brought some down-

and-outs into church the other day. I tell you, Dick is having a hard time keeping her in line.'

This was news to Professor Bullen. Up until this conversation with Alan he had rather thought that things were going well at St Godric's. It had been he who had been one of the prime movers in getting the Masonic grant for the organ and, with the arrival of the new organist, he had been among that group who expected to hear great things. He still expected to hear great things – broadcast recitals on Radio 4, perhaps even a *Songs of Praise* . . . which reminded him, he had a friend at the BBC. An evangelical curate who favoured guitars did not sound at all the thing. 'I see,' he said. 'Sounds like Dick needs a bit of help all round.'

'You could say that.'

Professor Bullen swallowed the bait. 'She's coming to do our Christmas service up at St Thomas's this year,' he said reflectively. 'From what you're saying, I'm not going to enjoy it very much.'

'No, shouldn't think you will,' agreed Alan. 'It might even make you feel moved to complain to the Bishop.'

They sniggered together like two naughty schoolboys and then Professor Bullen said abruptly. 'Good to talk to you, Alan. We must do lunch soon. Leave things with me.' And he rang off.

By four o'clock in the afternoon Father Trumpington was feeling murderous with rage. He had passed from shock to depression to hate, and now all that remained was a small core of icy and irrational fury. Not against Jackie – he could not yet think about her – but against Norman. Norman had been having an affair with Jackie. It made his blood run cold. The snake! That viper he had taken to his bosom! He felt sick when he thought of him touching her. Malcolm had even said that Norman had his own key. Father Trumpington had never had a key, and his jealousy almost choked him as he realised what that must mean. Had they laughed at him? he wondered. Was he a joke? A cover to disguise their own little affair? Had Norman even planned it this way? And in his thoughts the organist was transformed from the rather good-natured fellow Father Trumpington had always thought him into a terrible Bluebeard-type character, who went about his exploits with low animal cunning, leaving a trail of seduction in his wake.

Worst of all, Dorothy's laughter echoed in his brain until he could stand it no more. He wanted revenge. Hardly knowing what he was doing – all thoughts of the evening service having long since been blown from his mind – he put on his coat as the first shadows of night began to draw on, and went out into the gloom. Dorothy heard the front door slam, but when she rushed out of the kitchen where she had been busy making biscuits in preparation for Christmas, she was greeted only by the mocking darkness of the hall. 'Oh, the fool!' she said. 'He's going to ruin us all.' She wondered briefly if she should run after him, but a little voice inside her head told her it would be no use and, besides, she felt so angry herself that a part of her now wanted him to do something stupid. Let the whole world know what a sanctimonious idiot he was, she thought viciously. Let Amelia know! And she felt so overcome that she slumped down on the bottom tread of the stairs and burst into tears.

Father Trumpington walked quickly. His footsteps took him in the direction of the church but, hardly knowing what he did, he passed beyond there to the little house at the back – the house where Norman and Gudrun lived. He had no fixed plan in his mind, he simply wanted to see Norman now. He had to! In this, however, he was frustrated, because when he got there the house was dark and there was an empty feel about it. Still without any clear intention of what he was going to do, he sat down on the doorstep to wait.

The first sight that greeted Norman and Gudrun when they finally returned from the hospital was what appeared to be Father Trumpington's cossack hat perched on their front gate. Norman got out of the car, pulled up short, and peered into the gloom. At the same moment Father Trumpington staggered to his feet, like some terrible spectre rising from the grave, and Gudrun, who had just come round the side of the car, uttered a shriek.

'My goodness! You startled me,' she said, recoiling and clasping her throat. And then, uncertainly, 'Father Trumpington?'

Father Trumpington ignored her. 'You bastard!' he said, staring straight at Norman.

Norman gazed back at him in total bewilderment. Like Gudrun, it had taken him a second to recover from Father Trumpington's rather startling appearance and now, try as he might, he could not make sense of the words. 'Pardon?' he faltered.

'You bastard!' repeated Father Trumpington in choked tones. He appeared to be having difficulty expressing himself.

Gudrun, with rather more presence of mind than her husband, guessed something of what had happened. At least, she guessed that Father Trumpington had found out about the affair, and rather imagined that he had stormed round now in righteous anger to demand Norman's repentance and expel him from the church.

'Norman,' Gudrun hissed, groping for her husband's hand, 'he knows.'

Her intervention seemed to release Father Trumpington's tongue. 'Yes, that's right,' he snarled, 'he knows! *I know*! Thought your little game was safe, did you? You swine!' This last was uttered in tones of loathing and Norman could only stare at him in terror. Who had told him? he wondered. Jackie, or her husband? His mind raced. If it was indeed Jackie, and her presence across the street that afternoon might suggest that, what had she been driven to say? Even now, with some last shreds of chivalry, Norman wanted to protect her, but hard on that impulse came the realisation that all his worst fears seemed to be coming true. What was this revelation going to mean for him? How would Gudrun react?

'N-no,' he stammered, wondering if it was still not too late to deny everything. 'It's not true. It's a mistake.'

It was possibly the worst thing he could have said. Father Trumpington knew exactly what had happened and Norman's words simply fanned the flames of his already burning rage. 'What do you mean?' he shouted. 'Do you deny it?' He took a flying leap forward but quick as lightning Gudrun interposed herself between them.

'Stop!' she commanded. 'You can't do this.'

Father Trumpington found himself momentarily checked. 'I suppose you don't know,' he said bitterly, taking account of her for the first time. 'You don't know what this swine's been up to.'

'Yes, I do,' said Gudrun coolly.

Father Trumpington goggled at her. 'What?' he said.

'That's right,' said Gudrun. 'I know *everything.*'

'You can't!' said Father Trumpington.

Norman meanwhile cowered back. He hardly knew which was worse, Malcolm or Father Trumpington, but he discovered he felt petrified of them both. He could not understand why Father Trumpington was so angry. Surely he should not be so upset by the discovery of an affair between two of his congregation, even if one of those involved was his organist.

'Look, I'm sorry,' he said. 'I don't understand all this. I didn't know she was still married. I thought they were separated – at least, that's what she told me. How was I to know her husband was going to turn up?'

At his side, Gudrun went ominously still. 'What do you mean? Whose husband?' she demanded.

'I thought you knew everything!' said Father Trumpington snidely.

Gudrun ignored him. 'Norman,' she insisted, 'what are you talking about?'

Norman could hardly bring himself to look her in the eye. 'Jackie,' he mumbled. 'I'm sorry. I went round there after church this morning. I let myself in, like I always do, only this time he was there. We had a row. He was so angry, I just ran.'

Gudrun looked as if she could hardly believe her ears. 'You went round this morning?' she repeated. Norman nodded miserably, and she glared at him. 'So that's why she was there?' she said fiercely, waving a hand accusingly towards the street corner.

'Yes . . . no . . . I don't know,' said Norman. 'I guess so.'

'And you thought she was telling Antonia what had happened?'

Norman nodded his head miserably. 'I guess she was,' he agreed.

'And it's all right for you to have an affair when you're married, but not for her?'

Throughout this exchange Father Trumpington had been standing frozen with his hand upraised in the air, as if searching for a likely candidate to hit, but now he suddenly jerked into life. Their words had served only to make the whole situation more burningly real to him. *He* had been cuckolded, he thought bitterly, not Malcolm. 'How could you do it?' he blurted out. 'She's my lover, not yours.'

Norman had been staring miserably at Gudrun, but at these words his head jerked round and his jaw dropped. 'I beg your pardon?' he said.

Father Trumpington was beyond caring. 'Jackie,' he snarled. 'We were going to go away together, till you stepped in and spoilt it all.'

And with that he thrust Gudrun aside from the path and lunged again at Norman, catching him by the throat. Gudrun seemed stunned. She did nothing this time, just stood back and stared in disbelief. Released from all constraint, Father Trumpington gave a wild scream and began to hit Norman frenziedly. For a second the organist stood his ground, trying to fend the priest off, then he squirmed and tried to break free. 'Mind my hands!' he shouted.

'Mind your hands! I'll break every bloody finger you've got!' yelled Father Trumpington.

And then they both fell on each other, scuffling and shoving, and trying vainly to get a grip on each other's coats. It ended when Norman, seizing his chance, suddenly sprang back and raised his fist. He brought it crashing down on Father Trumpington's eye. The priest staggered, and then fell back on to a dustbin beside the front door. It rocked, and then keeled slowly over, and there was a terrible smell as rubbish cascaded down the path. Father Trumpington thrust out a hand to save himself, but it was too late. With a strangled cry he fell heavily and ended up sitting in the flowerbed with a banana skin on his head.

Norman stood back panting. 'You mean you've been seeing her too?' he demanded.

Father Trumpington nodded dumbly. He had no energy for more.

'She said I was the only one!' said Norman, in tones of outrage.

Father Trumpington glared at him.

'You've both been made to look fools,' said Gudrun.

At that moment the church bell began to toll. 'Evensong!' gasped Father Trumpington, horrified. He staggered to his feet, panting for breath and gripping his side.

'Oh my God,' said Norman.

'Help me,' said Father Trumpington. 'Everyone'll be arriving in a minute.'

Gudrun removed the banana skin from his head and Norman brushed him down. 'We'll get there,' he said. 'I just need my music.' He shot into the house and reappeared a moment later carrying a bulging case of music. 'I shoved in everything,' he panted. 'I can't think straight. I don't know what I need.'

'You'd better pull yourself together,' said Father Trumpington grimly. He winced as he tried to move, and then reached out a hand and grasped Norman's shoulder for support. The organist squirmed under his touch, but he allowed himself to be used, and together they began to limp slowly towards the church. Norman had a tear in his jacket, and as he walked he was awkwardly cradling his hand. Gudrun heard him say, 'My knuckles! They're raw, I'll never be able to play.'

Father Trumpington's right eye looked so swollen it was almost closed and he was obviously having difficulty standing up straight, but as they disappeared into the twilight, she heard his voice float back, 'You'd bloody better!'

Chapter Fifteen

The music that evening was not good, and Father Trumpington insisted they turn off half the lights in the church and instead use candles, which, he said, would be a foretaste of Christmas, a living symbol that they were going to pass from darkness into light. 'Dang silly!' muttered Slynne, who was entrusted with the task of digging out the cobwebby holders left over from the carol service last year, and then finding enough candles to go round. On the whole, however, even he was not displeased. He had avoided coming to church earlier because of a deep sense of shame engendered by the events of the night before. His dream coat had already been consigned to the bin, along with muttered imprecations that it should 'burn in 'ell' for all he cared. Now he lived in mortal dread that he would see Jackie, conscious that he had made a fool of himself. But Slynne was no coward, and after eight hours of feeling thoroughly miserable, he was bristling with raw courage to face the world – especially Gloria Sunnington, whose insults after Jackie had rushed out, had stung him to the quick.

Antonia thought Father Trumpington did not look quite himself, but it was by now so dark that she could not see, and he ordered her to lead the service in such a peremptory voice that she did not dare inquire if he was all right. She led the service clutching a half-burnt candle in one hand and a prayer book that she could not see in the other, praying that she would not go wrong, while Father Trumpington himself cowered in the back stalls, hoping that no one would see his painfully swelling eye. Afterwards he did not come down to the porch as he was accustomed to do, to shake hands and inquire after people's health, but instead scuttled off to the vestry, curtly ordering Antonia to take his place.

'Bit gloomy tonight,' said Dave, sauntering casually down the aisle as he made his way out. He gave his books to Gloria, who was looking particularly sour, with a seraphic smile. 'An' may I say how very nice ye're lookin'!' Gloria glared at him suspiciously and, oblivious, Dave went on, 'Mind you, it's difficult tae see.'

'Thank you,' said Gloria stiffly, and turned away.

In the vestry Father Trumpington was tearing off his robes as fast as he could, desperate to get away before Alan should come in with the collection, ready to enter it in the book. He did not feel up to a conversation with Alan who, unlike ninety per cent of the congregation, had exceptionally good eyesight. All he wanted to do was get back home and think. He discovered that his confrontation with Norman had not in any way eased his pain but had, quite irrationally, encouraged him to hope. After months spent trailing round after Jackie, he found he could not yet relinquish the dream. Norman he despised as spineless, and Malcolm he categorised as a fool, but he felt that if he himself were now to act with determination, he might still pull it off. He was at a loss to know why Jackie should have consorted with Norman, but he felt that there were perhaps things here he did not understand, and he was ready to forgive. After all, Jackie, he reminded himself, had been lonely. She had taken it upon herself to care for Norman while his wife was in hospital. If that spineless seducer had taken advantage of her good nature . . . well, he could easily understand what had happened. It was all Norman's fault; he ought to be castrated!

From the shadows of the choir stalls his eyes had raked the congregation back and forth, searching in vain for Jackie. He wanted to go round to her house – if he could only see her and they could talk, then it would all be straightened out. He had never told her, he realised, that his intentions towards her were honourable, and it occurred to him that maybe it had been that that had driven her into Norman's arms. Yet when it came to it, he could not quite summon up the courage to go down that path. He still had a lurking fear that Malcolm, despite what he had said earlier about never wanting to see his wife again, might be there at the house and might realise what had happened. So instead he went home, scuttling furtively along the shadowed edges of the pavements so that no one should see him, till he made it to his front door. And when he pushed it open, there was Dorothy waiting for him.

* * *

202

Like Father Trumpington, Gudrun was a prey to confusion, indescribably angry with Norman that he had not told her what had happened earlier, and amazed by the revelation that Father Trumpington was also involved with Jackie. She had gone into the house, her brain reeling, and then lain on the bed, fully clothed, trying to make sense of what she had just witnessed. Try as she might, however, she could not come to a point where everything seemed all right. The central axis of her world had been rocked, and she could not pull it back on course.

Norman found her there two hours later. 'I'm sorry,' he mumbled, coming and sitting on the edge of the bed. She turned on him limpid eyes; two dark, fathomless pools, at the bottom of which lurked horror.

'Did you know?' she asked.

He shook his head. 'No, not at all . . . I thought she loved me.'

There was a painful silence. 'And you?' asked Gudrun. 'Did you love her?'

Norman bit his lip and looked down at his knees. 'I don't know,' he said. 'I thought I did. It was madness. She was so different . . . I just wanted a change.'

'You certainly got that,' said Gudrun bitterly.

Her anger washed over him. 'I didn't know about that old goat,' he said, 'honestly. I can't really take it all in.'

She reached out a tentative hand and laid it on his knee, and after a second he covered it with his own. The knuckles were scraped raw and there was a swelling over his thumb. 'Your poor hand,' she said, and then, 'Was it all right? Could you play tonight?'

'Not very well.'

She moved slightly and he lay down beside her on the bed. 'I'm so sorry,' he said again. 'I feel I've been out of my mind. I've really let you down.' She said nothing and after a second he said, 'Can you ever forgive me?' He turned and looked at her, but her eyes were fixed on the ceiling.

At last she said, 'I don't know. I'm just not sure any more. I thought I could, but tonight . . . Everything went mad. He was so angry. I can't make sense of anything.'

'But there's Otto,' he said. He said it plaintively, as if somehow Otto was a lifeline.

'Yes,' she agreed.

'There's still hope.' Norman did not know what to do. He clutched her hand, as if trying to will determination and life back into her, but she remained unresponsive and at last he said, 'Why don't you go and see Antonia?' Norman actually disliked Antonia intensely. She made him feel uncomfortable. But somewhere, in the deep recesses of his brain, he understood that she had helped his wife. He had no idea what Gudrun had told her – he rather imagined it was everything, and that in itself made him uneasy – but he knew that with Antonia, Gudrun had grown more calm, and even he himself somehow felt, when she was around, that things made sense. They did not always make the kind of sense he wanted, but he somehow felt it was right. 'Go and see her,' he urged.

At last she looked at him. 'Do you think I should? Are you sure you won't mind?'

He grimaced. 'It seems it's a bit late for that. No, I'd like you to see her. I want to get this sorted. And I don't want you hurt.'

The next day Gudrun went round to see Antonia. 'I've got to talk to you,' she said timidly.

Antonia laughed. 'Oh dear, that sounds serious,' she said.

Gudrun, however, did not smile. 'It is serious.' She sat carefully down on Kathleen's overstuffed sofa and nervously twisted her hands.

Antonia regarded her anxiously. 'Whatever is it?' she asked. 'Is it Otto? Has something happened?' Gudrun shook her head. 'Has something happened with Norman?'

Gudrun could take no more, she burst into tears. 'Yes . . . no,' she began. 'Last night . . .' And with that she poured out the whole tale of Father Trumpington's attack on her husband.

Antonia's jaw dropped. 'Do you really mean,' she asked incredulously, when she could get a word in, 'that Father Trumpington has been having an affair with Jackie?'

Gudrun nodded.

'But that's impossible!'

'No it isn't,' said Gudrun miserably. 'Think about it. I've been doing little else all night. He's always following round after her and going to her house – he even does her garden for her. And he takes her to his choir. We've all been thinking it was pastoral concern. I overheard Gloria Sunnington saying the other day how good he was, but all the time he's been chasing round after her. He's been besotted. We just none of us knew.' She shuddered. 'But he was so jealous last night. I thought he was going to kill Norman.'

'Jackie's husband came back on Saturday,' said Antonia slowly.

'Yes, I know, that's how Dick found out. Malcolm went to see him.'

'Did he?' Antonia's brain was racing. Jackie had called upon her, and Malcolm had been to see Father Trumpington. She felt puzzled. Did that mean Jackie knew that Malcolm had been to see the priest and, if so, had she been afraid of the effect the news would have upon him? Or was she playing some deeper game altogether? Did she even know yet that Father Trumpington knew?

She put the question to Gudrun, but Gudrun shook her head. 'I don't know,' she said. 'I don't know if Jackie knows or not. And if she does, I don't know what she'll do.'

'Well, at the very least,' said Antonia reflectively, 'she must know now that her marriage is over, and I think she's a rather dangerous lady.'

'What are you suggesting?'

Antonia shrugged. 'I don't know, but I wouldn't put anything past Jackie. She's saying Malcolm hit her.'

Gudrun looked shocked. 'No,' she said decisively, 'Norman said Malcolm was really angry with him, but he didn't seem at all angry with Jackie. Just upset. Norman said it was Jackie who seemed angry. He heard her shouting as he ran down the stairs, but he didn't say she sounded afraid. He said she sounded cross. I don't believe he'd have hit her.'

'But that's what she's alleging.'

They gazed at each other, and Gudrun said quietly, 'Why did he do it, Antonia? Why has Dick had an affair? How could he?' All the turmoil that she had been experiencing throughout the night came through her voice and Antonia looked at her narrowly. Gudrun went on, 'How could a priest act like that?'

It was a cry for help, Antonia knew. 'I don't know,' she said gently, taking Gudrun's hand. 'He's just been weak, I guess. Or maybe he's lost faith. I've often felt he doesn't really believe.'

'Do you think so?' said Gudrun eagerly, as if that explained everything. 'But if that's so, he shouldn't be a priest at all.'

Antonia shrugged. 'I suspect there are quite a few priests like Father Trumpington around. But if it upsets and hurts us, think what it does to God. It's his church.'

'You mean God doesn't want this?'

'Of course he doesn't.'

Something like relief seemed to sweep over Gudrun. 'He is a very bad priest!' she announced.

The priest in question was at that moment on his way to see Jackie. He had had an unpleasant interview with Dorothy the night before. She had told him in no uncertain terms that she was not going to stand it for much longer, and he had retorted bitterly, 'Good!' and that the sooner she went the better. But Father Trumpington's mouse of a wife had long since disappeared. She snapped back at him that it would not be her who was going, but him. Father Trumpington was astounded, and felt moved to point out to her that they were residing in a clergy house. She dismissed this. 'Not this mausoleum,' she announced. 'You can keep this dump and welcome. I'm talking about the cottages. You leave me, and I take them, along with everything else we've got. I'll divorce you for adultery – and I'll name that slut too!' Father Trumpington was shocked, but there was no reasoning with her, and finally she delivered herself of an ultimatum. 'You stop seeing her now,' she said, 'or I'll tell the PCC. I'll ruin you!'

Father Trumpington had not told her about his encounter with Norman, but it occurred to him that after that fracas her threat might well be redundant. 'And how did you get that eye?' she had asked him scornfully at that point, no trace of sympathy in her voice. He had mumbled something unintelligible and Dorothy had grunted, 'Well, whoever it was, I wish he'd killed you!'

Father Trumpington was not, however, thinking of Dorothy as he turned into the road where Jackie lived. The street looked quiet, he thought, staring up and down and scenting it like a wild animal on the look-out for danger. From the corner he could see

Jackie's house and he peered at it closely. He could see her car outside, and he could see the curtains of the lounge pulled close – like a sign, he thought, telling everyone to keep away – but apart from that there was no sign of anything untoward. Certainly no sign of Malcolm. Breathing a sigh of relief, he began to walk as fast as he could, without actually breaking into a run, towards the front door, hoping against hope that no one would see. He rang the bell and stood waiting, chaffing for her to come and answer the door so that he might get safely inside. All around, the lace curtains of the other houses stared at him blankly, and he imagined faces peering at him – all, no doubt, wondering what the vicar was up to. All, no doubt, ready to go and whisper the news to Dorothy!

It seemed an age before he heard a slight movement from the hall and then there was a rattle as the chain was put on. Seconds later the door was drawn back two inches, and Jackie's haggard face appeared in the crack. 'Oh, it's you,' she said dispiritedly. He stared at her and she heaved a sigh. 'I suppose you want to come in.' Wearily she pushed closed the door and slid off the chain, and then stood back to let him in.

Swallowing uneasily, Father Trumpington stepped through into the hall. Her greeting was not quite what he had been hoping for. He had rather imagined that she might throw herself into his arms and beg him to take her away, but she seemed positively cold. He bit his lip, but it occurred to him that, with the events of the day before, she might still be feeling rather upset. Also, he wondered if she was maybe scared that he had found out about Norman, and if it was fear that was making her so apparently hostile. He decided to put her out of her misery, and at the same time assure her of his undying devotion. 'Malcolm came to see me,' he said, in what he hoped was a reassuring tone.

The effect was electric. A look of fear came over her face. 'Ssh!' she warned. 'Elspeth's upstairs. She doesn't know.' She bundled him unceremoniously into the darkened front room and hastily shut the door, then turned to him. 'Yes?' she said. 'So what did he say?'

Father Trumpington was put out. She seemed neither surprised nor even greatly interested by his news. In fact, she seemed to be asking simply because she felt it was expected of her; her manner implied that she wished he would go. 'He was very upset,' he said admonishingly.

'I'll bet he was,' said Jackie bitterly. She turned, and to his immense surprise took a small cigar from a packet lying half open on the coffee table. Then, to his even greater surprise, she lit it and inhaled deeply, watching him all the while through narrowed eyes.

Father Trumpington had not known she smoked. His jaw went slack and he gazed at her in bewilderment. He had never seen Jackie like this before. To him Jackie was fragile and neat and soft, but now there seemed something hard and unnatural about her, almost wanton, as if she did not care. 'He told me what happened,' he said.

'And what was that?' she inquired sweetly.

Father Trumpington swallowed. It was Jackie who should have been feeling guilt, he thought, and yet, quite unaccountably, he felt as if it was he who was in the wrong. He squirmed under her cool gaze. 'He told me about Norman,' he said.

'And?'

His eyes goggled. 'Isn't that enough?' he said, outraged.

Jackie yawned. She seemed bored. 'I really don't know,' she said. 'I suppose it depends really . . . on exactly what you're interested in.'

There were serious cracks appearing in Father Trumpington's world. 'But Jackie,' he said, in a strangled tone, 'what about me? What about us?'

'Us?'

'Yes! You and I . . . all we've meant to each other. How could you have done this with Norman?'

Jackie shrugged and flung herself down on the sofa, stretching out her legs. 'I don't know,' she said. 'I just like him, that's all. He's romantic.'

'He's married, Jackie.'

She looked up at him coolly. 'So,' she reminded him mockingly, 'are you.'

It was beyond him. He sat down opposite her, dazed, trying desperately to take it all in. 'But what about me?' he asked at last. 'Don't you like me?'

Jackie shrugged again, 'You're OK . . . I guess. Bit old though, for me.'

He looked at her through the ashes of his dreams. 'You're a bit old for him, aren't you?' he said tartly, gathering his forces. And then he shuddered. 'Jackie,' he tried again, 'I love you. I want us to get married. Doesn't that mean anything to you? What could Norman give you that I can't?'

She stared at him cruelly. 'Sex,' she said flatly. 'He's good in bed. He's imaginative. And as you keep reminding us all, he's going to go far. He *is* somebody.'

'I'm somebody too,' protested Father Trumpington miserably, 'and I can give you sex if you'll give me a chance!' He looked at her pleadingly. 'I can be imaginative. We've only ever done it once, but give me a chance. You'll see!'

To his intense chagrin she laughed and then, leaning forwards, very gently blew smoke into his face. 'I very much doubt it,' she said.

In the course of the previous night Jackie had come to a lot of decisions. Her marriage to Malcolm was well and truly finished. The house, she supposed, would have to be sold, and he would obviously, from what he had said, try and get Elspeth – but she would fight that one. She would spread it around how cruel he had been. She would blacken his reputation so much that he would not be able to return, and she would make sure that he paid – he would pay for having dared cross her. She and Elspeth would have a comfortable life now. But what had struck her most forcibly was that this was a turning point in her life, and that meant opportunity. She was determined not to waste it. In the small hours of the night, she had stood back and coolly surveyed her life, and it had come to her that, whatever else happened, she did not want a future of living death with an old man. She did not want Father Trumpington.

The priest stared at her. For one painful and soul-searing second he saw himself through her eyes, a pompous, spent old man who was unfaithful to his wife. He felt a strangled cry of anguish uncoil itself in his stomach, but he sat there motionless, simply gazing at her silently. 'Is there nothing I can say?' he asked.

'Not really,' she replied. 'No.'

He finally left only after she had asked him repeatedly to go. He felt dazed, all the horror of the previous afternoon welling up in him anew. She did not love him, he knew that now, and yet he had been ready to throw up everything for her. He felt like an old, burnt-out wreck; the one emotion still smouldering amongst all the debris was bitter hatred for Norman, who alone had destroyed his dreams – his one last chance of happiness, as he kept reminding himself.

He walked down the pavement with deadly intent. If he could not have her, then Norman certainly would not! His footsteps again took him in the direction of the organist's house. He had determined exactly what he was going to do. He was going to sack Norman this very instant and turn him and his family out on the street, and if anyone dared ask why, he would tell them that Norman had been found committing adultery, and that he was not a fit person to grace their church.

He arrived at the corner of the church, breathing fire.

Gudrun had returned some fifteen minutes before, but Norman was up at the school where he taught part-time, leading the girls through one final rehearsal for the Nativity play they were to stage later that day. She was not expecting him back before four, and planned to grab a quick bite of lunch and then head for the hospital, to be with Otto.

Father Trumpington, who had totally forgotten Norman's teaching commitments, marched up the front path and banged furiously on the wooden door. There was a perfectly good bell, but he ignored that and instead beat on the panels with his fists. 'Norman, you creep!' he bellowed. 'Come out here at once! I want a word!'

Gudrun, sitting in the kitchen desultorily nibbling a cheese sandwich, almost choked, and then leapt to her feet in concern.

'Come out!' screamed Father Trumpington. 'I know you're in there, you lily-livered swine!'

Gudrun felt so frightened, she began to shake. She wondered whether she should run out through the back door and try and escape, but it occurred to her that Father Trumpington might catch her before she could reach the gate, so instead she turned the key in the lock and wedged a chair up against the handle.

Next, she crept out into the hall. The hammering was still continuing, along with the shouting and abuse, and she wondered how long the door would hold. Very timidly, and cringing before the blows on the wood, she stooped down and shot the bolt. Then she reached up and did the same at the top.

'You filthy coward!' screamed Father Trumpington.

Gudrun prayed and prayed that Norman would not return. She was frightened what Father Trumpington might do. At all costs, she thought, she had to get rid of him, but how? She thought if maybe she stayed very quiet he would lose interest and go away. But that did not seem very likely, because from the sound of it he was becoming more and more angry, and his blows had become a regular pounding, as if he was trying to knock the door down. Heart in mouth, she crept up the stairs and went into the front bedroom from where she could look down on him. The sight that greeted her eyes filled her with terror. He had thrown off his coat and was dancing up and down on the path, intermittently hitting and kicking the door and screaming insults at the top of his voice. She pushed open the window and in a quavering voice called out, 'What do you want?'

'Your spineless sod of a husband!' shouted back Father Trumpington, looking up and catching sight of her.

'He's not here,' she responded.

'Don't give me that!' Bang went his fist on the door.

'No, really,' said Gudrun. 'He's working.'

'Where?' shouted Father Trumpington suspiciously.

Gudrun would not tell him that and have Father Trumpington go round to the school and attack her husband there; they had their livelihood to think of. 'That is none of your business,' she said imperiously.

'Oh, isn't it?' he said, mimicking her tone. 'Well, let me tell you, my lady, I won't have your fornicating husband in this place a moment longer. I want him out. I want you both out. Today!'

'It's Christmas,' said Gudrun, startled.

'I don't give a damn if it's the last day of the apocalypse,' roared back Father Trumpington. 'You're out! The lot of you! I won't have these filthy goings-on in my parish!'

At least he had now stopped banging on the door and Gudrun

took advantage of this to say, 'It's your jealousy speaking. You can't do that.'

He looked up at her, dangerously quiet. She had never noticed before how piggy his eyes seemed. 'Oh, can't I?' he inquired, smiling evilly, the light glinting on his irises. 'I think we might see about that.'

'And Jackie?' yelped Gudrun, now seriously frightened.

'What about Jackie?' he snarled.

'Are you going to turn her out of the parish too?'

'Why?' roared Father Trumpington. 'Do you want to set up house with her or something? A nice cosy little menage à trois! What's it got to do with you?' And he suddenly launched himself again at the door, kicking and flailing at it with his fists. Gudrun screamed, and then ran into her and Norman's bedroom to phone the police, but her hands were shaking so much that she dropped the phone three times and could hardly manage to punch the numbers. The whole house seemed to be reverberating under Father Trumpington's blows. She heard the wood splinter on the door downstairs, followed by a shout of triumph, and gave a low moan. 'Hello, police?' she said, when a voice answered at the other end. 'Please, I need your help . . . Please come quick . . . Someone is trying to break in!'

She sounded so strange that she might have been written off as a nutter, except that the officer at the other end of the line could hear the noise and the manic screams behind. 'Hey, Sarge!' he yelled. 'I think there's a murder going on here!'

Gudrun could hardly speak, but somehow she gave her address, and then collapsed sobbing beside the bed. 'Please hurry,' she whispered. 'Please, I think he's in.'

It was true. Father Trumpington had finally managed to smash his way through the front door and was now conducting a systematic search downstairs. Gudrun could hear his roars of rage and the challenges he kept flinging out. 'He's not here,' she sobbed. 'He's not here.'

Outside there was a sound of sirens. The police had not had anything as exciting as this for weeks. There was a screech of brakes and two pandas hurtled crosswise on to the pavement. Policemen spilled out of the cars and threw themselves towards the broken door. 'It's OK, luv!' yelled one. 'We're here.'

Father Trumpington, in the act of dismantling Norman's piano with a small chopper that he had found in the kitchen, froze, and then two policemen fell on him and literally pinned him to the floor. 'You're nicked, mate!' a voice shouted in his ear. 'You do not have to say anything . . .' and for the first time in his life Father Trumpington found himself being told his rights. Then he was hauled unceremoniously to his feet and a voice said incredulously, 'Blimey, he's wearing a dog collar.'

It was with difficulty that Father Trumpington persuaded the police that he had been in the house at Gudrun's invitation, carrying out necessary repairs, but he was helped by the fact that she refused to press charges and so regretfully, after five hours, they let him go on condition that he pay for the damage he had caused. Overall he had found their attitude most unpleasant, especially when one of them had pulled him aside as he was leaving and hissed in his ear, 'Just don't forget, mate, we'll be watching you from now on.'

Meanwhile, Antonia had found herself summoned to take care of Gudrun who, said the police, was in something of a state, although she had refused point blank the offer of a doctor, and did not want her husband to know. A car duly arrived to fetch Antonia, and a young WPC escorted her into the wrecked house. 'Bit of a mess,' she remarked dispassionately. 'He went berserk. He's hacked the piano to pieces.' She looked at Antonia curiously. 'He claims he's the vicar.'

'Really?' said Antonia.

'Oh yes,' said the WPC, 'and he was wearing a collar, just like you. Big chap, going bald.'

'Hmm, he could be the vicar then,' said Antonia.

Another policeman appeared. 'She's upstairs,' he said laconically. 'Won't stop crying. Rum business. Won't tell us what it was all about.'

Antonia followed him upstairs and found Gudrun, still shaking, sitting huddled on the bed, tears streaming down her face. 'Oh Antonia,' she wailed, looking up and catching sight of her. 'Thank God you've come. It was terrible.'

The officer nodded and withdrew, and Antonia sat beside Gudrun on the bed. 'What's happened?' she asked. 'The WPC said it was Dick.'

Gudrun nodded, her eyes huge. 'Yes,' she breathed, 'he was looking for Norman. It was like yesterday, only worse. He said he was going to throw us all out on the street. He wouldn't believe me when I said Norman wasn't here. And then he broke down the door. He kept shouting that Norman was a fornicator, and that he was going to kill him. I was so frightened.' And she again began to cry.

Antonia waited for her to stop and then said, 'So where is Dick now?'

'They've taken him down to the police station to ask him some questions. But I've refused to press charges.' She looked at Antonia defiantly. 'They'll let him go.'

'Is that wise?'

Gudrun sniffed. 'I don't want my family dragged any further into this mess. I don't want all the questions or the publicity there'd be. Norman's career will suffer if this gets out, and I just want to forget it all, and for us to get on with our lives.'

Antonia looked concerned. 'Is that going to be possible?' she asked. 'It sounds like he's gone totally over the top.'

Gudrun, however, was pursuing her own line of thought. 'He said Norman's fired.' She turned and gazed at Antonia. 'He can't do that, can he?'

Antonia grimaced. She wanted to reassure Gudrun, but felt unable to. 'I wouldn't put anything past him,' she said slowly, 'not after what's happened the last few days. His normal way of carrying on is just to tell the PCC what to do. He might simply tell them to sack you – and they might do it.'

'But he can't!' Gudrun's lower lip jutted and she appeared to come to a decision. 'I will not allow him to put us out on the streets. We would like to leave, yes, and I'm sure now that's best. But I will not allow him just to throw us out. When we leave it will be because Norman has another job. And a good job. I will not allow him to wreck the lives of my family, nor deprive us of our home.'

Antonia looked at her curiously. 'But if you refuse to press charges what else can you do?' she asked.

For the first time Gudrun smiled. It was a bit watery and weak, but nevertheless it was a definite smile. 'I am going to write to the Bishop,' she announced.

Chapter Sixteen

Professor Bullen had spoken to the Archdeacon who discovered he had a considerable interest in the young man who was acting as the Bishop's chaplain. He summoned him round to tea, and there discovered that Nigel felt that God was maybe calling him to be an evangelist. 'How wonderful,' said the Archdeacon sympathetically. He wasted no time in making a few phone calls and discovered, to everyone's amazement, that there was a marvellous post going in the Szechuan province of China. 'You know, I think this would be just the thing,' he said, bumping into Nigel two days later. 'I really feel God may be calling you there. Now!'

Nigel blinked. He had not envisaged quite so speedy a summons to the mission field; in fact, he had not felt he was being called overseas at all. The Archdeacon, however, was insistent. 'This is for you,' he said. 'I felt it the minute it landed on my desk.' In vain did the Bishop's chaplain protest. All around him people were saying, 'God's calling you to Szechuan, is he? How wonderful!' And it was said to him so often, and with such insistence, that he began to believe it himself – which was not at all easy, because, as he was a young man of very great faith, he wanted, above all, to be obedient to God. He spent lengthy periods in agonised prayer, pouring out his dilemma to God and asking for some sort of sign, but on this occasion the Almighty seemed maddeningly quiet. Finally he determined to lay down his golden fleece; he would go to see the Bishop and, dependent upon what that worthy said, he would stay or remain. The Bishop, he told God, was to be His mouthpiece, let him but speak the word and he would obey.

Unfortunately the Archdeacon had also been to see the Bishop and, in the course of their conversation, he had casually let drop how much he admired that 'fine young man, Nigel', and what a pity it was that God was calling him to China when they needed him so much in the diocese. The Bishop was dumbfounded.

'Calling him to China?' he repeated, shocked.

'Oh yes,' the Archdeacon assured him. 'I had a letter from **Save the People** – you know, the missionary organisation operating out there. It arrived the other day. They were asking if I could supply the name of anyone who might be suitable for a post in Szechuan. Sadly for us, Nigel saw the letter and immediately said he felt it was for him.' He twittered sanctimoniously. 'Such commitment. I have unbounded admiration for him. But,' and here he looked at the Bishop closely, 'the one thing that he said bothered him was leaving you.'

The Bishop gazed down at his hands with a divided heart. The last thing he personally wanted was to lose Nigel, who in every sense had seemed to him to be the answer to his prayers. They were so similar in their theology and belief; the difference between them lay, as he very well knew, in Nigel's steely determination to follow whatever he felt the Lord was saying. The Bishop felt a similar commitment, of course, but in his case he was fatally hindered by his desire to be nice to people, and not to cause them any upset. Time and again he had found himself agreeing to things that he really knew he ought not – to things that were actually preposterous – and closing his eyes to the most glaring faults in others, simply because he wanted above all to avoid conflict. 'We must not split the body,' he was fond of saying. But even he knew, in his heart of hearts, that that was merely an excuse because he was terrified of upsetting people. Nigel, however, with his gentle courage, had no such inhibitions. It was not that he actively sought conflict, or even demanded that everyone share the same sort of belief as himself, but he believed that it was important to honour God in line with Biblical principles, and from that position he would not be moved.

The Bishop had been impressed by both his strength and his skill, and had come to rely upon him heavily to enforce those difficult decisions that he knew had to be made but lacked the courage to carry out himself. Nigel had become a kind of shield for him, but at the same time he had faithfully expressed the Bishop's views, as for example had happened in the unhappy situation with Father Trumpington. For years the Bishop had been saying that he felt Freemasonry was wrong, and that his clergy had to choose in order that they might be an example to the flock, but he had got absolutely nowhere – mainly because, whenever it came to any kind of face-to-face discussion, he had always ended up agreeing that it could not be so bad after all, because senior clergy had been Masons for decades. Then Nigel had arrived, and he had been absolutely clear on what their stance should be, and gratefully the Bishop had begun to allow him to try and purge the diocese of what he felt to be the unhealthy stranglehold Freemasonry had.

Weighed in the balance against these feelings, however, was the Bishop's desire not to stand in the way of God. If the Lord really was calling Nigel to China, then of course he would have to go. The good Lord would provide for all their needs. So it was that when Nigel finally came to see him and broached the subject, the Bishop had already determined not to stand in his way. 'We shall miss you dearly, my boy,' he said, looking him firmly in the eye but with an inwardly wracked heart, 'but if this is what the Lord is calling you to now, then go, with my blessing. God's kingdom will be richly served.'

Nigel swallowed, but he had already committed himself to abiding by the Bishop's words. 'Then,' he said, 'I must, most regretfully, tender my resignation.' God, he felt, had spoken.

Nigel was to travel two days before Christmas. The day of his departure, Gudrun's letter arrived on the Bishop's desk. 'Goodness gracious me!' that worthy said, reading its contents in ever increasing dismay. 'Good Lord . . . Good heavens! God help us!' And then he called loudly for Nigel, before realising he was no longer there. 'Oh,' said the Bishop, his heart sinking. 'Oh dear.' He spent the next two hours locked in his study, praying and trying to work out what to do. He knew that he must summon Father Trumpington and try and find out the truth of the matter. Something, he knew, had to be done, but his heart quailed at the prospect. The Bishop was terrified of Father Trumpington, he was so pompous and bombastic, and so unreasonable in his attitude. The Bishop had not the slightest difficulty in believing the allegations the letter contained. He just rather wished that the police had charged the man, and maybe even locked him up.

219

Then it hit him what a terrible scandal this would be, and the damage it would do to the diocese if any of it ever became known. Never had he missed Nigel more. His former chaplain, he thought, would have known exactly what to do. But he was no longer here, and the Bishop knew that this problem he had to solve alone.

He sent for the Archdeacon and, having carefully closed the door and instructed his secretary that on no account were they to be disturbed, he laid the letter before him. 'What's this?' said the Archdeacon jocularly, and then his jaw dropped as his eyes travelled down the page. 'Oh my God,' he said, in slightly less reverential tones than had been employed by the Bishop. 'What on earth are we going to do?'

'I don't know,' said the Bishop.

But the Archdeacon was thinking. 'This can't possibly be true,' he said. 'The woman must be mad!'

'Do you think so?' asked the Bishop hopefully.

The Archdeacon bit his lip and once again looked at the letter. 'Maybe not,' he admitted. 'She says the police were involved. You don't make up things like that. But maybe we should at least check that part of the story. I've got a friend down at the police station. Have you got a phone directory?'

The Bishop handed him one and the Archdeacon looked up the number. Then he dialled the police station and asked to speak to Detective Inspector Lauder. The Bishop could tell from the Archdeacon's face when the other man came on that the news was not good. 'Um, yes,' he kept saying, 'I see.' Finally he said, 'Look, can we ask you to keep absolutely quiet about this? We'll take the necessary steps to sort it out, and if there's any discipline needed, we'll do it, but can we ask you, for the good of the church here in this diocese, to forget the matter completely and say nothing.' There was another long pause, during which the Bishop could hear the low buzz of a voice at the other end, then the Archdeacon said, 'At all costs we want to make sure this doesn't reach the press. They'd get things out of proportion, and that's not going to help anybody.'

He put down the phone. 'It happened,' he said briefly, 'but since there were no charges brought, they're happy to keep quiet. He's

going to instruct his men that they are to say nothing, especially
to the press, should that situation arise.'

'Thank you,' said the Bishop with heartfelt gratitude. 'What
shall we do next?'

The Archdeacon thought for a minute. 'Well,' he said at last,
'it's Christmas in two days. I suggest we do nothing until after
that's out of the way – things may be a little clearer by then
anyway. Then we write this woman a holding letter, asking her to
keep quiet but saying we'll deal with it, and then I suppose we'd
better have him in.' He looked unhappy. Removing opponents of
Freemasonry was one thing, but covering up this kind of a scandal
was quite another. He rather hoped there would be some adequate
explanation, or that at least some of the charges would be proved
to be untrue, but his imagination could not quite envisage that
one.

'But she's worried about losing her home,' pointed out the
Bishop. 'Shouldn't we at least do something to reassure her on
that point?' He thought of his own palatial lodgings and
shuddered. He could well imagine the state his own dear wife
would be in if faced with such a problem.

The Archdeacon, however, lacked the same ready sympathy
as his superior, and his thoughts were not so much upon Gudrun
as on the problem posed by Father Trumpington, and the need to
keep the whole affair quiet. He looked again at the letter. 'If this
really is true,' he said judiciously, 'I doubt even Dick could move
that fast. But perhaps you're right, we should maybe drop him a
line to the effect that we've received this and that he's to do
nothing.'

'Oh, what a good idea,' said the Bishop. 'I'll get somebody to
drop it round by hand this afternoon. I don't think we can trust
the post at this season.'

The letter duly arrived at half past three that afternoon, pushed
through Father Trumpington's letter box by some unknown hand.
Father Trumpington went pale as he read it, and Dorothy, who
happened to be in the room at the same time, said waspishly,
'What is it? What's happened now?'

A change had recently come over the Trumpington household.
Father Trumpington had been subdued when he had finally

arrived home after his sojourn at the police station, and when Dorothy had peremptorily demanded where he had been for so long, he had told her. There had seemed nothing to hide any more. 'You did what?' Dorothy said, horrified. But then, seeing his daze, she took command of the situation and bundled him off to bed. 'He's not well,' she announced to parishioners. 'I think he's got flu. He's been in bed all day, but a few more days should do it.' And a steely glint had come into her eye. 'Don't worry, he'll be around for the Christmas services. You have my word!'

From that story she would not budge. The following day she had phoned the bank and told them too, she could not come in because her husband was ill, and then she had gone up to Father Trumpington with a cup of tea and, perched on the side of the bed, had told him exactly what they were going to do. 'You're going to forget all this,' she said commandingly. 'It never happened. I agree with you, Norman and his wife have got to go, and so has Jackie Newberg, but we've got to be a bit careful about this.'

'What do you suggest, dear?' he asked meekly. Dorothy liked that, it had been a long time since he had used any kind of endearment that held a hint of sincerity towards her.

'I suggest,' she said, 'that we let it be known Norman's been having an affair, and with whom. They can't deny it, and from what you've said about Jackie Newberg, I suspect it'll be a while before she comes back to church. So I don't think we need worry too much that *your* little infatuation is going to come out. What we can say to Norman is that if he'll keep quiet now, you'll give him a good reference and help him find another job.'

'Do you think he'll go for it?'

'Yes,' she said. 'I shouldn't think they'll want to hang around here. Not now. And he's got a family to support. I think he might jump at it, if you can come up with an attractive alternative.' She looked at him. 'I think you ought to ring up some of your contacts and see if anyone's looking for an organist at the moment.'

Then she took it upon herself to go and see Norman, who by this time had not only taken in the full devastation to his house but had heard, too, the whole sorry tale from Gudrun.

'You're in a bit of a mess,' Dorothy told him flatly.

'So are you,' he retorted.

Dorothy ignored that. 'I have a proposition,' she stated, 'that I think will help all of us.' She gave him a brief outline of her plan.

'So I'm going to have to take the blame, am I?' he said bitterly.

She shrugged. 'It's going to come out anyway from what I hear. Apparently Jackie's husband is going to name you in divorce proceedings. You should be receiving something any day now.'

He swallowed. 'Vindictive sod!'

'Maybe,' Dorothy's eyes were hard. 'But that being so, you can't hope to keep this quiet, so why not try and make the best of a bad job? You keep quiet about Dick, and we'll help you.'

Norman agreed.

Father Trumpington felt a great weight of anxiety roll from his shoulders when she got back and told him her news, and since then he had been content to allow her to take charge and direct him in what to do. He was like a child again, feeble in her hands, grateful for her strength. In this way their marriage seemed, if not exactly reborn, to have been transmuted into something wondrous and new. They were talking again, plotting, and Father Trumpington discovered he was amazed by the steely qualities this new Dorothy possessed. He might not be exactly fond of her, but he discovered that under her rather amazing hairdo (which he still disliked) there lay the mind of a brilliantly devious tactician – almost as good as himself. And so, in his shipwreck, they began to work together to cover over the yawning holes that had appeared, and so ensure that the truth would not be known.

Now Dorothy took the letter from his inert hands and peered at it closely. 'You never told me about this,' she said incredulously.

He shrugged helplessly. 'I never knew. How could I? I didn't know what the stupid woman was going to do!'

Dorothy thought rapidly. 'It's all right,' she pronounced, 'just stay calm. We'll deal with it.' Father Trumpington gazed at her in awe. 'We just keep denying everything,' she said after a minute. 'I'll stand by you and I'll say it's all rubbish. We can say Gudrun's unbalanced and that it's all malicious. We can say that the bit about the affair between her husband and that Newberg woman is true, but that she couldn't face it, and that's why she's accusing you. We can say that you found out about the affair and were shocked.' She looked at him speculatively, weighing in her mind if this was the time to push home her advantage. She decided it was. 'It's going to cost you,' she said flatly, 'for me to support you like this. Things are going to have to be different now.'

'Anything, dear,' blubbered Father Trumpington.

She smiled. It was not a nice smile. 'Good,' she said. 'From now on I want our joint account to be exactly that. I want unrestricted access. But I want more than that. I want to take over the running of the finances, which means that if you want anything from now on, you ask me. And you do nothing without fully consulting me.' Father Trumpington nodded dumbly. 'Right then,' she said briskly, 'first things first. I think you should reply to the Bishop.'

'What about Antonia?' hazarded Father Trumpington. He hardly dared mention her name in face of Dorothy's whirlwind organisation, but the Bishop's letter had referred to her particularly as having been called upon to give Gudrun pastoral support. Father Trumpington knew exactly what that meant.

Dorothy turned on him a steely eye. 'Antonia?' she queried. She was not very skilled at deciphering church-speak, and had not realised the implications of the inclusion of Antonia's name, but she had long since realised that the curate was a thorn in her husband's flesh.

Father Trumpington nodded. 'She knows everything,' he said. 'Gudrun's obviously been talking to her.'

'Really?' Dorothy regarded him. This put a very different complexion on matters. If Antonia knew, then she was a threat too, perhaps even greater than Norman and Gudrun. 'Well then,' she said, 'the answer's quite simple. She just has to go. You must find a way of sacking her for incompetence.'

Later that same afternoon Amelia and her family arrived to spend Christmas with her parents as they had done for the last ten years. 'Good heavens, Mummy!' squeaked Amelia, bouncing over the threshold and then pulling up short when she took in Dorothy's changed appearance. 'You really have had a make-over, haven't you!'

Dorothy, who had been on the telephone to Gloria about

flowers for Christmas Eve, carefully replaced the receiver and looked her only daughter levelly in the eye. 'I took your advice,' she said.

'You did, didn't you?' said Amelia faintly.

Sebastian, six, and Charlotte, five, tumbled through the door with excited squeals of delight. They loved Christmas, and in particular they loved racing round the rambling old rectory, playing all the games they were not allowed to at home. 'Coo, look at Granny!' said Charlotte now. 'Doesn't she look funny? Why has she got that funny thing on her head, Mummy?'

'Ssh,' said Amelia, going pink. 'It's her hair, darling.'

'Why is Granny's hair purple?' demanded Sebastian.

'Because it's Christmas,' said Torquil, Amelia's husband, coming in behind them and taking in the situation at a glance, 'and jolly pretty I think she looks too!'

Amelia was not so sure. In fact she was rather horrified. She thought her mother's hair looked as if she had had a rather unfortunate encounter with a power socket, and as for the leggings, Amelia was not convinced that leggings were wise on someone with so ample a posterior, whatever the fashion magazines said. She swallowed uncertainly. 'Well, it's certainly different,' she conceded at last.

'I'd like purple hair,' announced Charlotte, 'and I'd like my face made up like a cat too!'

Amelia decided to change the subject before things got even more embarrassing. 'Where's Daddy?' she demanded. 'Is he out visiting, or is he in his study?' All the time she was watching her mother covertly. She did not like the change, she decided, but she had to admit that Dorothy was looking better than she had in a long, long time. It was not the externals, she thought, but some inner quality. Her mother looked glowing, even excited. She went up close and squeezed her arm. 'Is everything all right?' she whispered.

Dorothy smiled back. 'Yes, dear,' she said quietly, 'things couldn't be better!'

Amelia reflected that men were strange creatures. Her father had obviously liked the change, even if she did not. 'I'm so glad,' she said. 'I told you things were all right.'

225

'What are you whispering about, Mummy?' demanded Charlotte.

'Nothing, darling.' Reassured, Amelia's eyes again darted round. 'But where is Daddy?' she insisted. 'He's usually here to meet us.'

'I'm afraid he's not very well,' said Dorothy. 'He's upstairs in bed.' She had decided that to add veracity to their story, Dick had to stay in bed till Christmas Eve.

Amelia, who recalled her father's last bout of heart trouble, was immediately all concern. 'Oh dear,' she said, 'nothing serious, I hope.'

'No, no, of course not,' reassured Dorothy, 'just a touch of flu, that's all. But at his age, you can't be too careful, and we do want him well for Christmas. It would be awful if he weren't around on Christmas Day. There are all the Christmas services, for a start.'

'I suppose so,' said Amelia doubtfully. She felt worried her mother was concealing something. 'Has he had the doctor?'

Dorothy pooh-poohed the idea. 'Good gracious no, of course not,' she laughed. 'What use is a doctor with flu? A few days' rest, that's all he needs. He'll be as right as rain tomorrow.'

Amelia could not be reassured till she had gone upstairs and seen for herself. She found her father sitting in state in bed, surrounded by the newspaper, books, and a jigsaw that Dorothy had suggested he might enjoy. It was a mark of his subdued state that he had actually attempted it. Amelia was horrified, immediately convinced that there was something terribly wrong, although she could see no sign of flu. 'Poor Daddy,' she whispered to Torquil, 'you know, I think he might really be ill. I've never seen him like this. He looks like all the stuffing's been knocked out of him. Do you think there's something seriously wrong?'

Torquil, not much given to introspection, was reassuring. 'No, of course not,' he said. 'Flu does that to people, that's all. He's obviously getting over it. Looks like he's doing pretty well to me. Your mother's quite right, if one takes care, there's no problem.'

Amelia's face cleared slightly. 'Of course, you're quite right,' she breathed. 'But he must have had a terrible time to have gone to bed like that. Daddy never goes to bed if he's unwell. He says it's namby-pamby, and that he doesn't hold with mollycoddling. He's so brave.' And here, for some obscure reason that was unclear even to herself, she wiped a tear from her eye.

'There, there, old girl!' said Torquil, giving her a quick hug. 'Don't take on. He's going to be all right. And we're here now, you know, so your mum can rest too.' He looked reflective, or at least as reflective as he ever managed to achieve. 'If you ask me, you know,' he said confidentially, fixing Amelia in the eye, 'she's the one who looks like she could do with a bit of a break. She seems tired to me.'

Amelia swallowed. 'You know, I'm not at all sure that things are going well for them at the moment, although,' she paused and looked up at him, 'they do seem happy together, don't they?'

'Course they are, old thing!' Torquil, not noted for his sensitivity, laughed. He had always assumed that Amelia's parents, being church people and all that, were a model of conjugal bliss. He had of course in the past noted that they did not talk to each other very often, but in his rather blundering way, he had simply assumed that that was the way they were. Today, if anything, he had been surprised at how much they seemed to have changed. Nevertheless, he knew what Amelia meant. There was something in the air. 'Tell you what, old thing,' he said, 'why don't we ask them?'

Accordingly, after dinner, when Charlotte and Sebastian had gone to bed, and Father Trumpington had been allowed downstairs, Torquil, with no great preamble, said, 'What's wrong then? What's up?'

Father Trumpington and Dorothy looked at each other, and Father Trumpington swallowed. Dorothy, however, was ready for this. Indeed, she had been expecting the inquiry, and had been working out what to say ever since they arrived. 'You're quite right,' she said now, 'there is something wrong. We must have been stupid to think we could hide it from you.' Father Trumpington looked at her with horror, petrified at what she might be about to reveal, but she ignored him. 'Your father's having a lot of troubles in the parish,' she announced. Father Trumpington closed his eyes. 'He has a most troublesome woman curate who's been causing all sorts of problems and trying to stir people up against him. She's causing a lot of division. But on top of that, which is difficult enough,' Father Trumpington opened one eye and looked at her, 'we've just discovered that the new organist is having an affair with someone from the congregation. And to make matters worse, his wife has written a letter to the Bishop complaining about the way Daddy's handling the affair.'

Amelia's eyes grew round. 'Poor Daddy,' she said excitedly, relief flooding over her, 'it's just like one of those dreadful church scandals you hear about in the rags, isn't it? No wonder you're both looking so tired.'

'Good Lord,' said Torquil, 'yes, I see. Bit of a tricky one, isn't it? What are you doing about it?'

Father Trumpington opened both eyes and looked helplessly at Dorothy. His expression seemed to say, 'You got us into this, now get us out!'

Dorothy was equal to the challenge. 'There's not a lot we can do, at the moment,' she said, not looking at him, 'but your father's trying to find a new position for the organist, out of the goodness of his heart, while we sort all this out. And as for this dreadful woman,' now she too closed her eyes, 'well, I don't know, Daddy's working on it. We're praying the congregation's not going to be irrevocably split, that's all, before we can get rid of her.'

Amelia decided that she hated this woman curate. She had never liked the idea of women in the Church anyway, they ought to know their place. This just confirmed what she had thought all along. 'What a terrible woman,' she said. 'How can she, when she claims to be serving God?'

'I really don't know,' said Dorothy piously. 'We just have to accept that some people are totally unsuitable, and yet they manage to get in. Somehow they manage to hoodwink the selectors. And then we have to deal with the mess they create. All we can do is pray for them, and trust that God will bring good from the evil they create.'

'Well, I think you're just too good-natured,' said Amelia. 'I hate her.'

Chapter Seventeen

Gloria was surprised to receive a phone call from Dorothy asking her to sort out the Christmas flowers, but then Dorothy explained to her that Father Trumpington had flu and had said that she, Gloria, would rally round and then she felt pleased. At the other end of the line, her ample bosom swelled. In his hour of need, Father Trumpington had turned to her – and not to his silly blob of a wife. Gloria was not able to resist allowing a patronising note to creep into her voice. 'Oh yes, that's quite all right,' she responded. 'Just leave it all to me. I can sort that out. No problem.'

If Dorothy noticed, she gave no sign, but then she was too busy trying to ensure that the Christmas services were going to be all right to waste time worrying about uppity churchwardens. 'Thank you very much,' she said crisply, and rang off.

Gloria put down the phone with a simpering look on her face.

'Who was that?' demanded Griff, at that moment banging his way in noisily through the front door. He had just come back from the pub and was overflowing with rather too much Christmas cheer.

'The vicar's wife,' said Gloria tartly. She looked at him with distaste. 'You're drunk.'

Griff smiled tipsily and then belched. 'Yes,' he agreed, 'isch loverly!'

'Oh God,' said Gloria. She thought rapidly and then announced, 'I've got to go out. I've got to do the flowers for the service tonight.' Normally, if asked to sort out the flowers, Gloria would simply have phoned up someone else and told them to do it, but now, under the combined effects of Griff's drunkenness and the warm glow of feeling she was needed elsewhere, she decided to do them herself. Anything to get out of the house for a while. 'You,' she said, 'can go and sleep that off. I want you sober when I get back. So no more boozing while I'm gone.'

Griff decided she was wonderful. There was no one like his

Gloria. Staggering forwards, he threw his arms round her and planted a big kiss on her nose.

'Ugh! You stink,' said Gloria, pushing him away violently.

Griff interpreted this as affection. 'You're wonderful,' he hiccupped. He swayed uncertainly, a huge smile on his face, and then subsided gently on to the floor. Gloria stared at him in disgust, and then kicked him viciously in the side. He gave a low moan but did not stir, and she glared at him with real hatred in her eyes. From past experience she knew that he would sleep now for hours. Nothing would waken him; he would be like a corpse. Well, let him lie there then, she thought angrily. She did not care. Without a backward glance, she grabbed her coat and bag, stepped over him and flung out through the door.

The church, when she got to it, was dark. She let herself in through the vestry and carefully locked the door after her. Many women would have been frightened to go into that echoing, dark building alone, but not Gloria. As she stepped through into the gloom, she bristled like a tiny destroyer and then ploughed her way into the darkened nave, her stilettos ringing on the red tiles. She found the switches to the lights at the back of the church, and flicked on the one to the kitchen behind the vestry. Through the pale gleam that shone out through the opened doors, she saw that someone had been before her. They had left piles of holly and white, gold and red flowers standing in buckets ready to be arranged, but no one as yet had come to put them out. Tutting to herself self-righteously, Gloria gathered them up and then set off back towards the kitchen.

Forty minutes later, as Gloria was putting the final touches to her arrangements, Norman arrived. He let himself in through the front door and immediately went to the small cloakroom off the entrance and flicked on the lights to the centre aisle and organ console. The pale glow from the kitchen was lost and, not realising anyone else was there, he made his way over to the organ and sat down ready to begin his practice. But just as he was unlocking the console and setting out his music, Jackie arrived. She had been waiting for him to visit her the whole week, and had been first surprised and then annoyed when he failed to appear. Then it had occurred to her that he might be worried about running into Malcolm and so, that morning, albeit rather chagrined, she had decided to take the initiative herself.

She came down the side aisle noiselessly and, just as Norman was striking up, laid a proprietorial hand on his arm.

Norman let out a startled yelp and his hands shot back from the keys. As if in sympathy, the organ made a deflated sound and then wheezed to a stop. 'Good God,' he said, spinning round. 'Why did you do that? I didn't know there was anybody there.'

Jackie looked at him aggrieved. She had rather expected him to fling his arms round her. 'You haven't been to see me,' she said, pouting.

He looked at her as if she was mad. 'Does that surprise you?'

Jackie gaped. 'Well, yes,' she said. 'Actually, it does.' In all her thoughts on how to deal with the problems posed by Malcolm and Father Trumpington, it had not yet occurred to her that Norman might no longer share quite the same feelings as herself. Also, she was ignorant of all that had happened over the past few days. As far as she was concerned, she had given Father Trumpington the brush-off, and that was that. She was free now for Norman. She knew that Father Trumpington knew about Norman, of course, but she knew absolutely nothing of the fight there had been, or of the priest's jealous rage. And she certainly knew nothing of the threats that had been made against Norman and his wife, nor of the proposition put to them by Dorothy. So now, when he stared at her so coldly, she felt stunned. 'What is it? Wh-what's wrong?' she faltered.

Norman glowered. 'Where would you like me to start?' he inquired bitterly. 'With your husband perhaps? Or shall we have a change of subject and begin with Dick?'

Jackie went white. 'What do you mean?'

From the kitchen Gloria had heard the organ strike up and then abruptly stop, and now she came quietly out to see what was going on. Her eyes immediately fell on Norman sitting at the organ console, with Jackie standing rigid at his side. Gloria felt her skin prickle with excitement. Their stance was so awkward that she knew straightaway that something momentous, and illicit, was going on. Agog with curiosity, she crept forward and hid behind the nearest pillar, straining to overhear what was being said. 'I mean I know everything,' she heard Norman say. That sounded promising.

'What?'

'Oh, come off it, Jackie! It's a bit late to start playing the innocent. I mean he told me what had been going on!'

From behind the pillar Gloria heard Jackie make a mewing sound. She leant out as far as she dared, straining to see, her excitement mounting. It occurred to her that this was better than anything she could possibly have imagined, and of late she had been imagining rather a lot about Jackie, none of it good. In particular she had been wondering how to discredit this woman whom she had to come to regard as her rival, and so leave the way clear for herself with Father Trumpington. But from what she could hear now, it sounded as if fate was about to do this for her. Norman and Jackie were obviously having the most frightful row, and the organist had clearly found out something that had upset him. Gloria's nose, always ready for scandal, twitched. Good, she thought viciously. She had always hated Jackie. She inched forward till she could see the pair clearly and saw Jackie wring her hands, as if disclaiming all knowledge. 'Nothing's been going on,' she heard her say.

'He told me!' shouted Norman. 'You've just been playing me for a fool.'

'No!' said Jackie desperately. 'Never! I love you!'

'Me and the rest of the football team! Why didn't you tell me that your husband was around?'

Gloria's ears pricked up even more. Jackie's husband? This was a turn-up for the books if he had come back. No wonder Norman was annoyed, and her eyes grew round. From her vantage point behind the pillar she saw Norman start to his feet and Jackie launch herself at him, flinging her arms round his neck. Norman tried to push her away, but Jackie clung to him and gave a strangled sob.

'Why?' she shouted out. 'Why do you have to believe him rather than me? He's jealous, can't you see? Why do you have to take any notice of what he says? Why couldn't you ask me?'

'Ask you?'

'Yes!'

'OK then. Who? Who are you sleeping with?'

Gloria's jaw dropped open.

'You,' Jackie said, 'just you, I swear.'

'Pgh!' muttered Gloria. 'Believe that and you'll believe anything!'

'What was that?' said Norman. The pair looked round, startled, and Gloria dived back behind her pillar.

'Nothing,' said Jackie after a minute. 'There's no one there.' She laid her hand again on Norman's arm. 'Norman,' she said pleadingly, 'you've got to believe me. It's you I care about, that's all. No one else.'

Norman stared down at her. 'You were in bed with him, Jackie,' he said mulishly. 'You told me it was all over between you two.'

'It is,' she insisted, 'but he came home suddenly. You know how it is. He wanted us to sleep together – and we are still married.'

Norman did know how it was. He thought of Gudrun. He still slept with her of course, but somehow that was different. Jackie had told him that her marriage was over. 'Did you tell him about us?' he asked at last.

'No,' she said. 'I was going to, but then you came, and it was just all so awful. We ended up having the most ghastly row.'

'Dick told me.'

'Did he?'

'Yes.'

At mention of Father Trumpington's name, Gloria went rigid with attention. Now, once again, summoning up all her courage, she peered cautiously round the pillar.

'He said Malcolm's going to name me in divorce proceedings.' In this Norman was not being strictly accurate, but he saw no reason at this point to let Jackie know that Dorothy also knew. Explanations, he felt, would be too involved.

From her vantage point, Gloria saw Jackie's eyes grow round.

'Is he?' she said. 'I don't know. I haven't heard yet . . . I suppose he might.'

Gloria was so astounded that she collapsed back behind the pillar, a hand upraised to her face. Divorce, that was what Norman had just said – Jackie was getting divorced, and he was going to be named. He had said that Dick had told him! It was so sudden that Gloria found it hard to take in. Norman and Jackie were having an affair, that much was clear, and matters appeared to have come to such a head that Malcolm had come home. Gloria was puzzled. When had he come back? How was it that she had not realised? Her thoughts flew to the Christmas party and Jackie's odd behaviour that night. It must have been then, she decided, and Father Trumpington had obviously known. Like the sun coming out from behind a cloud, her thoughts suddenly cleared. She saw it all now. Father Trumpington had never been interested in Jackie, her suspicions had been misplaced. It was simply that he had known what was going on and, like the good priest he was, he had tried to have a word with Jackie in order to help. But clearly it had been to no avail, because the couple were now divorcing and Norman . . . what would happen with Norman now?

Gloria stood there, catching her breath and trying to work out what course of action would best serve her own interests.

Behind her Norman was saying, 'Look, Jackie, I can't. I don't want to. It's over. There's Gudrun—'

'Gudrun!' Jackie spat out the name. 'Don't be stupid, please. Don't destroy what we've got!'

'We haven't got anything,' said Norman, outraged. 'I realise that now. I've been an idiot.'

'No,' protested Jackie. 'Don't you see? It's all coming right now. We can be together.'

'What?' said Norman. 'What do you mean, together? I don't want to be together. I'm married to Gudrun.' There was a small silence and then he said, 'In any case, I'm going away. I'm getting another job.'

Jackie looked at him in pure outrage. 'You can't,' she said. 'I won't let you. What about us? You can't leave me now.'

Before he knew what she was going to do, Jackie wound herself up against him and bit, almost fiercely, at his neck. At the same time, the scent of her perfume wafted up and struck him full in the face. Norman caught his breath, feeling as if he was drowning. He felt plunged suddenly into a deep pool of indecision. Trapped by her presence, he found he wanted to believe her; that he was the only one. Yet in the same moment he thought of Gudrun and of all that had happened in the past week. He thought how close he had come to losing her, and he knew now that he did not want that, and that what they had was good. But at the same time, there was something so exciting and enticing about Jackie . . . he wanted that too. He was not ready to give her up. Sensing that he was weakening, Jackie let her lips slide up and locked them on to his mouth. Norman's good intentions creaked and began to bend. 'No,' he said, making a feeble attempt to push her away.

'You want it as much as I do,' muttered Jackie. 'You know you do. We're meant for each other.'

The quiet brought Gloria out of her reverie and, very cautiously, she peered out from behind her pillar once again to see what was going on. She saw Jackie pouring herself over Norman, smothering his face with kisses, and she saw him, with his eyes closed, drinking it all in. So that's how it is, she thought. She had seen enough. Taking advantage of their preoccupation, she stole quietly back to the kitchen and let herself out through the vestry door. She would return later that evening to put the flowers out.

Norman finally went home feeling sick. He had not managed to get any of his practice done. When he had tried, after Jackie had finally gone, he had found that he was unable to play. He felt totally drained and confused, all his certainties of the past few days once again dangerously undermined. At the back of his mind was the feeling that he had to escape, but he was no longer sure that that was possible. He did not feel Jackie would let him go. He had been insistent that he had to get another job, and had told her what had happened with Father Trumpington, but then Jackie had said that if he moved, she would move too, she would follow him wherever he went. On top of that, she wanted him to tell Gudrun that it was all over and that he was leaving her. But Norman did not want that and, though he lacked the courage to tell Jackie, he was fully determined not to cause Gudrun any further hurt.

When he got back to the house he found Bethany and Iwan there. Gudrun, still frail and suffering over her fears for Otto, had nevertheless insisted that the children come home for Christmas, and Phoebe had brought them round that morning. Now as Norman came into the house Bethany ran and flung her arms round him, almost knocking him from his feet. 'Daddy!' she screamed, and she hugged him so tightly that Norman felt tears start to his eyes.

He stooped down and buried his face in the little girl's hair. 'Where have you been, tiddler?' he asked when he had regained sufficient command of himself, but it was Iwan who answered.

'We've been to see Otto,' he yelled. 'He's gorgeous, but there are all these funny tubes coming out of him, and he wouldn't open his eyes!'

Norman looked up inquiringly and saw Gudrun biting her lips. She shrugged helplessly. 'It's his breathing,' she said, 'it's bad again. They've put him back on the drip.'

Gloria got to the church a good forty minutes before the midnight service was due to start, and busied herself putting out the flowers and lighting the candles on the altar and down the centre aisle. The church looked almost magical in the low, flickering light, and for once even Gloria felt a mystery there, as if the spirit of Christmas had come and breathed its life tangibly into the air, but then she thought again of Griff, and a sour look came to her face.

As she had expected, he had slept for a good five hours, still sprawled inelegantly across the hall floor, and then, when he had awoken, he had hauled himself up by the coat hooks and announced he was going back to the pub because there was something that he had to get. 'Yes, pie-eyed,' Gloria had responded tartly. But he had looked at her with an injured air and informed her that it was nothing like that, and that she would be very pleased. He had then left, promising that he would not be long, and that he would come along afterwards to church. Gloria had cringed, and found herself hoping that he would get pie-eyed again; anything rather than embarrass her. Nevertheless, she found herself keeping a wary eye on the door.

Father Trumpington arrived ten minutes before the service was due to start and, even to Gloria's undiscerning eye, he looked terrible, a shadow of his former self. He was indeed feeling extremely apprehensive. The events of the last few days had taken their toll upon him but, even more than that, he had a lurking dread that everybody knew what he had done and that he would

236

be a laughing stock. 'Don't be silly,' Dorothy had assured him, 'nobody knows. Only the Pilkingtons and us, and they're not going to say anything!' But all the same, she promised to be at his side and, for the first time in his life, Father Trumpington had felt grateful. Now she came in with him and, squeezing his hand reassuringly, went to sit at the front of the church while he went to robe.

'My, you don't look too good,' said Gloria as he came into the vestry. She was getting out the Communion things and had just locked the safe.

Antonia was there too, putting on her stole and trying not to react as Gloria ostentatiously waggled the keys to the safe under her nose. Though she had been here for three months, Antonia had still not been given any keys to the safe, and Gloria never tired of flaunting what she felt to be her superiority.

Antonia turned away, determinedly ignoring the churchwarden, and said, 'Yes, you do look a bit pale. Are you sure you're going to be all right?'

Father Trumpington grunted. He remembered suddenly that Antonia also knew, but he did not think that she would say anything, for Gudrun's sake as much as anything else. 'Perfectly all right, thank you,' he rasped. 'I wouldn't be here otherwise.'

'Yes, but you mustn't overstrain yourself,' chided Gloria. 'Flu's nasty.'

Father Trumpington set down his bag and began to take off his coat, prior to putting on his robes. 'Go and check the stalls,' he said curtly to Antonia, 'and then go and welcome people as they come in.'

Gloria waited till she had gone and then said, 'Funny attitude that girl has. She always does what she's told but . . . I can't stand that pious air she's got. It's so holier than thou!'

'Yes,' grunted Father Trumpington. 'She can be a bit of a trial.' His thoughts reverted to Norman and Jackie and, unable to help himself, he added, 'Though not perhaps as much as some.'

Quite unconsciously his eyes had strayed in the direction of the organ, and he jumped now when Gloria said, 'Yes, I do know what you mean.'

Father Trumpington felt his flesh crawl. He froze in the act of buttoning up his cassock and stared at her, his tongue cleaving to the roof of his mouth. He swallowed painfully and then, in a hoarse voice, said, 'I'm sorry?'

Gloria interpreted his strained manner as concern. She had not intended to say anything quite yet, but she was nothing if not an opportunist, and it seemed to her that the right moment had presented itself. 'Oh, it's all right,' she said reassuringly, and trying to inject warmth and sympathy into her voice. 'It's just that I know.'

'Oh, my God!' said Father Trumpington. He sat down heavily.

'Dear me,' said Gloria, 'you are still feeling weak, aren't you? Shall I get you some water?' Father Trumpington shook his head. 'You mustn't take it so much to heart,' went on Gloria. 'These things happen, after all.' She smiled. 'We just have to be careful how we deal with them. Make sure we take the right steps.'

Father Trumpington looked at her. He had felt mystified by his churchwarden ever since the Christmas party, and now it occurred to him to wonder if she was about to try blackmailing him. 'How much do you know?' he asked carefully.

'Oh, pretty well everything, I should think,' said Gloria cheerfully, 'but don't worry, I'm not going to say anything if you don't want me to.'

Father Trumpington closed his eyes. It was even worse than he had feared. She knew it all and she was threatening him. Unless he acted quickly, it could be only a matter of time now before the whole church knew.

'Yes,' Gloria was going on, totally oblivious of the effect her words were having, 'I saw them here in church. They didn't know I was here. I overheard them speaking to each other – and carrying on,' she added meaningfully. 'Disgusting, if you ask me, in a church!'

'In church?' said Father Trumpington faintly. 'When?'

'Today,' said Gloria, 'this afternoon. I was doing the flowers like you asked me to.'

'Of course,' said Father Trumpington.

'And they came in. They started off having a row. That was how I knew they were here. Shouting at each other, they were. I heard it all. They poured it all out!' Father Trumpington thought she looked at him menacingly. 'And then the next minute there they were, canoodling and kissing over by the organ.'

Father Trumpington's humiliation was complete. He felt he hated Jackie now, but nothing she did surprised him any longer. Yet far, far worse, was the fact that Gloria now knew too. 'What must I do,' he asked heavily, 'to keep you quiet?'

Gloria blinked. It seemed rather an odd thing to say, she thought, in the circumstances. 'Oh, you don't need to worry,' she said, puzzled. 'I'm not going to tell anyone, unless you say. I think you've acted wonderfully. I want to help.' He looked at her as if she was mad and again she smiled reassuringly. 'Oh, I know what you're worried about,' she said suddenly, light dawning. 'You're scared of the effect all this could have on the church. Of course, you're right. If this came out, there'd be a terrible scandal.' Father Trumpington looked at her in terror. 'Don't worry,' she breathed, and she chuckled conspiratorially, 'my silence is very easily bought!' With that, she leant forward and patted his arm, a terrible smile on her face. 'I'm going to support you,' she assured him. 'Whatever it takes!' With that, she whisked out of the vestry to go and arrange the chalice and patten on the altar. Father Trumpington sat stunned. He had been right. It was definitely blackmail. If he did not do now exactly what she said, it was all going to come out. 'Oh dear,' he muttered softly, 'this is terrible.' But at the same time, he felt that there was a light at the end of the tunnel. Very faint, it was true, but unmistakably there. He had been a fool, he knew that now, but Dorothy at least was going to stand by him and, although it appeared that Gloria also now knew, it seemed he could buy her silence – though with what he wasn't yet sure. Father Trumpington swallowed and made a resolution: he was willing to pay any price.

Out in the main body of the church, Gloria suddenly froze. She had looked up from the altar and had seen, coming through the doors and carrying a huge box, Griff. He caught her eye and waved cheerfully, at the same time pointing at the box and then at her. Gloria felt she wanted to run away. Why could he not just leave her alone? Why did he have to embarrass her like this? She scuttled as fast as her short legs would take her down the aisle, and caught up with him just taking a seat at the back. 'What on earth's that?' she hissed. 'Why have you brought that here?'

'Hello, luv,' said Griff beerily. 'It's for you. It's your Christmas present. Happy Christmas!'

Gloria was almost beside herself as heads turned to look in their direction. 'But why have you brought it here?' she repeated. 'It's not Christmas yet!'

Griff straightened his shoulders with immense dignity. It had percolated through to his beer-soaked brain that the light of his life did not appear overly pleased. 'I know that,' he said, with an injured air, 'but I told you, I had to pick it up from a bloke at the pub. Beautiful it is, I got it cheap.'

Gloria closed her eyes. 'What is it?'

'A microwave,' said Griff proudly, 'top of the range. Fell off the back of a lorry.'

'You mean it's stolen?' shrieked Gloria.

All down the church more heads turned to look.

'Ssh!' said Griff hastily. 'Keep your voice down.' Then he whispered, 'No, I mean literally, it fell off the back of a lorry. It's dented but it's only a very small dent and it works perfectly. That's why it was going cheap.'

Gloria looked at him. Words failed her. She raised a finger and waggled it warningly in his face, and then turned on her heel and marched smartly away. Off to the side she heard a small titter and, turning her head, saw Jackie, who smiled cattily and gave a small wave. Bitch! thought Gloria, taken aback even to see her there. But she recollected herself and, with only the barest pause, curtly nodded her head and sailed on. She would have her revenge soon enough.

It was three o'clock in the morning when Antonia finally got home and fell into bed, and then she had to be up at seven, ready to get down to church in time for the eight o'clock Communion. She had tried suggesting to Father Trumpington that they did not really need an eight o'clock Communion on Christmas Day, so soon after the midnight service and before Communion at ten, but he had dismissed the idea. 'Of course we do!' he said, and he ordered her to take it with reserved sacrament, saying that he himself would be along later. He also felt they needed a shortened

Communion at twelve, and a service of evening prayer at four thirty, all of which he ordered her to take, explaining that he himself would be unable to attend as he would have the family at home. That Antonia might also like to spend some time with those dear to her he appeared to consider irrelevent.

As it was, Antonia got to church by ten to eight and then, having waited forlornly for fifteen minutes for someone else to turn up, said the morning office by herself. She debated afterwards whether to go back home and have a cup of coffee, but it occurred to her that Kathleen might not be up, and that it would be selfish to disturb her any further, so instead she stayed at the church and read through the Nativity stories in Matthew and Luke, until it was time to start preparing for the ten o'clock.

She was not sorry to have the time alone, she felt it was a chance to talk things over with God; recently she seemed to have been so busy that she had had very little time for that. She wished that she was not a party to all the secrets Gudrun had shared. Each time she looked at Father Trumpington now, she felt a terrible weight of dark knowledge. She thought that someone in authority ought to know, so that she could be relieved of the burden, but she knew that it was not her place to tell anyone, because then she would be betraying the confidence placed in her. Yet she felt the terrible dishonour to the church and so, very soon, she lay down the Bible and began instead to pray, pouring out all her problems and asking God to do something to sort it all out. And somehow, sitting by herself in the tiny Lady Chapel, she felt calm and peace begin to return and the quiet assurance that, in the end, all would be well.

The certainty that God was in control comforted her and, almost without realising, her spirits took an upward turn and she found herself beginning to give thanks for the tiny babe born in the stable that Christmas time two thousand years ago. So it was that when Father Trumpington himself arrived some two hours later, he found her in an unexpectedly cheerful mood, which only further fuelled his unease and intensified his loathing for her.

'Is that her, Mummy?' hissed Amelia who had accompanied Dorothy to church, along with her husband and two very excited children.

'Yes,' whispered back Dorothy. 'But don't stare, dear. You'll draw attention.'

'I think someone ought to draw attention to her,' answered Amelia robustly. 'She looks really horrible. So full of herself. And to think she's causing Daddy so much trouble.' She glared at the curate's back and at that moment, as if feeling someone's eyes upon her, Antonia turned round. She had just been hugging someone and wishing them a merry Christmas and, perhaps unfortunately, at the precise moment she glanced round she laughed, so that as her eye fell on Amelia it looked for all the world as if she was laughing at her. Amelia bristled. 'Do you see that!' she said indignantly. 'She must have heard. She's laughing at me. What a cow!'

Antonia, recognising Dorothy, came over. 'Hello,' she said. 'Merry Christmas. Is this your family?'

'Yes,' said Dorothy faintly, and made the introductions she had been hoping to avoid.

'How lovely to meet you,' enthused Antonia. 'I hadn't realised Dick had grandchildren. Is it just the two? What are their names? What gorgeous long hair!' And she ruffled Charlotte's hair good-naturedly, while the child looked up, instantly besotted.

Amelia sniffed coldly and looked away. 'Please don't do that,' she said, 'it takes me ages to do her hair every day.'

There was an uncomfortable silence. 'I'm sorry,' said Antonia. 'It's such a pretty colour though, isn't it? It's like ripe corn.' She tried again. 'Who does she get the colour from?'

Amelia refused to answer and, embarrassed, Torquil said blusteringly, 'Think it must be from Dick, you know. It's certainly not from my side of the family. It's not obvious on Amelia's side either but Dick's bald, apart from those few grey hairs of his, so I reckon it's him!'

Amelia glowered. 'Be quiet, Torquil,' she said witheringly, and then she turned and stared at Antonia. 'I think you ought to be ashamed,' she said loudly.

Antonia gaped at her. 'I beg your pardon?'

'You heard what I said,' snapped Amelia. There was a sudden silence as her shrill voice carried down the main body of the church. 'You ought to be ashamed after all you've done!'

'All I've done?' repeated Antonia. She looked totally bewildered.

Amelia was beyond caring. She thought it was about time someone stood up for poor Daddy, and she was certainly not going to allow some jumped-up little curate, fresh out of theological college, to come in and set them all by the heels in the way Antonia seemed to have done. Dear Mummy might be worried about causing offence, but she wasn't. 'Yes,' she said, 'you know what I mean.'

'No, I don't,' said Antonia. 'I'm sorry.'

'Be quiet, dear,' said Dorothy.

But Amelia would not be quiet. 'I don't know how you've got the nerve to come in here and act like you own the place,' she shrieked, 'setting people against each other the way you do! You are only a curate, after all. If you ask me, you should never have been ordained. They made a big mistake when they selected you!' She became aware of the ring of shocked faces that had gathered round her and fell silent, although she glared defiantly at them. Her expression suggested that, though they might not know, she did, but she was not going to say any more, out of respect for Daddy.

Antonia stared at her, very white, and then, muttering 'Excuse me', turned and walked away. Behind her Alan Gunningham, who had been watching the whole proceedings with interest, smirked. Very good, he thought, let people think Antonia had been involved in something underhand, it would serve his purposes very well. He went off in search of Father Trumpington and found him on his knees before the opened doors of the choir cupboard, testily doling out sheet music and berating the choir boys for their noisy exuberance. 'Be quiet,' he heard him say, 'the whole church does *not* wish to know that you had a Biker Mouse this morning, Matthew!'

'Dick!' Alan hissed. 'A word.'

Father Trumpington, his head in a large cardboard box, turned round hastily, bumping his nose on the edge. 'Oh, it's you, Alan,' he said, rubbing the offended orifice with his hand. 'Of course.' He seized the nearest child and thrust a wodge of sheets into his hand. 'Make sure everyone has a copy,' he snapped, 'and I don't want to hear another sound out of any of you!' He staggered to his feet and turned to the Treasurer.

Alan drew him aside. 'It's all fixed,' he said softly. 'I've had a word with George.'

Father Trumpington stared at him. In all the turmoil of the last few days, he had completely forgotten about the plan to remove Antonia, but now it all came flooding back to him like a surprise present received on a particularly joyless day. 'Have you?' he gasped.

Alan nodded. 'She should be in for a nice little surprise after Christmas, if all goes according to plan. And I say, jolly good idea to get Amelia all fired up like that.' Father Trumpington looked blank and Alan laughed softly. 'She had a go at her,' he explained, 'at the back of church. Practically accused her outright of spreading sedition and anarchy. I almost felt sorry for the girl. She hadn't a clue what to say, just stared at her like an outraged kitten, and then walked off.' He squeezed Father Trumpington encouragingly on the arm. 'Take heart, old boy,' he said, 'we'll soon have this little problem sorted out.'

Father Trumpington wished all his little problems could be so easily sorted out. Nevertheless, he was grateful to Alan. Somewhat irrationally he blamed the onset of all his recent disasters on Antonia, and he had this lurking feeling that, if only he could get rid of her, everything else would come right too. The knowledge that George Bullen was now to intervene was balm to his soul. 'Thank you, Alan,' he said sincerely.

Alan winked. 'Now do your part,' he said. 'Make sure that she can't get up to the hospital on time. Give out a few extra notices. You know the sort of thing. Spin out the sermon. Anything. But hold her up!'

Father Trumpington did not need any more urging. He discovered that there were all sorts of things to tell people about the new year, while amazingly his sermon on iconoclastic representations of the Madonna in the Balkans (during which he as usual managed the difficult feat of totally avoiding all mention of Jesus) lasted a whole thirty-five minutes. Consequently, when the shell-shocked congregation finally staggered to their feet, it was eleven twenty-five and Antonia had all of five minutes to make a twelve minute journey up to the hospital. 'Did you come on your bike?' inquired Father Trumpington sweetly. She nodded. 'Then I suggest you get on it,' he said. 'You might be a tiny bit late if you don't hurry.'

Antonia ran for the door. But she had first to negotiate the congregation, all of whom seemed to want to hug her and wish her a very happy Christmas, and to inquire what she was doing for the rest of the day. 'Sorry,' she panted, 'can't stop. I've got to get up to St Thomas's.'

By the time she had found her bike and hoisted up her cassock, it was eleven thirty-two. She pedalled off as if her life depended on it, and was helped by the emptiness of the roads, but it was still eleven forty by the time she arrived. Then she had to lock her bike and run the entire length of the hospital to the staff dining room where the service was to take place. As she pelted down the final corridor she could hear the weak strains of 'Oh come, oh come, Emmanuel' just drawing to a close. She pushed open the door and almost fell in, and all round the room heads swivelled and stared. From the dais Professor Bullen glared at her disapprovingly. 'Ah,' he said loudly, 'our officiant has at last decided to grace us with her presence. Just in time to give us our address.'

Red-faced and fighting for breath, Antonia walked through the beds and wheelchairs down the length of the room. There was silence as every eye followed her progress, and she could see one or two of the doctors grinning at her discomfort. They had evidently themselves, in the past, felt the lash of the professor's tongue. Then, as she mounted the five shallow steps that led up to the stage, she stumbled slightly on the hem of her cassock and almost fell.

'Oh, come along,' said Professor Bullen testily. 'Are we supposed to sit here all day?' He waved an irate hand towards the lectern that someone had put ready for her to speak.

Gathering herself up, Antonia collapsed gratefully against it, leaning heavily on the wooden edge. A sea of pale faces stared up at her. Most of the patients went home for Christmas, leaving only those who were seriously ill behind. Some of course were too ill to be moved and had had to stay in the wards, but the rest had all been trundled in in wheelchairs or, failing that, in their beds, along with drips and hoists and whatever else of their medical paraphernalia they needed. They looked an odd sight, and odder still were the nurses standing anxiously poised around the sides, with bits of tinsel pinned to their uniforms.

'Thank you,' said Professor Bullen. He turned from Antonia and glared down the hall. 'Just to remind you all,' he said harshly, 'Father Christmas will be doing his rounds immediately after this service and would much appreciate help in distributing turkey and presents to the patients.' He sat down then with a peremptory nod of his head, and Antonia realised that everyone was now looking expectantly at her. She smiled uneasily, unsure at what point of the service they were. 'The sermon!' barked Professor Bullen, noting her discomfort. 'We've done the rest.'

'Ah, yes, of course,' said Antonia. His interjection had not helped, and she fumbled slightly with her notes and again looked around, trying desperately to collect her thoughts. It had not struck her, prior to this moment, how very demoralising it must be for the patients who would have to remain over Christmas. In the weeks leading up to the holiday there had been an air of excitement about the hospital, and she knew that every effort had been made to celebrate Christmas in a way that would ensure no one felt left out of the festivities taking place in homes throughout the land. But still it had not struck her before how very ill people would have to be if they had to remain and, as she looked at them now, a flood of sympathy and pity swept over her.

'I am so sorry to be late,' she began, 'and so very pleased to be with you all here today,' and she could not help adding, 'although I'm sure that most of you wish you were somewhere else.' Then she pushed away her notes and began to speak of the love of the tiny baby for them all; the love of the baby whose mother must have wished at the time that she was somewhere else too, rather than in a grubby stable.

Antonia had felt nervous as she rushed in, and was taken aback by Professor Bullen's obvious displeasure and the coldness of his manner. She had never actually met him before, although she had heard many horror stories about him from the staff and knew

246

that he was generally reckoned to be a bit of a tyrant. But now, as she spoke, she forgot about him, becoming lost herself in the Spirit that flowed from that tiny stable, and all around she saw an answering gleam reflected in the faces of the people lying in the beds or hunched over in their chairs. She found herself telling them about joy, and was rewarded by seeing hope flicker into life all around her.

Afterwards, she went down among the beds, and hands reached out and grasped her own as she passed, and over and over again people said, 'Thank you, it's really Christmas now.' One old lady, so frail and thin she seemed almost not to be there, a bag of bones tossed higgeldy-piggeldy on to the bed and then tidied away under a sheet, called out to her as she passed, 'Over here, dear! Come here!' She could not raise herself or even reach out an arm, but she lifted a frail hand about an inch off the bed and, very gently, Antonia took it.

'Hello,' she said. 'Happy Christmas.'

The woman smiled. Her breathing was shallow, and as Antonia looked at her closely, she saw that her body was hopelessly twisted. 'I can't move, dear,' she said, 'but I wanted to say thank you. I love Jesus too . . . you brought him here to me today.'

Antonia had no idea what to say. She felt tears start to her eyes. Very carefully, she squeezed the woman's hand. 'Bless you,' she said.

Professor Bullen was waiting for her at the door. 'I trust you have some reasonable explanation for the time of your arrival,' he said.

'I'm sorry,' said Antonia. 'It was just that the service at St Godric's went on – you know how it is, Christmas.'

He looked at her. 'No,' he said, 'I don't. For myself I make a very great effort to be where I've said I'm going to be on time. I suggest you learn that lesson. You were twenty minutes late and we had to start without you. You almost didn't make it in time for the sermon. There is absolutely no excuse for such laxity.' And, not giving her a chance to respond, he turned his back on her and began to talk to someone else.

Chapter Eighteen

As the confirmation drew nearer, Kathleen, Dave and Jude began to meet together to pray in the front room of Kathleen's house. That Christmas, for Dave, was the most meaningful of his whole life, and he felt a deep excitement at the prospect of his baptism in the new year. The day after Boxing Day, he checked again with Slynne that the jetty was now completely safe, and began to pray that God would keep from them any hint of rain or snow. The closer the baptism came, the longer Father Trumpington's list of conditions had grown. If it snowed or rained heavily, so that the level of the river rose, or if there were strong winds or it was too muddy, the baptism, he had informed the congregation, would be moved inside the church. Dave was in an agony of apprehension. All over Christmas he kept staring up at the sky and muttering incoherently to himself, but the weather seemed unable to make up its mind. Over Christmas itself it was bitterly cold and there were icy winds, then on Boxing Day the temperature went up, but it began rather half-heartedly to rain. The drizzle, it was true, did not last very long, but the clouds seemed then to settle lower, in a thick impenetrable blanket, heavy with threat.

Dave and Slynne bumped into Father Trumpington, who had dropped into the church to escape from the delights of home, as they trudged back up from the river. 'Yon jetty seems fine,' Dave was saying, and Slynne was rather cautiously agreeing when Father Trumpington loomed out of the gloom in front of them, like some baleful imp rising out of the mist.

'Seems a bit muddy to me,' boomed the priest, correctly divining where they had been. 'If this doesn't clear up, I'm afraid it's all going to be off down by the river.' He could not disguise the note of satisfaction that had crept into his voice and Dave looked at him in alarm.

'It's a'right!' he announced. 'It's perfect. The water's like a mill pond, and the jetty's jus' greet now!'

'But the mud,' admonished Father Trumpington, and he stared meaningfully down at Dave's mud-caked boots.

'No,' protested Dave, 'it's a'right, 'onest. I went down the bank. It's always muddy down there, but Edgar's a'right. He stopped up on the jetty, and his shoes are fine!'

Father Trumpington looked at Slynne's feet dubiously. 'I am not convinced, David,' he said. 'We shall have to see. I do not intend to take risks.' And with that he went off, even managing a little hum to himself. Indeed, his spirits had lifted considerably that day because he had received by the morning post a copy of the letter of complaint George Bullen had already sent to the Bishop. It was harsh in its condemnation of Antonia.

The professor began by stating baldly that she had been twenty minutes late for their most important service of the year, and that she had proffered no adequate explanation. She had made it clear, he went on, she did not want to be there, and had even gone so far as to say that she thought all of them probably did not want to be there either! He then said she had preached a highly inappropriate and offensive sermon, in particular that she had told a large group of sick people, many of whom were suffering from terminal disease, that Jesus would heal them! Words, he said, had failed him at the crass insensitivity manifested by this; she was clearly lackadaisical in her approach and displayed not the slightest understanding of pastoral care. He could only hope that she would now learn from a reprimand. He ended by saying he expected a full apology, made by Antonia in person.

In the midst of his gloom, Father Trumpington had been greatly cheered. Let her wriggle out of this one, if she could. The Bishop would almost certainly summon her in now, he reflected. Indeed, he could not do otherwise, given the standing of Professor Bullen in the city. As for himself, he could not wait to inform her of the enormity of her sin. He rather thought it was so serious that he should get together a little meeting with some of the more trusted members of the PCC, and that they should rebuke Antonia as a group. She would see then that it was not simply him, but that they all disapproved of her. Also, it occurred to him that criticism of Antonia would very effectively take the spotlight from himself, and he began to wonder, if he was very quiet now and kept his head down, whether the Bishop might not forget his unpleasant little fracas with the Pilkingtons. He had said as much to Dorothy, and she had looked at him sceptically, but even that could not for long depress his returning spirits. He might have made a fool of himself with Jackie but he was going to come out of this all right, he told himself. Let him just find a new and more suitable organist, and he could even carry on with his original plan to put St Godric's firmly on the ecclesiastical map.

The one fly in Father Trumpington's present ointment, apart from the wounds inflicted to his vanity by Jackie, was the resumption of conjugal relations that he had been forced into with Dorothy. She had made it clear that this was a part of the deal to maintain her continued support, and Father Trumpington had found himself pushed physically to the brink. In vain he had tried to protest to her that he was a much older man now and could not manage it more than once a night. Dorothy was relentless. With her aerobics and regular exercise classes, she had found a new lease of life. Regularly, at three o'clock every morning, she woke him up by heaving herself on top of him and blowing into his ear. Father Trumpington was not sure that he could take much more. Dorothy, however, appeared to be blooming. There was a spring in her step, and a remarkably determined glint in her eye which made Amelia simper and say it was all 'so sweet' and 'at their age!' It made Father Trumpington cringe, but he was running too close to the wind now to try to do anything to alter the situation.

The day before the Sunday set for Dave's baptism there was a light scattering of snow. But on the morning itself, the day dawned bright, crisp, and clear, with not a trace of a cloud in the sky. Dave phoned up Antonia early – in fact, he got her out of bed. 'He can't possibly object now,' he said jubilantly. 'It's perfect! Look at it!'

Antonia looked, peering bleary-eyed through a gap in the curtains that she had steadfastly resisted drawing back. 'Um,' she said, noncommittally. She was learning with Father Trumpington that it did not pay to be too sure. Still, as she peered out of the window and her eyes began to focus, she felt that even he would be hard put to object. 'It looks like it'll be all right,' she said cautiously, 'but don't build your hopes up too high. Just in case.'

'Don't be daft,' crowed Dave. 'It's almost a heatwave. Yon man can't possibly object!' But then he got down to the subject of his phone call. 'I want my bonfire. I want tae burn everything,' he said emphatically. 'I know I can't have it at church, but I want tae get rid of everything bad from ma old life. Clean slate now, and I'd like you tae be there tae say a prayer.'

Antonia groaned inwardly, thinking longingly of her bed. 'Where had you thought of having it?' she inquired, without enthusiasm.

'In the park. It's not goin' tae be very big, after all, and there won't be anybody about at this hour, so I don't think anybody's goin' tae mind!'

'Oh, I'm not sure about that,' said Antonia, coming fully awake as visions of angry park keepers leapt to her mind.

But Dave insisted. 'Look,' he said, 'we can light it where the gardeners usually light their fire. We won't be harmin' anything. It's just a small wee fire.'

He sounded so imploring that she relented. She met him in the park some half an hour later, and together they made a small fire on to which Dave piled a strange assortment of books, tarot cards, and packets of what, at first glance, appeared to be herbs but which Dave assured her were potent charms. Whatever they were, they had a strange effect on the fire because, as soon as they touched the flames, they blazed up and a shower of sparks flew into the air.

'Ah'm very sorry, an' ah'm givin' it all tae you, Jesus!' announced Dave.

And then Antonia obligingly said a prayer to separate him from all such things, proclaimed him freed by the sacrifice of Christ and, without more ado, they set off for the church.

Father Trumpington was already there when they arrived. He had just come back from an investigation of the river bank with Slynne and was evidently trying to find some reason why they should not go ahead. 'Oh, it's you,' he said without enthusiasm when he saw Dave. 'I really *do* feel it's too muddy, you know.' He looked at Slynne for confirmation, but Slynne shook his head.

'Oi don't think as ye need t' worry,' he said consideringly. 'Grounds rock-'ard. It'll be muddy later, when as the temperature goes up, but it's not goin' t' cause much of a mess at the moment. It's like iron.'

Father Trumpington glared at him and said, 'Yes, thank you, Edgar.'

'No problem,' Slynne responded, 'Oi loikes to 'elp.'

The priest tried a different tack. 'I fear it will be too cold for you, David.'

Dave grinned. 'No, I had ma porridge this morning. I'll be fine. It's only a quick in an' out. And Jude's bringing me along some spare clothes in case any of these get wet. But I'm planning on wearing ma swimsuit.'

Father Trumpington stared. 'Your swimsuit!' he repeated weakly. He had never heard of someone being baptised in a swimsuit before.

'Yep!' Dave nodded. 'I've got it on already.'

At that moment Gloria came up. Because Father Trumpington had from the first ostensibly agreed to Dave's baptism in the river, the churchwarden had convinced herself, along with most of the rest of the congregation, that the priest actually wanted it to happen. She imagined now, from the conversation that was taking place, that he was simply exercising his usual pastoral care for others – which was so like him, she thought adoringly. For herself, she thought the whole business was rather silly, but the mere fact that the light of her life wanted it made her determined to offer whatever help she could.

Overhearing Dave's last remark, she said approvingly, 'I like a man in a swimsuit.' Then she turned to Father Trumpington and smiled meaningfully, slightly puckering her scarlet lips. 'I've got all the baptism cards out,' she added, 'and the Mother's Union have offered to put on coffee afterwards in the hall for everyone, so I asked them to go ahead.' Her smile grew tender, and she looked at the priest with an expression in her eye that filled him with dread. He thought she looked quite threatening. 'Quite exciting, isn't it?' she purred seductively, pleased at what she felt to be his clear response. 'We're all looking forward to this.' And with that she sailed off.

Father Trumpington stared after her retreating back and Dave said jubilantly, 'Ya know, I think God wants this too. He's made the weather so perfect this morning, and everyone's being so nice.'

Father Trumpington did not share his sentiments, but as he stared after Gloria he wondered glumly what she might do if she felt herself to be crossed. For some strange reason, he reflected, she seemed to want this baptism. He swallowed and made up his mind. 'Yes, yes, all right!' he said testily. 'We'll have it in the river.' And then he glared at Antonia. 'I want a word with you later,' he hissed nastily. 'I'll see you in the vestry after the service.'

The church was unexpectedly full for that first service of the year. Word of the baptism had got around, and not only had all Dave and Jude's friends turned up to support him, but many of the curious from other churches in the city had turned out to see the spectacle too. Father Trumpington looked around at the long hair and leather jackets of Dave's friends and shuddered.

'After the first hymn,' he announced grimly, 'we shall process out in an orderly fashion down to the river. Please bring your hymn books and the baptismal cards with you, but leave your prayer books in the pews. At the river bank, we shall gather in an orderly semi-circle round the jetty, and David will make his promises there before you all, before going down into the water, when I shall baptise him.'

Somebody let out a cheer, and another voice shouted, 'Good on ye, Dave! Go for it!'

Father Trumpington glared. 'Please remember that this is a house of God!' he snapped. 'Let us approach the proceedings with some decorum!' Hardly had the words left his mouth, however, than there was a sound of boots scraping on the floor and books being dropped, and all over the church Dave's untidy friends began to rise to their feet and head towards the door. 'The first hymn!' bleated Father Trumpington feebly. They ignored him and, despairingly, he nodded towards Norman, who obligingly struck up the opening chords of 'Onward Christian soldiers'.

Despite all the priest's best efforts at restraint, the untidy mass that spilled out of church and down towards the river had more the feel of a rowdy triumphal march at a football match than a religious procession. In vain did Father Trumpington try to marshall them into neat rows and get them to be quiet. They defied his every effort, scattering noisily across the graveyard and along the river bank, pushing and shoving each other in an effort to get a better view.

Once arrived, Dave flung off his clothes and stood proudly on the jetty, clutching his baptismal card before his eyes. Father Trumpington abandoned all hopes of order and began, as fast as he could, to yell out the words. 'Do you believe and trust in Jesus Christ?' he bellowed.

'Yes!' bellowed back Dave.

'Do you believe and trust in the Holy Spirit?'

'I do!' shouted Dave.

'Use the right words,' snapped Father Trumpington, exasperated.

'I believe and trust in him!' cried Dave, managing to make himself sound like a revivalist preacher from the Midwest. Father Trumpington raised his eyes heavenwards.

'Just get in the water!' he said.

Dave needed no further urging. With a cry of euphoria he leapt in. He had not intended to. He had meant to walk down the steps sedately in a manner of which he thought Father Trumpington would approve, but somehow when it came to it he was unable to hold himself back. With a cry of triumph, he took a flying leap and threw himself bodily into the middle of the stream so that water fountained up and cascaded in every direction, saturating those unlucky enough to be near. Father Trumpington, who was standing slightly back, discovered he had three large splashes on his surplice, and he looked at Dave coldly. 'Please restrain yourself and come and stand here.' He indicated a spot just in front of the jetty and, crestfallen, Dave came and stood there while Father Trumpington gathered himself up and stepped forward for the final ordeal. Being careful to hold back his robes so as to stop them from trailing in the river, he leant down and scooped up a cupful of mucky water. 'David,' he began, 'I baptise you . . .' – He discovered Dave was standing further out than he had at first thought, and that he could not reach to tip the water fully over Dave's already dripping head.

Grunting, Father Trumpington pursed his lips, clutched his stole to his chest, and leant out further over the water. At the same moment Dave obligingly moved forward, and his head caught Father Trumpington's outstretched arm. For one frozen moment the startled congregation watched as Father Trumpington swayed and then, caught off balance, slipped and thrust out a hand in an effort to save himself. His groping fingers closed on air. He stood, ridiculously balanced on one leg, and then, with a wild cry that seemed a parody of Dave's, he toppled headlong into the river.

'I didn't know you were coming in,' said Dave, surprised. 'That's real nice of you!'

Father Trumpington surfaced, spluttering and gasping for air. A crown of weed circled his bald head. 'In the name of the Father, the Son and the Holy Spirit,' said Dave encouragingly, as the priest appeared to fight for breath.

In fury, Father Trumpington slapped his hand down on the water, at the same time spitting something green and slimy out of his mouth. 'In the name of the Father, Son and Holy Spirit!' he shouted savagely, as water cascaded all around and over Dave.

'Alleluia!' shouted Dave, flinging his arms up into the air.

As if in response to his cry, there was a sudden disturbance close to the bank, in the water off to his right, and both he and Father Trumpington turned to stare. In the sudden quiet, a large water rat suddenly popped its head above the surface and looked Father Trumpington straight in the eye.

'Hey,' said Dave, in tones of interest, 'a rat.'

'Oh my God,' said Father Trumpington. 'Weil's disease!'

Chapter Nineteen

Father Trumpington was brought home, dripping wet, by Alan. 'Fell in the water,' said the Treasurer apologetically to Dorothy. 'Sorry.'

Father Trumpington moaned softly and rubbed a hand across his eyes.

Dorothy waited till Alan had gone and then said grimly, 'What happened?'

Teeth chattering, he told her. 'And then this rat appeared,' he concluded. 'It was huge. Its body was all bloated. I'm sure it was ill.' He sneezed violently and Dorothy eyed him.

'With flu no doubt,' she said, her tone acerbic. She had long since decided all men were hypochondriacs. 'What you need,' she said crisply, 'is to get out of those clothes and into a good hot bath.'

He shook his head. He was convinced he was dying. 'No, dear,' he said softly, and in a failing voice. 'I think I should go to hospital now – the danger of Weil's disease, you know.'

'Nonsense,' said Dorothy firmly. 'If anything, I should think you've given something to the rat.'

Despite all his best efforts to be ill, Father Trumpington discovered she was right. He did feel better once he was in the bath. As he lay there soaking, Dorothy came in with a cup of tea. 'Antonia's on the phone,' she said crossly. 'She says you said you wanted to see her this morning, and what do you want her to do now?'

Father Trumpington closed his eyes weakly. If he was dying there really did not seem much point. On the other hand . . . He stretched his toes and discovered he felt immense anger against Dave. Someone ought to pay, he thought. 'Tell her to come round at four o'clock this afternoon,' he said grimly.

Dorothy put down the tea on the ledge beside the bath and looked at him with satisfaction. 'Of course,' she said. 'I told you you'd feel better, didn't I?'

* * *

Antonia had not the slightest idea why Father Trumpington had asked to see her, though she rather thought it might have something to do with the preaching rota for the next few months. She had had four days' break with Henry after Christmas. They had gone up to the Lake District, which was where her parents lived, and had spent hours talking as they walked the long lines of the fells. They had not talked about anything in particular; just themselves and God, and what they felt he might be calling them to, but the result was that she had returned feeling immeasurably encouraged. There were many good and exciting things happening, as Henry had pointed out, and somehow all the upsets with Gudrun and Norman and the problem posed by Father Trumpington's bizarre behaviour had fallen into place, dwarfed by the overarching splendour of the hills and skies. More than once she had thought to herself that if God could create all this out of nothing, then he could most certainly sort out the tiny bit of chaos in which she found herself. And the thought had been comforting, so that gradually all her anxieties had disappeared.

This morning was her first day back and, still borne up by the feeling of quiet certainty communicated by the fells, she found it hard to imagine that anything could possibly be wrong. Also she felt a measure of excitement that she was eager to share with Father Trumpington because, after the service that morning, four of Dave's long-haired friends had come up to her and, rather diffidently, had said that they would like to get to know Jesus too. They had been impressed, they explained, by what had happened to Dave, and they wanted it as well. So now she could not wait to talk to the priest about the possibilities of setting up an inquirers' group.

She arrived at five to four clutching assorted articles for an inquirer's course that she had dug out of her college ministerial aids pack. There was one short book that she thought looked particularly interesting, and she had brought along a video as well that she thought he might like to watch.

Father Trumpington decided to receive her in his study. The closer it had got to four, the angrier he had become. Everything was her fault, he kept telling himself; and as he turned all that had happened in the past few months over in his mind, her iniquities grew and grew. If she had not come to St Godric's, there would never have been that awful baptism in the first place. How dare she fill up his church with these uncouth louts. He rather suspected Dave had pulled him in deliberately! Consequently, when he at last walked magisterially in through the door, having made her sit waiting for ten minutes by herself, he was in a mood of unparalleled malevolence.

'Ah, Antonia,' he said, without preamble, 'there's been another complaint. But this one's rather more serious than the others.'

Antonia's jaw dropped open. 'Complaint?' she repeated. 'From whom? When?'

'From Professor Bullen.' Father Trumpington smiled nastily and seated himself opposite her at the desk, leaning back in his chair, fingertips resting lightly together across his chest. 'I'm afraid he's written to the Bishop. Not only did you arrive late at St Thomas's, he says, but your manner was extremely offensive, while the sermon that you preached was insulting.' Antonia appeared speechless and, not displeased with the effect, he went on, 'If he had spoken to me first, of course, I should have tried to dissuade him from writing to the Bishop, but as it is, I'm afraid there will be trouble over this. Professor Bullen is extremely upset.'

A feeling of unreality swept over Antonia. She felt bemused. She had been late, it was true – through no fault of her own – but apart from that she had felt the Christmas service had gone well. She had certainly noticed that Professor Bullen was rather brusque, but then again, after all the stories she had heard from the nursing staff, she had not really expected anything else. She could think of nothing that would merit so harsh a complaint. 'I'm sorry,' she managed eventually. 'I'd no idea. The last thing I wanted was to upset people.'

'That would appear to be the problem,' said Father Trumpington drily, 'that you have no idea! Professor Bullen says you appear to have absolutely no understanding of pastoral care.'

Antonia digested this. 'I'm sorry,' she repeated. She could think of nothing to say.

'The Bishop will obviously want to see you,' continued Father Trumpington, delighting in her discomfiture, 'and I think you had better make an appointment to see Professor Bullen as soon as possible, to apologise. See what you can do to clear up this mess.'

She looked devastated, but Father Trumpington felt no pity. He discovered that he wanted to see her totally humiliated and destroyed. He wanted to see her not only removed from St Godric's, but removed from the Church as well. He hated her, more than anyone he had ever hated before in his life. 'By the way,' he said, as she was still reeling, 'have you been to see Gloria and Alan yet?'

She shook her head. 'There wasn't time over Christmas with so much going on. I did try to see Alan, but he said he was too busy and to leave it till after Christmas, so I was going to give them both a ring this week.'

'Well, make sure you do,' said Father Trumpington glassily. 'Let's try and have a new beginning and wipe the slate clean now.' He reached forward to a notepad on his desk and cleared his throat noisily. 'While we're on the subject of new beginnings, I thought we should take the opportunity to tighten up your general approach to work. It's unfortunate that all this has happened, but I do blame myself to some extent. I have not exercised as tight an oversight of you as I should have done. I have therefore drawn up a list of guidelines for you.' He peered ostentatiously at the pad. 'In future, these will govern all that you do, and how you do it. I shall read them out to you.'

Almost involuntarily Antonia's chin had lifted, but she said nothing. He paused briefly and stared at her, as if expecting her to protest. When she did not, he turned, disappointed, back to the list. 'One,' he read out, 'you will in future show me a copy of every sermon you propose to preach. You will present it to me at least three days in advance, and I shall then make necessary deletions and amendments. Two, in these sermons you will avoid anything that might be construed as challenging.' He glared at her. 'You will preach only words of comfort. It is not your place to offer criticism or guidance.' Still she said nothing. 'Three, on no account are you ever to pray with anyone. You have caused enormous trouble these last few months, praying with people, and it has to stop. When you visit people, you will confine yourself to asking about their health and drinking tea. You will absolutely not talk about Jesus!'

Antonia could not restrain herself. 'I thought I was supposed to talk about Jesus,' she said, 'and pray with people. I thought that was what the job was.'

Father Trumpington looked at her as if she was a particularly low breed of vermin. 'Absolutely not!' he exploded. 'How dare you stir people up the way you do. You've caused no end of trouble. I've never known anything like it. The parish is by its ears!'

The overhead light glowed palely. In the gathering gloom, Antonia found the afternoon had taken on a surreal quality. She could not quite take in what was happening. She did not defend herself because she could not understand how the criticisms had been made. She knew how warmly so many people felt towards her, and she thought of the lives that she had seen changing as people became touched by God. She had not really linked any of these changes to herself. She had rather thought it was simply a privilege of ministry to see such things happening. So often she had felt that she was merely a spectator brought along by God, while he did whatever it was he wanted to. She imagined that it was the same for everyone in ministry. She had even thought it must once have been the same for Father Trumpington too. She could not understand how he claimed she was causing trouble.

'And what's that you're clutching?' said Father Trumpington suddenly, indicating the papers, books and video on her knee.

She looked up, startled. 'Oh, er, nothing. A few things for an inquirer's course. Some of Dave's friends came up this morning after the . . .' she was going to say baptism but, remembering what had happened, changed her mind, 'service,' she amended. 'They said they'd like to find out more about Jesus and could we set something up. So I brought along this stuff and was going to ask if we could set up a group.'

Father Trumpington went purple. 'Good God!' he exclaimed. 'That's exactly what I mean. Everything you do causes trouble. You want to bring more of these long-haired louts into church, do you? How do you think the rest of us feel?' He did not wait for a response. 'I tell you we're fed up. You should hear Gloria on the subject!'

Chastened, Antonia looked down.

'Look here, Antonia,' Father Trumpington went on, 'you've driven me to this. I'm going to have to call a meeting with the churchwardens and Alan, and give them a chance to put their point of view to you too. You have got to toe the line now.' His chest puffed out. 'I'm not going to have it said that I threw you out, but to stay you really must change your ways. You're here to serve. That's what a deacon is, a servant. It is not your place to go out and convert people or change things!'

Father Trumpington felt rather good after she had gone. He felt that overall the encounter had been an unqualified success. This feeling was intensified when halfway through tea the phone rang. It was his friend from St Butolph's-under-Lynne up in Carlisle, whom he had phoned on the off chance of their having a vacancy for an organist. 'Yes,' said Father Strawson, 'we are looking as it happens. Why? Do you know someone?'

Father Trumpington took a deep breath. 'Yes,' he said, 'I do.' And he told Father Strawson all about this wonderful young organist he had come across, who was actually with them at the moment but who was looking to move because of family problems. Here Father Trumpington's voice dropped. 'Got himself mixed up in a spot of bother,' he confided, 'with another woman. Wife's a bit neurotic. If they don't move now, the family will split up.'

'Ah,' said Father Strawson. He quite understood. 'Good organist, you say?'

'The best,' assured Father Trumpington. 'Trained at the Royal Academy.'

There was a silence, then, 'I'm definitely interested. Do you think you could get him to come up and see me next week?'

Father Trumpington put down the phone almost dancing with glee. He felt fairly certain he was soon going to be rid of Antonia, or, failing that, crush her to his will, and now it looked as if he was going to be free of Norman too. He looked forward to having parish life restored to the easy flow it had enjoyed before. He felt he wanted to celebrate. 'Dorothy,' he called, 'could you pour me another cup of tea, dear?'

* * *

There was still, however, the problem of the Bishop to be overcome, and that particular difficulty made itself felt the following day. At nine fifteen, Father Trumpington received a phone call summoning him in. He told Dorothy, who said, 'Don't make a mess of this. Remember, I'm going to back you all the way.' Then she got his coat and helped him put it on.

Despite her support, Father Trumpington felt nervous as he inched slowly into the crowded car park of Church House. He found himself wondering which car belonged to the chaplain, and felt a superstitious dread that he might park next to it, as if proximity might somehow adversely influence what was to take place. When he got inside, however, he found himself in for a surprise.

'Oh, yes,' said the secretary who came to fetch him. 'Nigel's left. He had a call to China, just before Christmas. Ever so sudden it was. Such a nice young man. We do miss him.'

Father Trumpington made a sound midway between agreement and denial, and the secretary looked at him sharply. 'Just wait in here,' she said, pushing open a door and standing back to allow him through. 'I'll come and get you when the Bishop's free.'

The Bishop meanwhile was having a quick glass of medicinal sherry to try to fortify his nerves. 'Do I really have to see him?' he quavered to the Archdeacon.

'Yes,' said the Archdeacon firmly, 'you do. But what are you worried about? I'll be here.'

'It's just that he's so . . . overbearing,' said the Bishop miserably. 'I always find myself agreeing with him.' He thought, not for the first time, longingly of Nigel who would have known just what to say and what to do.

'You're in control,' said the Archdeacon, fixing him in the eye, 'just remember that. We've got hard evidence here, but we've got to keep it all quiet.' He shuddered, wishing, as he had found himself frequently wishing of late, that Father Trumpington was not a Mason and that he had not been quite so hasty in engineering the removal of the one man who might possibly have been able to deal with him. For all his worldliness, the Archdeacon did actually retain some last vestiges of faith, added to which he was appalled that a brother Mason could have acted so dishonourably.

263

Like the Bishop, his one concern now was to prevent the truth from coming out. 'The best and most honourable thing of all,' he said reflectively, 'would be for Dick to resign. So let's put that to him. After all, he is sixty-two, he might be glad of the opportunity. We just need to be firm.'

'Yes,' said the Bishop dubiously, remembering the last time he had suggested that. He wondered whether to risk another glass of sherry to stop his hand from shaking, but decided against it. One more and he might find himself under the table instead of sitting at it. He pressed the button on the intercom and said tremulously, 'I think you'd better show him in now, Heather.'

Father Trumpington found himself ushered once again into the Bishop's private domain, and was surprised to find that the Archdeacon was there. His spirits lifted slightly. 'Hello,' he said, 'how nice to see you. We haven't met since—'

'Yes,' said the Archdeacon hastily, 'quite. Why don't you take a seat, Dick?'

Father Trumpington sat.

'Well,' began the Bishop. He stared unhappily at the letter before him on the desk and, summoning all his courage, managed, 'You know that we have had a most serious complaint about you, Dick. Perhaps you'd like to tell us what happened.'

Father Trumpington had always rather prided himself on his imagination. In his youth, indeed, he had harboured thoughts of writing a book but had somehow never quite got round to it. Now all his frustrated creative genius came to the fore. 'Well, it's really very simple,' he began. He told them that there had indeed been an unfortunate incident at the Pilkingtons' house, but that had occurred because he had been so enraged to discover that Norman, the organist, had been carrying on an affair under his nose, *in church*, with a woman from the choir – and he had independent evidence that would support that. He had felt so angry, he said, that he had been unable to restrain himself. It had been a little, he added, permitting himself a small laugh, like Jesus driving out the money changers from the temple.

'Quite so,' said the Bishop. 'Mrs Pilkington herself does not deny that her husband has been involved with another lady in the parish. But there is the more serious allegation that you yourself are engaged in a relationship with this woman.'

Father Trumpington squirmed, but long years married to Dorothy had taught him to lie, if not convincingly, at least effortlessly. 'Preposterous,' he said, 'the woman's deranged. I'm sure if you talk to her now, you'll find she no longer maintains that story.'

The Archdeacon and the Bishop looked at each other. They had been expecting this.

'We don't believe that,' said the Archdeacon flatly. 'We've been making independent inquiries. In particular, we have obtained a copy of the police report of the incident Mrs Pilkington is complaining about, and they support her account.'

Father Trumpington was speechless.

'Look here, Dick,' tried the Bishop, 'you must see the enormous damage this could do to the Church if it were all to come out. There is very damning evidence here, and the only answer that I can see is,' he swallowed nervously, 'you really have to go.'

Father Trumpington stared at him. 'Are you trying to sack me?' he asked, the slightest suggestion of a threat creeping into his voice.

'No, no,' said the Bishop hastily. He was all too well aware that he could not do that without the matter going to a consistory court, and that he wished at all costs to avoid. 'Of course not. But given the circumstances, surely, for all our sakes, it would be better now for you to retire.'

Father Trumpington fixed him with that peculiar look that the Bishop dreaded so much. He cringed.

'Come now, Dick,' he said feebly, 'if not of yourself, think of poor Dorothy. What would public knowledge of such a scandal do to her?'

'There is no scandal,' said Father Trumpington through clenched teeth. 'Dorothy knows all there is to know, and she supports me absolutely. I have not the slightest intention of resigning now. Why, that in itself would be an admission of guilt! And I am not admitting guilt. You are so anxious to avoid publicity, but if you want to get rid of me you're going to have to make a formal charge and bring me before a consistory court. I have absolutely no doubt that you will find no evidence to support such a proceeding and . . .'

'We have the police report, Dick,' said the Archdeacon softly.

Father Trumpington rounded on him. 'You'll have to bring that out in court then,' he said defiantly. 'What do you think the media will make of that?'

The Bishop passed a hand before his eyes. The interview seemed to be going precisely the way he had feared. It was true, short of the most fearful scandal there was absolutely nothing they could do, not if the man declined to take the honourable way out. He either resigned, or he sat there. 'Dick,' he protested, 'this really won't do. If you remain we might, if we are very lucky, avoid a public scandal, but what of the damage to St Godric's?'

'What damage?' said Father Trumpington.

In vain they pointed out the effects of it becoming known to the parishioners that their priest was carrying on an affair. 'I am not carrying on an affair,' said Father Trumpington, with absolute sincerity. Then they suggested that marriages in difficulty might disintegrate with such an example before their eyes, and the Bishop asked Father Trumpington if he really wanted that on his conscience. Father Trumpington shrugged. 'I have not the slightest idea what you are talking about,' he said.

Finally the Archdeacon said, 'Look here, Dick, you can't possibly keep this quiet now. Too many people know. It's bound to come out. We're into damage limitation here, and the most effective way of accomplishing that, as the Bishop has already said, is for you to go.'

'No,' repeated Father Trumpington. 'It never happened. End of story. Anyway, the Pilkingtons will be going soon.'

The Bishop and the Archdeacon exchanged glances.

'What do you mean?' asked the Bishop carefully.

'Very simple. Norman and his wife have decided that they would like a fresh start. He has an interview up in Carlisle this week and, between you and me, I would be very surprised if he doesn't get the job.'

The Archdeacon drew in his breath sharply. 'I don't know how you've managed this, Dick,' he said, 'but if it's true, you're running very close to the wind. What about the others?'

'Others?'

'Of course, man! There's this woman, for a start. This Jackie Newberg. Do you think she's going to keep quiet?'

Father Trumpington smiled. 'Jackie is being sued for divorce on the grounds of adultery. Her husband is naming Norman as correspondent. Jackie is fighting for custody of her daughter, Elspeth, and in the circumstances it is by no means certain that she will get it.' His smile broadened. 'I hardly think she will like the complication of *another* lover appearing on the scene.'

Neither the Bishop nor the Archdeacon drew attention to Father Trumpington's altered phraseology.

'What about the curate?' asked the Archdeacon. 'Mrs Pilkington's letter mentions that she has been talking to her, and that she knows it all.'

A change had come over the meeting, and they all knew it. The Bishop and the Archdeacon were no longer trying to evict or discipline Father Trumpington; rather, they were asking him what to do.

Father Trumpington cleared his throat. 'Ah, yes, Antonia,' he said. 'Have you received Professor Bullen's letter yet?'

When he rose to leave some three-quarters of an hour later, the Bishop and the Archdeacon both shook him by the hand, and the Archdeacon even went so far as to clap him on the back. If the truth be known, he was profoundly relieved that he was not going to have to admit in public a fellow Mason's misdemeanour. He had no desire to bring the craft into disrepute. All three, however, had agreed that, if the dreadful truth were not to become known, something would have to be done to ensure Antonia's silence as well. 'Leave her to me,' Father Trumpington had said, his expression wolfish.

The Bishop, however, remained troubled. Something in Father Trumpington's eye had disturbed him. As Father Trumpington went through the door, he said, 'By the way, Dick, I really feel I should see Antonia. Be a good chap and tell her to give my secretary a ring and fix up an appointment.'

Father Trumpington was taken aback. 'You intend to reprimand her, I take it,' he said. 'Professor Bullen's complaint was most serious.'

The Bishop merely waved his hand vaguely. 'Yes, I suppose she had better go and apologise to him.' And then, turning away, Father Trumpington heard him mutter, 'Never rains but what it pours, I suppose.'

All in all, it had not been a bad morning's work, the priest reflected as he once more clambered into his car. He put the key in the lock and turned on the engine, revving jauntily. He would go and telephone Alan, he decided, and set up the meeting of inquiry for Antonia. He had no fears that she might say something about himself and Jackie. He himself would not have hesitated to use such a weapon, and use it to advantage, but Antonia, he knew, would never betray something that had been said to her in confidence. But he must, he decided, act quickly. If he left it all to the mealy-mouthed Bishop, he might find himself saddled with Antonia for the next five years. No, he reflected, far better to make a pre-emptive strike and then inform the hierarchy that the PCC had decided she was unsuitable and had to go.

He smiled wickedly, engaging the car in gear. Soon, he promised himself, very soon . . .

Chapter Twenty

When Gudrun found out about Norman's arrangement with Dorothy she was furious. 'We can't keep silent,' she said. 'It's not right. He's done wrong.'

'But if we agree not to tell people what happened, he'll help me get another job,' Norman protested.

'And you'll take all the blame, I suppose,' retorted Gudrun. 'Everyone'll know then that you've been having an affair, but he'll get off scot-free!'

'They're going to find out about me anyway,' said Norman miserably. 'Jackie's husband is naming me in the divorce.' He bit his lip, wilting before her rage. If anything, his feelings about the two women had grown even more confused over the new year. He really wanted to finish with Jackie now, but he felt as if she had some kind of hold over him and somehow, whenever they were together, he found he was unable to break free. He had told Gudrun what was happening, he felt he owed it to her, but she had been totally unable to understand.

'You must just tell her,' she had said flatly. 'Tell her to leave us alone!'

But Norman could not do that, despite the little speeches he wrote down and the rehearsals he held beforehand in his mind. Whenever he was alone with Jackie, his will crumbled. It was terrible, and now all he wanted to do was run away. He had not taken seriously Jackie's threat to give up everything and follow him wherever he went. He could not imagine anyone behaving like that, especially not someone who had a lifestyle as comfortable as Jackie's seemed to be. He felt that if only he and Gudrun could go away somewhere and get a fresh start, Jackie would lose interest and leave him alone, and they would be free. His silence seemed a small price to pay for that. And now Father Trumpington had fixed up this interview for him in Carlisle. It was a long way away, but that to Norman seemed good, and the church sounded interesting too, but they had to keep quiet.

'What about me?' Gudrun suddenly wailed, breaking into his thoughts. 'Don't my feelings come into any of this? Everyone's going to know that my husband's had an affair with that bitch but he's going to be fine!'

Norman winced. 'Isn't it worth it?' he said. 'If we can just get away?'

Gudrun was not convinced. 'I don't like Carlisle,' she said petulantly.

'You've never been there.'

'I don't like the sound of it!' And then she said, 'Besides, what about Otto?'

It hung in his mind that Otto might not go with them anyway and, seeing his face, Gudrun said fiercely, 'No, you're wrong. He's going to be all right. I'm sure of it. But he needs proper care!'

Norman shrugged helplessly. 'We can't stay,' he said. And then, 'Look, whatever happens, it's going to take a few weeks to sort out, he should be stronger then anyway.' He did not add, 'if you're right', but they both thought it, and then he said, 'Please, Gudrun. I'll make sure there's a good paediatric unit, I promise. Otherwise we won't even think about it. But please, if there is, try it.' He looked at her pleadingly. 'For the rest of the family . . . For me.'

Norman went up to Carlisle by train on the Tuesday. He did not usually travel by train, but St Butolph's had offered to pay his expenses and, repressing the guilt he felt at squandering such a large sum of money, he caught the overnight sleeper to Scotland.

He was pleasantly surprised when he saw the church; and the organ, he discovered, was rather fine. Father Strawson was harder to digest. The priest wore a biretta and cassock for the entire time that Norman was there. He was a short, rotund little man with twinkling eyes. He lived alone in the large rambling rectory attached to the church, and had a woman in twice a week to clean. Norman discovered that what should have been the dining room had been turned into a private chapel, and it was there that he found Father Strawson, deep in prayer, when he arrived. Then when they went over to the church, the priest genuflected ostentatiously as they passed through the door, and crossed himself.

'Reverence the cross, Norman,' he admonished, 'reverence the cross.' Norman was not used to this kind of behaviour, and he bobbed awkwardly. Father Strawson beamed. 'Very good,' he said. 'Now let's go and have a look at the Lord's instrument!'

Minutes later Norman found himself seated at one of the most magnificent organs it had ever been his privilege to play. Father Strawson looked at him kindly as he launched into a thundering piece by Bach and then, as it came to an end, he said mildly, 'You've had a wee bit of trouble, I understand.'

Norman nodded, his heart suddenly transferring itself to his mouth. He had wanted to avoid this subject.

But the priest only looked at him for a moment and then said gently, 'Aye, well, we all run into problems in this life. Sounds like you need a bit of healing to me. You and your lady.' He looked at Norman sharply. 'But mind, I'll not have any of that kind of nonsense here. You've got to understand that!'

Relief flooded Norman. 'No, I . . . I don't want it,' he stammered. 'At least, I mean . . .'

Father Strawson laughed. 'Bit the apple and discovered a maggot, have you?'

'Something like that.' Norman hung his head. 'I think I've been a bit stupid. I just want a fresh start now.' And somehow he found himself telling Father Strawson all about Gudrun and the children, especially Otto, who was still in hospital, and their fears for him.

'We've got a good children's unit here,' Father Strawson said reflectively. 'I'm chaplain. I'm often up there. There's a very good high-dependency unit.' Then he tilted his head to one side and looked at Norman quizzically. 'But I'm not entirely sure they'd want to do a heart op on him.'

'That wouldn't be a problem,' said Norman. 'They've already told us at Carberry that he'll have to go to Addenbrooks in Cambridge for that.'

The priest nodded sympathetically and then said, 'OK, we'll try it. You can start in a month, or a bit longer if the babe's not strong enough to move. There's a house with the job, and the pay's twelve thousand a year. Not a lot, but enough if you're careful, and you'll find we all help each other here.'

Norman could not believe his luck. He went home on cloud

271

nine, eager to share all that had taken place with Gudrun and to tell her all about the strange little priest. Gudrun would appreciate Father Strawson, he knew, and he was sure she would not object to the move when she knew there was adequate hospital care for Otto. Overall, he felt that St Butolph's would offer them a real chance.

He bounded off the train as it pulled into the station and flung off as fast as he could down the platform, but when he arrived at the barrier, he found a surprise awaiting him. Standing there, wrapped in a long grey coat that came down to her ankles, the collar turned up against the cold, and with a large, shaggy fur hat pulled down low over her ears, was Jackie. She gave a twinkling laugh as he appeared and flung her arms round his neck. 'Hello,' she said breathlessly. 'I've come to meet you!'

Norman gaped at her. 'Why? I mean, how did you know which train?'

'I've met every one since two o'clock!' Her hold was like a vice about his neck and she planted a long, lingering kiss upon his mouth. Angry with her, he did not respond. 'You don't seem very pleased to see me,' she pouted, standing back and surveying him. 'I thought you'd be glad.' Then she laughed again. 'What a cross-patch you are! Come on, I'm going to take you off for a meal.'

Norman scowled. He disentangled himself with difficulty and stared at her. 'No, really, I can't,' he said. 'I must get back. Gudrun'll be expecting me.'

'Oh Gudrun!' Jackie pulled a face. 'I wouldn't worry about her, she'll still be waiting whatever time you get back. You can always say the train was delayed.' She looked at him appealingly. 'Come on, come and eat with me.'

'But I don't want to,' said Norman. 'There are things I need to tell Gudrun. I have to talk to her.'

That pulled her up short and she peered into his face closely. 'You've got the job, haven't you?'

He nodded, and as he did so a feeling of dread stole over him. He had not wanted Jackie to know; he felt afraid. But it was too late, her eyes were fixed upon him, and there was a curious expression in them.

'Are you going to take it?' she asked.

'I . . . I'm not sure,' he prevaricated, wanting desperately to keep the truth from her, and wishing for all the world that Gudrun was here.

Her eyes narrowed even more, till he felt he was being stared at by a cat; a cat that looked uncomfortably as if it was about to strike. 'I'm not sure I believe you,' she said. 'I think you have decided.'

'No . . . it's a long way . . . there are things we've got to talk about. Hospitals, for one thing. I don't know if Gudrun will want to go up to Carlisle.'

'Oh, Miss Goody-two-shoes won't object!' A spasm of anger crossed Jackie's face. 'Why aren't you telling me, Norman? Why don't you want me to know? What is it?'

He looked away awkwardly. 'Nothing,' he said.

She regarded him for another second, and then nestled up and slipped a hand through his arm. 'Let's go and discuss it over a meal,' she said appealingly. 'You can tell me all about it and we can work out what to do.'

Norman was lost. He wanted to say no but, faced by her insistence, he did not know how to. Numbly he allowed her to lead him out to her car and stowed his bag obediently in the boot. The next second they were off. She drove to one of the biggest and most expensive restaurants in town. 'We've got something to celebrate,' she explained, as he looked around askance.

'But people will see us,' he said, appalled.

She laughed. 'Does that really matter?'

'Yes,' said Norman fiercely, 'it does.' He did not want to have his indiscretion blazoned all over the town but, even more than that, he felt that if he gave in now, it would be a tacit admission that Jackie had won and that his marriage was finished, just as hers was. It might of course be finished anyway, he reminded himself, if Gudrun ever found out that Jackie had been waiting for him and had heard his news before she did, but some last remnant of fight reared itself in his spirit. He did not want Jackie to ruin everything now. 'We either go somewhere outside town,' he said firmly, 'or that's it. I'm going home. Now.'

She looked at him measuringly, and then switched on the engine and began to back. 'All right,' she said, 'as you wish. We'll go somewhere quiet.' But as she drove off, they both knew that Jackie had won, because now she was taking him somewhere that he had said he wanted to go.

It was after midnight when he finally got home and, as he pushed open the door, he felt that a stain had been cast over his news. It did not seem so good any more. Jackie had already begun to make plans. She had announced over dinner that she would put the house on the market next day, and that she would go up to Carlisle to begin the search for somewhere new, not too far from St Butolph's, at the weekend. Norman had tried to reason with her. He had pointed out that it would be the most terrible upheaval for Elspeth, and that she would be leaving all her friends. But Jackie had only shrugged. 'Elspeth'll be all right,' she said carelessly. 'She'll soon settle down. It'll be good for us; a new start.' Norman had been fully aware that by 'us' she meant herself and him, and that Elspeth hardly entered into the equation at all. Even so, he had been unprepared for her next bombshell. 'Why don't you tell Gudrun?' she had urged, leaning forward across the table. 'Tell her you're going to leave her here. Tell her it's better for Otto, if you like. Let's make it a new start in every way.'

They had argued for over an hour, and in the end she had burst into tears and said, 'If you really loved me, you'd do this!' It had reminded him curiously of Gudrun in some of her more clingy moments. But Jackie was not Gudrun and, unlike his wife, he found he could not get his own way simply by having a tantrum and flinging away from her. Jackie was absolutely determined to move to Carlisle.

As he stepped into the hall, he noticed a light on in the front room, and in the same moment a low rumbling snore reverberated through the house. Norman checked, startled. He had never heard Gudrun snore before, and would never have imagined it would sound like that anyway. Cautiously he crept towards where the sound was emanating from and pushed open the door. Sprawled across the sofa, pudgy hand awkwardly cradling her cheek, lay Phoebe. She started and jerked awake as the door creaked and opened her eyes. 'Ooh, it's you,' she said, pulling herself up. 'Thank the Lord you've come.'

'Why?' he asked, coming further into the room. 'Where's Gudrun?'

274

Phoebe's eyes filled with tears. 'Up at the hospital,' she said. 'They phoned about seven tonight. Said you should both go up. Gudrun waited for an hour, because she said you were due back, but then, when you didn't come, she went up by herself and asked me to wait here with the children.'

'I don't understand,' said Norman.

'It's Otto,' said Phoebe, 'he's taken badly. They said he might not last the night.'

On that same Tuesday afternoon Henry and Antonia had gone for a walk up on the chalk downs outside Carberry. Centuries before, some unknown hands had etched the figure of a huge naked man into the hillside. From a distance, it looked as if he was striding arrogantly across the hills, and that was where they went, to see what he looked like close to.

As they clambered up the steep hillside, Antonia at long last took the opportunity to tell Henry what Father Trumpington had said. He was furious. 'He can't say that,' he protested, panting slightly with the exertion. 'You're doing a good job. He can't order you not to pray with people or forbid you to preach.'

'He's not forbidding me to preach,' Antonia pointed out, 'he's simply saying I mustn't preach anything challenging.' She fell silent as she negotiated a particularly difficult bit, and then said, 'But maybe he's justified, what with all these complaints and everything. Maybe I *am* in the wrong.'

They paused and Henry looked at her. 'You don't believe that,' he said, 'and neither do I. He's just getting at you. He's a lousy priest himself, and he doesn't like it when someone else comes in and does a halfway decent job.' Overhead a gull screamed and flew down low, and Henry went on, 'The trouble is, he's running that church for himself, not God, and he doesn't like the prospect of a bit of work.'

As she looked out across the valley stretched out below, Antonia came to a sudden decision. She had been toying with it in her mind over the past few days but had been held back by feelings of loyalty towards Gudrun. Now, however, she felt that she could no longer simply hide from Henry all that had taken place. She felt it was unfair to him, and she felt, too, that it was a sin that there should be this dark secret at the heart of St Godric's life.

Very slowly, she began to tell Henry about Jackie and Father Trumpington. When she came to the part about Norman and Gudrun, and all that had happened over Christmas, she hesitated, but as she stood there on the hillside, looking down on the scurrying figures in the town below, she felt again, and more insistently now, that this was something that went far beyond them all and that Henry had a right to know.

As she drew to an end, he whistled softly. 'I guessed there was something going on between Norman and Gudrun,' he said, 'and it didn't take any wild intelligence to guess that Jackie was involved, but I hadn't realised Trumpington was sniffing around that quarter too.' He paused and, like Antonia a moment before, stared out across the valley. A thought occurred to him. 'Does Trumpington know that you know?'

'I'm not sure. I've been wondering that too, but I don't think that's why he's acting towards me the way he is at the moment. After all, he's been funny right from the beginning. I think he just resents what he calls my style of churchmanship.'

Henry rubbed his chin. 'The question is, what do we do now? He certainly seems to have got you into a corner, and he clearly feels that he's able to call the shots.'

They both turned and resumed their upward climb. 'I guess I'll have to go and see Bullen,' said Antonia.

Henry agreed. 'I think you should. Ask him what exactly the grounds of his objections are. Try and talk to him.'

She shrugged. 'Doesn't really matter, does it?'

'Maybe not. I just feel that all this is a little strange, and it would be good to find out what's going on.'

'He doesn't like me,' she said tersely. 'That's what's going on.'

They were on the tip of the giant's foot now and they paused again, this time to look up.

'I say, he's rather splendid,' said Henry, 'but it looks to me like he needs a bit of a weed.' It was true, close up the giant looked overgrown and unkempt, as if he was in danger of disappearing under the grass and back into the cliff. 'I wonder why they carved him here,' he said pensively.

'Some sort of worship, I should think. He looks a bit phallic. They were probably trying to bless the crops.'

'It's remarkable he's survived so long.'

'A dead tribute to a dead faith. Maybe they should stop weeding him and just let it go.'

'When's this meeting you told me about going to take place?' Henry asked suddenly.

Antonia pulled a face. 'Tomorrow night,' she said wryly. 'Dick can be very efficient when it pleases him.'

'Who's going to be there?'

'I don't know. He hasn't said, but I guess Alan Gunningham will be one of them, and probably Gloria too. I don't know about anyone else.'

'Well,' Henry turned and suddenly smiled at her innocently, 'I think you should tell a few people exactly what Trumpington said, and see what their response is. After all, if you really have been upsetting everyone, you'll soon know, and you'll know how to change. On the other hand, if some people actually appreciate what you've been doing, well, maybe it's right that they should be heard too.'

Chapter Twenty-One

In the event it was Henry who began to tell people what Father Trumpington had said. Antonia protested that she really couldn't, and Henry, seeing her turmoil, said all right then, he would tell them himself.

He lost no time. As soon as they got back he told a stunned Kathleen, and then he phoned up Ken Brown and told him of the criticisms Father Trumpington had made and of the conditions he had laid down. Ken Brown growled, 'It's his job to protect and teach the girl, not to try and destroy her. There's the devil in this if you ask me!' And then, his voice dropping, he said, 'Henry, I'm glad of the chance to speak to you. I think there's something you and Antonia ought to know too.'

There was a feeling of unease in the parish, he said, people were worried that something very wrong was going on. Father Trumpington had been seen on numerous occasions and sometimes quite late at night coming out of Jackie Newberg's house. And then there was the odd change that had come over Dorothy. 'You mark my words,' Ken said, 'Dick's up to something he shouldn't be – that no man of God should be! I don't like it at all. We've all of us been wondering what to do. In fact a few of us held a meeting only the other night. We didn't tell Antonia and you because we felt it was better for her not to be involved, but we really feel Dick can't be allowed to carry on like this. We're thinking of writing to the Bishop and asking for him to be removed.'

'Good God,' said Henry, his brain reeling at the speed with which things suddenly seemed to be happening. His mind began to race. 'Is that all?' he asked, thinking of Gudrun and Norman and the possible implications for them if Norman's involvement had been discovered too.

'All?' Ken's voice exploded down the phone. 'Isn't that enough? Do you want photographs or something?'

'No,' said Henry hastily, 'I didn't mean that. I was just thinking,' he groped for a plausible excuse and came up, rather lamely, with 'about Jackie's husband. He was over here at Christmas, you know.'

'I know,' said Ken grimly, 'and you're quite right. I suspect he's found something out too. This is a very nasty can of worms, if you ask me.'

Antonia was distressed to discover that the whole of the parish appeared to know what had been going on between Jackie and Father Trumpington. She felt as if the whole world had gone mad, and she was worried that Gudrun would think that the information had come from her and that she had failed her because of that. Very reasonably, Henry pointed out that it was entirely out of her hands, and that no one could blame her for the truth simply becoming known, and that it was therefore ridiculous to worry. 'They were bound to find out,' he said. 'It's just that it's sooner rather than later – and a good thing too, if you ask me. I don't like all this secrecy. It makes me feel bad.'

'Me too,' she agreed, but even though she knew he was right, the knowledge did nothing to contribute to her peace. She felt there was something more she should have done. Of one thing, however, she was determined; she would not allow Father Trumpington simply to browbeat her into submission to what she knew to be wrong, even if it meant that she lost her job. She was determined to stand by what she felt to be right.

She arrived at the rectory just as the clock in Father Trumpington's gloomy hall was striking the hour. Dorothy answered the door and, unsmiling, showed her into the front room. 'Go in,' she said curtly. 'They're waiting for you.'

Her manner did not seem to augur well and, if it was possible, Antonia's spirits sank even lower. There seemed a kind of fatality in the air, she thought, as if something darkly inexorable was drawing near and she was powerless to flee. She had the sudden feeling that if she failed now, something of life would be lost.

At first sight the room looked as if it had been set out like some macabre court of law. At the far end she saw three easy chairs ranged side by side, and facing them in splendid isolation in the middle of the floor, one single wooden dining chair. It looked most odd in the surroundings of that room, and seemed to stand a long way from anything else. At the same time an anglepoise lamp had been brought in from Father Trumpington's study and, whether by accident or design, it was trained now upon the chair, so that it looked as if whoever occupied it was going to be under interrogation. Then she became fully aware of the three people already there and the faint glimmerings of amusement she had felt at sight of the lamp died; they sat like judges, their faces grim. She was reminded of the cartoon of Judge Jeffries on the wall of her father's study at home; the hanging judge, as her father had explained.

Father Trumpington sat in the middle, with Alan on his right hand and Gloria on his left. They were evidently just finishing a leisurely cup of coffee because in front of them, on the small coffee table, stood a half-empty coffee jug, still steaming gently, and a plate of Dorothy's homemade biscuits. Gloria was just saying, 'Um, very nice, I've never had this Christmas coffee before. Is it a special mix?' Her words died as she became aware that Antonia had walked in, and she stared at her coldly.

'Ah, Antonia,' said Father Trumpington, looking up, 'thank you for coming.' He made no attempt to rise, nor to offer her a drink, but simply indicated, with a brusque wave of his hand, that she was to sit down on the chair.

Nervously she went over and sat down and, glaring at her, Father Trumpington began, 'You are here to answer for your conduct. You have been arrogant, self-willed, and opinionated, and you have stirred up people emotionally in a way that has never happened before in the parish. You have caused unending trouble.'

She almost expected him to ask, 'How do you plead?' but he fell silent, glaring at her malevolently instead, and Gloria took up the refrain.

'That's right,' she shrilled, 'you've caused terrible problems here!' She looked at the other two for support and they nodded agreement, and she went on, 'Some of us find your ministry really offensive. The only thing you seem interested in is people's souls – and it's just not right! You go around as if you've got God pinned on your sleeve!'

Father Trumpington sniffed his agreement, grateful, and Alan broke in quietly, 'Perhaps, more seriously, you seem to be filling up the church with down-and-outs, and some of us really don't like that. St Godric's used to be a very nice church before you came along.'

'Yes,' blurted Gloria again, before he could go on. 'They're horrible. Why, some of them even smell, and they don't know how to behave. They won't be quiet.' Her ample bosom heaved with indignation. 'If you ask me, you ought to forget about God and learn about Anglicanism. We don't want all those awful happy-clappy people in St Godric's!'

There was a stunned silence after this outburst, and then Father Trumpington said meaningfully, 'You listen to Gloria, Antonia. Gloria knows exactly what she's talking about. You can learn from her!'

'Ooh, Dick!' exclaimed Gloria in delight, and a slow stain of pink crept up her neck and disappeared into the line of her peroxided hair.

Father Trumpington was too preoccupied with the business in hand to spare a thought for Gloria. 'Your behaviour,' he said, his eyes fixed on Antonia, 'seems designed to split the church in two and turn people against me, and I will not have it!'

After that, all hell seemed to break loose. It was as if the floodgates had been opened and everything just poured out. Charge after charge was brought against her, some so ridiculous they almost made her laugh aloud – like Gloria's accusation that her 'meddling', as she put it, with Kathleen Earnshaw had made the poor woman totally unable any longer to receive Communion. She seemed totally ignorant of the fact that Kathleen was being prepared for confirmation and had herself chosen not to take Communion again until that had taken place. In vain did Antonia attempt to point this out, but it was no good, because they would not allow her to speak. 'You just listen!' Gloria kept saying. 'You hear what someone else has got to say for a change!'

Then at last, ominously, Father Trumpington said, 'And then of course there's St Thomas's. Heaven knows the trouble you've caused there.' He looked at Alan and said despairingly, 'Do you know, she still hasn't been and apologised to Professor Bullen yet!'

'You only told me two days ago!' protested Antonia.

Father Trumpington ignored her. 'We are going to have great difficulty patching up relations with St Thomas's because of her casual, lackadaisical approach. The professor tells me he is outraged!'

They all three nodded their heads sagely, and then Alan said, 'We're going to have to lay down some very firm guidelines . . . and I'm very sorry, Dick, because the burden is obviously going to fall on you, but you're going to have to make sure she sticks to them.'

They began to talk among themselves as if Antonia was no longer there. 'Yes,' chimed in Gloria, anxious for everyone to know they had her full support, 'her remaining at St Godric's must be made dependent on her compliance with very specific conditions.'

'I have already told her that,' said Father Trumpington.

'Exactly what conditions have you laid down, Dick?' inquired Alan.

Father Trumpington puffed out his chest and began once again to go through the list of stipulations he had delivered to Antonia a couple of days before. Alan grunted with approval when he heard that all her sermons were to be vetted and Gloria said, 'Ooh, that's good!' when she heard that Antonia was not to pray with people any more.

'You could also tell her she's not to bring in any more down-and-outs or long-haired layabouts, Dick,' remarked Alan. 'After all, they do lower the tone.'

It was too much. Antonia could restrain herself no longer. She had sat quietly while they had bombarded her with accusations, but they had been not the slightest bit interested in hearing her defence. It had all been agreed beforehand, she realised. She rose to her feet angrily. 'You can take your conditions,' she said loudly, 'and stick them!' Three heads spun round and looked at her in disbelieving shock. She had finally succeeded in getting their total attention. 'I have been ordained to preach the gospel,' she said, 'and to care for people spiritually. I fail to see how I can do either of these things if I am no longer to be allowed to preach and if I am forbidden to pray with people. I cannot and will not agree to such rubbish! And as for staying at St Godric's, I think you three are mad! I don't want to stay if those are the conditions.' Now she glared at them. 'I have this old-fashioned belief,' she said deliberately, 'that the Church belongs to God. Not you!' And with that, she turned on her heel and walked out, slamming the door behind her.

'Well!' said Gloria, as the shock waves reverberated through the house. 'I think we're well rid of her. Little madam!'

Father Trumpington swallowed uneasily. He was not quite so sure. He had a lurking suspicion that they had perhaps gone a little too far. He had wanted merely to cow her into submission, and then slowly winkle her out over the next few months, when the grounds for her departure would have been fully prepared and no one would have been surprised because he would have been able to say, with absolute sincerity, that she did nothing. He had not expected that she would simply tell them to get lost. He had thought that she would have to accept whatever guidelines they laid down, because it was her job and because she would need the money. Father Trumpington was not used to people acting on principle. He felt the first faint stirrings of apprehension as he thought of what the Bishop would say.

'You all right, Dick?' said Alan, noticing he looked a little preoccupied.

Father Trumpington started. 'What? Oh, yes,' he said, recollecting himself. 'I just hadn't expected her to react quite like that.'

Alan laughed. 'No, jolly good show, what? I thought it was going to be a bit harder than that.'

Antonia arrived back home in a towering rage. Henry was waiting for her, with Kathleen. 'What happened?' he demanded, taking one look at her face. She told them. 'He said what?' spluttered Henry. Then he said, 'I'll kill him!'

He began to shrug on his coat, his face a mask of rage, and both women leapt to stop him.

'No,' said Antonia, 'you can't!'

'I jolly well can!' said Henry. 'I'm not having him treat you like

284

that. I'm going to punch his silly face in!'

'Henry, no!' implored Kathleen, joining in. 'You mustn't hit him. Only think, the police may become involved! And you a solicitor!'

As they were struggling to stop him from going out of the door, Ken arrived. 'Hello,' he said, 'what's going on? You all look in a bit of a state.'

'It's that bloody man!' spat Henry, shaking Antonia's hand from his arm. 'I'm going to hit him for the way he's treated Antonia. He's not going to get away with it!' He lunged across the room in an effort to get through the door, but Ken planted himself firmly in the way.

'Ah,' he said, 'you mean Dick, I take it. What's he done?'

Antonia suddenly discovered that with all the upset of the evening, and faced by Henry's rage, she felt like crying. Struggling to keep back the tears, she told him briefly. 'I've left,' she ended up. 'I walked out and told Dick what he could do with his silly conditions. I'm not curate at St Godric's any more, and I'll probably never be curate of anywhere else now either.'

'Why?' inquired Ken mildly.

She sniffed. 'Well, it doesn't sound too good when you tell your vicar where to go, does it? I expect the Bishop won't have me in the diocese now.'

'Ah, I see,' said Ken. Then, after a moment, 'There has been a lot going on tonight, hasn't there? I've just come from a meeting too.' He scratched his head and looked at them all, and then said, 'Look, why don't we sit down and talk about this? Henry, take your coat off, lad. Go and hit him later if you like, but let's have a bit of a chinwag first. Things often look different after you've cooled down, and I think I've got some news of my own that you might be interested in.'

Henry looked mulish, but he allowed Kathleen to take his coat and sat down without further protest beside Antonia on the sofa. Every line of his body, however, seemed taut and Antonia had the feeling that any moment he was going to leap to his feet and rush out. She was rather touched.

'Right, now,' said Ken, seating himself too, 'I'm glad I've found you together, because I wanted to show you something. It was only given me tonight.' He fished in his pocket and brought out a small notebook. It was very old, and the edges were curling. He laid it on the table with satisfaction. 'There's a lady that lives opposite Jackie,' he said, 'she's called Mrs Moore. Funny lady – think she fancies herself as a bit of a Dick Tracy. She used to come to St Godric's a few years back, only she had a row with Dick over the Ladies' Club and swore she'd never set foot in the place again while he was there. Anyway . . .' He pushed the book very slowly towards them with his finger. 'She's been housebound the last couple of years, and she tends to spend most of her time sitting at the window of her front room, just watching people go by. Well, a few months back, she says, she began to notice that the vicar was a rather frequent visitor. She says she didn't think anything of it at first, but then the visits got very frequent – she even saw him doing her garden – and they began to be at odd times too, often quite late at night, and to last a long time.' He cleared his throat. 'She says it was so odd, she began to keep a diary. Said she thought someone ought to know, and that there needed to be what she called evidence. It's a diary of all his visits.' He laid his outstretched hand squarely on the book and looked from one to the other of them. 'It's all in there,' he said softly. 'All the dates and times. I don't think he's going to be able to wriggle out of this one.'

They stared at him in amazement, and then Henry picked it up and began eagerly to examine it.

'Do you think it'll stand up?' asked Ken quietly.

'Is she willing to say she saw all this?'

Ken nodded. 'She's prepared to tell anyone who's interested what she's seen. But that's not all she's seen,' he added. Henry looked up. 'Did you know about Norman?' Ken asked quietly.

It was Antonia who answered. 'I did,' she said. 'Gudrun confided in me after Otto was born. She was very distressed.'

'Ah,' said Ken. 'I suspected as much.'

They sat in silence, and then Antonia said, 'What are you going to do? Who knows?'

'Well,' said Ken consideringly, 'there's a good few of us know. Now. We'll try and keep the bits that don't relate to Dick quiet, of course, but we feel we've got to do something about this.'

'What are you talking about?' interjected Kathleen. 'I don't understand. Will somebody please tell me what's going on?'

Henry handed her the book. 'See for yourself,' he said. 'Dick's been having an affair with Jackie Newberg, but as you'll see from that notebook, so has our organist. Mrs Moore appears to have been very thorough.'

'I've been deputed to write a letter,' continued Ken, 'to the Bishop. We feel he's got to come into this now.' He looked at Antonia. 'Having heard what happened to you tonight, I feel that letter's got to be a bit longer now. I think we've got to complain about Dick's treatment of you, and make the point that you are not in any way responsible for any of the trouble that's occurred, despite what Dick's trying to say. And I think it can't hurt if others write too.'

Antonia looked down. She felt as if she had gone into the valley of the shadow but that there, unexpectedly, she had found others waiting for her. 'I don't think I can be a part of any of this,' she said.

'Nor should you be, love,' said Ken. 'You leave it to us now, and you just be quiet.'

Chapter Twenty-Two

Gudrun and Norman kept vigil two days and two nights by the tiny ventilator into which the medical staff had put Otto. 'The machine's breathing for him,' explained a nurse. 'Don't worry. It's just to help.'

But they did worry. They could not avoid it. He looked so tiny and helpless lying there, and there was absolutely nothing they could do. They talked a lot during the long, quiet hours of the nights. Norman tried to persuade Gudrun to go home, but she refused. 'Something might happen,' she said. 'I would never forgive myself if he died and I wasn't here.' So they both stayed, with Phoebe once again rallying to care for Bethany and Iwan, and they talked in whispers across the Perspex canopy under which Otto lay. Why they whispered, they were not sure, but they felt that if they spoke aloud they might wake him up before the time was right.

For the first time in his life, Norman found he was staring at death. He did not like the experience, because in the tiny shadow cast by Otto he was brought face to face with himself. Norman had always taken tremendous pride in his art. He had believed that he did not see as other men did. He had believed he lived beyond the shadows, staring into the formless light of what was real. That was what his music was. Now he found that that was an illusion. In those long hours he realised that only Otto was real but, trying to peer through the shadows that hung over him, he discovered he could not see him. Norman tried. He tried so many times but somehow he always felt as if there was something that lay just beyond his grasp, and he could not reach it. He could see Otto; of course he could. But at the same time he could not see him, had never seen him. And he felt that death lay like a curtain round the baby's fragile, almost transparent flesh. Beyond that curtain, thought Norman, lay what was real but he could not see it, and grief stabbed at him for all that he had lost.

On the morning of the third day he could stand it no longer. He turned to Gudrun and said, 'Don't take this wrongly, but I'm going to see Jackie.' She turned on him appalled eyes and he said quickly, 'It's not what you think. I'm going to tell her it's all over, and that she's got to leave us alone.'

His wife's face glowed with joy. 'Oh yes,' she said, 'please.'

'I won't be long,' he promised. He felt her eyes follow him as he fled, almost running, down the long central corridor of the ward. He had to be quick now, he knew. He had to see what was real, before it was too late and he lost it for ever.

He found Jackie at home. She was supervising the erection of a For Sale board outside the house, and her face lit up as he appeared. 'Norman,' she said, 'how lovely. I was hoping you'd come by. I tried phoning you yesterday to see how it had gone, but there was no one there.'

She entwined her arm through his, but he pulled away. 'Otto's ill,' he said stonily. 'I've been up at the hospital.'

Immediately her face assumed a look of false concern. A couple of days ago, Norman realised, he would have been taken in, but he could see her now for what she was.

'Oh dear,' breathed Jackie, 'how truly awful for you! Is he better now?'

Norman was revolted. 'No,' he said savagely, 'he's not. In fact, it looks like he might die.'

Jackie stared at him uncomprehendingly. There was something in his manner, she thought, that she did not like; that was not quite respectful. He seemed rude, as if he no longer cared. She had never seen Norman like this before. She looked at him measuringly, and decided it must be worry. 'So you came to see me for comfort,' she said. 'How sweet.'

His expression was dark. 'No,' he said emphatically, 'I did not. I came to tell you it is all over.'

The man sent by the estate agent was staring at them with interest, and Jackie looked at him sharply. 'Shall I put it here then, love?' he inquired innocently. 'Or would you like it over by the garage?'

'There will be fine,' snapped Jackie. Then she turned back to Norman. 'Come inside, we'd better talk. You're distraught, I can see.'

'I am not distraught,' said Norman, through clenched teeth, but he followed her into the house.

'Good luck, mate,' said the handyman sympathetically after him, and then under his breath, 'Blimey, I think you're going to need it!'

'What on earth's going on?' demanded Jackie as soon as they were inside. 'What's got into you?'

'Nothing,' said Norman. 'I've just come to my senses at long last, that's all.'

Her eyes narrowed. 'What do you mean?'

'What do I mean?' He looked as if he was about to explode. 'I mean I've realised just how pathetic this all is. I've looked at that baby, and I've seen a woman almost twice my age who won't let go!'

She was really stung. 'Norman,' she gasped, 'have you taken leave of your senses? We're in love, and I'm not twice your age.'

'No?' He almost sprang forward, grasped her by the shoulders and pushed her physically over to the mirror. 'Take a good look, Jackie,' he said cruelly. 'What do you see? Crepey skin, crow's feet! You're old enough to be my mother!' His fingers bit into her flesh, and he gave a quick bark of harsh laughter. 'You've lied to me, about your age, about everything. Nothing you've said to me has been true. And I've been fool enough to jeopardise everything for that.' He gave her a harsh shove, and then let go of her shoulders so that she fell back.

'Norman!' She stared at him aghast and two tiny spots of red grew in her cheeks. His accusations stung her to the quick, but she felt unable to face them – the more so because she knew that what he said was true. Picking on the most obvious cause of his anger, she said, through clenched teeth. 'I am not old enough to be your mother.'

'No?' he said jeeringly. 'Well, just how old are you then, Jackie? Forty-five? Fifty? More?'

'No,' she said, but it was a plea not a denial.

'How old are you really?' he said remorselessly.

She opened and shut her mouth once and then, closing her eyes, said softly, 'Forty-eight.'

'Huh!' His hoot of derision was like a knife going through her and he looked at her in disgust. Almost inconsequentially he demanded. 'Do you know how old I am?'

Still with her eyes closed she said, 'Yes, twenty-six. A beautiful age.'

He ignored that. 'Yes, twenty-six,' he repeated bitterly. 'And I think I've been a fool. I just never saw the truth.'

Her eyes flew open at that. 'What do you mean?' she said quickly. 'It doesn't matter. What difference does age make? We're in love.'

'No,' he said, 'no, we're not in love. We've never been in love. I don't think you even know the meaning of the word. You've lied to me the whole time. Let's face it, you're an old bag trying to grab at life before it's all too late, and I was fool enough to get taken in.' He made a flinging movement as if pushing her away and then said, 'It's over, Jackie. Just leave me alone. I never want to see you again!'

And the next minute he was gone, the house reverberating with the violence of the slam he gave to the front door. Shocked, she sank to her knees. 'It's not over,' she whispered hoarsely, 'it can't be. I'm not old.' But it was, she realised . . . and she was. Sinking even lower, till she lay sprawled on the floor, she burst into tears.

Norman ran non-stop back to the hospital. He was seized by a nameless dread that Otto should have died while he was away. He flung in through the main doors and raced up the three flights of stairs to the children's ward. Then, fighting to still his breath and to restrain the hammering of his heart, he began the long walk down the corridor that led to Otto's room. His dread, how-ever, grew and as he drew near, his footsteps slowed. What if he is dead? he wondered. What if it's too late? He stopped outside the closed door and fought to clear his head. Then, with a trembling hand, he quietly pushed open the door.

Gudrun looked up and smiled. 'You're back,' she said. 'Is it all right?'

He nodded, but found he was unable to speak.

'Still holding his own,' she said quietly, following his gaze. He came forward then and went round to her side. The tiny baby still lay there motionless, but there was a delicate flush to his skin that Norman thought had been absent before. 'Oh, Gudrun,' he said, burying his face in her neck, 'I've been such a fool.' He began to sob.

Her hands went up immediately and she embraced him. 'Yes,' she said softly, 'I know. It's all right.'

The Bishop was surprised to receive a whole pile of letters, all from the same parish and all, apparently, saying the same thing.

'St Godric's!' he said despairingly and closed his eyes, then he pressed the intercom for his secretary and said, 'Heather, have we heard from Antonia Beecher-Henty yet?'

'No, Bishop,' crackled Heather's voice down the line, 'not yet.'

The Bishop tutted sadly. 'Ring her for me,' he commanded, 'and fix up a time for her to come in. Oh, and Heather, as soon as possible.' He flicked off the machine and sat back. There had to be easier ways of serving God, he reflected, than being a bishop. Just at the moment, he rather fancied entering a monastery. He surveyed the untidy pile spilling over his desk and sighed again, beginning to wonder if there was anyone in St Godric's who did not know about the affair. The trouble was, the whole sorry business, like some rogue computer virus, seemed wholly out of control, spiralling to more and more bizarre depths. Why, one letter he had received that morning had even implied that Jackie Newberg was keeping a brothel and that Father Trumpington was acting as her pimp! A week ago and he would have dismissed it out of hand – he might even have laughed about it – but now he was not so sure. 'Oh dear, oh dear!' he said aloud. 'Whatever am I to do?'

There was no one else in the room, so it may justly be inferred that he was asking God. God, however, did not answer, and after a moment the Bishop leant forward and buried his head in his hands. Whatever could have possessed Father Trumpington, he wondered, to throw out his curate (which was what he imagined had happened) after all that they had said to him about keeping the affair quiet? The whole parish appeared to be in an uproar. The Bishop was only surprised that so many had rallied, and so vociferously, to the girl's support. He had only met Antonia twice before; once when he had ordained her, and the other time for the obligatory chat when she had come under his jurisdiction in the diocese. She had not appeared to him then to be anything very special, simply another bright-eyed and eager ordinand. He could not imagine how she could have provoked such strong reactions. One thing, however, was becoming clear to him, and that was that Father Trumpington hated her. Why, he could not imagine, but the letters spoke of victimisation and intense anger. The Bishop began to wonder, not for the first time, if Father Trumpington was going mad. He picked up one of the letters at random and read, 'There's been a lot of trouble over the last few months, and a lot of excitement too. God seems to be moving in St Godric's at long last, only the vicar appears to have taken leave of his senses! There *is* division, it's true – some want to move on, and some don't want things to change at all. Dick Trumpington, very unfairly, is blaming Antonia for all of this but we want to make the point now that she is in no way to blame. She has a very deep and lively faith. She has been the catalyst for all that is happening, not the cause . . .'

'Oh my God!' said the Bishop weakly. 'That's all we need – a saint!'

The intercom crackled again. 'I've managed to get hold of Antonia Beecher-Henty, Bishop. She says she didn't know she'd been asked to come and see you but that she was going to ring and ask for an appointment anyway, and can she bring her fiancé along too?'

'Her fiancé?' repeated the Bishop, his mind still on the letters. 'Ah yes, I suppose so.'

The intercom crackled again, 'In that case, I'll make an appointment for them at four o'clock this afternoon. You've got the Burundi Archdeacon earlier, and there's a deputation from the Boy Scouts at three, but I think you should be well clear by then.'

'Thank you, Heather,' said the Bishop weakly, 'that will be fine, I'm sure.'

'Poor old duck,' said Heather as she flicked off the machine and turned to her colleague. 'He does sound low.'

The Bishop was indeed extremely low. He could see no way out of the present dilemma, and the one thing he dreaded above all else was that the press was going to become involved. He could imagine lurid and sensationalist articles in the tabloids, howls of outrage from a censorious public, and a camera crew encamped on the steps of his own house, demanding a statement for the *Six O'clock News*. It was his worst nightmare. If only the dreadful man had resigned, he thought bitterly, there would have been an end to the problem, but the Bishop knew that, short of a miracle, Father Trumpington would never do that. He would hang on like grim death to the bitter end, hopelessly entangling them all in his grubby little concerns, doing endless damage. The Bishop wondered if he should talk to the Archdeacon again, and then dismissed the thought. There would be no point. He knew exactly what the Archdeacon would say, and in his mind he heard again the Archdeacon's measured and judicious tones, 'Keep it quiet, Matthew . . . deny everything.' The Archdeacon always said that, but the Bishop did not particularly like the advice. He kept wondering what Jesus would have done; the trouble was, he was not sure. He felt he knew what was right, but he could see no way to get there.

He decided that at least one thing was clear. Antonia would have to go back. He would not allow Father Trumpington just to throw her out like that, it was most unChristian. And then, too, it occurred to him that if she did go back they could at least preserve an outward appearance of normality, even if internally things remained a mess.

The Bishop sighed and prepared to write an answer to every letter before him on the desk. He would tell them that he was dealing with the matter personally, and he would beg them on no account to talk to the press, because of possible damage to the Church.

By the time Antonia arrived with Henry, later that afternoon, the letters had been cleared away and some semblance of that order so dear to the Bishop's heart had been restored to his desk. 'Come in, my dear, do,' he said, with an attempt at joviality. 'Sit down.' He moved a chair closer to the desk for her, and looked at Henry. 'And this is your fiancé, is it?'

'Yes,' said Henry, 'I'm Henry,' and he held out his hand, smiling. Henry was feeling much encouraged by the Bishop's willingness to see him as well. He was certain that now the Bishop was involved, everything was going to be sorted out, which from his point of view meant that Father Trumpington was going to be removed.

'Well,' said the Bishop sympathetically, as soon as they were seated, 'tell me exactly what's been going on.'

Antonia drew a deep breath and began to recount all that had taken place since her arrival at St Godric's. She held nothing back. She told the Bishop how strange Father Trumpington had been from the beginning, and how he had seemed to resent anyone new joining the congregation. She told him too all about Norman and Jackie, and the terrible effects on Gudrun, and then the horror of them all as they realised that Father Trumpington was involved too. The Bishop sat transfixed. It was true he had already heard the main ingredients of the story, but only in outline, bare and cold; never in his wildest dreams had he imagined how truly awful it had all been. 'Good heavens!' he said. 'Yes . . . I see.'

'And finally,' said Henry, unable to restrain himself any longer, 'Trumpington called Antonia in to this kangaroo court he'd set up.'

'Kangaroo court?' queried the Bishop.

Henry nodded. 'Yes, you know, a mock hearing where the defendant's not allowed any form of defence.'

The Bishop blinked. 'You're a lawyer, aren't you?' Then he cleared his throat and said apologetically, 'I am sorry, I'm afraid I still don't quite understand.'

'It's really very simple,' said Henry patiently. 'He arranged a meeting with two of his sidekicks in order to discipline Antonia. He wouldn't allow anyone else to go along with her or to be present, and he wouldn't hear anything that went against his view. He wouldn't allow her to speak. They presented a long list of faults and things that she was supposed to have done wrong, and then said that she had to abide by certain conditions or she'd have to go.'

The Bishop's eyes bulged slightly. 'Conditions,' he said. 'Ah, yes.' He remembered some of the letters mentioning conditions. 'And exactly what were these conditions?'

Something in his tone did not sound quite right, and Antonia swallowed, suddenly apprehensive. 'Well, first of all,' she began, 'he said he wanted to see all my sermons three days before I was due to preach.'

The Bishop looked at her, and the faintest of smiles crossed his face. He had been imagining something absolutely horrendous – he would not have put anything past Father Trumpington – but this sounded relatively mild to him. The poor child, he decided, had obviously overreacted. 'It's quite normal, you know,' he said gently, 'in a deacon's first parish, to help them in this way with sermon preparation.'

Antonia looked at him, undecided. 'Secondly,' she said, 'he said I was only to preach words of comfort and nothing that could be construed as a challenge.'

The Bishop nodded. 'It might be said our job is to comfort people,' he suggested.

This time both Henry and Antonia looked at him, and then Antonia went on, a chill creeping into her own voice, 'Third, he said I was not to pray with people.'

The Bishop at that moment was looking out of the window, his hands splayed across his chest. 'It might be said . . .' he began tranquilly, and then the full import of her words hit him and he stopped. 'Not to pray with people?' he repeated.

'That's right. He said it was my praying with people that was stirring everyone up, and that I mustn't do it any more.'

The Bishop had never heard anything like it in his life. He had come across many shades of churchmanship, but never had he heard it suggested, even by the most cross-grained liberal, that a Christian priest should not pray with a parishioner. 'He can't say that,' he protested feebly, 'it's part of the job. We're supposed to pray with people.'

'That's what I said,' said Antonia grimly.

'What did you do?' asked the Bishop. He dreaded the answer.

'I left,' said Antonia.

There was a small silence, during which the photocopier from the next door office could be clearly heard, and then the Bishop said, 'I'm sure there's been a mistake. He can't possibly have meant that.'

'He did,' said Antonia.

'I'll talk to him,' said the Bishop. He thought for a minute. 'What we need here is reconciliation!' Then he heard himself promise her, with a lot more conviction than he actually felt, that he would sort it all out. 'And then you must go back,' he said firmly, 'and resume your ministry at St Godric's.'

'No,' said Antonia.

'I beg your pardon?' said the Bishop, wondering if he had heard aright.

'No,' she repeated. 'I will not go back while that man is still there and has not repented for all that he's done. He's not fit to be a priest, and if I were to go back now with those situations unresolved, then I would be as guilty as he is.'

The Bishop stared at her. 'Do you mean you're resigning?' he asked incredulously.

Antonia's chin lifted. 'No,' she said, 'I'm not. I'm just not going to go back while he's still there!'

Chapter Twenty-Three

Faced by what he felt to be Antonia's intransigence, and unable to think of anything else to do, the Bishop phoned up the Reverend Elizabeth Marshall. 'Go and see her,' he commanded. 'Women are your responsibility!'

The hair on the back of Elizabeth's neck prickled; she scented the imminent downfall of her foe. She wasted no time, and rushed round to see Antonia.

'Hello, my dear,' she bellowed, as soon as Antonia opened the door to her. 'I hear you're having a bit of trouble with Father T. I told you this would happen. I warned you what he was like!'

The fact that she was right did nothing to endear her to Antonia, who was just then not in the best of moods, having had a row with Henry as soon as they had come back.

'He's not going to do anything!' Henry had said, outraged. 'They're going to do a cover-up job and that sod's going to get away with it. It stinks!'

Upset herself, she had rounded on him. 'It's a difficult situation. What do you expect them to do?'

'Boot him out!' said Henry. 'Defrock him!'

'They can't do that unless the matter goes to a consistory court, and they want to avoid that.'

'Why?' demanded Henry. 'What's the matter with taking it to a consistory court if it clears it all up?'

She looked at him. 'The scandal would damage the Church ...'

She had sounded unconvinced, even to herself, and Henry had flung off in anger, shouting over his shoulder, 'That kind of a church ought to get damaged! It's corrupt!'

Elizabeth, with the sensitivity of a bulldozer, failed entirely to register the fact that Antonia was upset. She stood back now and regarded her benignly, a smile playing about her lips. She was, if anything, rather pleased that this had happened; it vindicated all her worst suspicions about Father Trumpington and imparted a warm glow of self-righteous satisfaction to her chest. It was a pity, she reflected, that Antonia had got caught up in it all but Elizabeth was, above all, of a practical nature. She fully realised that, although Antonia should never have gone to St Godric's in the first place, it would be better now for all concerned if she were to go back. The Bishop had not needed to warn her of the dangers posed by the press. She was fully alive to the damage a scandal could cause, and knew that at all costs the truth had to be suppressed and that everything must appear to go on as before.

'Why don't you go back?' she demanded, as soon as they were both sitting down in Kathleen's front room. Not noted for her pastoral skills, Elizabeth smiled brightly and said, 'After all, at the outside it'll only be for another three years, and then you'll get another parish. How's it going to hurt you to keep your mouth shut? Why can't you just do what he says? Thousands of people before you have had to do that.'

Fresh from her argument with Henry, Antonia shuddered. 'I can't go back because it wouldn't be right,' she said.

Elizabeth tried a different tack. 'You do realise that there isn't another job for you in the diocese, don't you? Refuse to go back to St Godric's, my dear, and that's it.'

'If God is for me,' muttered Antonia, stung, 'who can stand against me?'

But the Reverend Marshall would have none of that nonsense. 'The salaries allocations board, my dear,' she said crisply. 'They want to see some return for their money. They're not going to pay you just for sitting around, you know, and there won't be another job. Not with this hanging over you.'

Antonia did not answer and, exasperated, Elizabeth glared at her, but then, after a second, her expression softened. 'Then what are we going to do?' she asked more gently.

Antonia could only shrug. She had been asking herself the same question all day, but so far had come up with no very satisfactory answer. 'It seems so unfair,' she said bitterly, 'that he's done what he's done and can stay there, and I've done nothing but am out and can't carry on my ministry.'

Elizabeth thought, and then an idea struck her. It was so sudden that she thought perhaps it was divine inspiration. She could not understand why she had not thought of it before. 'Antonia!' she said eagerly. 'Why don't you just go back to law?' She felt herself warming to the suggestion with every word. 'After all,' she enthused, 'you'll make a lot more money at the Bar than you ever will in the Church.'

Antonia shook her head. 'I feel God's called me into ministry,' she said flatly.

Elizabeth began to see why the Bishop had felt at such a loss. It was becoming borne in upon her that Antonia would never go back to St Godric's while the situation there remained unresolved. She stared at her, exasperated. 'Then you'll just have to marry your young man,' she said abruptly, 'and live off him.' Her tone suggested that she was now bored with the whole business. 'I could easily get you a non-stipendiary position then, I suppose. People aren't so choosy if they're going to get a helper for free, and of course some people say that married women shouldn't have paid jobs anyway.' She eyed Antonia narrowly. 'You could have children then too, my dear. They fit in very nicely if you're part-time.'

Antonia looked at her as if she was mad. She could not believe the crass insensitivity being displayed by the other woman, who was so casually planning to relegate her to the ranks of the unemployed. She could not stop herself. 'Has it ever occurred to you,' she said quietly, 'that I feel I have a calling from God, and that the labourer is worthy of hire? I have no desire to live off a husband and fill in my days with school runs, aerobic classes, and the occasional pastoral visit to the sick. I happen to believe that I have a genuine calling in life, a calling for which God has both prepared and trained me. And I am not just going quietly to disappear because it makes life easier for all of you!'

There was not a lot left to say after that. Antonia showed the Reverend Marshall out, her lips steely – but that was because she felt she wanted to cry. As she shut the door and crept up to her room, unable for the present to face anyone else, she had to admit that her prospects looked grim.

The Bishop decided to pay Father Trumpington a visit. He had toyed with the idea of yet again summoning the recalcitrant priest to his office but had finally rejected it. He knew that he must act now without delay, and he could not be certain that Father Trumpington would comply. Besides, he did not like the atmosphere after Father Trumpington had been around. He felt in some strange way as if the air had been polluted. Gloria Sunnington was ahead of him. She had come round, she explained to Dorothy, to sort out service details for the parish magazine for the coming month. 'Now that Antonia's gone,' she said brightly, 'we've got some difficult gaps to fill.' As soon as Dorothy had left the room, however, Gloria tossed aside her notebook and, throwing all caution to the wind, sidled round to the other side of the desk and sat herself firmly on Father Trumpington's knee.

Father Trumpington felt himself grow hot with horror. He had known of course that there would be a price to pay for Gloria's silence, and had been wondering what it would be. He had even been preparing himself and had withdrawn a large sum of money from the building society, but that her demands might be of a sexual nature had not occurred to him. He had always thought of her as rather a midget, and an unattractive midget at that, and he had pitied her for the way she always appeared to try so hard, yet get everything so dismally wrong. He had felt, too, that her husband must be a trial, but never in his wildest imaginings had it occurred to him that he himself might be the object of Gloria's erotic fantasies. He had assumed that because she herself was so unattractive to him, he must be equally unattractive to her. What had happened at the Christmas party had disturbed him, it was true, but thinking about it later, and preoccupied as he had been with Jackie, he had finally put it all down to drink. The blackmail, he had thought, was entirely different in kind.

However, as Gloria wriggled her plump behind into his genitals it became obvious that her expectations were rather different to his. She had come round that morning with a mission. She had decided that she could stand it no longer. He was a god to her! She burned for him, her flesh yearned for his touch, so she had decided to grasp the bull, as it were, by the horns. 'Oh Dick,' she panted now, 'don't be shy. We can't go on like this.'

Father Trumpington agreed, he was getting the most terrible

cramp in his leg. 'Gloria,' he began, and discovered he could think of nothing to say.

'Yes, Dick,' she cooed, misinterpreting his speechlessness as joy. 'One of us had to take the initiative!'

'What about your husband?' managed Father Trumpington.

'Oh Griff!' Gloria dismissed him. 'He doesn't matter. It's only you and me . . . I want you . . . I adore you . . . I . . .'

It was at this point that the Bishop walked in, with Dorothy, intent on offering them all coffee, close behind. To say that Father Trumpington was glad of the interruption, while accurate, would perhaps be putting it in a rather misleading fashion.

'Good God!' said the Bishop. 'What on earth are you doing, man?'

He advanced grimly into the room and behind him Dorothy said, 'What *are* you doing, Dick? I thought we'd finished with all of this!'

'We have, dear,' began Father Trumpington. 'I . . .'

The Bishop was peering at Gloria intently. 'This, I take it,' he said, 'is Mrs Newberg.'

'What?' said Gloria. Of the four of them, she had seemed the least put out by the interruption up to that point; indeed she had been so intent on what she was doing before they came in that it had taken her a moment to register that there was anyone else there at all. Now, however, she leapt to her feet, pulling her skirt awkwardly down over her knees. 'Jackie Newberg?' she said indignantly. 'No, I'm Gloria.'

'Gloria?' said the Bishop. 'Gloria who? Not another one?'

'No,' said Father Trumpington desperately.

'What do you mean another one?' demanded Gloria.

There was a shocked silence and Dorothy advanced into the room. 'What was she doing on your knee, Dick?' she asked imperiously. 'Are you up to your little tricks again?'

With her aubergine hair and crimson leggings, so obviously furious, she looked like some kind of scarlet terror, and Father Trumpington quailed. 'It's not what you think, dear,' he said.

'What little tricks?' said Gloria plaintively. 'What are you talking about?'

The Bishop, who was still standing there looking from one to the other of them uncomprehendingly, said, 'If this woman is not Jackie Newberg, will someone please tell me who she is?'

Gloria, although not gifted with lightning intelligence, was beginning to register that there was something seriously wrong here, quite over and above the fact that she and Father Trumpington had been discovered in a compromising embrace.

'Exactly why should I be Jackie Newberg?' she demanded ominously.

The Bishop looked impatient. 'Surely if you are a part of this benighted man's congregation, you'll already know. Mrs Newberg is the lady with whom he has been having an affair.'

'What?' shrieked Gloria. She turned to Father Trumpington. 'Dick, is this true? It can't be!'

Father Trumpington looked down at his shoes, his ears scarlet. Life, he felt, was playing a cruel trick. 'But you already knew,' he whispered.

'No, I didn't!' shouted Gloria. 'You disgusting old pig!' She turned from him in outrage and grabbed at her coat, and they all three stared at her as she shrugged it on angrily and began to head for the door. 'You . . . you Bluebeard!' she spat, turning at the last moment. 'To think I was letting you sweet talk me like that, and all the time you were carrying on with that slut! Jackie Newberg indeed! That's it, I'm leaving!' And the next second, true to her word, she was gone, the house echoing with the angry slam of the door behind her.

'I still wish to know who that woman was, Dick,' said the Bishop quietly.

Father Trumpington slumped back down in his chair. 'My churchwarden,' he said hoarsely. He appeared stunned. He looked up at Dorothy. 'You've got to believe me. I never did anything to encourage her . . . I never knew.'

The Bishop seated himself opposite and drew off his gloves. He looked unconvinced. 'Is there anything else I ought to know?' he inquired frostily.

In spite of all the evidence against him, Father Trumpington still refused to go, and nothing could be done to remove him without the most appalling scandal. The Bishop was not prepared to pay that price. The only positive action he took was to say, once again, that Father Trumpington would never be allowed another curate. Antonia, he at long last acknowledged, would not have to go back. It would not be fair. But he still had not the slightest idea what to do with her and, perhaps unwisely, mentioned to Father Trumpington his fears that the girl herself might talk.

Father Trumpington took these words to heart. He wanted her to come back, he said immediately. She *had* to come back. The Bishop regretfully told him that that was not possible because she had refused. Father Trumpington was so enraged that he later phoned up Antonia himself. 'You've got to come back,' he insisted.

'I'll never come back,' she replied. 'Not while you're still there and all of this has been suppressed.'

But Father Trumpington, though cowed, was not defeated. 'If you don't come back now,' he snarled venomously, 'I'll make sure you never work in this diocese again. I'll make sure you never work in the Church again. You're finished!'

'Try it!' she said, and hung up.

The unhappy result, for St Godric's, was that over the next two months more than half the congregation left. Some went to new churches, and some decided they wanted nothing to do with such a body ever again. But at least, as all acknowledged, the public face was intact. Privately, of course, there was horror that the Bishop had not done anything. But then again, as the disaffected parishioners said to each other, 'What *can* you do?'

Chapter Twenty-Four

Three weeks later Dave, Jude and Kathleen were all confirmed, as had been arranged, at St Etheldreda's, Carberry's one and only charismatic Anglican church, which stood in the centre of town. The service was packed. St Etheldreda's regularly had a congregation of five hundred or more at all its services, and that night there were thirty-four of their own young people wanting to make a public profession of their faith. There was a lot of singing, and from all over the church people stood up to pray and give prophecies out loud. Kathleen felt rather unnerved by it all, but Dave was unabashed. He thought this was the way church ought to be.

At Dave's request, Antonia found herself taking part in the service, robed and standing next to Peter Dunn, St Etheldreda's priest. Halfway through the intercession time, a man stood up and delivered a long prophecy that he said he felt came from God. It began with a picture of a young woman standing in the centre of the church and ministering to the people. Power flowed from her, said the man, and he felt the Lord himself stood over her, with his arms outstretched. There was a description of pain, and much suffering, but the man said it was the blessing of the wilderness, and that the Lord himself would make a pathway through the desert. 'Thus says the Lord,' proclaimed the man, 'there is balm in Gilead. I am able to restore you a hundredfold!' A chorus of alleluias went up, and somewhere a woman began to sob. The Bishop looked rather taken aback by it all, but the man had not finished. 'Upon the lady,' he cried, now thoroughly caught up in the words, 'the Lord speaks blessing. I will use you, he says. You feel that all your work has been destroyed, but I am moulding you. I will take you. I will use you. I will give you a greater work . . .'

Antonia became aware that the Reverend Peter Dunn was looking at her closely. After the service he came up to her and said, 'Sorry to hear about all the trouble you've had.' Antonia flushed, but he went on, 'As it happens, I'm looking for a curate at the moment, and I think the Holy Spirit is telling me to ask you . . .'

Antonia could hardly wait to tell Henry. She was still living at Kathleen's while the diocese tried to sort out what to do with her. Kathleen was delighted and had said Antonia could remain for ever as far as she was concerned. But the diocese clearly wanted to have something rather more definite sorted out, and the Bishop had said very firmly that as he did not want Antonia to suffer from all that had happened, they must find her another position as soon as possible. None of this had pleased Henry, however. As he had pointed out, just finding Antonia another job was hardly going to heal all the emotional hurt that had been done. He had been profoundly affected by what he saw as the cover-up of what had taken place at St Godric's. In particular, he was furious that Father Trumpington still remained in post and that outwardly everything appeared to be going on as before. Henry's one consolation was that so many of the congregation had left and that the choir had fallen apart as soon as Norman and Gudrun had gone; try as he might, Father Trumpington seemed unable to find another organist. Henry felt there was at least something of justice here.

But nothing could lessen the deep anger and disillusionment he felt, and he had declared his intention of never again supporting the Anglican Church. He had even gone so far as to try to persuade Antonia to leave the ministry entirely and to marry him straightaway. They could join a house church, he said, if she really wanted, after all that had happened, to belong to any church at all. But Antonia had resisted this. Like Henry, she too felt enraged and hurt, but unlike him she felt she ought to stay within the structure and try to work for change. 'I do want to marry you,' she kept saying, 'but not like this. I don't want it to seem like I'm running away. And I still believe that God's called me for a purpose. I can't just give it all up the minute things get tough. People still need help, after all. Even people like Jackie. Heaven knows what's going to happen to her and Elspeth now, after all of this!'

Henry grimaced. 'She'll survive. That type always does.' Then he added, 'Her husband's instructed my firm, by the way, to handle the divorce. He's absolutely determined to get custody.'

'Oh God,' she said, 'what a mess.'

It was, and Henry, if it were possible, seemed to feel it even more deeply than herself. He raged and cajoled, but still he could not get her to change her mind, and finally he said, 'OK, we'll give it three months. That's plenty of time for God to sort something out if he wants. But if nothing's come up by then, we'll get married. That's it.'

Something about the set of his chin had made her agree. And it had occurred to her, too, that if indeed nothing had happened within three months, then it might be reasonably inferred that God himself was trying to say something. Now, however, Peter Dunn was asking her to be his curate.

It was so totally unexpected, it knocked her for six. And she was not entirely sure it was right. For a start, St Etheldreda's was so near to St Godric's and that would surely make for problems later on. Also, she wondered if Henry would be able to bear living in such close proximity to Father Trumpington. All the same, something about the suggestion excited her.

When Henry dropped her and Kathleen back later that night, she stayed behind with him in the car. She had already alerted Kathleen to what had happened and wanted to be able to tell Henry when they were totally alone, without the feeling that they had to be careful what they said in case they were overheard. Henry should feel able to speak without constraint.

Kathleen understood completely. As soon as they pulled up, she jumped out of the car and said, 'Thank you very much, Henry. I'm going straight to bed.' And she scuttled off before either of them had a chance to say anything more. Henry stared after her, puzzled.

'Henry,' said Antonia, 'I've got something to tell you.' And heart in mouth, she related to him Peter Dunn's proposal.

'You can't be serious, Antonia,' he said when she finally faltered to a stop. 'You'd be next door to that swine Trumpington. There'd be no end of trouble.' And then when she said nothing he went on, 'I'm just not sure about any of this. How do you know this bloke Dunn is going to be any different?'

In the dark, she looked at him. 'Oh, come on, Henry. You know he's not like Dick. He believes in God, for a start!'

'So does the Bishop,' said Henry glumly.

She stared at him and sighed. 'I really want to do this,' she said, groping for the right words. 'I still feel called to ministry, and I really think that this is of God.'

He shrugged. 'You said that about St Godric's once too.'

'But maybe that was right.' She leant forward across the brake till she was almost touching his arm. 'Maybe,' she said insistently, 'what was at St Godric's had to be exposed. Maybe God wanted to give us all a chance of dealing with the wrong that was there.'

'But it hasn't been dealt with,' he said obstinately.

'No, but that's God's problem now, not ours.' She at last reached out and laid a hand on his arm, and immediately felt the tension pulsing through his sleeve. 'We tried,' she said softly, 'we really did do all we could. That was all God wanted of us. The outcome isn't really our concern. But now we've got to be obedient to the next thing he wants us to do.'

He turned on her such haggard eyes that she was momentarily appalled. 'I don't think I can ever forgive that man,' he said. And she knew that he was talking about a betrayal that went far beyond all the petty infidelities and the lies. 'I don't think I can ever trust anyone in the Church ever again.'

'I'm in the Church, Henry,' she said softly. 'Dick Trumpington isn't the Church. We've got to allow God to do what he wants to do.' She became urgent. 'And we've got to be faithful now or he won't be able to.'

Henry looked at her for a long moment, and she saw the anguish still lurking behind his eyes. 'I still wish I'd hit the sod,' he said, 'I think I'd feel better now.'

She laughed. 'Not if you'd been charged with assault.'

He reached out a hand and brushed the hair back from her face. 'Antonia,' he began. He paused and looked at her, and then said, very slowly, as if the words hurt, 'I do love you, and I love God, you know . . . it's just all that's happened. I think the Church stinks but I know what you're saying. Maybe you should go there. But,' he took a deep breath and she stared at him apprehensively,

'I want us to get married straightaway. If you go there, I want to be your husband. I want people to know that I've got a right to be a part of things, and that I've got a right to protect you.'

She smiled. 'Oh, Henry,' she said, 'you're being feudal again. You make it sound as if you're going to do battle.'

'No,' he said soberly, 'but you may be, and this time I'd like to be right beside you.'